Sweet Second Chance

Sweet Second Chance

Windy City Publishers
2118 Plum Grove Rd., #349
Rolling Meadows, IL 60008
www.windycitypublishers.com

Published in the United States of America

First Edition: 2013

ISBN:
978-1-935766-74-2

Library of Congress Control Number:
2013932197

Cover Art by Joann Mariahazy
Appleton, Wisconsin

CHICAGO
www.windycitypublishers.com

It's ridiculous. I cry at the most stupid things. I cry at inopportune times. I cry when I have no tissues available. I cry at weddings of people I don't know. I cry when I see old people holding hands. I cry at almost any movie with a plausible love story. I am a hopeless, sappy romantic. But I needed this book to be more.

I also laugh at stupid things. I laugh at inappropriate times. I laugh hard enough to cry when I have no tissues available. I grew up in a house where we tried not to laugh at each other, because that would be admitting someone else was funnier than you were. It is to these folks, grandparents, parents, and five funny siblings, Jan Stage, John Fancher, Jerry Fancher, Joann Mariahazy, Jeff Fancher, my son Andrew Danalewich, Stacia Danalewich, and Mariah Stewart that I dedicate the humor in this book. I hope you like the characters. And I hope you laugh.

Acknowledgments

So many people encouraged me to squeeze this project out of my brain and onto paper. There is no way to thank them all. But know that if you ever, inadvertently or deliberately, try to make people laugh, you have a special place in my heart. I believe God put us on this planet to live life abundantly and to be happy. A sense of humor is a gift. Thanks for sharing yours.

Many thanks also to the professionals at Windy City Publishers: first, to Lise Marinelli who convinced me this would be an enjoyable, very doable process; she was correct. Secondly, to Alice Refvik and Shelly Aschkenase, editors extraordinaire. They were kindly brutal. I needed it and I appreciate it. Finally, to Dawn McGarrahan Wiebe for patience and good direction in navigating this course. You are treasures.

Sweet Second Chance

Jackie Fancher

WINDY CITY
PUBLISHERS

CHICAGO
www.windycitypublishers.com

Early October

He stood tall, head bowed, autumn sun warming his dark hair and black suit. Dark glasses hid red eyes; a lone tear creeping out, bravely escaping down his clean-shaven cheek. Muffled sobs joined the sounds of feet uncomfortably shuffling in recently fallen maple leaves.

"From dust we came, and to dust we shall return," the pastor somberly spoke.

His words were lost in the heartache of the day, mingled with the acrid scent of burning leaves carried on a gentle breeze through the old cemetery.

It should have been me. Why wasn't it me? The words repeated in his brain.

At a signal from the pastor, he laid two roses on the casket, one a deep velvet red, the other purest white, tied together with a linen handkerchief still damp from his tears.

Friends and family quietly left the graveside, some greeting him with condolences, others offering help with anything he might need, and several just touching his arm to help ease his grief and their own. He stayed a few minutes alone, finally releasing a shuddering sob that echoed amid the rustling leaves. He walked to his car and drove home.

CHAPTER 1

October, One Year Later

A my Sweet turned the key in the lock of her front door at the same time she saw the red tip of her fingernail flick to the floor. She stomped into her condo, slammed the door behind her and threw her out-of-season white purse onto the couch.

"My life is crap!"

She kicked off her left shoe. It hit a vase filled with murky water from daisies that had turned to dust and slime. Surprisingly, the vase defied gravity, rocked slightly and righted itself. She kicked off her right shoe. It found the target. Margaret Gibson carefully opened the front door and peeked in.

"Amy, are you okay?"

No answer.

Gibby stepped in cautiously. She wrinkled her nose as the smell of the toxic floral arrangement reached her.

"What happened here?"

"My life stinks worse than those flowers, that's what."

Gibby went to the kitchen and came back armed with paper towels and baking soda.

"I'll clean that up," Amy growled, knowing that by the time she did, most of it would have evaporated and the rest would be absorbed by the carpet pad.

"No, you won't. You know it and I know it." Amy's friend dabbed, changed towels, dabbed, changed towels until it was as dry as could be expected then sprinkled the spot with the baking soda.

"You're so freaking domestic, I could puke!"

"Don't bite my head off, Amy Sweet. You don't have friends to spare. Now, are you going to tell me why your life is crap or not?"

Amy took a deep breath, stood up, lifted her skirt and wiggled out of her panty hose. She looked for another target. Gibby snatched the hose out of her fist and threw them into the hallway, halfway to the hamper.

"I'm out of work."

Gibby's eyebrows rose as she gasped. "You've been there eight years!"

"Doesn't matter," Amy mumbled. "Funny how just a few words from a moron can smash your self-esteem like a bug. I'd been there long enough to know my job, my boss's job, most of my coworkers' jobs and I guess I was just too damn comfortable."

"Do I know this moron of whom you speak?"

"Charlie Burgone. The Great Downsizer. I've been downsized. Too bad he couldn't downsize my ass."

Gibby covered her mouth with her hand and laughed. "You mean Charlie who smells like sweaty man-ass?"

Amy nodded. "The one and only... let me take that back. He's not the only one who smells like sweaty man-ass, but he is the only Charlie that I worked for who smells like sweaty man-ass."

"So," Gibby started. "You no longer have to work for a person you never liked, who smells bad. And this has you upset?"

"You know better than that. I had a great paycheck from Baxter Brothers. I was good at my job, and I don't feel like standing with the other slugs of the earth in the unemployment lines."

"Maybe you'll meet a man there," Gibby offered, always the optimist.

"What do I need with an unemployed man? This brings me to part two of why my day is crap. Crane called me at work." She cocked her head. "Seems he's going to be a father." She snarled. "Thought I might like to know."

"I take it that you're not the mother?" Gibby knew Amy and Crane were having a tough time, but she thought they'd pull through as they had before. "So, Crane is going to be a dad."

Gibby moved to the arm of Amy's chair and put an arm across her friend's shoulder. "I'm sorry. You're feeling awful. Come on across the hall and I'll reheat a couple pieces of meatloaf and some green beans and we'll crack open a bottle of wine."

"You know," Amy said pensively, "I'm not as upset as I thought I'd be. The relationship with Crane was on very shaky ground. I used to like my job, but I really didn't enjoy it the way I used to. I think I got stuck in a comfortable rut. Maybe this is a good thing. Maybe I can turn crap into something good."

Gibby hugged her. "Did I mention the meatloaf is Martha Stewart's recipe?" Amy threw her hands out to her sides, "Well, there ya go!"

*

Gibby came from the bathroom, hands washed, long, blonde hair tied back, ready for food preparation. She was a nurse in the maternity ward at St. Mary's Hospital where she fought the daily battle against germs. This naturally carried over into her home life. Amy knew her way around her neighbor's kitchen. Their condos may as well have been a suite, because door-knocking and bell-ringing were unnecessary. They felt equally at home in each other's places. With a stack of three plates, three knives, three forks, three spoons and three napkins, Amy set the table. Gibby's roommate, Beth, would be home from work soon and ready for supper.

"Get the cloth napkins. And the nice wine glasses. This will be a celebration."

"Of what," Amy shouted over the roar of potato peel going down the disposal, "my unemployment or my status as dumped girlfriend?"

Gibby, hands on her slender hips, said, "Your freedom from a boss who doesn't bathe and your freedom from that cheating skunk, Crane. You can't tell me there isn't a little part of you that's breathing a sigh of relief."

The front door opened and Beth walked in, arms full, bouquet of flowers from the blind (she thinks) man at the train station in her right hand, briefcase in her left hand, three books from the library in the crook of her arm, and coat draped over her shoulder. She was breathing heavily as she dropped everything on her rocking chair.

Amy rushed to help her. "Good grief girl, you're not homeless. You don't have to carry all your belongings with you. Did you leave your grocery cart in the hall?" She gave Beth a hug. "How was your day?"

Beth, rushing through her daily homecoming routine, shouted back over her shoulder as she went to her room to let Punkin out. "My day was fine. I expected to see you on the train." She'd lived and worked in the Chicago area for about five years and had yet to lose any of her sweet, sultry Virginia accent. She scurried into the bathroom, took care of urgencies, washed her face and pulled her silky, black hair into a ponytail with a yellow scrunchie.

Amy shouted back. "I took an earlier train. The one with the cute-but-married conductor you're always sweating over."

"The nerve!" Beth yelled from her room while changing into snowflake flannel pajama pants and a black tank top. "You didn't flirt with him, did you?"

"I had to sit in an aisle seat. You know how the train gets that little side-to-side rhythm? When he was punching tickets, I leaned just a little." She mimicked Beth's accent. "Mah, oh mah, it was thrillin'! He asked me if I wanted to see his whistle."

"Amy Sweet, you lie like a dog!" Punkin, fat orange cat of unknown sexual orientation, glared at her. "Sorry, Punkin, Sweetie. It's just an expression."

Gibby raised her voice at both of them. "Please, ladies, can you finish this conversation in the dining room? I have just about had my fill of hollering babies today and would like a little quiet time in my own home. Now let's get this celebration underway."

"What are we celebrating, Gibbs?"

"We are celebrating freedom. Amy, fill her in on the events of your exciting day."

"Well," Amy started, "first I get a phone call from Crane letting me know that since he will soon be a father, we should probably break up."

"Slime!"

"Exactly." Amy continued. "After I come back from the ladies room—had to fix the mascara after the very brief crying jag—Charlie Burgone downsized me."

"The fragrant Charlie? What a dog!" Punkin glared again. "Sorry, Sweetie Pie. It's just an expression." Beth looked over at Gibby.

"Beth, here's a vase. Did the charlatan trick you into buying flowers again?"

"He's blind and very kind, and his flowers are always fresh. Besides, he can make change really fast when I'm in a hurry." Gibby and Amy rolled their eyes, silently mouthing "sucker." They were helpless to resist the laughter that followed.

"I don't care what you say, he's blind. I'm sure of it," Beth insisted.

Gibby changed the subject. "Amy, open the Galena Cellars Red. I'm sure it will be perfect with Martha's meatloaf."

"Don't tell me you're recycling that meatloaf for a third night," Beth feigned insult.

"You know the rule," Gibby said, "don't like it, don't eat it."

"I'll eat it. I need something to cushion the wine. I assume there's some Cherry Garcia for dessert? After all, if it's a true celebration, ice cream is a necessity. And we need to pray first."

Amy and Gibby knew better than to argue. They reached across the table and held hands. "Lord, thank you for another day in your creation, even though Amy hit a rough spot in the road. Bless her, our friendship, this food, and Martha Stewart, even if she was in the slammer. Amen."

The three friends raised their glasses. Gibby toasted: "Here's to the freedom of starting over and the blessing of second chances."

The three glasses clinked. "I love you guys."

*

Amy went back to her place after dinner and picked up the phone to call her best friend, to tell her about the events of the day. Hillary Samms, former college roommate, lived in a small apartment just north of the Loop. The two friends could be found lunching together several times a week and starting the morning off at Starbucks. Amy realized it was getting late, but she knew Hillie would want to hear the news.

A groggy Hillary answered the phone.

"Sorry, Hills... I know it's late, but I wanted to talk to you before the morning."

Amy told her of the breakup, losing her job, and how Gibby was thinking of this as a good thing.

"Face it, Amy, Crane just made it easy for you. Being gorgeous just doesn't make up for cheating and acting like a jerk. I think you know you two would have split up within two or three months anyway. Who's the mother-to-be?"

"Don't know. Don't care. Didn't ask. And he didn't say."

"You're a terrific woman. Let nature take its course, and when the time is right an awesome man will step into your life. We've been at this long enough to know you can't force it. Love will happen when it's meant to happen." Amy let her speak without interruption, knowing from experience that when Hillie had a message, it would be delivered. "I know being out of work is scary and interviewing is scary. But you know you're smart. You can make a complete sentence, and you have clean fingernails. That's half the battle. Have you looked around you lately? You worked for a stinking slob. He didn't respect you. I think he was intimidated by you. He knew you could do his job, and probably do it better than he did. I say good riddance. Good riddance to Charlie and Crane."

"I knew I'd feel better if I called you before I went to bed. Now maybe I'll sleep."

"Yeah, but I won't. That's okay. The four of us need a little get-together planning session." These friends from four different backgrounds seemed to mesh into an entity that gave strength to each individually. When one of the foursome had a problem, they would meet, eat, have a little wine and chocolate, and talk it out. They each considered the other three a blessing in their lives. Yes, a get-together was in order. This time Amy would be the recipient of support, advice and comfort.

"Get the girls together and come on downtown. I'm free all week, so pick a day. Let me know. I'll stop at Godiva's. We'll bulk up."

"Thanks, Hillie. You guys are terrific." She hung up the phone. She had awesome friends. They sure made her life easier. She wondered how she could be so lucky.

*

After the obligatory trip to the unemployment office, Amy spent two days doing things she had put off for months. She swirled through her condo with cleaning supplies, mops, rags, buckets, and all forms of new dusters that recently showed up in stores. She dusted, scrubbed, waxed, polished and vacuumed anything that couldn't move out of her way. She even threatened to bathe Punkin. She put a Faith Hill CD in the player and sat on the couch with a kitchen towel around her neck and a can of Pledge in her hand. The intent was to take a ten-minute rest. She woke up when Gibby gave her shoulder a shake. It was dark outside. Faith Hill had been silent for hours.

"Well I hope you got that out of your system."

"Oh, crap! I must have been tired."

"I'm sure you're exhausted. You've had quite a week. The place looks great.

You better stop now or you're going to make my place look bad. Actually, if you get another burst of energy like that, you can come across the hall and spend a few hours."

"Ten dollars an hour. I need the money."

"Deal. I talked to Hillie and we're on for tomorrow night. We'll have supper downtown with her and then go to her place for brainstorming under the influence of wine and chocolate. Bring an overnight bag. We're having a sleepover."

"Am I in such dire shape that I need an overnighter?"

"You're a mess, Amy dear."

"Have you had supper?"

"Beth is across the hall broiling chicken and buttering noodles. You're welcome to join us."

"Give me a minute to wash up and I'll be over. I feel like I should be having breakfast."

*

Amy, Beth and Gibby dropped their overnight bags off at Hillary's place and took a short cab ride to Café Ba-Ba-Reeba!, where, luckily, they discovered the wait for a table wasn't going to be long. Known for tapas specialties, the café was the perfect place for the four friends to dine. They ordered several small plates to share along with a pitcher of passion fruit sangria. The discussion centered on the day's events, not Amy's situation.

Beth asked, "So, what's new on the maternity ward?"

"Two sets of twin girls today. They're all healthy and doing fine. Days like this are what I dreamed of in nurses training," Gibby responded. "How about your day?"

Hillie answered. "Well, I had to start the day at Starbucks by myself." She gave Amy an apologetic look.

"Sorry. I thought of you as I stirred the Coffee-mate into my cup of Folgers. I was spoiled rotten."

Beth called the waitress over. They ordered another pitcher of sangria, halibut frio with garlic aioli, beef tenderloin brochettes, shrimp in olive oil, and red peppers with manchego cheese and citrus-soaked olives. They passed the plates back and forth, sampling everything.

"Our treat tonight, Ames." Hillie waved her off as she reached for her purse.

"I'm not a pauper yet, you know."

Gibby spoke up. "Don't argue. We discussed and we agreed: our treat tonight."

"You discussed?" Amy asked, incredulous. "You've been discussing me? I feel like a slug."

"You are; but you're *our* slug, and we care about you."

Amy chuckled. "Good grief. Can we go now?"

They had another cab ride back to Hillie's place. This trip was three dollars more than the first; probably because the cabbie smelled the sangria and figured they wouldn't know the difference. They took the elevator to the seventeenth floor and staggered down the hall to Hillie's apartment. Amy opened the curtains. The apartment was a small one-bedroom, but the view of the lake made up for the lack of space. She stood with her hands on her hips and took in the sights of the city she had grown to love. "This view just blows me away."

Hillie reminded her. "Wait until the morning when the sun comes up. That view alone is worth half my rent. I'm making a pot of decaf to go with dessert, after the business part of our meeting."

Beth spoke up. "I'll take notes."

"Notes? Why do we need notes? I thought this was a friendly get-together. Maybe we should get a court reporter!" Amy seemed confused.

"I figure if we have suggestions and can get a plan of some sorts for you it would be too bad if we forgot due to the effects of sangria." Hillie stated this as if it should be obvious to everyone.

Gibby carried the carafe full of coffee, cream, napkins and four mugs painted with purple and yellow pansies. Hillie made a presentation with a gold colored box of Godiva chocolates as if she were carrying in the Thanksgiving turkey. She set the box on the coffee table and chuckled at the harmony of the "ooo" "ahh" "mmm" sounds from her friends. Sometimes there are no words. This was understood by the friends when responding to chocolate, Ben and Jerry's, or Cubs' shortstop Alex Gonzales.

Hillie started the conversation. "I suppose we need to know what your immediate plans are, then we can go from there."

Amy answered. "You mean, like what am I doing tomorrow?"

"Sure, let's start there."

Amy crossed her legs in the soft brown leather overstuffed chair, held her mug with both hands and sipped her coffee. "I'm getting up early to go to my cousin's cabin to help her paint. I'll probably spend the night and finish up Sunday morning. It's a two-hour drive. I'll stop and get groceries and do some laundry. That's where my plans for the rest of my life end."

Hillie asked, "Is she paying you to paint?"

"Well, no, I just volunteered to help her. I like to paint and you know how it is. Sometimes projects will wait forever until you get some help, then the whole thing just takes off. I know she's wanted to do this for a while. We may even do a crackle finish on a couple of the interior doors."

"She's buying the paint?"

Amy answered, "Yeah, most of it, except for the crackle stuff. I have that from one of my own projects. I wouldn't think of asking her for money."

Beth chewed on a dark chocolate caramel, her pen a frenzy.

Gibby asked her, "What are you writing?"

Beth held up the paper. "I wrote 'paint' and drew a bunny."

"Bunny on crack," Hillie critiqued. "So, have you thought about what you'd like to do to make a living? This is the perfect time to take a chance. If money didn't matter, what would you like to do? If training didn't matter? If geography didn't matter? What have you dreamed of doing?"

Amy looked thoughtful then laughed. "I'd like to work for the tailor shop where Kevin Costner shops and measure inseams."

Gibby joined in. "Getting paid money to run your hands up a man's leg. Sign me up."

Beth added, "Not just any man…Kevin Costner. Could it be the same place where Alex Gonzales shops? Or Tom Cruise?"

Amy answered, "Sweetie, it's your fantasy. You could be inseam checker to the stars!"

"Okay," Hillie tried getting control, "before we feel up all the cute men on earth, can we get back to the issue here? Really, Ames, haven't you ever just wanted to do something different? Chuck reality to the wind here. Say you have no bills, no rent due, no ComEd, no van payment."

Amy thought and answered. "I actually like to do work. Not hard, sweaty, dangerous work. No climbing telephone poles, but physical stuff. I like the computer for playing, but I really don't want to sit behind one all day for a paycheck. I could do gardening, but that's pretty limited in this part of the world, where we have to deal with winter."

Hillie reminded her. "Remember, in fantasyland, geography is not an issue. Besides, there are greenhouses, indoor gardens, conservatories…"

"Okay, then. I could do that. I like to make things pretty. I like to fix stuff. I'm pretty good with my hands."

Beth added to her notes and reached for a coconut truffle. "My behind is getting bigger by the minute."

Amy added to her list. "I like to deal with people in person, not on the phone and not through email. Actually face to face. I like to use my brain. I like to figure stuff out. I want to make a difference in someone's life, but I guess I've just looked past that for a paycheck."

Gibby reminded her. "There's nothing wrong with a paycheck. It lets you do the stuff you want to do when you're not working. Hmmm…that made sense to me in my brain, but didn't seem to translate well after leaving my lips."

"I know exactly what you mean," Amy answered. "That's what I've been doing. I put up with crap at work so I can take the money and do something I enjoy on the weekends. Meanwhile, only two out of seven days are fun, and life is too short. Help me out here, ladies."

"Write this down." Hillie pointed to Beth. "Buy a newspaper this week and just scan the want ads. Circle anything that sounds like you might enjoy it. Ignore the pay, the hours, the location and prerequisites. Just ask yourself if this is something you could do for five days a week and not wish that it was only for two. Ask yourself if this is something you could enjoy so much that you would consider taking less money to do it. I'll be down to your place on Wednesday, and we'll check out your selections."

Gibby raised her hand volunteering. "Dinner at our place. Write that down, Beth."

Beth nodded, scribbled final notes and licked the bottom of the page with a chocolate tongue. "Binding. Sealed with chocolate. Be there or be square. Now get the Kleenex and put *Steel Magnolias* on."

Chapter 2

When Wednesday came, Amy grabbed the newspaper and a bottle of Octoberfest wine and headed across the hall to Beth and Gibby's place. Hillie was already there and was setting the table.

"Have a seat, neighbor. Dinner is almost ready."

"It sure smells good. It lured me from across the hall. Corkscrew please."

Gibby handed her the corkscrew and Amy filled four glasses. Dinner was devoured like the four hadn't eaten in days. Twenty minutes later, the dishwasher was loaded and the friends moved to the living room.

Amy and Hillie sat on the couch and spread the newspaper on the coffee table. Beth and Gibby looked on, anxious to see what Amy was checking out.

Hillary counted. "Eighteen pages of want ads and you only circled six jobs."

"I figured reality had to enter into this somewhere. I'm not trained to be a nurse, teacher, ironworker or car mechanic. I have absolutely no interest in about seventy-five percent of these ads. The others I considered carefully, ignoring the location and the pay. I came up with these six, three of which I could actually do and may even call on," Amy reasoned.

Hillie read the first ad. "You could drive a semi cross-country."

"I could if I were trained. I think it would be fun once you get out of the city."

Gibby asked, "So, you could drive your van to Iowa, get in a truck, drive it around, come back to your van and drive back to the city?"

Amy answered. "Remember, geography doesn't matter. I've always admired lady truckers. It's like breaking into a man's world. Big rig, big guy. But when you think of it, it's just driving. I like to drive."

Beth agreed. "Makes sense to me. What's next?"

Hillie answered. "I see a trend here. CTA bus driver? You won't drive a truck in the city, but you'll risk the life of forty people on a bus?"

"Okay, here's my thought…trucks get no respect in the city, they're a nuisance. Buses, on the other hand, are a necessity. People actually stand outside and wait for them. Not only that, they give you money when they get on."

"You don't actually get to keep the money, you know," Gibby reminded her.

"I'm not an idiot. Plus, that big wheel right there for you to hold onto, there's just something about making the perfect corner…"

Hillie rolled her eyes. "Next."

"Car detailing." Amy waited for remarks.

Beth shook her head. "I don't know what that means."

Amy explained. "Well, people bring their cars in to get washed, vacuumed out, waxed, buffed, you know, cleaned up. Plus, it could include some painting."

"Like what," Gibby asked, "painting those flames shooting out of the hood, or lightning bolts down the side of the car so that you think a Chevette is actually fast?"

"Maybe. This is actually one of the ads I'm calling on tomorrow."

"Next." Hillie was determined to keep the discussion on track.

Gibby read the next ad and fell over onto the floor holding her sides laughing. "Cake decorating at an X-rated bakery? Is that frosting on your pants or are you happy to see me?"

Hillie couldn't resist. "Maybe you could use memories of Crane as a model!"

Beth joined in. "Can you whip up another batch of that creamy white filling?" Her Virginia drawl made it sound lewd.

Amy came to her own defense. "I thought it could be on-the-job training for a real bakery, and I know there are classes I could take." She couldn't help but laugh with her friends. "Some support from you guys would be nice."

Gibby couldn't let it rest. "Lovely wedding cake. Are those boobies?"

Hillie continued. "What else ya got here? Painter. Not a lot of details."

"I'm calling on that one tomorrow, too. Thought I'd get the scoop. I like to paint. I just don't know if it's a house, a canvas or graffiti."

"Last one. Another painting job. Interior large home. Minor remodeling." Hillie looked hopeful.

"I'm calling on that one, too," Amy said. "I'll send emails tomorrow to let you all know how I did. I have to report in for the unemployment office, too. I get a check in two weeks. Keep your ears open. I'm not desperate yet, but I do get a little nervous when I think about the future."

"I'll pray for you every day, Ames," Beth assured her.

"Thanks. I'll need it."

Gibby thought out loud. "You know, Friday we never did address the Crane issue."

Amy answered. "What's to address? I'm out of his life and he's out of mine."

Gibby added, "Just like that."

"Just like that. I don't want Crane back. I don't care about him or his family-to-be. Obviously, he hasn't cared about me for a while. I just feel stupid that I missed the clues."

Hillie came to her rescue. "Don't you dare take his buttheadedness onto yourself. You deserve better. Let's just hope he's happy with the situation he's in for the sake of that baby."

*

Amy got up early, showered, and dressed as if she actually had a job to go to. She had toast, strawberry yogurt and coffee for breakfast, took her vitamins and sat at the kitchen table with the phone in one hand and the newspaper in the other.

Why am I nervous? These people have no idea who I am. If they say no, that's okay; there were hundreds of jobs in the paper. If they say yes, I'll update my resume and go for an interview. Nothing ventured, nothing gained. No pain, no gain. A bird in the hand…am I insane? Shut up and make a call.

After six phone calls, she went to the computer to email Beth, Gibby and Hillie.

Buds,

Job search went as follows:

1. Just wanting to drive a truck is not enough. I'd have to go to truck driving school. Forget it.

2. CTA bus…hmmm. Something about quotas. I'd have to be a woman of color with English as a second language, over age 45, with no traffic tickets for a year. Disqualified on all counts.

3. Car detailing…flunky at a carwash. Might be fun in the summer—you can wear a bikini. But I have a feeling my boss would be male. Nah.

4. Bakery wanted to know if I was familiar with male and female anatomy in larger than life situations. I told the owner that my own ass is larger than life, but I have only seen it in a mirror; and most male anatomy I've seen has actually been smaller than life. No sense of humor. Fugetaboutit.

5. Painter...white dotted lines on the highway. Need I say more?

6. House remodel/paint job. Have appt tomorrow to check it out. In the northern 'burbs.

Love, Amy

Amy needed a vehicle, and the white Chevy van was priced just right. She had no kids to haul to soccer practice. She wouldn't be hauling two weeks of groceries for a family of six. Fortunately, she wasn't planning to sleep in it and wouldn't be called on to use it to help friends move. Originally just a way to get around, the trusty van suddenly had a new purpose. It turned out to be perfect for hauling a stepladder, paint cans, rollers, brushes, drop cloths and other tools she needed when helping someone out on a painting project. Little did she know how useful it would be.

She found the address: shiny brass numbers embedded in a six-foot-tall brick post that used to support a gate. She followed the curving brick driveway up to the front of the house, shut off the engine and walked to the front door. She checked her watch. On time. The shiny brass knocker was heavy. Knock, knock, knock. Three ought to do it. Four would be too much. Two, not enough. *Why am I nervous? It's just another painting job.*

No answer. She knocked again. There was no doorbell. She waited. Knocked again. No answer. She tried the knob. It was locked.

Amy followed the brick path around to the back door and pressed the doorbell. No answer. Pressed again. No answer.

The "Hello!" she called out was met by silence.

There was a large building on the back of the property. Maybe a garage or workshop. She walked across the lawn and knocked on the door. No answer. She could hear activity inside, so she knocked again. No answer. She tried the knob. The door opened. She poked her head inside and shouted over the din. "Hello!"

A man was standing at a circular saw toward the back of the building. The saw was screaming its way through a large piece of wood balanced very carefully by two muscled arms and a very nice back in a white t-shirt. The workshop smelled like wood—the fragrant aroma that reminded one of construction—of progress being made. In the sunlight, she noticed sawdust in the air, despite a vacuum system hooked up to the saw.

"Hello!"

Obviously he wasn't going to hear her over the grinding of the saw. Amy walked carefully over the concrete floor, slick with sawdust, toward the carpenter. He finished the cut and set the wood aside. She tapped his shoulder.

"What the f…!" He jumped out of his skin, saw Amy, and cut off his last word. He reached over and shut off the saw. "Who the hell are you? You scared the crap out of me! How did you get in here? What do you want?" His face was red and he was breathing hard. All Amy could think was that she would like to brush the sawdust out of his fluffy dark hair.

"First of all, I am Amy Sweet. I got here through that door." She pointed. "I'm here about the painting job we discussed over the phone. I'm sorry I scared you. I knocked and rang, and hollered, and knocked again."

"You didn't scare me, just caught me off-guard." He clarified.

"You said I scared the crap out of you."

"Obviously you didn't. Can we start from the beginning?"

"Please. I called yesterday about the painting and remodeling work. My name is Amy Sweet." She held out her hand. He took it and gave her a firm shake. "I have a 2:30 appointment."

"I'm Logan Carson. That's my house. It needs some work. How many men do you have?"

"I just broke up with…oh, you mean men that work for me?" She blushed, realizing that he thought she just did preliminary work for the "real" painters. "I am the man…er…uh…I'm not a man. I'm the painter." *Idiot!*

"I was pretty sure you're not a man. I'm not an idiot."

"Did I say that out loud?"

"What?" He looked puzzled. "Well, Amy Sweet, I have never had a conversation like this before in my life. Come on into the house, and we'll see if we can't get to the bottom of this over some beer."

She watched as he took a brush that hung by the door. He brushed sawdust off his arms and jeans. He stepped into the yard and banged his boots against a tree, grabbed the bottom of his shirt and with one swift move, pulled it over his head. He shook it out and fluffed his hair, dislodging more sawdust. *I want that to be my job. Fluffing sawdust out of beautiful hair of handsome men. I'll check the want ads again.* She smiled at the thought. *He thinks I'm an idiot.* He pulled his shirt back on and pointed her toward the house.

*

"Wow!" Amy stopped just inside the back door. The kitchen was black, white and red with restaurant-quality appliances. There was a huge butcher-block island with a double sink. Amy detected a wine cooler under the counter, which appeared to be very well stocked. The refrigerator, she determined, was bigger than her kitchen. The cabinets were beautiful, and she wondered if he had made them. Logan flipped three switches and lights popped from the ceiling, oozed from under cabinets, and sparkled across every glossy surface. "I'm very impressed! Did you make the cabinets?"

"You can pretty much assume if it's wood, I made it."

"Mr. Carson, you do beautiful work. So you're a carpenter by trade?"

"Logan, please. I'm not old enough to be Mr. Carson. And no, I just do woodworking as a hobby. I found out long ago that people would like me to make things for them for the cost of the wood. Unfortunately, I'm a bit of a perfectionist, so I take my time and when I'm done with a project it's worth a lot of money. Not many people are willing to pay, so I do it for my own enjoyment."

"You have a great workspace out there. Too bad you can't make a living at something you enjoy."

"What makes you think I don't enjoy what I do for a living?"

"I certainly don't know you well enough to know how you feel about most things, but you just seem so at home amidst the sawdust."

"How long were you watching me?"

Amy blushed. "Just a minute or so, while I was trying to get your attention."

"You know, I'm sorry, please, have a seat." He pulled out a chair for her at a table he probably made. "Didn't mean to leave you standing there. Beer okay?"

"Beer's fine. In a glass, if you have one."

He opened two cabinet doors. A light came on inside the cabinet. The back wall was mirrored and the shelves were glass. Everything sparkled. He smiled. "I believe I have glasses."

"You're showing off!"

"Sorry, I'm proud of this kitchen. I worked hard on it, and I love just sitting in here sometimes with all the lights on. Unfortunately, it's the only room in the house that's finished. I guess that's why you're here, right?"

"Yes, I'm answering your ad for a little remodeling and painting. If this is what you expect, I'm terribly under-qualified." Amy was preparing herself to be politely dismissed.

"Well, yes, I am a perfectionist, but I don't expect others to be. I'd just expect you to be professional. I'll do any woodworking, but I don't have the patience for painting."

"I guess I need to see the house. I'll take some measurements, make some notes, and get back to you with an estimate. Do you have time now for a tour?"

"I can give you half an hour, then I have an appointment. So, living room first."

Logan led her into the huge open space with a ten-foot ceiling. There were no drapes, no personal touches, just a couch and chair and a coffee table. She knew he was not the craftsman of this space.

"What am I matching here? Do I need to check with your wife?"

"I'm not married. I have no emotional attachment to anything in this house. I have a few functional pieces, but nothing you have to strain yourself to match. Just stay away from pink and purple, and we should be fine. And if I see mauve, you're fired."

"If you make me paint something brown, I quit," she retaliated, coyly.

"Deal." He walked past her and she followed him through a huge dining room and up a wide staircase that narrowed as it got to the second floor. Her hand slid lovingly up the silky finish of the banister, certain that Logan made it. He saw her appreciating his sanding and buffing efforts.

"Walnut."

"It's beautiful."

"Thanks. There are four bedrooms up here. Paint the hallway and the closets in the hallway. Don't worry about the bathrooms yet. I'm having them tiled and we can catch up on any painting that remains after that's done."

"Something nice and neutral for the hall?" Amy queried.

"Not white. Something a little warmer, but not dark."

"Mauve might be nice."

He gave her a piercing look. Words weren't necessary. She passed him in the hall on her way to another bedroom. As she got close to him she inhaled his masculine sweat and sawdust scent. He turned and looked at her, caught in the act.

"Did you just sniff me?"

Amy stammered and blushed. "I uh, well, you just smell so woody…um… no, I mean, not like a woody, woodsy. No, not like the woods, not oakey, but, well, it's a good smell. I was just appreciating it."

"You're a peculiar painter, Amy Sweet."

"You don't know the half of it!"

"Do you need more time up here?"

"No, thanks. I'll just take my notes home and work up some numbers for you." She knew she'd have to add in the cost of renting some equipment. "Any deadlines? Parties? Special occasions that I need to be aware of?" She continued.

"This decade would be nice." He took her pen and jotted his phone number and cell number on her notebook. "Call me when you're ready. I'll make it a point to be here in the house so you don't have to knock on so many doors. And a word of warning: never touch a man while he's operating power tools. It could result in the loss of important parts. Some of them might be yours!"

"I'll take that to heart." She held out her hand. "It was nice meeting you, Logan. Hope I'm not up against too much competition."

He took her hand, gave it a squeeze, and held it for a second longer than he should have. "I'm counting on you to come out ahead. Call me."

He closed the front door behind her. That's when Amy realized she had been holding her breath.

Amy got in the van and pulled down the visor, flipped the mirror open, and put her hands on her pink cheeks. She was talking out loud to no one but herself. *What the hell happened in there? Manly man. He's a manly man. Why am I talking like Arnold Schwarzenegger? Not married. He acted married. Not a clue that a woman had anything to do with that house. Except maybe the kitchen. Does he cook? Awesome ass in those jeans. Could be my boss…boss…that means I might have a job. I go from smelly ass to awesome ass. Perfect. I love life. Life is good. Yes it is. Time for oldies on the radio.* She needed to sing to clear her brain.

*

Amy was desperate to share the news that she was sure she had a painting job. No one was home at Beth and Gibby's but Punkin. Hillary was at work, and

Amy didn't want to disturb her. She spread her paperwork on the kitchen table and the paint chips on the counter. She rearranged them several times and set aside the mauve selections just to torment Logan. She had to figure out how to choose bold colors that wouldn't knock you down when you walked into the room. She wanted her selections to be masculine, but not so much that the house felt like a sports bar. She wanted peaceful, quiet, and comfortable for the bedrooms. *His bedroom. What am I thinking!* After struggling for a few minutes, she realized she was not a decorator, she was a painter, and obviously there was a big difference between the two. She didn't want to lose this job. Logan wanted neutral for the hallway upstairs. That would have been her choice as well. That seemed like a good place to start. Should one of the bedrooms be a little more feminine? *Not married. Hmm…but had he ever been?* The first meeting was not the time to delve into Logan's private life. There was something very serious about him, but she also felt there was a sense of humor hiding just beneath the surface of this mysterious man. *He had sad eyes. Beautiful, but sad. Paint*, she chided herself for digressing. *Back to the paint.*

Amy put together a very nice presentation for Logan. She had sketches of each room, including measurements, and had taped the appropriate paint chips to each sketch. They were removable, so last minute switching was easy. She started thinking about dollars. Would there be enough money for her to hire a helper? Did she want a helper? She really did want to do this job herself, but would it take too long with just one person painting? After considering an hourly rate along with the cost of the paint, supplies and equipment, she came up with a total. She added a little cushion that she was prepared to remove if Logan balked. Amy stacked her papers neatly and read the phone number Logan had written on the top page. She called and got an answering machine. She left a brief message that included her phone number and the fact that she had an estimate and some ideas she'd like to discuss. *Now I wait.*

*

Gibby stopped by after work. She had a later-than-usual shift at the hospital and was very tired, but wanted to see how the interview went for the remodeling job. Amy was sitting on the couch in her pajamas watching a rerun of a Cubs game.

"Isn't baseball over for the year?"

"ESPN has reruns sometimes."

"Isn't that kind of stupid? I mean you know who won, don't you?"

Amy looked at her like she was from another planet. "Who cares who won. I mean, I did care at the time the game was live, but now I'm just watching to slobber over the shortstop."

"You're not well. My grandmother would say you need an enema."

"Your grandmother isn't here, and I wouldn't let her come within ten feet of my behind if she were. So, do you want to hear about my project? Where's Beth?"

"Beth is asleep already." Gibby reached under shirt and unfastened her bra. With a few deft moves, she pulled it out of a sleeve and tossed it over a chair. "Waste of fabric. So you're saying an interview turned into a project? That sounds positive."

"It's an old house, four or five bedrooms, although I only saw four. Ten-foot ceilings on the first floor. Huge living room and dining room. It could be beautiful."

"What do you mean, could be? Is it trashed or water-damaged or something?"

Amy shook her head and answered. "It's empty. I mean bare-bones furnishings, nothing on the walls, no pictures or curtains."

"Has it just been prepared for painting? Maybe things are stored away so you wouldn't have to work around them."

"I don't think so. It's like the house has no personality yet—unlike the owner."

"So tell me about her. Do you actually have the job?"

"I have to turn in my estimate and ideas to *him*. And *he* is gorgeous. He's single, a carpenter, mid- to late-30s, I think. Kind of sad, but funny in a way. His name is Logan Carson, and I don't think he has lived there very long. He has a huge workshop and makes beautiful things."

"The name sounds familiar. Are you sure you have the job?"

"No, because he didn't come right out and say I did, but it was just a feeling I had. I think I was the first or only person to answer the ad. I mentioned competition and he pretty much just blew past it. I think if I want it, the job is mine."

Amy tossed the proposal to Gibby. "I know the drawings are primitive, but I think you can kind of get the idea of what I want to do, can't you? Please tell me you see what I'm trying to do."

"Simple, I'd say, but he's not paying an interior designer. This is fine." She handed the proposal back to Amy and picked up her bra from the chair. "See ya tomorrow. I'm dead-dog tired. Congratulations!"

"Thanks! Good night."

Chapter 4

The phone was on its third ring when Amy woke up. She looked at the clock. She knew she wouldn't make it to the phone before the answering machine came on, so she walked to the kitchen and stood next to the phone, waiting while the caller left a message. It would probably be a hang up or wrong number at 6:30 in the morning.

"Amy, this is Logan Carson. I got your message, and this is the first chance I've had to call you back. I'll be home from work today by 1:00 or so, and have the rest of the day free, so if you want to stop by today, give a call back with a time. Thanks. Looking forward to seeing you…your proposal."

Looking forward to seeing me? Suddenly she was energized. She made a pot of coffee and sliced a bagel. After one bite she knew it would need to be toasted to be edible. She plugged in the toaster and crammed the bagel into the slots that were made for white bread. She poured orange juice into a jelly glass that had dinosaurs on it and arranged her vitamins on the counter. Just before the bagel began to smoke she unplugged the toaster. Armed only with a fork, she dug around and the bagel came out in four pieces. She slathered it with apple butter and had eaten half of it when the coffee was done. Sweet and Low and Coffee-mate: highly nutritious additions to caffeine. She poured the coffee into a Baxter Brothers mug—a less-than-cherished souvenir from her former employer—added the necessary chemicals, and stirred. By the time she had taken her vitamins and finished the bagel, the coffee had cooled enough to drink. She chugged down half of it, refilled the mug, and took it into the bathroom with her.

Amy had about five hours to work on her personal hygiene. She sat on the lid of the toilet with her foot over the waste basket. Most of the toenail trimmings went in the basket. The others were fired off randomly and she knew the only way to find them was to walk around in her bare feet. She dabbed her cuticle softener on each toe. She slathered fluffy cleanser on her face and brushed her hair until it was smooth and glossy and all the snarls were out. She swung her legs over the edge of the tub and shaved her legs. She ran the shower water until it was hot, stepped in, and spent twice as long on her shampooing as she normally did. Amy rinsed the cleanser off her face, conditioned her hair, and shaved under her arms. She grabbed the loofah, added plenty of moisturizing cleanser, and scrubbed until her skin glowed. The thick, fluffy towel had been hanging over the heating vent and was nice and warm. She turned off the shower and snuggled into the big towel. She wrapped her hair in another towel and plodded off to her bedroom to finish getting ready for…for what?

"This isn't a date," she told herself. "This is about painting. It's a job, and I'll be dirty and smelly every day." She fluffed her hair and tossed the towel aside. The rant continued. "I just cut my toenails for work. No. No. This is still a job interview. I haven't even been hired yet." Amy wanted to look good. First impressions are important. Except this wasn't the first impression. Amy groaned. She looked in the full-length mirror and addressed her reflection aloud: "I am not doing this because he's cute. I'm doing this because I need the job." *Yeah, right.* She called Logan back and left a message on his machine.

Amy's bed was covered with cast off clothing, as she analyzed her wardrobe possibilities. Pinstripe suit: too stiff. Jeans and sweatshirt: too casual. Jeans and a sweater: maybe. Leopard halter top: too slutty. Gray wool slacks… hmm. Perfect crease, perfect pleats, pockets didn't pull, and the seat wasn't split. They looked great with the little black boots. Add the pink cashmere sweater…well, partly cashmere, partly something else, she wasn't quite sure what. She looked good in pink…wait…he didn't like pink. "He doesn't like pink on his walls, but I bet he'll like it on me." She pulled the sweater over her head and smoothed it over her body. "Don't lie to me, mirror!"

Amy stood up straight, pulled her shoulders back, and sucked in her stomach. Not bad. She reached down and lifted her breasts up, pushed them together, and spoke to them. "That's where you should be. Memo to self: go bra shopping."

Amy carried nail polish, nail file, makeup, tweezers and mirror to the kitchen table where the lighting was the best. She finished the coffee and started the fine-tuning.

*

Logan pulled his 1980 black Mercedes into the garage and shut off the engine. He felt a little on edge and wasn't sure why. He knew that finally doing something with the inside of the house was ending another chapter in his life with Sam. He was sad about that, but excited, too. Would he have been as excited if the painter was a man and not Amy Sweet? Perfect name for her.

Nothing in the refrigerator looked appetizing, but Logan was hungry. He grabbed a handful of baby carrots, a dill pickle and three slices of bologna. He stuffed a slice of bologna into his mouth, bit off a third of the pickle, chewed and repeated twice. He popped the carrots into his mouth one at a time as he bounded up the stairs two at a time. As he undressed he threw his clothes over a chair making sure shorts and socks went into the hamper, just in case Amy looked in his room again. He showered, shaved, trimmed nose hair, brushed and flossed. He scanned for zits and brushed his hair. He picked up the Aqua Velva, set it back down, and went for the more expensive scent. He questioned his mirror. "What are you lookin' at? You got a problem with this?" He poured a little Royal Copenhagen into his palm, rubbed his hands together, and slapped himself on the cheeks. "Yikes! I will never get used to that." He wiped his hands in his armpits, dressed in jeans and a Bob Vila t-shirt, and waited for Amy's arrival.

*

Amy stepped out of the van, purse in one hand and Logan's estimate in the other. She took a deep breath and headed for the front door. She lifted the knocker and the door opened.

"Right on time. That's a point in your favor. Step on in. Kitchen table okay for spreading out?"

"The kitchen table is fine. I notice it's a mauve-free zone."

Logan pulled out her chair and moved a basket of apples.

"Would you like something to drink?"

"So you could show off your fancy cabinets again? No thanks. I'm just fine."

"What do you have for me, Ms. Sweet?"

"First I have a few questions. I basically have colors picked out, but was wondering about some details."

"That's what this meeting is for. Better to know up front, yes?"

"You said there were four bedrooms upstairs, yet I counted five doors. Is one of..."

"You don't need to concern yourself with the fifth room." Logan's voice went from friendly to curt, almost rude.

"No problem. I was just wondering if you wanted one of the bedrooms to be used as a library or maybe a den. I would probably change the colors. Or would you mind if one of the bedrooms was a little more feminine than the others?"

"I don't really need an office. I have a small computer table in my room. I don't have enough books for a library. But the den idea might be nice. You mean it would be darker, cozier?"

"That's what I was thinking. You could move your computer table in there and it might be easier to stay organized."

"Who told you I wasn't organized?"

"Well, uh, no one."

He was teasing.

"I just know from experience that when you start dragging your bills into the bedroom, eventually something ends up in the hamper and then your phone is being shut off."

"I'll take your advice. Take the smallest room and let's plan on it being the den. I'll have to buy a bottle of port. Isn't that what always happened in the old movies? The men retired to the den for cigars and port, while the women discussed doilies or something useful like that?"

"Something like that," Amy said, raising an eyebrow. "Den it will be, then. If you could take care of the trim in there, that would be helpful. A nice rich color, something like the banister?"

"Amy, are you putting me to work?"

"You're the one with the magic touch when it comes to woodwork. It's all yours. I know you said you're not married, and I really don't see evidence of anything too feminine around here, but I was thinking about lightening up one of the rooms. I know you don't want pink, but just something pastel, airy feeling. What do you think?"

"Can we call it cheerful instead of feminine? If I end up sleeping in there for whatever reason, I don't want girl cooties."

Amy smiled and made a deliberate note; "cootie free zone. So, here's my rule for painting: when you can see other rooms from the room you're standing in, it's always nice if they sort of match. Like when you said you want the hall upstairs to be neutral. That's good, because any room you look into from the hall won't clash. The living room and dining room could be different colors as long as they sort of go together. They could be very different if you have something like trim, artwork or drapes that visually connect them. Do you see what I mean?"

"I get the idea. I guess this is a challenge because there isn't furniture, there are no drapes, and you have no clue what is going to end up on these walls."

"True. But I'm willing to jump in with both feet and go for it." Amy handed the proposal to Logan, adding the dark green paint chips to the room that would soon be a den. She stuck pastel blue and yellow chips in the feminine... oops..."cheerful" bedroom. He raised his eyebrows and tried not to smile.

"My number is there. Call me either way, if you would, please. If I'm not doing something right, I'd like the chance to fix it next time." Amy picked her purse up from the chair next to her and started to get up.

Logan asked, "Where are you going?"

"I was going to give you a little time to read this over and think about the time and money in private."

"Well, I do have a problem with the money."

"Oh, I'm sorry. I think I could come down..."

"You're not charging enough. You have no idea what you're getting yourself into here, do you? If I paid what you're asking, I'd be robbing you. You're hired. When can you start?"

"Hired? Really? Great! I guess I can start tomorrow. I'll have to get supplies and paint. I didn't want to assume, you know."

"Are you a painting virgin, Amy? Have you done this before?"

"Virgin? No, I uh, just never charged for it before. I've just done it for free, you know, for friends." She was blushing and he wasn't going to let her off the hook.

"Are we still talking about paint?"

"I am." She stood up, ready to leave.

"Do you have a date? What's your hurry? Sit down a minute. I'll be right back." He took the stairs two at a time and came back downstairs with a check. "This is for half. I'll give you the rest when you're done, unless you run out of paint or brushes or something. Just ask. I'll give you more."

She stared at the amount on the check. "Are you sure? You haven't seen my work."

"I'm taking your word for it. Besides, there isn't a dishonest bone in your body. I can tell by your eyes." He walked her to the door. "Amy?" She turned around and looked at him leaning on the door frame. "Don't buy cheap paint."

"Okay, Boss."

CHAPTER 5

Amy stopped at the bank on her way home and deposited the check from Logan. The next stop was the paint store. She bought primer and supplies and decided she'd come back for colors as she did each room. She was expecting more argument from him on the "cheerful" bedroom. The second-biggest room had the big double windows facing the east. It would be light and cheery. She knew it would be her favorite. She still wondered about the fifth bedroom…or closet, or whatever it was. Maybe in time she'd get to see it. It was probably just storage, she thought, but he had gotten weird when she brought it up.

Back at her condo, Amy called Hillie at work to give her the news. Hillie was her biggest fan. "I knew you'd have something within the week. Good for you. Keep me posted on the progress."

Amy hung up the phone and started out into the hall to see if Gibby or Beth was home. Gibby was at the door in her robe kissing a man. Amy did a double-take. That was no man! That was Martin. Gibby and Martin had been divorced for years.

Gibby was pushing him gently out the door.

"…and you don't have to hurry back…ever!"

"And you don't need to be such a little bitch. Hey, Amy."

"Hello, Marty. Leaving, I hope?"

"Did this one poison your mind against me?"

"No, it's your cheap aftershave."

"Women!"

Amy and Gibby watched Marty swagger down the hall as he headed for the elevator.

"Margaret Gibson, how many times are you going to let that man back into your…house…bed…whatever?"

"He was here thirty-three minutes. You know we can only tolerate each other for half an hour. Longer than that and the name-calling starts."

"Why? Aren't you meeting doctors at work? You have Marty as your fall-back plan? I don't get it."

Amy walked in, sat at the kitchen table and Gibby cinched the belt on her robe. "First of all, I love him, and he loves me. We just can't stand each other." Amy rolled her eyes. She'd heard this story before. "Second, I had an itch that just happened to need scratching and here comes this knock on my door...it was fate."

"Did he ask for money?"

"Yes, but I didn't give him any. And Amy, he's just so darn cute. And third, half the doctors spend most of the day with their heads and hands halfway up some woman's twat. You think they want to look at mine when they come home?"

"I think they're smart enough to separate the two."

"You'd like to think that, wouldn't you? And fourth..."

"There's a fourth?"

"Marty is good and he has stamina."

"What good is stamina if you can't stand to be in his presence for more than thirty minutes?"

"Ames, we've been through this before. He's my ex. Now and then we get together to bump uglies and that's probably the way it will be until one of us ends up in a serious relationship with someone else. Sex is good for your blood pressure."

"Who told you that?"

"I'm a nurse, remember?"

"You're a baby nurse. That has nothing to do with sex."

"Speaking of babies, I'm on my way to the hospital for the late shift. Beth should be home soon if you want to hang around, but I have to get ready."

"I got the job."

Gibby spun around. "What? Really? That's great! When do you start?"

"Tomorrow. He paid me half. I get the rest when I'm done."

"Does he know that it's just you?"

"I told him. I think he's fine with that. He gave me more than my estimate. He said I undercharged and he couldn't rob me."

"Amy, good for you. This sounds like a good opportunity for you. I can assume you shopped already?"

"I shopped and paid the electric bill, the water bill, and bought stamps."

"So, once again, the power of four! Our little sessions helped. Problem solved."

Amy started for her own place. "Have a good shift. Give the babies a hug for me."

Amy walked into her kitchen and saw the answering machine light on. One message. She hit the play button.

"Amy, this is Logan. I may have already left for work by the time you get here tomorrow, so I'm leaving the back door open. There will be a key for you on the kitchen table. Use whatever you need. Make coffee, whatever. Lock up when you leave. Looking forward to seeing progress. Bye."

She played it again and didn't delete it.

CHAPTER 6

A my arrived at Logan's home at 7 a.m. The back door was open, Logan was gone, and a key was on the kitchen table as promised. Logan left a package of gourmet coffee beans on the counter next to the grinder and coffee pot. The thought of smelling a fresh pot of coffee was more than she could bear, so Amy ground some beans, filled the pot with cold water, and pressed the "on" button. There was half-and-half in the refrigerator. *Mmmm. Fat and caffeine.* The way to her heart.

While the coffee was brewing, she began unloading her van. Most of the equipment she would be leaving in the house until she finished. There was no point in loading and unloading every day. She would have to ask Logan if this was okay. After the living room floor was covered with drop cloths, she went into the kitchen, checked several cabinets before she found a mug and fixed the coffee the way she liked it—a little heavy on the cream. It smelled wonderful and she savored the first few sips.

Amy carried the mug with her into the living room. All the walls needed a light sanding, then rinsing before the primer was applied. It would be boring work for a while. It wouldn't get interesting until she started adding color.

It was a typical autumn day in Illinois. The sun was shining, a few trees still had some color, and there was a cool breeze blowing. Amy struggled with a window that had been painted shut. She opened it and let the fresh air in. She was wearing jeans and working up a bit of a sweat. Her hair was pulled back into a tortoise shell banana clip. She hadn't bothered with makeup except for a touch of mascara. Her t-shirt had a picture of Rosie the Riveter and stated that "Girls kick ass." She acted differently in this shirt than when she was wearing the leopard halter top or a silk blouse. The first day on a job where she really had to prove herself called for the Rosie shirt. Not only did she have to prove herself to Logan, she had to prove to herself that she could handle this. She was actually earning money doing something she enjoyed, something she thought she was good at.

Amy was using a rubber mallet to close the lid on the can of white primer when the back door opened and Logan walked in. He took a deep breath, smelling the fresh paint.

"Smells like progress to me!"

"Hello, Logan. Is the smell going to bother you? I opened a window in hopes of clearing out some of this smell out before you got home. Plus, I was a little warm and didn't want to fool with your furnace."

"No problem. I'll be out in my workshop most of the evening. Besides, I never mind the smell of work being done. Especially when I'm not the one doing it."

"Logan, it will take me a while to do this, especially if I do it right. I can hire a helper."

"And I told you, there are no deadlines. Take your time. I'm gone almost every day and spend a lot of the evenings in the workshop. I'll try to stay out of your way."

"Oh, you're not in my way. I don't mind the company. I can actually do two things at once; like paint and talk."

"If you need things moved, let me know the night before, and I'll help."

Logan left for the kitchen, where he opened the refrigerator, leaned on the door, and browsed for something that looked appetizing. He just didn't have the heart for cooking when he was the only one eating. Amy came in and rinsed out the coffee pot and threw away the grounds. She washed out her mug and placed it in the dish drainer.

"Amy, do you cook?"

"I have a good grasp of the basics, but have to follow recipes precisely for something fancy. You're not going to tell me you have this awesome kitchen and don't cook."

"I cook. I just don't plan."

"Here's the key," Amy explained. "Find two recipes you'd like to make per week. Write down the ingredients, and what you want for sides. You know, green beans, salad, corn. Go to the store, buy the stuff, and fix both things on the same day. This keeps dish-washing to a minimum. Then when you get home, you have two choices in the fridge. Alternate days, and you won't get bored. It's great: you don't have to cook every day, you get good meals, and you save money." Suddenly she got embarrassed, realizing she was lecturing a grown man on how to manage his weekly meal plan. He had his arms crossed over his chest, grinning at her.

"Sorry. Didn't mean to tell you how to run your kitchen. I'll go now. I assume I can take the key with me?"

"Yes, you can take the key. I leave pretty early and would rather not leave the door open. And I appreciate your cooking advice, Rosie."

Amy glanced down at her shirt, ready for the laundry. "That's me! Kick ass and take names! Good night, Logan."

"See you tomorrow."

CHAPTER 7

A my walked into her apartment and stripped her work clothes off as she walked toward the bathroom. A shower would feel good. Her shoulders and upper arms ached from reaching all day. She gave Logan good advice for meal planning, but she was too tired to eat. Well, too tired to cook. She'd pick at something—probably cheese and crackers with sweet pickles. She let the warm water soothe her strained muscles. It had been quite a while since she had undertaken physical labor for an entire day.

"I can do this," she thought out loud. "I had a good day. I have a great boss…myself! And a gorgeous client…I have a client! Life is good."

She climbed out of the shower, fell into bed and was asleep as her head hit the pillow.

*

Logan popped the top on a Michelob longneck, placed the bottle to his lips and took a long swallow. He picked up a Betty Crocker cookbook from the collection of cookbooks on the counter. Sitting at the kitchen table, he ran his hand across the cover, remembering how many times he'd seen Sam planning meals, flipping pages and looking for something new to tempt his taste buds. He took a deep breath and thumbed pages to the section titled "main dishes." Carefully poking through the trash, he pulled out an envelope that contained part of his overabundance of junk mail. Scanning recipes, he decided on a chicken-and-rice casserole and baked short ribs. On the scrap, he made note of the ingredients that were not in his pantry, added salad (already cut up in the bag would have to do), and planned to stop at the grocery store after work the next day. He left the list on the kitchen table and went upstairs to change into clothing more appropriate for sanding. He worked for two hours, ate a banana to stop the growling in his stomach, and went to bed.

*

Amy had been asleep for about an hour when she heard a knock on her door. She stumbled out of bed, tripped over her towel and grumbled, "Just a minute." She looked out the peephole on her door and saw Gibby, still in her nurse's uniform, cheerful green with a teddy bear print. She was a mess, face wet with tears, eyes red.

Amy opened the door. "What's wrong?"

Gibby walked over to the couch and sat down. Amy handed her the tissue box and sat down in front of her on the edge of the coffee table. "Tell me."

"I hate my job, Ames."

"You love your job. What happened?"

"We had a preemie that I've been taking care of for two weeks. The parents had been trying for years to get pregnant. They were so happy. Her little lungs just couldn't do it. She died this evening. The parents are crushed. It's so pathetic. Sometimes I think I just can't stand watching the suffering. It beats me up. I feel so useless when something like this happens. I'm sorry to dump on you, but Beth was asleep, and I know she has to get up at the crack of dawn."

"I don't mind. I can be pretty flexible with Logan."

"Logan, is it? I still think I know that name from somewhere." She blew her nose and came back to the reason of her visit. "Why is it Ames, that people who want so badly to have babies just can't make it work?"

"It's not a perfect world. Life isn't fair. Pick your favorite platitude. I don't have an answer."

"I know that, and I don't expect you to. I just had to fall apart for a few minutes." Gibby took another tissue out of the box. "Got any wine open?"

"That won't help."

"In the long run, no, but my feet are cold and I want to go to sleep and not toss and turn about this whole thing."

"How about we split what's left?"

"You're a pal. I'm just very sad. Distract me. How did your day go at the big painting project?"

Amy took a deep breath. "Well. First, I'm sore. My shoulders are killing me. Maybe this wine will help me, too. Second, I embarrassed myself by lecturing a grown man on how to budget his food preparation time. Third, I really like this job. The only one that smells bad is me by the end of the day. I can come and go as I please and work at my own pace."

"Not every client will be that flexible, you know."

"I know, but for now, this one is, and I'm going to take advantage of it to make sure I do this job right. I'll need him for a reference, I'm sure. Besides, he's easy on the eyes."

Gibby questioned her. "Did you ever say if he was married, divorced or what?"

"I asked. He's not married. I didn't ask if he was divorced, but I have a feeling that at one time there was a woman involved in his life. The kitchen is beautiful and he doesn't seem that thrilled about cooking."

Gibby tipped her glass up to get every last drop. "Yummy. I'm going home. Thanks for being my dumping ground." Amy took her glass and set it in the sink with her own. She walked her neighbor to the door.

"Give me a hug, Gibbs. You're a good nurse. You wouldn't care so much if you weren't. Those parents were lucky to have you taking care of their baby. You're a blessing to them, though they may not realize it right now."

Gibby hugged Amy hard and patted her back. "It's just hard."

"I know. Have a good sleep."

Amy locked the door and headed back to her room. She picked up her wet towel, tossed it over the shower curtain rod, brushed her teeth, and set her alarm for 8 a.m. instead of 6 a.m. Logan would understand.

CHAPTER 8

The light sage-green on three of the living room walls had the effect Amy wanted. It was calming and went well with the carpeting and the bluish-green of the juniper bushes that were visible from the front windows. She hoped Logan would like her vision for the room. Ten-foot-high walls are a bit more overwhelming than a paint chip. The fourth wall and part of the dining room would be just a touch darker. She'd pick up there the following day. She planned to stay a while since she had gotten a late start, but this seemed like a good place to stop for the day. She was in the process of cleaning up when Logan came through the back door. His arms were full of groceries.

"Good. You're still here. I was hoping you could get me started here before you leave."

"Started with what? Are there more bags in the car?"

"No, thank goodness. I don't know if I'll have room for all this as it is."

"Logan, you have a huge kitchen. You have room. Believe me. What did you want me to get started?"

"I followed your advice." He put meat in the refrigerator and some cans in the pantry. "I went through a cookbook and found two recipes that appealed to me at the time...of course, last night I was starving, so anything would have looked good to me. I made a list and shopped after work."

"I'm impressed. What are you making?"

"A chicken thing and some kind of ribs that I never had before. They sounded good and I think they bake at the same temperature. I can bake them together, can't I?"

"Unless you have some kind of strange religious dietary laws, yes, they can go in the oven together." She smiled at his lack of kitchen experience, but was impressed at his effort to try.

Logan pulled Betty Crocker off the shelf and opened to the pages he marked. Amy looked on and agreed that the recipes he chose sounded good to her, too, especially since she had finished lunch almost five hours before.

"So? What do you think? Do they seem too hard to follow?"

"You have an excellent book for less-experienced cooks. Do you want me to help you get started?"

He breathed a sigh of relief. "Would ya? You're not too tired? I don't think it will take too long. You won't have to stay while they bake, just nudge me in the right direction."

"Okay. First, wash your hands. I have a nurse friend who has pounded this into my brain. Always wash your hands. Then, since chicken is a little more fragile as far as bacteria goes, we'll leave it in the fridge, and do the ribs first." Amy read the recipe while Logan gathered all the ingredients on the counter.

"Amy, have you ever seen ribs like this? They're so wide."

"I suppose you're thinking spare ribs or baby back ribs?"

He nodded.

She explained, "These are beef, not pork, and they're called short ribs."

"Short on meat, if you ask me."

"That's why they're so cheap and why you need so many pounds of them for a recipe. Now, I'd rinse them off. You don't have to, but the way they're cut, sometimes you get these little bone chips. If you're a manly man you'd probably just swallow them whole, but…"

"Rinse them. It has nothing to do with my manliness." He flexed his biceps and grinned at her. "Certain things shouldn't crunch."

"I'll rinse ribs, you slice onions. Peel them and slice them thin." She patted the ribs dry with paper towels and admired his pile of onion slices. "Now mix the wet ingredients and prepare to massage your ribs."

"Wouldn't you rather do that?"

"What, massage your ribs?" Amy blushed. *Yes, oh yes, indeed I would.* "You can do it. If it was baby oil maybe I would, but mustard? Not touching it." She handed him a baking dish, he layered the coated ribs and she covered them with the onions. As Logan placed the dish in the oven Amy took the chicken out of the refrigerator.

"Gather your ingredients while I wash the chicken."

"You seem to enjoy washing meat. Do the breasts get massaged, too?"

"Mr. Carson, you are deliberately baiting me or trying to embarrass me, aren't you?"

"I just made an observation and asked a question. I'm a manly man, remember? I'm good at massaging breasts."

"This is a cooking lesson, not an anatomy class."

"Just another observation, by the way. You have green paint on your cheek. It clashes with the blush."

She ignored him. "Measure the rice and mix your wet ingredients. I'm removing the skin. You don't need the fat," she instructed.

"You think I'm fat? I've only gained fifteen pounds since high school. I'm in good shape."

"Chill out, Chubby. I didn't say you were fat. I meant you don't need to eat fat. Big difference."

"So you think I'm chubby?"

"Oh good grief! I think we're done here. Put the lid on and set the timer. I have to get home. I feel icky and sweaty."

"You smell great."

"Logan, were you sniffing me?" Hadn't he accused her of that very thing when they first met?

"I smell paint and a hint of something else."

"Onions."

"Maybe. Good enough to eat."

"You have a nice supper. I'll see you tomorrow."

Logan watched her walk down the front sidewalk to her van. He reached through his shirt and pinched a little belly skin. "No more doughnuts for you, fat boy."

CHAPTER 9

A my walked down the hall to her condo and noticed her door was open. Punkin was sitting in front of it like a guard cat.

"You big orange pig with fur, what are you doing here?"

Beth was standing in the kitchen holding up two dresses from Amy's closet.

"Well, what do you think, the black or the black?"

"Since my legs are longer than yours, you should probably take the black with the slit. Your boobs will look better in that one, too. What's the occasion?"

"I have an honest-to-goodness date. Some fool man is actually going to buy me dinner."

"Do I know this fool man?"

"Well, no, and neither do I. He's the brother of the boyfriend of a girl I work with. We're going to double. How queer. I thought I grew out of double dates in high school. Anyhoo, he thinks southern accents are so charmin'. Really, Ames, I've been a northerner for so long you'd think my little drawl would be hardly noticeable, but I guess a little of it still hangs on."

"You think so, shugah?"

"Don't mock me, friend," she warned jokingly, "not if you want the scoop when I get home."

"Beth, does this man have a name?"

"I'm sure he does, I'm just not sure what it is. I think it starts with a T. And it's short, like Tom or Ted. Barbara, my friend from work, her boyfriend's name is Kirk, and he's pretty cute, so I'm hopin' this is a genetic thing. I'm sure we'll be introduced, and I'll make it a point to remember his name."

"Remember, that dress is dry-clean only, so don't go pulling a 'Monica' on me."

"You get your horny mind out of the gutter. If this man is lucky, he may get a goodnight kiss on the cheek from me. And maybe I'll give him my phone number."

"You want to borrow my black slip?"

"No thanks, Ames. I bought a black thong, of all things, and I want no visible lines, straps, bulk, etc."

"He doesn't know it yet, but he's already lucky. Have a good time. Take notes."

"Come on, Punkin, Sweetie. We have a little prep work to do."

*

Amy closed her door and tried to remember the last time she had dressed up to go out. She and Crane had fallen into the 'comfy' rut and went on most of their dates in jeans. He must have been bored with her, she concluded. *Was it my fault? No. He cheated. Bored or not, he cheated.* She picked up the dress Beth rejected and carried it back to the closet. The answering machine was blinking. Caller ID showed Hillary calling, probably just before Beth arrived for the dress. Amy dialed her number and Hillie picked up on the first ring.

"Hey, stranger, been busy painting for the mystery man?"

"Busy painting and massaging ribs and breasts."

"What? Are you taking massages instead of cash? Who's doing the massaging? This is more interesting than I ever thought painting could be!"

"Actually, it's a long story, but the painting turned into a little cooking lesson."

"I have time for the long version." Amy sat cross-legged on the couch and started from the beginning.

"So you see, it's all very innocent, just a little innuendo to try to make me blush…and he succeeded."

"Come on, Amy, it doesn't take all that much to make you blush."

"Logan's cute and mysterious and I work for him, so anything beyond painting is pretty much out of line, don't you think?"

"You got half the money?"

"Yes."

"Problem solved. Do half the work, throw him to the floor, and go for it!"

"Believe me, Hillie; I've mentally thrown him to the floor many times. I'm kind of afraid of him. Not afraid that he'd hurt me, but there is something about him that I can't figure out. I think it has something to do with an old girlfriend or ex-wife. He has this barrier I can sense…like you'd get just so far asking personal questions, and then be shut down."

"You have plenty of time to finish this job, right? So, little by little, just ask a little something to get a clue."

"Gibby thinks his name sounded familiar to her. I don't know where they could have met. Maybe I'll start there. Maybe she knows him from the hospital. I could ask if he has ever been to St. Mary's."

"I was just wondering, have you ever had a spinal tap?" Hillie mocked. "Medical stuff is kind of personal. Just take clues from conversations. Share a little about yourself and maybe he'll open up."

"I'm not going to force anything. If he wants to talk, I'll listen. Another goal is to get back out to that workshop. He has several projects started and I'd love to watch."

"There's a good opening for you. Ask him to show you his power tools. Tell him you're interested in a good long screw."

"You speak the truth, my friend. But I'm going to let things move along at his pace …until I can't stand it anymore!"

"So, Crane is history?"

Amy smiled. "Ancient. Gotta go. My shoulders need the heating pad."

"See you this weekend?"

"Maybe. We'll have to hear about Beth's blind date."

"Is she dating the flower guy?"

"Goodnight, Hillie."

CHAPTER 10

Amy stopped at the hardware store on her way to Logan's the next day. She bought a textured roller that would be nice for the wall along the stairs in the dining room. As usual, Logan was already gone. He had started leaving the coffee and a mug on the counter for her. Today there was also a note.

Ms. Sweet,
Thank you for the cooking lesson.
Check the fridge.
Lunch is on me.
You can have either the ribs or the chicken. Or both.
I'll be late. Don't wait up.
Ha ha.
L

She tucked the note into her purse and made coffee. After four hours of painting, she headed for the kitchen. Her yogurt and cheese crackers could wait for tomorrow. She placed the individual serving of the chicken and rice in the microwave and waited for the buzzer. She found the silverware drawer, took a fork and dug in. Not bad. She finished the coffee and went back to work.

Amy came to a place in the room where she needed to change colors or sand. There was too much wet paint to sand and she knew she didn't have the energy to do another whole wall. It seemed like a good time to clean up. She remembered the note from Logan. *I'll be late.*

She was dying to get another look into the workshop. Would he show her if she asked? Probably. She was sure it would be locked. He had a lot of tools and equipment. There was a key ring by the back door beckoning her. She checked her watch, her stomach flipped, and she picked up the key. She followed the path worn in the grass from Logan's frequent trips to the workshop. When she got to the door she looked at the lock, and then looked at the keys. The first one didn't turn, but the second one did. She opened the door and had a brief scare that there might be an alarm. Nothing buzzed.

She took a few steps inside. There was wood everywhere and it smelled wonderful. He was very neat and organized. Several projects were in different stages of completion. Some almost done, a dresser, a shelf, others she couldn't yet recognize because they were just parts, unfinished and not assembled. She decided to ask Logan for a tour. He'd probably do it. If he said no, she'd take Hillie's advice and use that for a good place to start a conversation. She locked the door and went back to the house. After wiping a little mud off her shoes, she went in, found a notepad and left Logan a note.

L,
Thanks for lunch...the 3 of us done good (you, me and Betty).
See you tomorrow.
ASS

"Ass?" Logan asked himself out loud. "Is she calling me an ass? Probably her initials. Obviously the product of cruel parents." He opened the refrigerator door and noticed that Amy had eaten the chicken for lunch. He chose a container of ribs, put them in the microwave and thawed two pieces of garlic bread. Knowing he would be in the workshop, he opted for iced tea instead of beer. He inhaled the garlic bread and noticed that the ribs were better the second day. He ate fast and wrapped the bones in his napkin. He threw the napkin away and tied up the trash bag. He took it with him on his way to the workshop. That's when he noticed the mud by the back door. He didn't think too much of it until he noticed small footprints in the sawdust on the workshop floor. They were obviously not from his shoes. He would have to remember to interrogate...uh, no...*quiz* Amy about it tomorrow.

CHAPTER 12

Amy was sitting on the edge of the couch with bills spread out on the coffee table in front of her. She had them arranged in due-date order, then decided to put them in dollar-amount order, smallest to largest. It made sense to her. You could pay more bills if you paid less to each. That would mean that fewer people would be calling you to remind you that you missed a payment. However, it would also mean that if you didn't make the mortgage payment, you'd be spreading your bills out on a park bench or moving back home. Yikes. Her accounting strategy was interrupted by Punkin jumping onto the middle of the table, sitting on the phone bill, and proceeding to lick himself—or herself, whatever. Beth was a few steps behind.

"Please remove your mutant cat from my paperwork."

"Come on, Punkin, we're going to let Aunt Amy pay her bills," Beth said.

"How pathetic! I'm the aunt to a cat. By the way, have you ever discovered the sex of that beast?"

"Well, you know we went to the vet. He said Punkin had extensive surgery, maybe from an injury or something, and probably had been neutered. There are several scars on his/her belly and beyond and he wasn't quite sure what to make of it. Punkin's so shy that I've never witnessed litter box usage, so that's no help."

"So there's no way to tell the sex of this fur ball?"

"We could have an autopsy done, but frankly, Amy, I don't have the heart for it." Punkin stretched, yawned and rolled over the bills.

"Freak of nature, get off my bills!"

Beth picked up the cat and sat on the floor next to the couch. "Terry."

Amy looked at her. "What?"

"Starts with a T. His name is Terry. The blind date…remember?"

"Did you have a good time? Start at the beginning."

"I'll give you the abbreviated version. I went through the whole thing with Gibby and I don't have the strength to do it again."

"Let's hear it. Is he cute?"

"Yes, in his own way. He has some endearing flaws. He looks like Richard Gere's uglier brother."

"I didn't know Richard Gere had a brother, and how do you know what he looks like?"

"Terry looks a little like he could be Richard Gere's brother if he had one, but not as cute as Richard. That doesn't mean he isn't cute, because he is, but I'm just explaining what he looks like."

"Got it."

"Anyway, he has a little scar on one eyebrow and it kind of looks like Morse code, you know, dashes. He has an inch-long hair shooting out of his earlobe. I don't know how he missed it if he was even close to a mirror, but I'm not going to consider that a flaw since it's so easily remedied. Nose hair was neatly trimmed, though. That's always a plus. Keeps the whistling down to a minimum. He crossed his legs and I noticed that his leg looked clean-shaven. I thought that was odd, but maybe he's a swimmer and shaves to reduce resistance in the water. He has a nicely shaved neckline. You know how important the clean neck is to me. He has nicely shaped nails on manly hands. You know what I mean?" Amy nodded. "Not really manicured, but clean nails and little tufts of hair above each knuckle."

"So, you're saying he was like a sampler of hair. You didn't follow him into the men's room, did you?"

"You're nasty, Amy Sweet. No I did not."

"What about his head? Does he have hair there, where it belongs?"

"Yes and no. That's where the similarity to Richard Gere ends, I'm afraid."

"So he's bald."

"Did I mention he has a very healthy scalp?"

"Did he shave his head, like to reduce resistance in the shower, or is this a naturally occurring condition?"

"Quite natural, I'm sure. He has a lovely wreath of brown hair around his head…actually more like a hula skirt."

"Please don't tell me he's doing the comb-over."

"I'd have walked right out the door. Give me some credit. You know how I feel about bald. As long as the scalp isn't lumpy and crusty I kind of like it."

"Did you ever get beyond the hair? Is he nice? Details, please!"

"He sells John Deere tractors in Iowa. He has a beautiful smile, which of course, tractor salesmen need." Amy didn't see the connection, but she let Beth continue. "He comes to Chicago about four times a year. He drives a pickup truck with a gun rack."

"Are there antlers mounted on the hood?"

"He's a farm boy, not a hillbilly. And the gun rack holds an umbrella and a baseball bat. You know how I feel about guns, so he's okay on that count. I don't have a problem with bats, considering Alex Gonzales and all."

"Don't get me started. I'm having withdrawal and it will last until spring."

"I gave him my number, but I'm afraid, Ames."

"Why? You're a grown adult woman…if he's nice, if he likes you and you like him, and he calls, what are you afraid of?"

"I like him. He's so sweet. He goes to church. He respects his mother. He has a savings account. He cooks on the grill. He's never had a speeding ticket. His favorite movie is *The Sound of Music*."

"Now that scares me."

"Don't you see? He comes here four times a year. How can a relationship develop when you see someone four times a year?"

"Well, there's this new invention called the telephone. You can talk to people far away. There's email. You could go to Iowa to visit. You can write letters."

"I'm afraid to get involved in something that I can't nourish. You know how relationships are. You have to care for them. It takes a little effort. I think I'm willing to put forth a little effort here, but I'm afraid I'll be hurt."

"Sometimes feeling nothing is worse than feeling a little hurt. Give him a chance. Do you have his number or are you waiting for him to call you?"

"He said he'd call me, but he also gave me his business card. It's so cute. It has this little green tractor in the corner. And it does have an email address. And a fax number."

"How long is he in town?"

"Three more days. If he doesn't call me tomorrow, I'll call him. I think I have to be brave and just jump into this thing."

"Did he get lucky? Did you give him the kiss on the cheek that you mentioned?"

Beth stood up and Punkin got up with her. They walked to the door together.

"Absolutely not. He gave me a very soft, sweet kiss right on the lips and I licked his pretty little teeth."

Amy laughed. "You shameless hussy!"

Beth turned around before she closed the door. "And he patted my behind."

Amy was happy for her friend and hoped she'd get a phone call soon. She picked up the mortgage bill, wrote a check and tossed the rest of the bills on her kitchen counter.

*

Amy had Logan's key in her hand, and as she aimed for the lock, the back door opened. She jumped back a bit, startled at seeing him home that time of day.

"Good morning! Didn't expect to see you here."

"Come on in. I'm working at home today and usually do on Fridays. Hope I won't disturb your painting."

"Hope I won't disturb your work. I'm pretty quiet, usually, unless I turn on some music."

"Just do whatever you usually do when I'm not here. Coffee?"

"Please."

He already had her cup out on the counter. He poured and she added cream.

"Can I make you some breakfast? I'm having raisin toast with peanut butter."

Amy winced. "No thanks. I ate at home."

The toaster popped. Logan spread the creamy-style peanut butter in a haphazard pattern and took a big bite. He took his coffee cup and headed for the stairs. "See ya later." Amy put her yogurt in the refrigerator and headed to the dining room to continue where she had left off the day before.

Maybe he wasn't a morning person. He was usually chatty at the end of the day but he seemed rather aloof that morning. Was he mad at her? The painting was going well. Maybe she should go.

"Logan?" she hollered up the stairs. "I think I'm just going to go and let you work in peace."

"Stay. Really. You won't bother me one bit."

"Well, if you're sure…"

"Positive. Let's plan on lunch about noon. I'll come out of hiding then. But if you need something before then, feel free to disturb me." He walked back into his room and closed the door behind him.

Amy dug in and got to work so Logan would see some progress when he came down for lunch. She opened the window in the living room and propped the kitchen door open to get a little air moving. It helped the paint dry and got some of the smell out of the house. She was at the kitchen sink rinsing out a roller, getting ready to change colors, when Logan walked in. She looked up at the black-and-chrome clock. Noon. He was prompt.

"It's freezing down here." He rubbed his arms.

Amy closed the back door. "Sorry. I needed a little ventilation. The primer seems to smell a little stronger than the regular paint. I'll close the living room window, too."

"No, really, that's okay. Obviously you're working harder than I am."

"I don't know about harder, but maybe more physical labor, unless you're moving furniture up there."

"No, just brain strain."

"It's nice that you can work from home. I assume you use the computer?"

"It saves me a commute, and you know, Friday traffic. Everyone trying to get on the expressways for the weekend at the same time, in a hurry, distracted by weekend plans. Who needs it?"

"I used to take the train, so I didn't really mind the commute. I got a lot done on the train. My best friend lives downtown so her commute is painless. I have another friend who works at St. Mary's as a nurse. She has the same complaints you do."

"St. Mary's?" His expression changed. Nothing obvious, just something Amy sensed.

"Her name is Margaret Gibson. Do you know her?"

"No. Soup and grilled cheese okay?" Subject changed.

"Sounds good. Can I help?"

"Go in the pantry and pick out the soup du jour. Your choice." Her favorite was bean and bacon, but she wasn't risking that with Logan home. Vegetable beef and grilled cheese sounded good to her.

"Rye bread with provolone okay with you?"

"That sounds like some kind of gourmet grilled cheese sandwich."

"I put sweet pickle slices on mine. I also have sliced tomato."

"I'll have tomato on mine."

"Paper plates and napkins are under the sink, unless you insist on china."

"Paper is fine with me. Logan, are you mad at me? Did I do something wrong? Don't you like the paint?"

"I am not mad at you. I like the paint."

"Did I do something wrong?"

"You mean like going into my workshop when I wasn't home?"

"Oh boy. How did you know about that?"

"You left delicate little footprints in the sawdust."

"I'm sorry, I was…"

"Please don't make something up. If you want a tour just ask. If you need tools just ask. You know where the key is. I don't mind that you went out there, but I don't want you feeling like you have to sneak around."

"I wasn't going to make something up." She was, but he changed her mind. The truth always works. "I've been fascinated by it since that first day when I saw you working. Your craftsmanship around here just made me want to see more. Yes, I'd love a tour. I'd love to see your projects." *I'd love a good, long screw.* "I doubt that I'll ever need to borrow tools. It was just curiosity that went out of control."

"We'll go out after lunch. I'll show you the rocking chair I'm working on."

"Great. I saw spindles and wondered what they were for."

"Those are for another project. The rocking chair is almost ready to be stained."

"What's the other project?"

"Want to grab a couple of soup bowls? This is almost ready."

Hmm, subject changed again.

"And why did you call me an ass?"

"What are you talking about?"

"In your note." He pulled the paper out of his shirt pocket. "See you tomorrow, ass."

Amy laughed. "See you tomorrow. Period. A.S.S., my initials: Amy Sue Sweet."

"What could you have possibly done to piss off your parents before you were even born?"

"You know, I thought when I got out of high school the childish business of making fun of someone's name was finished, but I guess not."

"Come here, ass, and get your sandwich."

"You can kiss my ass, you power tool geek."

"Now is that any way to speak to your favorite client?" *I'd love to kiss your ass,* she thought.

"What makes you think you're my favorite?"

"You're just itching to check out my wood. And if you're nice, I'll let you do it right after lunch."

"In your dreams." *And mine,* she thought.

*

After lunch Logan wrapped up the trash and Amy put bowls, spoons and glasses in the dishwasher.

"Are you sure you have time to give me the tour of your inner sanctum?"

"I'm positive. Let me run upstairs and get shoes. Did you bring a jacket? I don't keep it very warm out there."

"I'll be fine. I have sleeves and a protective coating of paint spatters."

Logan bounced down the stairs, looking forward to showing off his favorite place. He took the key that Amy had used the day before and held the door for her. She followed him to the workshop and waited while he opened the door. He flipped on the light switch and motioned for her to go in before him.

"I love this smell. It's so new and fresh."

"I agree. I love the stain, the glue, all of it. I love the feel of the wood as I'm sanding. You run your hand across it and it feels smooth, but you change grit on the sandpaper and just when you think you're done, it feels silkier. So you rub a little longer. It only gets better. You can see some nice furniture in stores, but the truth comes home when you rub your hand across the finish. Machine work just can't compare to hand-sanding."

"But obviously, you do a lot of machine work here."

"Cutting, sure, and initial sanding, but you can't beat the hand-rubbed finishes. Come here and I'll show you what I mean. You'll never get a sliver from something I've made."

She walked over to the rocking chair that was almost finished. He dusted the seat off and motioned for her to sit. She did. Her arms fit perfectly and the shape of the back just drew her head naturally to rest.

"Logan, this is wonderful. It's so comfortable and it isn't even padded."

"The person I'm making it for is about your size, so I knew it would feel good to you."

"You measure people before you make chairs for them? I thought you didn't make things to sell?"

"Well, yes, you sort of measure. A chair for a child would be smaller than a chair for a football player, but you don't have to be precise, just close. And I'm not making it to sell. It's a gift."

"Lucky recipient." She rocked gently, reluctant to stand up.

"I'll show you what I mean about the sanding. Stand up and feel the arms." She did, feeling both and enjoying the tactile sensation.

"Very nice. Smooth and silky."

"Now feel the seat." She rubbed with both hands.

"Oh, Logan, this is like butter! I want to put my face on it."

"The arms aren't finished yet. The seat is oak. The back is walnut. Feel the spindles. Can you tell the difference in the wood?"

She ran her hand up and down with no fear of splinters. She closed her eyes as she stroked. "Yes. The grain is closer. It feels harder, almost as if it's coated with something."

He watched her stroking and realized he had stopped breathing. "It isn't. It's just the difference in the wood."

Amy looked up at him and smiled. "Are you warm? You look a little flushed."

"No, I'm fine."

"Mr. Carson, you are a master with wood and I'm honored to know a true craftsman. I'd love to watch you work sometime."

"I usually don't have an audience, but I suppose that could be arranged, maybe some day when you finish up early. I might even let you help."

"You'd let me touch your tools? A mere mortal like me who doesn't know maple from mahogany?"

"There are very few people who I even allow in here and even fewer that have permission to touch my tools, but I think we can work something out. Of course, you'll need some hands-on training from me."

"Whose hands on whose tools? I think you're trying to make me blush again, Logan. Some day your teasing is going to get you more than you bargained for."

I look forward to that day, she thought. "You're quite the bargain."

"I'm pretty good with the smaller tools, but the big, powerful ones scare me." She winked. *Two can play at this game*, she thought.

"Big ones are fine for some things, but precision, quality and durability are usually more important."

"Is that your way of saying size doesn't matter?"

He laughed out loud, being caught off-guard at his own game. "I guess it is. I have to get back to work, unless there's something else you need to see."

She pointed to a box with small spindles. "What are those for?"

"Nothing." With his hand on the small of her back, he directed her to the door, locked up and went back upstairs to his work.

She enjoyed the tour of the workshop and being allowed into a part of his life where not many people were privileged to go. It was obvious to her that there were just some things he wasn't willing to share. Yet.

Amy realized they really had not yet had a personal conversation. He was very good at changing the subject. *This is a job. What should I expect? You don't sit down with co-workers or your boss and spill your guts after knowing them for a week,* she thought. Was it only a week? She was very comfortable with Logan. She walked in and out of his house the way she, Beth and Gibby walked in and out of each others' homes. And he was a tease…and she liked it. He would be fun if he weren't so guarded. Then she decided she would go home early and not paint on Saturday. She planned to, but maybe she just needed to step back. She realized she felt a little chemistry with Logan. Did he tease others the way he teased her? Was it simply manly-man banter, or was he really interested in having her touch, rub, massage. *Good grief! I need a break*, she thought. She finished another wall, cleaned up, and ran up the stairs. She knocked lightly on Logan's door.

"Come in, Amy."

She opened the door. "How did you know it was me?"

He looked over the top of his glasses and raised his eyebrows. "Did you let someone else in?" *Duh*, she thought.

"Well, no. You wear glasses."

"Yes I do. Was this something you needed to announce?"

"Don't be a butt, Logan. I just came to tell you that I am taking off. I'll see you on Monday."

"You're not coming over tomorrow?"

"No, I need a break. I have stuff to do at home that I haven't done all week because I'm sore at the end of the day. I get home, put on my jammies, and crash on the couch until bedtime."

"Well, now I feel bad. If I'm working you too hard, just shorten your day. I told you there is no deadline on this painting project. I don't care if it takes a year. Don't beat yourself up over this."

"There sort of is a deadline. And please don't think that I don't appreciate what you're paying me, but it won't last me for a year, so I will eventually have to line up another job."

"Right. I didn't think of that. You don't have a regular job? Just painting for me?" He motioned for her to have a seat on the bed.

Was this an honest-to-goodness conversation about something besides food, paint or wood? "I got fired from a job I had for eight years because I was a threat to my boss," Amy explained. "He was a dope and knew that I could blow the whistle on his ineptitude. Besides, he smelled like sweaty man-ass."

"What?"

"He smelled like…"

"I heard what you said and I'm aware of the condition. There's a cure for it. It's called 'haul your stinking ass into the shower.' It's guys like him that give men a bad name."

"You're my hero." She stood up to leave.

"Sit a minute…do you have time?"

She sat back down. "Sure."

"So you got fired and just decided to paint houses for a living?"

"Not exactly. I have three very good friends, and whenever one of us is plopped in the middle of a dilemma, we get together and brainstorm…usually under the influence of wine, chocolate and ice cream."

"That's quite the combination. Four women and three powerful drugs. Could be deadly for your enemies."

"It was quite a day…seems so long ago now. I also got dumped by my boyfriend on the same day."

"I'm sorry to hear that." *Not.*

"He got his girlfriend—who apparently was not me—pregnant."

"I see." He was just letting her ramble, not quite ready to have her leave the house for the day.

"That's when we decided that life is too short to spend it doing a job you don't like. I like to paint, so if I can make a living at it, yada, yada, I'll be happier."

He took off his glasses. "That sounds like a good plan and I totally agree."

"Then why are you in here and not out in your workshop earning your living making beautiful things from wood?"

"What makes you think I don't?"

"For one thing, you're here all day sitting in front of a computer without a speck of sawdust in sight."

He motioned to her with his finger. "Grab a chair. Take a look."

She pulled up a chair and sat next to him in front of the computer. He pressed the 'enter' key and the screen filled with a gazebo. "Logan, it's beautiful!"

"I'm glad you like it. I worked on it for four months."

"You built it?"

"No, I designed it. Someone else built it. We pack them as kits and contractors order them for their clients and assemble them on their property. You can choose the style, the wood, the finish and the accessories. We sell a lot of them."

"Who is 'we'?"

Logan pressed several more keys. The screen filled with the company logo.

"Carson Creations. You're that Carson? I've heard of you."

He smiled. "Good. Glad to know the advertising works."

"You do more than just gazebos. You make decks and lawn furniture and stuff."

Logan typed in another command and a catalog of sorts popped up.

"This is your website. I'm impressed."

"Sometimes I have to pinch myself to make sure it's real."

"Was this your father's company?"

"My father was a plumber. He's retired."

"So this is all yours? Your own company? Logan, I'm very proud of you! How did this come about?"

"I got fired from my job one day and I decided that life is too short to spend eight hours a day doing work you don't love. Story sound familiar?"

"I'm speechless!"

"I understand. I actually have people that work for me. I'm a boss. People actually do what I tell them to do."

"You have the power. How many people work for you?"

"I have another design person, a couple people who work on prototypes, and a few people who actually make the parts for the kits. There are shipping and packing people and a small office staff that does payroll and stuff. At first it was me and another guy and we did everything. Then when I discovered that people were willing to pay big money for quality products, I hired a few more people. I still approve everything and actually have to see the finished product before we start making enough to sell. This is all top-of-the line stuff. The warranties are substantial. We stand behind our work. If I find someone slacking on quality, they're gone before they can steal a pencil. My name is on this stuff, and seconds don't leave the facility."

"Good for you. What an awesome success story." She put her arm around his shoulder. He flinched, hit a few keys in error, and the screen went blank.

"Shit."

"Logan, I'm sorry!" She moved her arm.

"That's okay. It didn't go far…I hope."

"I didn't mean to startle you. It was just an impulse." *Or an urge,* she thought.

He patted her hand. "Don't worry about it. I was just a little…uh…I didn't expect it and…um…you just…never mind."

"Why Logan, I do believe I flustered you a bit. Maybe I shouldn't have acted so familiar."

"That's fine, Amy." *Please touch me. It's been so long,* he thought.

She stood up. "I sure do appreciate you letting me into a little corner of your life. It just makes me even more certain that I did the right thing. Life is too short. You're right about that. I just hope I can be successful enough at this to keep my modest lifestyle together."

He stood up and put out his hand. She put hers in his and he shook it. "You'll do fine, Amy Sue Sweet. Thanks for the support." *Please stay,* he thought.

She grinned. "Monday then?"

"Sure. I'll walk you down."

She stopped in the dining room, picked up brushes, rollers and some towels. "I'm going to clean this stuff and do some laundry over the weekend. You need to take a break and relax, too."

"I'll be working on the rocker an hour after you're gone. That's my form of relaxing."

And you'll have sawdust in your hair, and you'll smell so good, and I'll probably spend the entire weekend wishing I were here, she thought.

"Amy? Did you say something?"

"No, I don't think I did, did I?" *Did I say that out loud?* she thought. "See you Monday, Logan."

"'Bye."

CHAPTER 13

Logan went into the house, picked up the phone, and made himself comfortable on the couch. He hit speed dial and his brother's secretary answered the phone. "Good afternoon, Bolin Carson's office. May I help you?"

"Hey, Doris, it's Logan. Is Bo in?"

"Well, hello there, Sweetie. I haven't talked to you in ages. Are you okay?"

"I'm fine, how about yourself?"

"I'm a grandmother for the third time."

"Good for you. Is Bo in?"

"He sure is. I'll put you right through. Take care."

Bo picked up. "Hey, Logan! How's it hangin'?"

"Don't ask. How are you?"

"Oh, you know me, attorney to the stars. I just did a will for Alex Trebek's cousin's boyfriend's mom."

"Well, aren't you just all kinds of connected!"

"Make fun if you must. Some day Robert DeNiro will be at my door."

"Yeah, probably to beat the crap out of you."

"No kidding. So, I assume you wanted to do more than poke fun at my client list?"

"Got a few minutes? I just want to dump. You know how just speaking out loud gives you a different perspective sometimes?"

"True."

"Well, I met this woman."

"Lord, let me sit down and get a glass of water."

"Not funny, Bo. She scares the shit out of me."

"So, stay away from her or buy a gun."

"Not that kind of 'scared' you derelict. I mean I lose my mind around her. I stutter and stumble. I feel like I blabber on about nothing, and she looks at me like I'm preaching the gospel. I actually asked her to help me cook."

"You mean like in the kitchen?"

"Yes, like cook. You know, food?"

"Where did you meet her?"

"She answered an ad in the paper."

"You had a personal ad? 'Horny white male seeking female who likes power tools?'"

"Not a personal ad. God, why do I bother talking to you? It was an ad to hire a painter to do the inside of the house."

"You hired a chick to paint? Cool."

"Are you still in high school? Chicks can…Women can do anything these days, including paint, and this one is very good at it."

"So what's the problem, she wants to paint everything mauve?"

"No, we have an understanding about color choice. I'm feeling things for her that have me very unsettled. I actually flirted with her and it was kind of fun. It's been so long since I've done anything like that. I want to touch her, but when she put her arm around me to make a point, I totally freaked. Then we both felt stupid. I tried to apologize. I didn't want to go into details. You know there are days the Sam thing seems like yesterday to me. My heart still hurts so bad sometimes, I'm incapacitated."

"What's her name?"

"Amy Sweet. And she is, by the way."

"You want me to check her out?"

"No! She's not a stalker or a terrorist. She's a painter. I don't know what to do."

"How long have you known her?"

"I've seen her almost every day for a week. She has the run of the house during the day and I usually see her before she leaves in the evening when I get home from work. We discuss the day, the progress of the house, blah, blah, blah."

"What does she look like?"

"Pretty. Brown hair, not too long, very silky, usually tied up with some kind of apparatus, probably to keep it out of the paint. Brown eyes, nice lashes. She smells good."

"What?"

"I sniffed her."

"You're an idiot."

"She sniffed me first."

"So are you using the dog method for finding a mate?"

Logan put his head back and banged the phone on the couch cushion. "Cut me some slack here, please. I'm in a conundrum."

"A conundrum. You're in a fucking conundrum. You're the only person I know who can say conundrum with a straight face."

"Actually, I'm in a lack-of-fucking conundrum. I want to make a move on her but I'm afraid. It's been a long time."

"Are you saying you can't get it up?"

"Bo. All parts are in working order. It's the whole emotional thing. I don't feel like going into the whole Sam story and if I'm going to get involved with this woman she deserves to know the whole thing."

"Body?"

"She has one, yes."

"Details…tits?"

"Two. Nice. Not huge, not small. Just right."

"Legs?"

"Two…long and tan. She thinks her ass is big, but I think it's fine."

"Does she like you?"

"I think so. She responded nicely to a little good-natured teasing."

"Did you give her your 'size isn't everything' speech as you showed her your power tools?"

Silence.

"You did, didn't you? God, some things never change. Just preparing her for the shock when she sees your little…"

"Enough from you. I needed a little sympathy and advice and you make fun of my…whatever. Not funny."

"Well, I suggest you take Amy up to your room, have her bring a roller with her and show her your little 'whatever.'"

"Thanks, Bo. Big help you are. Gotta go. I have a rocker to stain."

"Hey, Logan, just giving you a hard time. Take your time with her. If it's meant to happen it will. You have no deadlines. Make sure she's quality. You're worth it."

"She's quality. Thanks. See ya."

CHAPTER 14

A my stopped at the bookstore on her way home. She headed for the magazine section, selected some home decorating magazines and looked for the most comfortable chair in the place. The afternoon with Logan had mentally set her back and she just wanted to think about what she had learned about him. She should have guessed by the size of the house, the lot and the workshop that he was more than just a data-entry person who fooled around with wood in his spare time. She had mistaken his unwillingness to sell his creations for lack of drive or insecurity. She knew his furniture would sell if he really wanted to sell it. People were getting tired of mass-produced furniture and were taking the time to search in antique stores or resale shops for those hidden treasures that were made in a time when workmanship was important.

Logan did have drive. He definitely had talent. He obviously wanted people to buy what he made; he just did it in a way she never would have guessed. He was an artist, though she doubted that he would describe himself that way. She thought it was cute how he was still so surprised at his success. He said he had to pinch himself to make sure it was real. She wondered how much positive feedback he got about his work. The company must have been doing well.

Why did he jump when I touched him? she thought. *Maybe it was inappropriate. It felt right at the time…at least it did for me. He responded with a handshake. Probably letting me know that the touch was okay. I need to know more about him. How could I supposedly have been in love with Crane, if this stranger I've known for a week has me so unsettled? A week with Logan has tossed my insides around. I want to be with him at the house, but feel I need to take the weekend off. Why? Am I testing myself? Am I testing him? He has my phone number. I think he'll call. Will I be disappointed if he doesn't? Yes. Yes I will. Must be time for a visit with the girls.* She paid for one of the magazines and went home.

*

Gibby and Beth's door was open and so was Amy's. Punkin was sitting in the hall between the two doors.

"Are you the vicious guard pig?"

"This is braless Chinese night," Gibby announced. "Hillie stopped in Chinatown and brought forty pounds of food. We're eating at your place because Beth has travel info on Iowa spread all over the table. Bus and train schedules, road maps, you name it."

"So, she's tracking down Terry after all."

Hillie came in with several square white containers with wire handles. "Personally, I think she just wants sex. There are more containers next door if you'd care to help carry them."

"Did I hear correctly, that this is braless Chinese night?"

"Yes, Ames, the bra on the couch is mine. Gibby's is so small you can't see it."

"I heard that. You're just jealous that I can wear a wet t-shirt and no one notices."

Hillie laughed. "Yeah, jealous, that's the word."

Beth came in loaded down with paper plates, plastic forks, packets of soy sauce, sweet and sour sauce, hot mustard and a bag of fortune cookies. "At least my bra doesn't look like a flotation device."

Hillie stopped in the hall, put her hands on her hips. "Was that remark intended for me?"

"If the life vest fits…" Beth stuck her tongue out and arranged the items she was carrying on the table.

Amy chimed in. "I'll settle for semi-perky." She went to her room, removed her bra and put on exercise shorts and a t-shirt that said, "Do you think I actually give a shit?" She'd never leave home in it, but it seemed to fit the mood of the evening.

Hillie started opening cartons and placing serving spoons in them. "I got a pretty good selection, I think. The orange chicken sounded good to me, vegetable fried rice, egg rolls, crab Rangoon, kung pao chicken extra peanuts, Mongolian beef extra hot, something funky on a stick that I don't remember what it's called, and Beth, your favorite, shrimp in lobster sauce, even if it does smell like underwear. You have to keep it in the far corner with the lid on or I'll gag. And you have to eat it fast, and destroy your dishes when you're done." Beth knew she was banished to the far side of the room while she ate the foul stuff, but the banishment was worth it.

Gibby started. "So, what's on the agenda tonight, or is this just recreational eating?"

Beth whined, "I don't have to take notes, do I?"

Hillary answered her. "Probably not necessary because alcohol is not involved yet, but if anyone gets an MSG rush you may have to step up. I want to hear about Beth's man."

The "Virginia" popped immediately into Beth's voice. "Oh, my." She blushed.

Amy started for her. "Well, he has quite an assortment of hair, some of which Beth has not yet seen. He has a healthy scalp, and she licked his pretty white teeth."

"Well, you certainly have twisted that around a little, now haven't you?"

Hillie helped her out. "Then you better tell it yourself, because we need to know details. Is he cute?"

"In his own way. The more I think about him the cuter he gets. He's kind, he doesn't use bad language, he goes to church…"

Gibby jumped in. "That clinches it."

"Now don't make fun just because we both claim Jesus Christ as our personal Lord and Savior. It's one less point of contention in the future."

"Does he know you're thinking of him with the word 'future' in the same sentence?"

"It's hard to explain, Hillie. We connected, that's all I know. I'm just not all that experienced at this dating thing, probably because I'm so picky. We have a little distance issue, but I keep telling myself that it may not be an issue if he doesn't call me."

Hillie, never missing an opportunity, jumped in, "Call him."

"He gave me his business card, so I don't think he'd mind if I did. And maybe I will."

Covering all bases, Hillie considered it her responsibility to ask the nasty questions. "Is he married?"

Beth stuttered, "N-no. I don't think so. I don't know. I didn't ask. I just assumed if he were, he wouldn't be going on a date. He doesn't wear a wedding band. I better find a way to get to the bottom of that issue…but my money says he's not. We talked all evening, and I think I would have figured that out. We have a lot in common. He was very polite and respectful."

"Are you seeing him again?"

"Well, actually, he called me at work, but of course I couldn't talk because I had an audience of busybodies. He was on a fifteen-minute break from a meeting and couldn't really talk anyway, so we set a little phone date for 10:30."

Gibby had been in the kitchen refilling her plate and missed part of the conversation. "You're having phone sex with Terry at 10:30?"

"I'll be taking his call in my room, and if it turns into that, it will be none of your concern. I'll give him until 10:40 and then I'm calling him."

"Good for you," Amy added. "Can you conference us in on that?"

"Ya know, sometimes y'all are just not funny."

They all laughed.

"Hillie, anything new in your life?" Amy was putting off the discussion of Logan. She wasn't sure why.

"No. I work too damn hard. My favorite men are gay. I love my job, but I need a break. You guys are my only distraction. Maybe it's time for a little vacation."

"That sounds like a healthy decision. Did you know that Gibby got another poke in the whiskers from Marty?"

"Amy, you are determined not to talk about your boss, client, whatever-he-is, aren't you?" Gibby tried distracting Hillie from the Marty situation.

"Good for you, Gibbs. Sex is good for the circulation, or something, isn't it? Are you using condoms?"

"Yes ma'am. Double-bagging."

"Case closed. Amy, what's up with the Logan situation?"

Amy took a big bite of an egg roll, needing the time to chew and think. "He's a client I currently work for, not a situation. We had a little chat today. I thought he had some kind of go-nowhere job working on a computer all day, then he comes home at night and builds stuff in his workshop. He invited me into his bedroom slash office and…"

"Ooooo!"

"Shut up. He showed me a project he's working on. He actually owns his own company. He designs and builds decks, gazebos and stuff like that. His designs were beautiful and very expensive. I also got a tour of the workshop."

Hillie asked, "Did you get the good long screw?"

"No, but I thought about it. We had a good visit. He actually started his business for the same reason I started painting. He got fired from a job he didn't like. I still have plenty of questions for him, but I don't want it to seem like an interrogation. This is moving slowly. That's good, I think, for the long run, but right now, if he walked through that door and gave me the 'come hither' look, I'd hither all over him."

Gibby asked, "What does he look like?"

"He's about 5'9", just a little taller than me. He has fluffy dark hair, eyes that are several shades of green depending on the light, no facial hair, good teeth, ample bottom lip, good body, great body, nice ass in jeans."

"Probably nice ass out of jeans. What's with the lip…ample?"

"I want to bite it."

"You're in trouble!" Hillie sang.

Gibby added, "I think I might know him. I'll have to ask around."

"Gibbs, is it bad? You have to tell me. You've mentioned this before."

"Amy, it's a hunch. Nothing to worry about. Are you working tomorrow?"

"No, I need a break. My shoulders have turned to rubber. I have so much to do around here that I thought a Saturday off would be beneficial. I have laundry to do, shopping, bill-paying…"

"What's the name of his company?"

"Carson Creations. Have you heard of it?"

"I've seen signs on fences and stuff, and ads in the paper."

Beth joined in. "Me too." She stood up and headed for the door with her paper plate in her hand. "I'm going to get rid of this offensive plate and go primp for my phone date."

Hillie rolled her eyes and said after the door closed, "Lord help us. If he doesn't marry her I'll kick his ass. And as for you, Margaret, you better be damn careful with Martin. He'll hurt you all over again."

"It's purely recreational."

"Whatever. I've gotta go. I have a date."

"What?"

"With Keneth–one n. We're going dancing."

Amy seemed puzzled. "I thought he was gay?"

"He is. Just try to get a straight man to dance. It's purely recreational."

"Don't forget your bra." Hillie went to the couch, picked up her bra and stuffed it in her purse. "And take some of these leftovers."

"No. You guys can finish it off tomorrow."

Amy and Gibby looked at each other. "When it rains, it pours."

"I'll help you clean up and then I'm going home. I need sleep and a shower—in reverse order."

"Me too."

CHAPTER 15

Just the sun shining through the window would have been sufficient, but the phone ringing at the crack of dawn is what woke Amy up on the day she planned to sleep in—if one can consider 8 a.m. sleeping in. She rolled over and let it ring, knowing it was probably Beth excited over her call from Terry, or Hillie wanting to discuss dancing with Keneth. She put the pillow over her head. Then she heard the low mellow voice of a man. A manly man. It was Logan. As usual, he spoke as if he didn't quite know what message he wanted to leave.

"Amy, gosh…surprised you're out at this hour. Oh, sorry, if you're still sleeping! Hope this doesn't wake you up, but I decided you're right about the study. I know you're not painting today, but…" beeeeep.

"Poor guy's gonna have to learn to speak faster," she mumbled. The phone rang. She let the answering machine pick up again.

"I'll try to talk faster this time…it's me, Logan. I think I'd like you to work on the study, or den, or whatever we're calling it. I mean, do that room next. I really do need to get…" beeeeep.

Amy laughed into her pillow, knowing the phone would ring in another few seconds. It did.

"Amy, me again. You really need to get a machine that takes a longer message. Call me…if you want to, I mean, I know you've got the day off, but maybe we could do…" beeeeep.

Amy sat up, wondering do *what*? Lunch? Tai Chi? The Nasty?

She rolled out of bed knowing there was no way she could go back to sleep now. She stumbled into the kitchen, started the coffee and headed for the bathroom. She stood close to the mirror, looked at the sheet wrinkles on her cheek, her severe bed head and some kind of Chinese herb that was stuck between her front teeth. She spoke to the mirror. "You look like shit."

Amy showered, dressed in sweats, grabbed a cup of coffee and banged on Beth's door. She and Gibby were already up discussing Beth's phone call with

Terry. Amy would have to get the update later. She just wanted them to know that she would be "doing something" with Logan later. Doing Logan, or doing lunch, but she wasn't sure which. She just wanted them to be as mystified as she was.

She went back home, sat at the kitchen table and made a list.

> SATURDAY—Crap To Do
> - laundry
> - change two lightbulbs
> - put up new shower curtain
> - make iced green tea
> - defrost chicken
> - call Logan
> - do Logan
> - sniff Logan
> - lick Logan
> - nibble on Logan

Obviously, number one had to be *call Logan*. She picked up the phone and dialed his number.

"Hello."

"Is this the power-tool geek who has to call three times to leave a message?"

"Yes, it is. Who's calling? Amy with the cheap funky-ass answering machine that only allows a person three inches of tape to leave a message?"

"That would be me, sleeping soundly when you rang my phone three times at the crack of dawn."

"Sorry, I couldn't sleep. I started thinking about the den. I'm looking forward to getting some furniture and stuff. I think it will look a little more like an office than my bedroom."

"Logan, your bedroom looks more like an office than a bedroom. I'll be glad to work on the den next. I need to tell you this, though, and this pretty much goes for the whole house. It's easier and cheaper to buy paint to match furniture than to try to find furniture to match paint. Neutral is nice, but eventually you want your house to reflect a little of your personality. A den or office would be a nice place for some richer colors."

"Amy, I know it's your day off, but I'm excited about this." *Any excuse to spend time with you,* she thought. "Can we meet for lunch? I'd like your opinion on a few things. Will you help me shop?"

"You trust me with that?"

"I trust you with my whole house. I will trust your opinion on some curtains and furniture."

"Window treatment."

"What?"

"It probably won't be curtains. So, we'll shop for a window treatment."

"So, now you're getting fancy on me."

"Not really, but if you go shopping for curtains, that's what you're going to get and I don't think that's what you want. Hence, we will treat the window."

"Are you still sore?"

"I need a couple of days where I'm not hefting that roller around."

"No painting today. I have a friend I want to introduce you to."

"Are you picking me up or am I meeting you somewhere?"

"I'll pick you up. Wear comfortable shoes and a shirt that's easy to remove."

"What's your skill level?

"In shirt-removing…pretty low, actually. I'm really out of practice."

"What are you up to, Mr. Carson?"

"You'll be moaning before the day is over. One hour. Be ready."

CHAPTER 16

Logan stopped the Jeep in front of her building, checked his teeth and hair in the mirror and cleaned off the passenger's seat for Amy. She had been watching for him from her window. When she saw him get out of his car, she grabbed a jacket and her purse and met him in the hallway. He looked disappointed.

"You didn't need to see my house, did you?"

"There'll be time for that some other day. We can get started." He held her jacket as she put it on. His hand brushed her back.

"Thank you. No Mercedes today?"

"That's my serious car. This is my fun car."

"So I guess we're having fun?"

"Let me know if you're not and I'll change plans."

He opened her door; she stepped up and in and latched her seat belt. "Where to first?"

"I want to show you a furniture store. I'm not going to buy a desk there, because I want to make my own, but I want to show you what I'm thinking about."

"You don't have a pattern?"

"I'm not making a dress. No, I don't have a pattern. Or a plan. But I do have an idea. We're not looking for details here, just general shape and size. And maybe color. I would like a nice deep reddish-brown stain. I haven't decided on wood yet. I know I want a leather desk pad. That's another stop later in the day."

They drove for about twenty minutes, chatting about the weather, office furniture and any cravings that needed to be satisfied at lunch. Logan stopped in front of an unmarked building that looked like a warehouse. He got out of the Jeep and grabbed a clipboard from the back seat. He walked behind the car to Amy's door, offered his hand and helped her out.

"What is this place?"

"This is my closest competitor as far as quality goes in furniture-making.

I'd like him to work for me, but he insists on running his own little shop taking custom orders. If I couldn't do the work myself this is where I would come. I'd work and scrimp and save to buy his stuff. He's Swiss. Quite a rarity in the States. He traded the Alps for the El."

"What was he thinking?"

"I think he was following the money trail. There are a whole lot of people here with a lot of money. A lot of people are looking for that European craftsmanship, even though Freddie would be one of the first to admit that there are excellent craftsmen in America. It seems there are some bragging rights that go with having something European."

"Where is he?"

"Freddie!" Logan shouted.

"Logan, my friend. One minute."

"Is this the friend you wanted me to meet?"

"No, that will be after lunch."

A short, stocky man with pure white hair and neatly trimmed beard stepped through a door from a room that appeared to be an office. His hand was outstretched as he hurried across the floor toward Amy and Logan. Amy noticed he had very well-developed arms, probably from carrying wood around. He reached out to shake Logan's hand. They gripped, shook, slapped shoulders and did a typical manly greeting. If they were women they would have hugged.

"Freddie, I'd like you to meet Amy Sweet. Amy, this is Manfred Berg, master carpenter."

His hand dwarfed Amy's as he greeted her. "What a pleasure to meet you, Miss Sweet."

"The pleasure is mine, Mr. Berg. Logan speaks very highly of your work."

"Please call me Freddie. Logan recognizes good work because his is excellent."

"I've seen some of Logan's work, and you're right about that. Please call me Amy."

Freddie put an arm across each shoulder, Logan on one side, Amy on the other. "Now that formalities are out of the way, I'll show you that computer desk I was talking about. It's tough to make something to serve the purpose of such a modern piece of equipment while still looking classic and dignified. See what you think about this. Keep in mind, this is just the piece, with no details or finish on it yet."

Logan took out a pencil and paper. "You don't mind, do you, if I just sketch a general idea?"

"My friend, you know I have borrowed enough ideas from you. Feel free to sketch. Besides, knowing you, it won't resemble mine very much when you're finished with it."

Logan walked around the desk, sketching all sides. It was actually three pieces. The part of the desk for writing had an old-fashioned roll top. Logan pointed. "Now *that* I will copy. It has a classic look with a modern purpose. You're still not looking for work are you? Because you know I'd hire you in a minute."

"I have more work than I can handle...well...I would have more than I could handle if I didn't turn so much work down. I would like to see you get busier in that workshop of yours. I could send you plenty of work, my friend."

"I enjoy it more when I do it for fun. How's that gazebo holding up?"

"My daughter got married in it."

"Small wedding?"

"Very, but the setting was perfect. We got a lot of compliments and probably sent some business your way."

"Thanks. Send me a picture. I'll put it on the website, if your daughter doesn't mind."

"So, Amy, you're Logan's..."

"I'm painting his house."

"Oh. I was hoping that he'd start seeing someone again since..."

Logan put the pencil back in his pocket and cut Freddie's comments off. "Well, Freddie, we have several other stops, including a visit with Olga."

"God help you, girl."

Amy looked puzzled. "What are you getting me into, Logan?"

Freddie winked and smiled. The friends shook hands again. "Stop by any time, and feel free to bring this pretty little lady with you whenever you do."

"It was nice meeting you, Freddie. You have some beautiful things here."

"Call me if you need work."

Amy and Logan got back into the Jeep. "What a nice man. He's a perfectionist like you."

"He was a good friend during a tough part of my life."

"Anything you want to share?"

"Not right now. This is supposed to be a fun day."

"Who is Olga?"

"You'll find out soon enough."

"Where's our next stop? Will I have to take my shirt off?"

"That will be up to you. I'm sure the people at the Merchandise Mart will be thrilled."

"So that's why I need comfortable shoes. What are we shopping for?"

"I'm ordering a desk chair. It will be delivered, but I wanted you to see it."

"Logan, I have to remind you, I'm a painter, not an interior designer."

"I know, but you have a good eye. If I get something upholstered, I'll need you to help with the fabric. If I pick leather, it's a done deal. I really have no preference. Comfort is all I care about."

"Have you looked at any of the ergonomically correct chairs? If you'll be sitting a while at the computer, it will help keep you from feeling fatigued."

"A lot of my time in front of the computer is just staring off into space while an idea formulates in my brain. I'd like to be comfortable while I do that, so I'm not really worried about carpal tunnel issues. Besides, I can only do it for so long and then I get the urge to go to the workshop. If my brain goes blank, it gets refreshed around the wood and tools."

"If my brain goes blank I eat chocolate."

Logan found a parking spot on Kinzie Street. He and Amy visited the display of the manufacturer of the desk chair Logan had at work. He tried several and chose a very comfortable, handsome, brown leather chair. Amy knew he'd choose the leather, so she was never concerned about having to make a fabric decision. She was, however, getting hungry enough for lunch.

She asked, "Are you ready for lunch?"

"That's our next stop. Do you like Italian beef sandwiches?"

"Extra juicy with hot peppers."

"Then our next stop is Mister Beef, just a few blocks north on Orleans."

"I've heard of it, but never eaten there."

"I'm surprised, with you working downtown for so long."

"It was too far for me to go during a lunch break."

Logan pulled up in front and got out.

"You don't mind if I order for you, do you? We can take the sandwiches to the park by the Water Tower. We won't have many more sunny weekends left. Would you rather eat inside?"

"I'd love to go to the park. Get plenty of napkins."

Logan came out in just a few minutes holding a bag that already showed some grease smudges, and two bottles of water. She took the bottles through the window and offered to take the bag.

"I'm setting this on the floor. I'd hate to see you get your clothes messy."

"Is this when I have to take my shirt off?"

"You can if you want to."

They drove about seven blocks east and parked on a side street. They walked to the park surrounding the original Water Tower that survived the Chicago Fire. Most of the trees had lost their leaves, but some autumn flowers were blooming and the sun was bright and warm. They found a bench perfect for people-watching. Amy sat sideways with her legs crossed and watched Logan as he unloaded the bag.

"It smells wonderful! If I wasn't hungry before, I sure am now."

"Just wait." He handed her a sandwich wrapped in several layers of paper. It was very heavy and smelled of Italian seasonings and garlic.

"Logan, this is huge. I'll never be able to finish it all."

"I'm counting on that." He grinned at her and took a bite of his sandwich. He groaned and his eyes rolled back in his head from the gastronomic ecstasy. "It raises hell with your breath, though."

"Who cares? It's delicious."

They ate and watched a street performer. Actually they watched other people watching the street performer. This was an excellent spot for watching the foot traffic that testified to the diversity that made Chicago such an interesting place.

"It's almost like people are out to absorb the end of the nice weather before winter."

"I know that feeling. It's why you open your jacket; hoping that it will be easier for the sun to warm up your soul."

"Logan, that's quite poetic."

"I have my moments. Are you going to finish that?" He had his eye on the last three inches of her sandwich. She handed it to him and he picked up right where she left off.

"Not afraid of girl germs?"

"Garlic kills 'em," he said with his mouth full.

She bent her head down toward her lap and let the sun beat down on her back. The warmth felt good. She rolled her shoulders and winced at the stiffness.

"You okay, Amy?"

"The sun feels good on my back. This is a great day. Thanks so much for lunch. This isn't exactly what I had planned for my day, but it has been fun, just like you promised."

"I don't think I promised…and the day isn't over yet. What did you have planned at home?"

"Just some projects that I've been putting off. Changing lightbulbs, that kind of thing."

He threw the bag and napkins in the nearest trash can and grabbed her hand. "Let's go." He pulled her up off the bench, let her hand go, finished his water and threw the bottle away. Amy tucked the rest of her water in her purse. They headed off in the direction of the car. When they reached the car, Amy stopped at the passenger's door. Logan kept walking.

"Where are you going?"

"We have one more stop in the city, and then we can go home." He stopped and waited while she caught up. He took her hand, passed two more businesses, and walked into the third.

"Logan, dahlink!"

"Olga, good to see you!" Olga gave him a bear hug until he grunted.

"I see you bring me another victim today, yes?"

"Olga, meet my friend Amy. Amy, Olga gives massages to die for."

Olga put her arm around Amy's shoulders and walked her and Logan to the back of the room where there was a space divided with curtains.

"Chairs today, yes?"

"Only chairs today, Olga, I'm afraid Amy would take advantage of me if I got naked."

Amy glowered. "Logan, you are as mean as a snake."

"Amy, sit!" It was a command, and she did. It was a peculiar-looking chair.

She wasn't comfortable at all. Logan sat in the chair next to hers, facing the opposite direction. Amy watched him, got up and turned around. "Your first chair massage?"

"Yes, actually."

"Good. Take off your shirt and bra. Put this around your front." Olga handed her a very fluffy and warm white towel. Logan pulled his shirt over his head and assumed the position. His head and arms rested lightly on the chair. "Maria!" Olga called toward the back of the building. "Logan is here for you."

A beautiful, dark-haired woman parted the curtains and walked in. The smile temporarily disappeared when she saw Amy with Logan. "Hello, Logan. How are you today?"

"I'm fine, Maria. I'd like you to meet my friend, Amy. We're here today because she's having a little arm-and-shoulder pain from overwork."

Maria answered. "Lucky for you, Amy. Olga will make you feel like a new woman."

"I was kind of fond of the old one. I'm just a little stiff, that's all."

Logan couldn't leave it alone. "Me too."

"Mr. Carson, turn your head please." He did, and Amy removed her shirt and bra. Olga took them from her and Amy covered herself with the towel.

"Olga, we'll both have the lotion, please."

Maria turned on some generic but soothing music. She and Olga could have been an Olympic event in synchronized massaging. The lotion was warm and smelled of lavender...very calming. After about thirty seconds Amy was as limp as a noodle. Olga pressed just the right spot on her sore shoulders and Amy moaned.

"I told you before the day was over you'd have your shirt off and you'd moan."

"Shhhh!" Olga scolded. She and Maria massaged for fifteen minutes and then left the room. Amy thought Logan was asleep because he was so quiet. She turned her head. He was watching her.

Amy whispered, "Thank you." Logan winked.

After a few minutes, Olga came back into the room and handed Amy her bra and shirt. Logan took his shirt from Maria and left the room so Amy could have some privacy. While Amy was dressing, Logan paid and generously tipped Olga and Maria. Amy came out dressed and grinning.

"Olga, thank you so much. Now I know why Logan thinks of this as a treat."

"You be good to my man or you answer to me, yes?"

"Yes!" Amy smiled. "Goodbye, ladies."

Logan held her elbow and led her out the door. They walked to the car in silence. Logan opened her door and went around to the driver's side. He buckled himself in. Amy leaned over and kissed him softly on the cheek. He held the steering wheel and stiffened.

"That was wonderful and very thoughtful, Logan. Thanks. Really. It was my first. If I were rich, I would do that every day."

He stared straight ahead. "You're welcome." He started the car and they headed back toward the suburbs.

*

After almost twenty minutes of driving in silence, except for an occasional grunt or comment on crazy drivers from Logan, Amy heard the blinker. Logan exited the expressway and after a couple miles of suburban streets he turned in at the Morton Arboretum. Although the trees were past their autumn prime, its walking and driving paths still made it a pretty place to visit any time of year. Logan pulled into the farthest corner of the parking lot. He shut off the engine and rested his forehead on the steering wheel.

"Are you okay?"

"I'm fine. I need a minute."

"Do you want me to drive?"

"No, I just need to think for a minute."

He unbuckled his seat belt and turned in his seat to face her. She did the same and faced him, as her heart began to pound in her chest.

"I have a few things to say, and I'm afraid I'm going to screw it up, so I really need you not to interrupt me. The main thing is that the last thing on earth I want to do is hurt you, so I have to choose my words carefully. Can you just listen to me for a few minutes?"

"Of course." She reached out and patted his knee. He flinched and she drew back.

"Sorry. That's one of the things I need to talk about. And as they say, 'it isn't you, it's me' really applies here, so don't think it's trite. Just wait until I'm done to ask questions, holler, walk out, whatever."

"You're scaring me."

You should be scared, he thought. "I don't mean to and I'll do my best not to hurt you."

"Talk to me Logan. I don't bite and I'll do my best not to judge."

"I don't know where to begin. That's why I've been so quiet. I guess I could just jump in…sink or swim." *I killed my wife,* he thought.

"The beginning is always good."

"Okay." He took a deep breath, looked into her eyes until he couldn't stand the question there and looked away. "I was married. She died. There are details that I'm still dealing with. You should never be afraid of me, Amy." That wasn't so bad. "It was a terrible time in my life. I never expected to meet someone that I'd connect with." He stopped. "Just a minute." He opened the car door and got out. He closed the door and leaned on it with his back to Amy. He was muttering to himself. She watched him shaking his head and scuffing at the dirt under his feet. *Why can't you just do it? If she leaves, she leaves. Don't wait until she's trapped and hates you. You're a fucking coward,* he thought. He shoved his hands in his jeans pockets and hung his head, obviously done beating himself up for a while. He got back in the car and Amy looked concerned.

"Are you…"

Logan held his hand up and she stopped her question. "Sorry. You walked into my workshop and turned my life upside-down. I didn't know how to respond. I've been alone about a year and I've just wrapped myself in some kind of armor against connecting with another person…a woman. There are days my heart hurts so bad I can't work. Then there are days when I want a life I can share again. I didn't think that would ever happen. I just expected a male to answer my ad. Amy Sweet, you scare the shit out of me. You did that day in the workshop and you have every day since." She opened her mouth to speak and he touched her lips with a finger. "I have to finish while I have the nerve." She smiled and didn't speak.

"I know I seem to pull away every time we touch, whether deliberate or inadvertent. I'm working on that, really. It's just, you know, touching is, um, kind of contagious. The more you do, the more you do. Then eventually the touching takes on a life of its own. It's something that you live for and can't live without. Then you find that you can live without it. It's just that I feel kind of awkward about it right now. Would you like to take a walk?"

Amy nodded and got out of the Jeep. She met Logan at the back and he chose a trail with sunlight sneaking through the trees. They walked close but he didn't hold her hand. "Is there more, Logan?"

"I feel like I'm overstepping my bounds, like I'm making more of this," he said motioning back and forth between them with his hands, "than there is for two people that have known each other for such a short time."

"Just talk and I'll tell you if you overstep."

"I just want you to know that there's a reason I pull away when you touch me and I'm working on that. I know you get mixed signals because I can tease you in fun, and I guess I expect a reaction. Then when you respond, I flinch."

"You said it yourself. The more you touch, the more you touch. Maybe you just have to step outside your comfort zone for a few minutes. It will get easier. After all, it's a perfectly natural action. Touching feels good. That's why we do it."

"Touching got me into trouble. I did a bad thing."

She stopped walking. He motioned to the side of the trail where a tree had fallen many months before. She sat down and folded her hands in her lap. Logan straddled the trunk and faced her. The sun lit her face and red highlights sparkled in her chestnut brown hair. Logan looked at her. *God, you're beautiful,* he thought.

"Logan, I haven't known you long, but I doubt that you could do anything bad. Certainly not anything that's unforgivable."

Because the person from whom I need forgiveness is dead. Just blurt it out, he thought. "Amy, I killed my wife."

Strange, she thought, she wasn't surprised or scared. Probably because she didn't believe him. She looked at Logan, his head bowed, too humiliated to look her in the face. This was the sadness in his eyes that she first noticed when they met. She put her finger under his chin and lifted his face. When he blinked a tear pushed out and rolled down his cheek. She brushed it away.

"Tell me about it. Were you driving?"

"No. She was in the hospital. She hemorrhaged and bled to death."

"Were you her doctor?"

"I'm not a doctor, you know that."

"But you think you could have saved her if…if what?"

"Amy, I have run this through my head hundreds of times. I was in the room with her. I watched the life seep out of her. I did nothing. She was screaming. I tried to comfort her. She was in pain. I didn't know she was bleeding. God, there was so much blood. By the time doctors or nurses noticed it, there was nothing they could do. I watched her die. I was with her and I did nothing."

Amy swung a leg over the tree, straddling it, facing Logan. "Logan, the common-sense part of your brain knows there was nothing you could do. You're not a doctor and you didn't know she was in trouble. In time that part will win out over the emotional part that has you convinced it was your fault that she died."

It was my fault. She was there because of me, he thought.

"Logan, I'm so sorry." Their knees touched. She leaned forward and rested her forehead against his. He closed his eyes and whispered.

"Touch me. Please."

Her hands were cold but she held his face between them. He looked into her eyes and saw no fear. She saw the beautiful green specks that were always there, and the sadness that she hoped to drive away, if he would let her. She leaned forward and kissed him very gently on the lips. He didn't pull away. Amy rested her cheek on his. He needed a shave, but this was not the time to mention it. She rubbed one arm, warming her hand while she wove her other hand into the thick hair on the back of his head, holding his face next to hers. She inhaled his scent, something very fresh and natural. She committed it to memory in case this never happened again.

He whispered in her ear, "Amy, did you just sniff me?"

She grinned. "Yes, I did. You smell wonderful."

"Lavender. The lotion at Olga's."

"Of course. You let Maria touch you without a problem."

"Part of my therapy. There was a problem, you just didn't see it. I go there twice a week."

"What punishment."

Logan took her hands in his. "Let's walk."

They held hands as they took the trail into the trees. It was peaceful, fragrant and beautiful. Leaves were sprinkled in their path by a light autumn breeze. As they walked, the leaves crunched beneath their shoes. Amy concentrated on the feeling of Logan's hand. It wasn't too much bigger than her own, but it was stronger. He held her firmly yet gently and gave a squeeze now and then.

"Logan."

"Hmmm?"

"There's more, isn't there?"

He stopped, dropped her hand and turned to face her. "Yes, but I can't go into it now. Oh God, Amy, please be patient with me. I need you to hang in there with me for a little while. I promise you I'll tell you everything."

"Logan, this," she said, motioning with her hands back and forth between them, "us, could it be more some day?"

"I hope so."

"No secrets."

"None."

"I hope so, too." She took his hand and they walked again. She noticed that the path had led them in a circle and she could see the Jeep in the parking lot. "Maybe we can do this again in the spring."

If you still want me in the spring, he thought. "That would be nice." They got in the Jeep and headed for her house. On the way, they stopped at the paint store and picked up new paint for the den. She was prepared for Monday.

"Do you want to come up for a glass of iced tea? I made it fresh this morning."

"You could give me the grand tour."

"That will take about a minute. You'll take the paint home. Or did you want to leave it here?" They got out of the Jeep and headed for Amy's building.

"I'll take it in when I get home so you have it first thing Monday, okay?"

"Good." They stepped into the elevator, the door closed, and the contraption groaned its way slowly to the fourth floor. Amy was hoping no one was at her place. Or in the hallway. Or looking out of the peephole. She wasn't in the mood for introductions. It had been a fun but exhausting day, and she just wanted time to contemplate Logan's story by herself before she dumped it in front of the girls. She wanted their opinions, but didn't want to be put in the position of having to defend him just yet. And she was sure she would defend him. He tugged at her heart strings.

She was thankful her door was locked. She used her key and let them in. "Have a seat in here." She pointed Logan toward the living room. "I'll be back in a minute." She headed for the bathroom and closed the door. While sitting with her pants around her ankles she was struck with terror. The list! It was on the kitchen counter. *Please, oh please, Logan, don't go into the kitchen,* she thought. "Logan, I think I left my purse in the car. Could you go out and check for me, please?"

"No, it's right here on the counter."

Crap!

"The rocker is comfy, have a seat."

"I'm fine, thanks. You have a nice view of the garden."

Good, he's at the window, she thought. She flushed and was washing her hands when he asked, "Where are your spare lightbulbs?" That was on the list. Maybe she'd get lucky and have a stroke in the next ten seconds and drop dead before she had to face him.

"Why?"

"You have two bulbs burned out in your kitchen fixture."

There was still a chance he hadn't seen the list. "I'll get the bulbs. It would be nice if you could change them."

She came out of the bathroom, stepped across the hall to the linen closet and picked up two sixty-watt bulbs. She dreaded what she would see in the kitchen, but it was only Logan, standing on a chair, removing the burned out bulbs. She took them from him and handed him the new ones. After they were screwed in she flipped the switch. "Great! I can see again." She noticed the list on the counter and breathed a sigh of relief.

"You had other projects for today? I know I took you away from your Saturday duties. Is there something I can help with?" *Lick Logan? Indeed!* she thought.

"No, I think I got just about everything done before you got here. But thanks for asking.

"Where's your new shower curtain?" He grinned, knowing that was the giveaway.

"You're a dirty dog, Logan Carson. How dare you…"

He stepped closer. "How dare I? Embarrassed, huh? How dare I. How would you like to be on someone's list of 'crap' to do? Lick Logan? When were you going to fit that into your schedule for the day? Sniff Logan. Done. Cross that one off. Nibble on Logan. I can't even think about that." He stepped even closer and whispered, "*Do Logan*."

"Now just a minute, I uh…there was this…um…you called and…"

"How much time were you setting aside to *do* me?"

She covered her red face with her hands and groaned. He was enjoying every minute of this. "Logan, I'm sorry."

"Oh, don't be sorry. I look forward to being on your list; just don't consider me 'crap.'" He stood toe-to-toe with her and she could feel his breath on her hair. He whispered, "So, you want to do me?"

"Oh, for Pete's sake."

"You want to do me for Pete's sake. How about do me for *my* sake? Keep me on your list Amy Sweet. We need to work on getting our projects done, don't we? I like being on your 'to do' list." He kissed her on the forehead. She didn't even have the nerve to look up. "Goodbye Amy."

"'Bye." He closed the door and she crumpled on the couch, humiliated.

Chapter 17

"Amy! Who was that? Was that Logan?" Beth burst through her door, having the decency to wait until Logan took the elevator down.

"Yes." She buried her face in a green satin throw pillow on the couch.

"What happened? What's wrong? Did he hurt you?"

"No, he didn't hurt me. What I did, I did to myself. Look on the counter."

Beth picked up the list. "Lick, sniff, nibble on, DO? You have some interesting plans for today. I assume Logan saw this?"

"I have never been so embarrassed in my entire life. I'll never be able to face him again."

"You need to save this. Look at it again in six months and have a laugh. This is probably a turning point in your relationship."

"I didn't think we had a relationship. I mean, I was hoping for something some day, but now he thinks I sit around here planning ways to *do* him."

"You do." Beth put the list in Amy's junk drawer.

"Beth, he was standing inches from me and said, 'So, you want to do me?' Do you know how bad I just wanted to press myself into his body and say, 'Yes, I do.'"

"From the looks of him, I don't blame you. Maybe it's good he knows how you feel. It will probably save time. He certainly doesn't have to sit around wondering and guessing how you feel. If nothing else, he knows you lust after his body. Lick? Sniff? You sound like a bitch in heat. And I mean bitch in the true meaning of the word. So, don't take it personally."

"You call me a dog and I'm not supposed to take it personally? It's a good thing you're my friend and I know what you mean. How can I face him Monday morning?"

"Simple, get there after he leaves and leave before he comes home. Isn't that what you usually do anyway?"

"I need to change the subject. How was your conversation with Terry?"

"Ames, he hit me like a ton of bricks. For so long I have no one in my life, then suddenly I have this person that I feel like I've known for years. I've never been so comfortable with a man in my life. You know how I am. I stutter, blush, fall all over myself, say stupid things."

"I've seen you in action."

"Well, now I do the same things, but he thinks that is just part of me, which of course it is. I can relax and be myself, so I stutter less, blush less and say fewer stupid things. How can this happen so fast? I had supper with him. I critiqued his hair. I had two phone calls with him and he leaves tomorrow morning, early."

"What did you talk about last night?"

"We talked about our families. He's not married, by the way, and never has been; however, he was engaged for a while."

"What happened with that?"

"They realized they were too young and mutually broke it off. They're still friends, and sort of family, because she ended up marrying his cousin. His family has a farm and some cattle, not really a big herd, but they make some money. He may get the farm when his folks die, but he has no plans on that now since they're pretty healthy. He likes the tractor business, partly because he gets to spend part of his day visiting with other farmers, driving around in the country and stuff. He likes the social part of it. I guess that's what makes him a good salesman."

"He seems to have sold you."

"Oh, baby! I bought it, big time!"

"Think back two weeks, Beth. How different our lives were then."

"The Lord had plans for us and we didn't have a clue."

"We were blindsided, alright. Is the Lord going to let you have sex with him? 'Cause I know you want to!"

"Please! I've known him for two days. Although I must admit my heart does skip a beat when I think about him. Someday, maybe. But we'll see how it goes. He hasn't suggested it. He's too much of a gentleman to do that."

"Want to borrow my 'to do' list? Lick Terry, sniff Terry…"

"Stop it right now. I can't even let that thought into my mind. If I build this into something that isn't ever going to be, I'll be crushed, which, if you remember, was my first concern after our dinner together."

The door opened, and Punkin stalked through, followed by Gibby.

"Having a gab session and didn't invite me?

"I got to see Logan!"

"Really! Is he cute?"

"Very. And Amy's gonna do him."

"When?" Gibby stared at Amy.

Beth answered. "Time is yet to be determined, but he is on her 'to do' list. I saw it, and so did he!" Beth retrieved the list from the drawer and showed Gibby.

"You actually put your horny little thoughts down in writing?"

Amy shrugged. There was nothing to say.

"Just be careful."

"Gibbs, why do you keep saying that? If you know something about Logan, please let me know. He's mysterious enough as it is. We had a very long talk today and he told me some personal stuff. It was very hard for him. I know there's more to tell and he promised me we'd talk again, but I think he could only take it for so long. It was painful. He got really emotional, but I think we had a little breakthrough."

"What did he tell you?"

"Why does his name sound familiar to you? You tell me first."

"His wife died at St. Mary's. I did some checking when you first mentioned his name."

"Why didn't you tell me?"

"I thought that if he was a stand-up guy, he'd tell you himself."

"He did. Today."

"Did he give details? Because a lot of what I heard at the hospital is probably just rumors."

"What did you hear?"

"What did he tell you? I'm not contributing to the rumor mill at that place."

Amy sat up on the couch and decided to tell the story based on the facts from Logan, not the "feelings" that he had. She would keep that information to her self since she felt it was given to her by Logan in confidence. "His wife was in the hospital. I don't know why, but I think eventually he will tell me about that, so please, don't say anything. I want to hear it from Logan himself without him thinking that I have been checking up on him." Gibby nodded. "He was in the room with her. She started hemorrhaging, and he didn't know it. She was in pain, and he didn't know why. And by the time the medical staff got there, she had lost too much blood and died."

Gibby nodded. "That's pretty much it."

Amy was relieved that his story was accurate, and felt a little guilty that she may have doubted it. "What do you mean, 'pretty much'?"

"I mean that there are more specific details in her medical records, but that isn't information I could ever share."

"But you would tell me if it was something bad? No, never mind. I know you can't say anything. I'm just going to trust him to tell me the whole story. He'll just have to do it in his own time, in his own way. And I know he will because he told me so today."

"Take your time and get to know him. I think he's had a rough time of it but will come around if he has someone patient to help him out."

"I think I'm the person to do that, Gibbs. He's a good person and I'm trying hard not to just throw myself at his feet. Which I could do in a weak moment."

"What did you do today that put him in a talkative mood?"

Amy thought. "Well, I wouldn't exactly call him talkative, but I nudged a little, and he needed to get some issues in the open. I met two of his friends today, had a nice lunch at the Water Tower, had a chair massage, and we took a walk at the arboretum. We had a little quiet time among the trees, and that's when he told me he killed his wife."

"What!" Beth almost fell off her chair.

"He told me he felt responsible because he was there and didn't do anything."

Gibby added, "What could he have done?"

"That was my point to him. And in his reasonable brain, he knows that, but he was her husband and should have protected her. And she died with him standing at her side. Naturally, he feels responsible. There's no convincing him otherwise. He'll have to work on that himself, and he is. I think he's been seeing a therapist. He alluded to it but I didn't press the issue. He's also working on his touching problems."

Beth asked, "What kind of touching problems?"

"Oh, the way he kind of jumps out of his skin when I touch him. He always apologizes and assures me it isn't my fault. That's why he's seeing the massage therapist. She massages and touches in a legitimate way so he gets used to it. Logan told me that touching leads to more touching, and if he touched too much, bad things would happen. I don't quite understand that, but I suppose he can clear that up for me, too."

Gibby looked at her and didn't speak, but had a knowing look on her face.

Amy pressed. "What do you know? What does that mean?"

"Amy, there are confidentiality issues involved here. He will have to tell you whatever you need to know. But just think about it. Touching leads to more touching. Where does more touching lead. To more intimacy. Which leads to what? You have to work on this with Logan."

"Intimacy leads to what—what married people do, I suppose. Married people have sex. Logic. I'm trying to be logical in a situation where logic doesn't even apply. Sex leads to…what? Sex leads to trust, being comfortable with another person. Sex is a connection, a way to express love. Sex…oh my God! Sex makes babies! Did she miscarry? Never mind. I know you can't tell me. Maybe, just maybe this is the key. She miscarried. And he feels like it's his fault, since he touched her, which got her pregnant, and she died because of that. In other words, he killed her."

Amy stood up and ran her hands through her hair. "Oh, God! I want to go to him. He's tormented by this. I'm sure of it."

"Amy, he's had a hard day if he told you what's been on his mind. Give him some time alone to deal with it. It's probably better for him to take little steps in this whole process. That way you won't be overwhelmed either. Work through this at his pace. Let him tell you his story. Don't drag it out of him."

"Okay. But that's what you think it is, right?"

Gibby just looked at her with an understanding smile. "Do you trust him?"

"Completely."

"Then let him come to you with the details."

"I want to go to him and hug him and tell him I know. I want to tell him it's okay to touch me. It won't lead to bad things. I won't get pregnant and die."

"Amy, that isn't a promise you could or should make."

"What are the chances…?"

"It doesn't matter what the chances are. It already happened in his life once, and it sounds like he isn't willing to take the chance again. It doesn't matter what kind of chances you're willing to take for him. It's the chances with his heart that he may not be willing to take again. Just respect that."

"Gibbs, I know you're right. It's just tough."

Beth joined in the conversation after listening, engrossed by the discussion. "That's God's gift to you, Amy. It's the female, comforting, mothering DNA we have an abundance of. Just use it at the right time. You can be a blessing to Logan. Be gentle with him. Be careful of his heart."

"You two are a blessing to me. This is perfect. I have an insight to his heart and mind without badgering him. I wanted to know so badly, but I knew there were certain things I just couldn't ask him yet."

Gibby got up to leave. Punkin followed her to the door. "Just remember, I told you nothing, but this isn't necessarily the end of his anguish."

"Gibby, what was her name?"

"Ask Logan. Good night."

Beth got up and headed for the door. "Terry's meetings are done this evening and we're having a late supper. Wish me luck."

"Need the list?"

"No. I think I can remember. Sniff, lick, nibble, do."

"You'll be okay as long as you remember *do* is always last."

"Gross." She closed the door behind her.

*

After Logan dropped Amy off, he went home, changed clothes and went to his workshop. He had to finish the rocker so it could be shipped off to California to Bo and Ginny. Their baby wasn't due for another month, but having the chair sit in the workshop was just another reminder of his failure. Amy fit perfectly in the chair. She was about Ginny's size. He imagined Amy rocking a baby in that chair. *No. Won't happen. Can't happen*, he thought. He opened a drawer and pulled out sandpaper to finish the arms. Tomorrow he would stain it. Two weeks for the finish to dry and it would be shipped in plenty of time. He sat on a stool next to the rocker and thought of his day as he worked.

Divine meddling. What else could it be? Amy gets fired and looks for work at the same time he decides to work on the house. Dumb luck? What is Amy calling it? Rebound from…whatever-his-name-is, boyfriend? He wondered how serious they were. Was she planning on marrying him? He must have been a supreme loser to let her go. He hadn't known anyone like her since… What was he thinking? Was it true? Since Sam. Could he even use their names in the same sentence? Not yet.

He needed to get to know Amy better. He thought he knew the kind of person she was, but really knew no details of her life. She lost a job. He didn't know what kind of work she did. Her boyfriend cheated on her. What was their relationship like? What kind of music did she like? Could she dance? Did she have hobbies? Painting, obviously. She painted for friends. Did she play the piano? Sisters? Brothers? They needed to have dinner and a nice little time to chat. But then, she'd probably ask questions of him. Bad idea. But she needed to know. No, he needed to tell. If this was going any further…*did he want it to*? He was going to have to be honest with her. He'd already told her that. No secrets. She'd find out sooner or later. Better for her to find out sooner and dump him, than to have him totally hooked on her. Was he hooked? God help him, he was hooked. *Amy, what have you done to me?* he thought.

Chapter 18

Amy spent Sunday doing everything in her power to avoid thinking about Logan. She was torn between wanting to avoid him because of the "to do" list and wanting to talk to him because of the information she, Beth, and Gibby discussed regarding his revelation about his wife. Amy wanted details, but was willing to wait for just the right time. As a distraction, she and Hillie went out and watched back-to-back movies and had supper. At Amy's instruction, they stuck only to the topic of the movies they had just seen and the food they were eating. It killed seven hours of the day.

Monday morning came much too soon, and Amy was determined to arrive at the house after Logan had left. She got there later than usual, got busy with some prep work in the den, skipped lunch, and left before he got home. He must have pulled in shortly after she left because when she got home there was a message from him on her answering machine.

"Amy. Logan. Sorry I missed you today. I'm making a meatloaf tonight and will leave a sandwich for you so you won't need to pack a lunch. I had a good day. Hope you did too. Bye."

She hit the erase button. "Now I feel like a jerk." She was talking to the answering machine.

She went back to her regular schedule on Tuesday but he was still gone before she got there. She ate the meatloaf sandwich and left him a note.

Logan,
thanks for lunch.
Did you have a date with Betty Crocker again?
ASS

Again, she left before he got home.

The next morning when Amy arrived, Logan was gone but there was a note from him on the counter.

ASS,
Take the key to the workshop.
The rocker is stained. Look but don't touch. Thought you'd like to see it.
I'll be late again tonight.
L

*

Thursday she almost ran into him in the driveway. He was speeding out as she was pulling in. He rolled his window down and motioned for her to do the same.

"I'm running late. Can we plan to have supper tomorrow? Plan for casual and bring dessert." He waved and she nodded.

Amy painted the first coat in the den. It took longer than she planned because there was so much trim to tape around. There was a depth of color that she wanted in that room, so she would paint a second coat on Friday.

*

On Friday, Amy took the pint of Ben and Jerry's Cherry Garcia out of her freezer. She wrapped it up, put it in a plastic bag and tossed it in a small piece of luggage. She planned to shower and change at Logan's. She didn't want to sit around in work clothes when she could be comfortable and clean. She packed a change of clothes and left for Logan's.

He was spending his usual Friday working from home. She walked in the back door, took the ice cream from her bag and put it in his freezer. She put her bag in the closet. He could be ready to move some stuff into the den by the weekend. She wondered how long it would take him to make the desk he was planning. Logan had already made coffee, so she poured herself a cup and took a couple sips. She carried a new roller, a utility knife and her coffee cup with her up the stairs. She thought Logan would be in his room in front of the computer. She turned the corner at the top of the stairs and headed for the den. Then the bathroom door opened and Logan stepped into her path, hair wet from the shower, wearing only a fluffy yellow towel. She jumped back and spilled a little coffee on his bare foot.

"Oww! I didn't hear you come in. Do you always sneak up on people when they're the most vulnerable?"

"You mean like when they're half-naked?"

Logan walked back into the bathroom to wipe the coffee off his foot. He grabbed some tissues to soak up the few drops that landed on the carpet.

"That's exactly what I mean." He tightened the towel and watched her as she checked him out from head to toe. "Perhaps you'd like me to do a little spin so you can check out all sides?"

"Yes, please." She'd already seen him without a shirt at Olga's, but this was different.

He glowered at her and walked past her to his room. "You're watching, aren't you?"

"Of course! Thank you." *Thank you very much*, she thought.

She went into the den, opened the paint and got started.

Logan had spent the morning in his room at the computer. Amy worked hard in the den and was surprised when he stuck his head in.

"Ready for a mid-morning break?"

"Sure. My coffee cup is empty."

Amy followed Logan down to the kitchen. He poured out the over-heated coffee, now too bitter to be enjoyable, and started a fresh pot. Amy sat at the table and watched him work.

"Changed clothes, I see."

"Despite what you might like to think in your little Logan fantasy world, I don't just wander the house in a towel all day."

"You think you're in my fantasies?"

"Amy. Don't make me mention 'the list.'"

She blushed and banged her forehead on the table. "When will I learn never to put things in writing?"

"Almond or chocolate?"

She picked her head up. "What?"

"Biscotti. Almond or chocolate?"

"Almond."

"That's my favorite."

"Then I'll take the chocolate." Amy didn't care. She liked both flavors.

"I was hoping you'd say that."

"Logan, I really don't know much about you."

"I think you know a lot of the important things about me, just not many of the little details. Like, I like almond. The nut itself, flavoring in cakes, cookies, biscotti…and candy bars. Almond bark, almond crescent sweet rolls. Now you know. And I know you like chocolate."

"I didn't have a lot of choice today, did I?"

"If you're going to whine about it, I'll let you take the almond."

"I'm not whining. You're right about the chocolate. I like dark the best, but not the cheap stuff. Milk chocolate is okay. I love chocolate milk, but feel guilty drinking it at my age. Like it's just for kids. Kind of the way I feel about eating Frosted Flakes."

"I love Frosted Flakes! But I'd never eat them in public, and I would never leave the box sitting around where someone might see it."

"I wouldn't make fun. Promise!" She continued the chocolate diatribe. "I could eat chocolate pudding every day, but only the cooked kind where you…"

"Where you get that skin on the top! Yes! I love to pull it off and wrap it around my spoon."

"Me too! But I don't care for chocolate ice cream. I like ice cream with chocolate things in it or on it, but not chocolate ice cream itself."

"I like it. Especially a big scoop in a cone when no one is watching. I like to get it all over my lips, and it gets all melty, and I feel just like a kid again. You know how it gets so far out on your face that your tongue can't reach it all? God, that's great."

"You haven't grown up yet, have you?"

"Part of me never will."

Amy smiled at him. "That's good to know."

Logan poured the fresh coffee and sat across the table from Amy. She bit into her biscotti and it broke in half. Logan broke his and swapped halves with her.

"Only seems fair."

"Thanks."

He dunked his in the coffee. She just crunched.

"Fruit?" He held out the basket of apples.

"No thanks. Wouldn't want to do anything too healthy."

They chewed and sipped, looking up at each other now and then. Logan refilled their cups and stood up.

"I have to get back to work. Lunch at 12:30?"

"See ya then." Amy waited a few seconds, took her cup and went back to her painting.

She knew she could have the room finished by lunch time. She carried a bucket of brushes and a roller down to the kitchen and began cleaning up in the sink. She wanted Logan to see the den before lunch. There would be just enough time to remove the blue tape from the trim. She liked it already and knew when the paint was dry the color would be even richer. This was her favorite room so far, mainly because of the comfy, cozy feeling it had, even without furniture. She knew Logan's handmade pieces would be perfect. She would encourage him at lunch to get started.

Amy knocked on Logan's door, opened it and stepped inside. The smell of latex paint was like aromatherapy to Logan. He inhaled and knew Amy was standing in the doorway.

"Lunch time. On your way down, stop in the den. It's finished. I'm really happy with the way it turned out."

"Okay. Wait just a minute while I save this." He pressed several keys and got up from his chair. He met her at the doorway and they walked down the hall to the den.

"I'm impressed! I thought the dark green would be too much, but there's plenty of window space in here. I don't want to cover the windows with anything too dark. It could get a little gloomy, don't you think?"

"You mean like heavy velvet drapes from an old Joan Crawford movie?"

"That's exactly what I mean."

"Do you like vertical blinds?"

"They always look kind of generic and boring."

"I agree, but you cover each slat with fabric. You can make a pattern, or stripes or anything, really."

"If you think you can pull that off, go for it. Let me see the fabric first or do a little sketch."

"My artwork is so lame, I'd be embarrassed."

"Then just show me the fabric and describe your idea to me. Better yet, I have a computer program that can help with that. We'll sit down and work on that next week some evening. Or maybe next Friday when I'm home."

"Sounds like fun. I'll start jotting down ideas."

They walked down the stairs to the kitchen.

Logan stood in the middle of the floor with his hands on his hips. "What do I feel like today? Salad? No. Waffles? Too much starch. Chili?" He looked at Amy. "Not while there's someone else in the house."

"Thank you."

"I have this awesome loaf of Italian bread. It has garlic chunks baked into it."

"Does it toast well?"

"It's great toasted, with butter, of course."

"Do you have enough eggs for omelets? I'm pretty good with omelets."

"I have plenty of eggs. I have cheese." He opened the refrigerator and began pulling out possible filling ingredients. "I have chopped onion. I have green pepper." He opened the green pepper container and sniffed. "Cancel the green pepper. I have a little chopped chicken."

"Smell it."

"It's fine."

"Give it to me." She unfolded the foil, sniffed and put a little piece in her mouth. She chewed and pronounced it edible. "Do you have salsa?" He set the jar on the counter and stood back.

"There's a great pan in the cabinet next to the stove and mixing bowls under the counter. There's a wire whisk in the second drawer over. Here's the butter and the eggs. Do your thing."

"Think you can manage toast?"

"It will be tricky. I have to actually slice the bread first."

"Maybe you could handle it better if you took it out to the workshop and used the band saw."

"How do you know I have a band saw?"

"I watch public television."

Logan picked up the loaf of bread and headed for the door.

"I was teasing." He stopped, turned around, and gave her a very sexy smile.

"So was I." He reached for the bread knife and cut four slices. "Enough?"

She nodded. She cracked the eggs like an expert, never dropping a speck of shell into the bowl. She was a master with the whisk. Mentally she assembled the omelet. Lightly cook the onion in the butter. Add the eggs. Gently lift the cooked egg so the uncooked pours underneath. While the top is still shiny sprinkle on a little salt and pepper. It was a large pan, but she used all the strength in her arms. She slid the omelet around, scooted it to the edge of the pan and while Logan watched, amazed, she flipped it in the air and caught it dead center in the frying pan. She added the cheese, chicken and salsa. She could smell the toast and the garlic would go perfectly with the eggs. After checking three cabinets she found plates. She took two, cut the omelet into two pieces, and held the plates out while Logan placed two slices of toast on each one.

"You're amazing."

"You make a mean piece of toast."

"I mean it."

"So do I." Amy bit into the toast and gave Logan the thumbs up sign. "Logan, have you thought much about the desk?"

"That's what I've been working on all morning. Come on up after lunch and I'll show you what I have so far."

"How long will it take you to make it?"

"Since it's three sections, the piece for the computer will be fairly easy to make. The roll-top part will take longer, and of course anything with drawers takes a while. I have the wood. The plan will be fairly simple and modern. If I worked on it every day, maybe two or three weeks, I guess, but there's no way I can spend that much time on it. We're working on a modular deck at work, and I need to spend a good bit of time getting that project off the ground. I'm in no hurry. I just need to be sure I have a workspace."

"The chair should be here Monday. So things are falling into place. New paint just doesn't seem like enough around here."

"I haven't done much for the last year or so. My heart just wasn't in it. Then one day I looked around me, decided I needed a fresh start and put the ad in the paper for help."

"How long did it take to do the kitchen?"

"Actually the basics were here. It just needed updated cabinets and all new appliances."

Amy decided to take a chance. "Was your wife into cooking?"

Logan stopped chewing and thought before he answered. "We did a lot together, you know, kind of complemented each other."

"Your specialty was toast?"

He smiled. "Pretty much. Actually I stayed in my domain. You know, the manly equipment—the grill."

"How long have you been in this house?"

"We moved here shortly after...actually, shortly before she died. We planned on remodeling together. She had the better eye for decorating. Would you mind if we changed the subject?"

"What's for dinner?"

"Steak on the grill, green beans with almonds and cranberries, and cornbread made from scratch. What's for dessert?"

"Ice cream."

"Homemade?"

"Dream on."

"Well, I have to get back to work. Come on up and I'll show you the desk so far."

"I'm going to throw the dishes in the dishwasher and I'll be right up." Logan went upstairs and Amy leaned on the sink. She looked out at the backyard and wondered how many times Logan's wife looked out that window watching him come in from the workshop. She wanted to know her name. Not that it was important, but it would help pull the picture together for her. Tonight was not the night to reminisce about Logan's dead wife. She wanted this to be her night. She wanted to get to know him and just the two of them together, without ex-boyfriends and spouses, would be the best way. She would spend the next few hours before dinner strategizing while priming another bedroom. Her goal would be to urge him to talk about himself. Not an easy task.

The door to Logan's room was open and he waved her in. She pulled up a chair next to him and he showed her the three-dimensional computer drawing of the desk he was designing for himself.

"Logan, you do beautiful work."

"Thanks. We'll see how it looks when it's done."

"You know exactly how it will look. You're too modest."

"Actually, sometimes I change things a little while I'm working. You know, details can be changed. Not measurements or anything crucial, but just little personal touches can be changed, depending on my mood at the time."

"Well, keep me updated. I'd like to watch you work on it in the shop. I better get back to work, too. I'd like to get a little priming done before dinner. I brought clean clothes to change into and would like to use the shower if you don't mind."

Logan groaned. "I guess I better get out the scrubbing bubbles."

"Don't be silly. Just point me to the towels."

He turned in his chair and pointed to the linen closet in the hallway.

"Thanks. See you later." She left and closed the door.

*

Amy was finishing up some prep work in the next bedroom so she'd be ready to dig in on Monday morning. She heard the distinct sound of an aerosol can and knew Logan had decided to clean the shower before she got in. She took her time and let him finish. He announced when he was done, "I'm going downstairs to start supper. Take your time."

She waited to hear him working in the kitchen and then ran down the stairs to the closet and brought her overnight bag up to the bathroom. How sweet of Logan. He had set out two towels, one big, one small, a matching washcloth, and a new bar of soap that looked kind of girly. He had a bottle of some manly smelling, slap-you-in-the-face shower gel sitting on the edge of the bathtub, so she was glad he offered her an option. She picked the bar up and read the paper: fancy-shmancy wrapper, French-milled lavender soap made in England. She wasn't going to spend one minute worrying about whose it was. Maybe it was a gift. Did he buy it just for her? No, of course not. He had no idea she would be showering there. Maybe it belonged to his wife. *Why must you overanalyze everything, you twit. Stop it right now,* she thought. He probably got it free with an oil change.

After showering and towel-drying her hair she dressed and applied just a touch of makeup. She combed her hair out, fluffed it with her fingers and looked in the mirror. Not bad. She shrugged her shoulders and went downstairs to join Logan in the kitchen.

But he wasn't in the kitchen. She smelled cornbread baking and the table was set. Once again, he impressed her. The tablecloth was black. The plates were white. The crystal was beautiful. There was an end-of-the-season yellow rose in a bud vase. She had seen the rosebush next to the house where it was protected from the weather. The rose was about two days past being a bud and it smelled wonderful. There was a bottle of merlot on the table, open, "breathing," and she decided to wait for Logan to pour it. Something was simmering in a pot on the stove. She looked out the back door and Logan, master of the grill, was flipping meat over. Steak. It looked great. There were thick slices of onion next to the meat with grill marks on them. Suddenly she was very hungry. He was standing under the light on the deck and waved when he looked up and saw her watching him. She opened the door.

"Can I help?"

"Turn off the fire under the green beans but leave the lid on. Take the butter out of the fridge. There's a bottle of honey in the pantry. Get that out, too." She closed the door before he could issue more orders.

Logan came in with the steaks and onions on a plate. He set it on the counter and went to the stove. He drained the green beans, tossed in a chunk of butter, a handful of dried cranberries and put the lid back on. The timer for the cornbread rang. He took the pan out of the oven and set it on the counter. Amy was amazed at his efficient use of movement. He seemed to be all over the kitchen at once. She just stood back and watched him work. He drizzled a little honey on the onion slices and added a fresh grind of black pepper. He handed her the salt shaker and the pepper mill and motioned for her to set them on the table. He dumped the green beans into a bowl that matched the plates and sprinkled on a handful of sliced almonds. He put a serving spoon in it and handed the bowl to Amy. He sliced the hot cornbread and placed several chunks in a napkin-lined basket. Amy, thinking ahead, took the butter dish and the honey and placed them on the table. He handed her the cornbread. He placed a steak and two onion slices on each plate and stood back to admire his work.

"Well, I'm tired just watching you!" He hadn't even broken a sweat.

Logan went to her chair and held it out for her. She sat down and placed her napkin in her lap.

"You're impressed, I can tell."

"The proof of the pudding is in the eating,' isn't that what they say? It looks good, but if it doesn't taste…"

He filled her glass. "I'm assuming you drink wine."

"Of course, thank you." She picked up her knife to cut her steak. Logan reached over and touched her hand. She stopped and looked up at him.

"Amy Sweet, painter extraordinaire, I'd like to make a toast." He picked up his glass and motioned for her to do the same. "Here's to friendships rich with promise, second chances, and a wonderful woman with a kind and patient heart." He touched his glass to hers and drank.

"And here's to a generous, courageous man, a man who has been a blessing in my life." They touched glasses again and drank. Logan leaned over, picked up her hand and brushed his lips across it. He looked her in the eyes and she knew she was blushing.

"Amy?"

"Yes?"

"I'm starving."

She glared at him and bit back a smile. "I didn't steal your fork…go for it."

They tasted, commented, passed dishes, cut, spooned, drank, seasoned, chewed and tried to chat in between.

"Logan, are you going to give me your butcher's name or will I have to spend my life eating inferior meat?"

"Stick with me, baby, I can get you the prime cuts."

"You're not going to tell me. This isn't grocery store meat. I'll just stalk you when you go shopping."

"So you're not giving the chef the credit for the incredibly tender, flavorful steak you snarfed down in record time?"

"I'll give the cow credit. And I did not snarf. I chewed ladylike-size bites."

"Cornbread?"

"Only if you pass the butter and honey. Logan, I'm getting stuffed but I can't seem to stop myself. Everything is delicious, as if you didn't know."

"You sit there and digest and I'll clean up. Then we can sit in the living room, put on a little music and wait until we have room for dessert."

"Logan, I'd really like to help."

"Then go pick out some music. It won't take you long. I don't have that big a selection."

Amy walked into the living room feeling the effects of a full belly and half a bottle of wine. There was a stack of CDs on the mantle next to Logan's stereo. As she flipped through the discs she chuckled to herself.

"No disco?"

"If I had disco, it would be with the Frosted Flakes—where no one could see it. I hope you're kidding."

"Too early for Christmas music?"

"Yes."

"Then that limits us."

"Don't make fun."

"Sorry." She knew this would be a perfect time for a conversation and didn't want to be bogged down with oldies and the urge to sing along. She filled the CD player with three discs: instrumental, classical, and piano. Then she turned the volume down low. She heard the dishwasher come on and Logan came around the corner appearing to approve of her choices.

"Can I get you something to drink?"

"Logan, I'm stuffed to the gills and don't have room for a drop, but I'll be sure and let you know if I get the urge."

"Okay, then come and sit by me. I'd like to get to know you a little better and this seems like a good time."

Does he read minds? she thought. "I'd like that."

He motioned her to the couch. She sat in the middle and he sat at the end. Just when she thought about moving closer, he pulled his legs up and rested his feet on her lap.

"And just what am I supposed to do with these monstrosities?"

"They aren't that big, and you can do whatever you want with them. I just want them up." Amy took her thumbnail and dragged it right up the center of his foot. "Anything except tickling. Not fair."

"So you're ticklish. Good to know, I suppose. I'm not really, unless you catch me off-guard."

"I'll remember that. What's your favorite cartoon?"

"Starting simple, huh? I know it sounds un-American, but I never really liked Mickey Mouse. Favorite? I'm torn between Chip and Dale and Chilly Willy."

"Amy Sweet…cheap. You go for the cute. I should have guessed. My favorite is Tom and Jerry. I like the whole blowing-up-rodents kind of thing. You know, pulling a bomb out of your skin. Dogs and cats, living together. Kind of kinky."

"I always liked Underdog."

"That's a chick cartoon. I loved Speed Racer."

"Logan, he was creepy with those big eyes."

"Cool."

She couldn't help herself. She started rubbing his feet with the tips of her fingers. He didn't flinch or pull back. This was good. "Favorite homemade cookie."

"No contest, chocolate chips no nuts, raisins or other foreign matter. Soft middle, crunchy edges."

Amy looked serious. "That would be my second runner-up. First would be plain butter cookies made with real butter."

Logan yawned. "I wouldn't turn them down."

"Are you sleepy? I could leave."

Logan straightened up. "No, really, this is just so relaxing. I've needed to do this for so long and it feels really good. Please stay. Three pizza toppings."

"On thin crust, cheese is assumed and not one of the three…black olives, green pepper, pepperoni. How about you?"

"On thick crust, sausage, onion, mushrooms."

"Logan, this could be a problem. We can't go out for pizza together."

"Of course we can. I don't mind compromising and I eat anything called 'pizza' no matter what's on it."

"That's a relief. Toilet paper."

"Not on pizza, thank you. Oh, you mean favorite toilet paper? I prefer pink, with the little embossed flowers. I feel so feminine and fresh."

Amy laughed out loud and was surprised at the sound it made in this huge house. She didn't think those walls had heard much laughter lately. "No, that's not what I meant. Over or under?"

"You mean how the paper is on the roller? I don't really care. If I need it, I'm not going to take it off and turn it around just so it faces the other way. It has a very short life span and comes to a miserable end…flush…who cares? People are starving in Ethiopia and we worry about how to put our overpriced, three-ply, soft, fluffy, scented pastel butt wipes on the roller. Amazing."

"So, how many men does it take to change a toilet paper roll? No one knows; it's never been done!"

"Not funny. Who do you think does it here?"

"Since your speech, I just figured you'd be advocating the return to corn cobs!"

"If you could flush them, I would!"

Amy leaned over and bit his big toe.

"That hurt, dammit!"

"It was just my attempt at changing the subject."

"Oh, I see! One more thing to cross off the list—nibble on Logan."

"Will I never hear the end of that damn list?" Amy rested her head on the back of the couch and closed her eyes. Logan nudged her under the chin with his foot.

"I'll help you tear it up. When we finish our chores. All of them."

Her breath caught in her throat and she didn't have the nerve to look at him. *If he asked, would I?* she thought. *No, of course not. Maybe. Depends on how he asks. Tonight? No. Maybe. If it was just a natural progression. Change the subject.* "Favorite season."

"Used to be fall. Spring, I guess. Everything comes to life. How about you?"

He seemed relieved the subject had changed.

"Fall. The smells are awesome; I love the colors. I love the crispness of the air—summer humidity is gone. It's very exciting for me. It's like nature goes berserk."

"Maybe I just need to work on some new autumn memories. Care to help me with that?"

Amy smiled at him. "Anytime." She rubbed his foot and kissed the toe she bit. "Best grade in school."

"A."

"Mine too, but that's not what I meant."

Logan looked pensive as he eliminated most years. "Eighth grade. We had an amazing class, excellent sports teams, some severe brainiacs, some hot chicks. We ruled the school…just before we got slam-dunked as freshmen the next year. Peons. It was humiliating. We were tight as a class. I had some of the best teachers ever in eighth grade. How about you?"

"Well, I know I asked the question, but I hadn't really thought about it. Third grade was the worst. We moved that year. The school I came from taught handwriting in third grade and the school I went to taught it in second grade, so I missed out on learning how to write. My grades were horrible. I felt really behind for a while. Fourth grade was next-worse."

"Grammar issue?"

"Shut up, smart-ass. Actually, a math issue. I had to stay after school for months to learn long division. I had my own little formula. The only problem was that it didn't produce the right answer. I guess fifth grade was the best. I loved my teacher, I could read, I felt semi-smart and I had two boyfriends."

"Slut."

"Of course, they didn't know I was alive. I wanted to get my period like so many other girls, but I…"

"Stop! Please! This is way more than I wanted to know."

"Peer pressure is very complex at that age. There are only so many things in life you can rush, and that isn't one of them. I wanted to be a woman."

"Well, you are! So, no more, please. You don't want me talking about wet dreams, do you?"

"Is this something you feel the need to discuss? Because I can go with that, you know, if it would help you out, Logan." He laid his head back and covered his face with his hands. Amy ran her hand up his ankle and under the hem of his jeans. He sat up so fast he got dizzy.

"I'm ready for dessert. Since you brought it and I slaved over supper, you can fix it. I assume it isn't too complicated…no fancy tools needed…just a scoop and a couple of bowls."

"Don't piss me off, Logan. I'll walk right out that door arm-in-arm with Ben and Jerry."

"You can't. Your part of the deal is dessert, and I'm ready. If you're nice to me, I'll tell you where the waffle cones are."

"I'll be *very* nice to you if you tell me where the waffle cones are." She remembered his conversation about enjoying ice cream as a child. *Cones…perfect.*

Amy went into the kitchen, opened the freezer and took out the pint container. She filled two cones and brought a stack of napkins to the table.

"Logan, you'll need to come in here. It's pretty soft."

Not really. "On my way," he called.

She sat next to him, rather than across from him.

"This is your favorite?"

"I'm addicted to it. Big chunks of black cherries, chunks of chocolate, creamy white ice cream. Mmm." She licked and he watched her. "See?" She stuck out her tongue with a big cherry on the tip of it.

"Oh, God."

Amy smiled and took a bite, closing her eyes as she savored every mouthful. "Heaven." She motioned to Logan. "Eat up before it melts."

He could hardly take his eyes from her. *She's doing this on purpose,* he thought. *Seducing me with this sweet, creamy, Sweet Amy Sweet. Two can play at this game.* He took a big bite, swallowed the ice cream, chewed the cherries and stuck out his tongue with two chocolate chunks on it. He looked up at her and winked. He took another bite and noticed that she was watching him. Again chocolate appeared on his tongue. He smiled and chewed.

"I think you got more chocolate than I did."

"I'm not greedy. I'll share." He stuck out his tongue. She reached for the chocolate chunk. His tongue disappeared like a frog with a fly. Amy pulled her hand back and laughed.

"I thought you were going to share?"

"I will." He showed her another piece of chocolate. She reached for it and he pulled away.

"Logan."

"No hands." He took another mouthful and showed the chocolate. Amy looked at him and leaned closer. He held his breath. She quickly took the piece of chocolate from the tip of his tongue with her lips. She smiled as she chewed it.

"Thanks."

"Anytime. More?"

Amy whispered, "Yes, please."

Logan offered another piece. She was not as shy this time and lingered slightly before she captured the prize. "Amy?"

"Hmm." She had a mouthful.

"Trade cherries for chocolate?"

She offered a cherry on the very tip of her tongue. Logan moved closer and took it very slowly. He chewed and backed up, noticing that her eyes were closed. Amy caught her breath and decided to slow down a little. She ate her cone a little further down and waited for Logan to offer her another bite.

As she knew would happen, Logan showed her two big chunks. She moved in to claim her reward and he slowly retracted the chocolate. She was determined not to be shy. This retrieval would basically be a kiss in any dictionary. She pressed forward, her lips on his. They were cold, sweet and wet. Her tongue went in search of chocolate that was a bit melted. While her tongue explored, Logan increased pressure on her lips, admitting to himself that he was actually kissing her. She backed away, breathing hard with chocolate on her lips and her heartbeat in her throat. She stared at her cone then looked Logan in the eye. She raised her cone to his face and pressed.

Ice cream covered him from nose to chin. They were both laughing. Logan returned the favor and moved in to help her clean up. He licked the tip of her nose and she licked his chin. They licked each other's lips. Logan nibbled chocolate off Amy's cheek and she chased a cherry that was on its way down Logan's chin. Suddenly he stopped and looked at her.

"You remembered."

"Just relax and celebrate the child in you, Logan."

Amy leaned forward and kissed him quickly on the lips. She stood up, tossed the rest of her cone in the sink and walked toward the bathroom. "I'm going to clean up. Meet you back on the couch?"

"You bet."

*

Amy came back and took the same seat she had earlier in the evening. Logan did too, but this time put his feet on the arm of the couch and his head in Amy's lap.

Logan spoke first. "Do you mind?"

Amy's answer came out as a whisper. "No." She had her hands safely on the couch cushions at her sides.

"Thanks for dessert. I don't think I'll ever think of ice cream in the same way."

She brushed at the wet spot on her shirt. "I had to wash up a little."

"I noticed. Can the quiz continue?"

"If you want it to. Unless you have to get up early."

"I'm the boss and I say I can sleep in. And so can you. You weren't going to paint tomorrow, were you?"

"Not unless you needed me to."

Logan looked up at her. "I can see up your nose."

Amy covered her face. "How many more times are you going to embarrass me tonight? Do I need…is there…?"

"Nope. Clean as a whistle."

She playfully punched him in the stomach. He grabbed her wrist before she could recoil for another blow. "Now be nice. Favorite power tool."

"Easy. The blender."

"That's an appliance."

"Vibrator. And don't ask for details because I just may give them to you."

"That would be a tool replacement, or a pseudo-tool, or quasi-tool."

"That's a faux-tool to you, fool. Say that ten times fast."

"Router."

"Why?"

"You can't see the blade, so it's kind of dangerous, but it's very useful for making things decorative."

"Pretty?"

"Ugh. If you must, yes, I suppose it can make things pretty."

"Fudge. With nuts or without?"

"Without. Brownies. With nuts or without?"

Amy got that dreamy look in her eyes. "Without, but frosted. Boxers or briefs?"

Logan looked thoughtful. "Depends on what I'm doing. Is lunging involved?"

"Forget it."

"No, really, Amy, this seems important to you. Like right now?"

"Oh please, don't tell me." She covered her ears with her hands.

"Boxers. Silk. Dark blue. They feel great." He wiggled his behind. "Thongs or bikinis?"

"That depends." She could turn it on him, which she felt sure he intended for her to do all along. "Is there lunging involved?"

"Oh God, I hope so."

She flicked his ear. "Victoria keeps her thongs hidden from me—that's the secret. My ass is too big for a thong."

"You have a very nice ass. If your ass was too big I probably would have already poked fun at you. Pantyhose or garter belt?"

"Pervert."

"Knee highs! I knew it!"

"A garter belt and stockings are purely for show. I'm more practical."

"Of course, they're for show. That's the whole point."

"Puppies or kittens?"

"Goldfish. They don't shed."

Amy picked up her hand and ran it gently over his hair. He closed his eyes. "Does this bother you, Logan?"

"Not in a bad way."

She nestled her fingers in his hair and watched as it gently curled around each finger. She remembered the first day she saw him. "Remember that day in the workshop when we first met?"

"A day that changed my life, I think."

She smiled at that thought. "The first thing I thought of was that I wanted to brush the sawdust out of your fluffy hair. It's so soft and silky."

"Like my boxers."

She gave a little tug. "Ow!"

"Sorry, I didn't mean to do that."

Logan picked up where they left off. "Zoo or museum?"

"That's tough. Which museum? Is there a special exhibit? What time of year? Are the animals sweaty and smelly?"

"Sorry I asked. White or wheat?"

"What kind of sandwich? Grilled cheese, white. Tuna salad, wheat. Turkey with mayo, white. Toasted with peanut butter, wheat."

"Nothing is simple with you, is it?"

"Nothing is simple, yet everything is simple. Life is as tough as we want it to be, I guess. Simple is always good to fall back on when you get tired of fighting."

"I think there's more here that I need to hear about, but you're sucking the power out of my brain with your scalp massage."

"I'll stop."

"No, but keep in mind it gives you an unfair advantage if these questions get tougher."

"What's the last movie that made you cry?"

"Amy, you go first. I have to think. Actually, wait. I want to change the question, since I can't remember when I went to the movies last. How about what movie always makes you cry?"

"My list is long. But I'll keep it short. 'Sound of Music.' What about you?"

"'Rudy' and don't make me talk about it."

"Lifelong dream comes true. Good movie. Cubs or White Sox?"

"Cardinals." She tightened her fist on a handful of hair and lifted his head off her lap. "Kidding!"

"That, my friend, is nothing to kid about."

"Do you put ketchup on a hot dog?"

"No. It should be against the law. Ketchup is for burgers and fries. Fabric softener or dryer sheets?"

"Dryer sheets."

"Me too. Spaghetti. Fat or thin?"

"Amy, you amaze me. Where are you pulling this stuff from? Thin, I guess. But if I'm not cooking, I'm less picky."

She knew that if she kept fooling with his hair and stopped asking questions, he'd be asleep in five minutes. He was very relaxed and his eyes were closed. Amy watched his face and couldn't resist. She took the tip of her finger and stroked his bottom lip.

She whispered, "So soft."

Logan grasped her hand. He kissed the tip of her finger, nipped it with his teeth and kissed it between each knuckle to her palm. She could feel his warm breath on her hand, a feeling she knew she would not soon forget. He pressed her palm to his lips and kissed it. His tongue made small circles in the center and she spread her fingers across his cheek. He kissed it again and clasped her hand in his. He placed her hand on his fly and pressed. She didn't pull away.

Logan whispered, "So hard."

"Logan." She leaned over and kissed him. She kept her face very close. She kissed each eyelid, the tip of his nose and his chin. He finally opened his eyes and looked into hers.

"Amy. I want a kiss. A real kiss."

He lifted his head to meet her. She knew once she started she would not want to stop. She parted her lips and pressed them to Logan's. He licked her bottom lip and drew it in between his. She relaxed against him then realized she had not moved her other hand. He sat up and put his arm around her, drawing her close.

"Logan, I feel like I'm eighteen again."

"No way. This is better."

They were both breathing faster. Amy concentrated on his bottom lip. She kissed it, sucked it in and licked. She nipped it gently with her teeth. She held Logan's face with both her hands and looked into his eyes. "I love that lip. I dream of it doing things to me."

"That can be arranged." He kissed her neck and she put her head back so he wouldn't miss a spot. He nuzzled her neck and sniffed her. "You smell so good."

"That's your lavender soap."

"I got it from a client in a gift basket." Amy stopped mid-kiss.

"You sure know how to kill the moment."

"You want me to lie?"

"Not lie, just embellish. An appropriate response is, 'I set it out just for you so it would blend with your essence.'"

"I got it. I set it out just for you so you could lather up your big behind."

"That does it! I have to leave now, Mr. Carson, and go home to my power tools."

"You'll be thinking of me." It wasn't a question. Logan stood up with her. It was late and they both knew that this was not going to be the night. She put her arms around his neck, looked him straight in the eye and rubbed against him.

"I'll be thinking of you all night."

Logan brushed her hair back. "This will happen for us, Amy. When we're both ready."

"Get ready, Logan. I have a list."

He kissed her softly, thoroughly, on the mouth, then once more on the forehead. "Thanks for tonight. I had a great time."

"Thanks for cooking. Everything was delicious. Maybe next time at my place, huh?"

He carried her suitcase out to her van, helped her in, and kissed her again through the window.

"Go put some shoes on before your feet freeze."

He looked down. "I didn't even notice. Good night, Amy."

"Monday."

She pulled out of the driveway. Her only goal was to get home and hope that when her head hit the pillow, she would dream of Logan.

CHAPTER 19

Amy didn't set her alarm for Saturday morning. She had no plans for the entire day. She had a message on her answering machine when she got home. Logan called to tell her he would be in the workshop all day starting on his desk. This was just an FYI. She didn't expect to hear from him all weekend. Nothing was pressing. She knew she'd be visiting with her neighbors, but there was no specific time.

It had been a while since she had slept late. She rolled over about 8 a.m. and heard the rain on her windows. The sun was up, but the clouds must have been very heavy because it was still dark outside. She heard faint rumble of thunder far away and now and then a flash of lightning brought out the details in the clouds. This was perfect weather for staying in bed with a book and a pot of tea. She was determined to stay in pajamas all day and give her brain and heart time to recover from the evening before. Maybe she would make a list. No. Not again. Nothing in writing. She would make a mental list of what she actually knew about Logan and what more she needed to learn about him.

There was at least one more mystery to be solved. She wanted to look in the room that he always kept locked. She wanted to know, even though she was fairly certain she did know the details about his wife dying. She felt she could prod only so far. She had proof of it. Logan had a knack for changing the subject. Now and then he would give her a little glimpse into his secrets, like the previous night commenting on autumn not being his favorite time of year. She knew his wife died in the fall because he had mentioned it once before. She was sure that he would open up in his own time and when he was ready, she'd be listening.

Amy plodded to the kitchen and put water on the stove for tea. She reached high in the cabinet for her grandmother's English china teapot. She set out the English breakfast tea, her favorite china cup and saucer and the blue-and-yellow plaid tea cozy, also her grandmother's. Nothing matched, but it didn't matter. The kettle whistled. Amy filled the teapot with hot water and put another kettle on to boil. When the kettle whistled the second time, she emptied the teapot of the first water, added the tea and filled the teapot again. She put the lid on, covered it with the cozy and looked at the clock. Just enough time to pick some music and magazines for the day. She put music on the stereo, tossed magazines on the coffee table, cleared a spot for her tea and dug a bar of dark chocolate out of the secret hiding place in the kitchen. She knew it was stupid to hide it from herself, but if she left it laying out it wouldn't last very long. She walked through the house and opened all the curtains and blinds. She loved to watch storms. She poured the tea, added a teaspoon of sugar and stirred. She took peach yogurt from the refrigerator and headed for the couch. Perfect. She should do this one day a week for her mental health.

She finally had a chance to go through the decorating magazine she bought the week before. She wanted some ideas for Logan's bedrooms. She knew she wasn't a decorator, and he wasn't paying her to be one, but he seemed to be fairly agreeable to some of her ideas. If she showed him some pictures, maybe they could order some curtains—oops, window treatments—bedspreads, something to hang on the bare walls. She had planned on one of the bedrooms staying rather plain—something he could turn into a nursery someday. *I can't plan his life for him,* she thought. She wondered how masculine he wanted his bedroom to be. The house needed a feminine touch. A yellow rose and a bar of lavender soap weren't enough. She would try sneaking her ideas into conversations and then find a way to make him think they were his.

As she got up to refill her cup there was a light tap on the door. Amy opened it to find Beth and Gibby in pajamas. They were carrying a pitcher of orange juice and a plate of freshly baked blueberry muffins.

"Good morning, ladies. I wondered how long it would take you to drop in."

"If you don't want us here, we can leave, can't we, Beth?"

"We'll just take our warm, buttery muffins with us and leave."

"Not so quick. I planned on this being a lazy day with no plans, so this fits into my non-schedule very well. I made tea. This kind of weather just doesn't seem to call for coffee."

Gibby passed out napkins, filled cups with tea for herself and Beth and sat on the floor in front of the coffee table. She broke a muffin in half and inhaled the wonderful, warm blueberry scent. "Beth, you have outdone yourself."

"Thank you very much. Help yourself, Ames."

Amy lit two candles since the sky seemed to have gotten darker. "I love days like this. Turning lights on just ruins it. So, Beth, how was the farewell to Terry?"

Beth and Gibby just looked at each other. "Do you want me to tell her? I don't want you blubbering all over the place again."

"I think I can tell it this time. Eight hours of sleep gives you a new perspective on things. Did you ever realize that? Nothing really has changed overnight, but just the fact that you're waking up, still alive, a second chance puts everything in a new light."

Amy was losing patience. "The story, please."

Beth started. "I was just so sad, you know, Terry leaving and all. This seems like such a crucial time, and I'd like what little momentum we have to keep going."

"What makes you think it won't?"

"Just distance. He called me this morning, but it just isn't the same." Beth's voice cracked. She sipped her tea and started again. "He hit me like a ton of bricks, Ames, and I can't stand not seeing him."

"How much vacation time do you have? Maybe you could plan a little trip?"

"I have plenty of time, but you know how it is with salesmen. If they aren't selling, they aren't making money."

"Is he feeling this same urgency you are, you know, to be together? Because if he is, there's got to be a way to arrange schedules to see each other a little more often. It's only Iowa, not Egypt, for Pete's sake! It's a four-hour ride to Iowa."

Beth had already done her research, so was prepared with an answer. "Four hours to the Illinois-Iowa border, then two more hours on country roads. The bus takes even longer."

Amy seemed to have the solution. "Okay, so assuming you drive faster when you're horny…"

Beth interrupted. "What? Maybe *you* do…"

"I would. You start work an hour early, work through your lunch and leave Chicago at 3:30 p.m. You drive like the horny little chick you are, cross the Mississippi River about 7:30 p.m. You make a pit stop and gobble a granola bar and get back on the road by 7:40 p.m. You check your map again. Allow a few minutes to get lost the first time, and arrive in Terry's arms before 10:00 p.m. You screw your brains out until dawn, he gets up, sells a tractor, and comes back to pick up where he left off, giving you time to shower and rest up. Totally do-able."

Gibby laid on the floor laughing. Beth was trying not to laugh, but did see some possibilities in Amy's scenario.

"Now Amy, you know I am beyond saving myself for my husband, but that's just a little more than we're ready for right now."

"I bet Terry's ready."

Beth blushed. "I must admit, I did see evidence of it, and felt rather proud of myself for putting him in that condition."

Gibby added, "But you didn't offer him any relief, did you?"

"Of course not, not yet. I just assume he'll handle that himself for a while. He'll be in St. Louis in two weeks. I suppose I could meet him there."

"Beth, find out where he's staying and meet him. Stay in separate rooms if you must, but it seems to me you need to work out the geography."

"I'll email him later and see what he thinks."

Gibby changed the subject. "So, Ames, where were you last night? I heard you get in kind of late."

"Well, you knew I was having supper at Logan's after work. He worked at home during the day. We had coffee together and he showed me some plans he's working on for a desk he's building. I know the computer is a miraculous thing, but his mind just sees things in chunks of wood and they turn into beautiful objects. I am so in awe of his talent that sometimes I find it hard to even speak about it. He made a rocking chair for his sister-in-law who's expecting. He made me feel the wood after he sanded it. He's such a perfectionist. He can make wood feel like satin. He takes such time with details."

"Is he like that in all parts of his life?" Gibby, always curious, wanted to keep Amy on track.

"I don't think so. He's actually pretty relaxed. I showered and changed clothes and…"

"You were naked in his house?" In Beth's drawl, the word came out sounding like "nekkid."

"Yes, Beth, I took my clothes off before I showered. I couldn't very well have dinner with him while I was all sweaty after working all day. I didn't see the point in driving home to change, so I took clean clothes with me."

"So, you *were* naked in his house."

"I was bareass, titty-floppin' naked in Logan's house. I was in the shower, not prancing through the living room. Why is this a big deal?"

"You were naked."

"That has been established. No clothes. Wet in the shower. Nude. I did, however, put on very nice underwear, just in case."

"You ate dinner in your underwear?"

Amy wondered where this was going to end. "Yes, I did wear underwear during dinner; however, it was covered with jeans and that cute little snug pink shirt with the scooped neck."

Beth seemed to breathe a sigh of relief and Gibby took it all in stride. She enjoyed Beth's southern accent when she got excited and just let her talk. Gibby imitated her. "You ate dinnah in yoah unda-waya?"

"Don't you make fun of me, Margaret. I have lived here too long to have that much accent left."

Amy rolled her eyes and continued. "Anyhoo...Logan did steaks and onions on the grill. He spun through the kitchen like a chef on speed. Everything was done at the same time, nothing was burned, nothing was overdone or underdone. The wine was perfect. If he was a troll I'd marry him for his cooking abilities alone."

Gibby reminded her, "But he's not a troll, is he?"

"He's drop-dead gorgeous and gets cuter every time I see him. He has an awesome body...he was actually naked in his house too. When I walked in this morning, I went up to work in the den and just assumed he'd already been working on his computer because I was running a little late. Needless to say, I walk into a delicious-looking Logan, all fresh and damp, wrapped in a towel. I spilled hot coffee on his foot, and that started our day off just right.

"I fixed lunch. If I had known what a good cook he was, I would have been intimidated. We worked a little longer. He showed me his desk plans. We had dinner and talked. We discussed little things, just kind of quizzing each other. It was easy. I enjoyed talking with him. He had his head in my lap and let me play with his hair. You know I'm obsessed with his bottom lip."

"The 'ample' lip." Gibby remembered.

"Ample and perfect. I had to touch it. We touched a little. It was nice."

Beth asked, "Just what did you touch?"

Amy smiled.

"Naked or through clothes?"

"Why are you so fixated on nakedness? We were dressed. Except he was barefoot."

Gibby couldn't resist. "How big are his feet?"

Amy knew where she was headed. "Big enough." She leaned her head back on the couch and took a deep breath. "We kissed." Her friends were silent. "It was a warm, long, tongue-sucking, lip-mashing kiss and it was wonderful. It took my breath away, and Logan's, too. Then he made fun of my big ass and everything came to a halt."

"When are you going to realize you do not have a big ass? And how dare he make fun of it!"

"Calm down, Beth. It was in fun, and a way of slowing things down, which we both wanted to do. He was teasing me and I let him. He is anxious for me to get back to 'the list' one of these days. 'Do Logan' is the only thing left. I left shortly after that and we agreed that we're headed in that direction. If he would have asked last night, I would have said yes."

Gibby reminded her to be careful. "You need the whole puzzle. There are only a few pieces left, but they're big pieces."

"I know that and I'm working on it. He can't be pushed. If I try, he changes the subject. But if he's on his own time schedule, he can be very talkative. I'm going to let him bring me slowly into his life. I'm not going to barge in. He knows we have issues, and we discussed not having secrets if this is ever going to be anything more. God, I want it to be more." She put her head in her hands and surprised all of them when she broke into tears. "Please, God, let it be more."

Gibby got up on the couch and sat next to her. She took Amy's hands. "You love him, don't you?"

Amy nodded and sniffled. Beth handed her the tissue box.

"What if he lies to you?"

"He won't."

"How does he feel about having children?"

Amy blew her nose and wiped her eyes. "I don't know. We never talked about it. I just remember our discussion here the other night thinking that his wife may have had a miscarriage."

"Find out, Amy."

"Why, Gibby, what do you know?"

"You have to talk to him. I can't tell you anything, you know that."

"He wouldn't hurt me, I know it."

"Not deliberately, I'm sure, but if you get too involved…well, you know the whole 'love is blind' speech."

"Gibby, I know right from wrong and so does he. He's very ethical. We've even discussed that regarding his business. He's very strict about the kind of person who works for him. I think once he even mentioned dealing with someone who deceived him or committed some kind of fraud or something. I didn't think twice about it at the time. How could that have anything to do with his wife's death?"

"It may have nothing to do with anything. I'm just reminding you that your heart is a fragile thing and you may want to protect it."

"And I know this: *his* heart is a fragile thing, and it's been crushed. Sometimes I can see the pain in his eyes. He loved his wife. They had a life planned. They bought a house, remodeled a kitchen. They had plans that came to a screeching halt. She's dead. He feels guilty. He's trying so hard to come back from all that. I want to help him. He's letting me."

Beth jumped in. "Maybe it's time we meet him! Invite him for dinner."

"Oh that poor man. I can't subject him to a grilling from the three of you."

"We're your best friends and he needs to meet us. Just as we need to meet him."

"Well, I did kind of promise him dinner. My terms this time. Which means hectic, burnt, undercooked, messy. I'm humiliated already."

Gibby got up to leave. "Well, enjoy your day off and your storm. I have to get ready for work. Beth, see you later. Don't hold dinner. I'll be late."

"Thanks, Gibbs, really. And let me know if you find out anything…anything at all, please."

"Amy, I'm leaving you, too. I'm gonna get started on that email before I lose my courage. St. Louis sounds good to me. If Terry isn't as excited as I am I'll be crushed."

"Give him a chance. Let him catch up to your page. Keep me posted."

CHAPTER 20

L ogan woke up early with plans to work on his desk. He ate a banana while the coffee was brewing. He filled a thermos, took an umbrella and headed for the workshop. When he stepped through the door he reached for the light switches. He'd need them all today because it was so gloomy. Normally he enjoyed a good rainy day, but today he was concentrating on the job at hand. He set his thermos down and began sorting wood. He watched for color, grain and thickness. He set some shorter pieces aside that would be perfect for drawers. Some of them still had dark edges from when they were burned, but he was sure they would sand down just fine. He remembered the fire as he stroked the boards. And he remembered the person who set it.

It happened almost two years ago. An outdoor play set that Logan had designed was being shipped to a family with three children. Although production was about two weeks behind, it was always Logan's policy to sacrifice speed for safety. Carson Creations' employees knew this, and although they would sacrifice bonuses for being behind, they knew they would lose their jobs if less-than-perfect products left their shop. Logan's name was burned into each piece and a small brass plate was attached at a prominent place on each object with the company name, logo and address.

Logan hired a man named Bart Winston. He had an impressive resume but Logan had trouble getting in touch with a couple of the references he listed. He was hired on a temporary basis, depending on the response from the references and the quality of the work he would do in the following two weeks. Logan watched him, checked his work and had his foreman watch him. Winston was an excellent carpenter. His work was precise. Logan never did get a response from the references, but he was so impressed with his work he stopped calling. Winston tended to keep to himself during lunch and breaks and didn't participate in the camaraderie that had become so common among the other employees. They were more like a family. They were proud of the work they did and were very supportive of each other.

Logan wished Winston fit in a little better, but his work made the grade so he thought no more about it.

One day, one of his workers let Logan know that the drill he used every day was missing. It was nowhere in the shop to be found. Winston got very defensive when questioned about it and made a big fuss about being accused. Within an hour, the drill showed up in the arms of a long-time employee who had borrowed it overnight. This was not uncommon, but the rule was to let someone know you were borrowing something. Winston was angry for the rest of the day. Logan was so surprised at his reaction that he decided to call the references again. After a call to the phone company he discovered both numbers were fake as were the companies that they were for. Logan decided to keep an eye on Winston. Trust was now an issue and Logan had no tolerance for unethical behavior.

Logan got a phone call one day from an attorney asking about Winston regarding check fraud. He gave the man minimal information and decided to call Winston in to talk to him. Logan would give him a chance to explain himself and would try to be fair. Still, he would reinforce the policies by which the other employees abided.

Winston walked into Logan's office.

"Have a seat, Bart."

"Thanks. What's up?"

"I just had a phone call from an attorney representing First Bank and Trust in…"

"Shit. What did that asshole want?"

"That gentleman had some questions about some checks and I told him I would have you get in touch with him. I really didn't feel it was my place to discuss your business with him." Logan handed him a phone message sheet with the information on it to make a return phone call. Winston didn't pick it up.

"That's right, it isn't any of your business. That son-of-a-bitch had no business calling here."

"He said he tried your home and never got an answer."

"My old lady is sick. Has to stay in bed until our kid is born. She can't be bothered with jerks calling on the phone."

"Bart, you're an excellent carpenter. If you made some mistakes and are trying to turn things around, I can work with you, but you have to be up front with me."

"You know, if you don't trust me, you can just shove your gazebo up your ass." He stood to leave.

"In that case, Bart, you're fired. Leave me a good address and I'll have your last paycheck in the mail to you in two days. Pack up your things. I'll pay you through the end of the day."

"Don't strain yourself, Carson."

Bart Winston walked out and slammed the door behind him.

Logan breathed a sigh of relief and entered an order in his computer for a final paycheck for Winston. This reinforced his trust in his intuition.

A week later he received a call in the middle of the night that there was a fire at the factory. The damage was minimal. Most of the wood could be used once it dried out and had the charred parts trimmed off. This was a lot of the wood Logan had in his shop at home. Insurance paid for two saws and a vacuum system. Since it was late, no one was there working. That was a huge relief for Logan. The fire department found no hard evidence as to who started the fire, but they were sure it was arson. A street person described a man running from the building shortly before the fire trucks arrived, but the description was very generic and it was dark out.

Winston popped into Logan's mind. He gave the police his name and address when he got into the office the next morning. No one answered the phone. Logan washed his hands of it and was content to just let the police do their job. New equipment was purchased and it was back to business as usual at Carson Creations.

A week later his tires were slashed on his Jeep. Again the police were called. No one saw anything. By the time the foreman noticed that some finished products had been tampered with, the outdoor play set that went to the Bronson family was already assembled in their yard. Their five-year-old daughter was injured when some hardware failed. Mr. Bronson made three phone calls. First, an ambulance. Second, the police. Third, Carson Creations. Logan joined the police in the Bronson's yard. He knew that this was a deliberate attempt to smear his name, not necessarily injure anyone. It was never proved that

Winston had anything to do with the tampering. Logan was being sued. He totally understood the anger of having a child injured. He agreed on a generous settlement out of court, paying for the medical bills, plus setting aside some money for possible future problems. He replaced the outdoor play set and built a deck for the family. Logan and the Bronsons ended on good terms.

Logan decided to tell Amy the story next time they were discussing business. He still felt he had to prove himself to her, especially after the "I killed my wife" speech. She trusted him. He knew that. He could tell her anything. She was a good listener. He would let her into another part of his life.

CHAPTER 21

Hillary knew it was past time for her weekly phone call or visit with Amy. It was a dreary Sunday and Hillary had no plans on leaving her apartment. She called Amy late in the morning and was surprised when she answered after the first ring.

"I'm glad you called. I was going to call you this afternoon if I didn't hear from you. What's new?"

"I signed up for a Tai Chi class. It's good if you're too klutzy for yoga."

"Is it co-ed?"

"Would I spend time doing this if men were not involved?"

"Why did I bother to ask?"

"How's things with carpenter-boy?"

"Logan is fine." She described her evening with Logan, and Hillary was very excited for her. She also told her of Gibby's warnings.

"Ames, are you busy Monday night?"

"No. I can leave Logan's whenever I want. Why?"

"Meet me at the coffee shop next to the library. We're going to do some research."

*

On Monday night, Amy left Logan's house before he got home. She changed clothes and took the train downtown riding against the flow of commuters. She walked several blocks in the rain to the coffee shop. Hillie was already there. She had ordered a veggie sandwich on foccacia bread for them to split and a bag of 'hot as fire' potato chips to share. Amy shook her umbrella off outside and joined Hillie at the table by the window.

"I'll get the coffee." Amy went to the counter to order their usual, then remembered it wasn't morning and Hillie may want something different than the kick-in-the-head caffeine blast she bought at the crack of dawn. She walked back to the table. "So, what are you drinking?"

"Get me a decaf, extra fat, extra sugar, extra chocolate with extra whipped cream and a sprinkle of cinnamon. I'll call it dessert."

"That's disgusting. Is this PMS-related?"

"Smart-ass. Just order."

Amy came back to the table with a small decaf for herself and the obscene concoction for Hillie. She made a production of setting it in front of Hillie so everyone else in the room knew exactly who ordered it. "You're a pig."

"Oink."

"So, what are we researching?"

Hillie ate the whipped cream off the top of her coffee and was too engrossed to speak for a minute. "Well, I figured there has to be stuff on the internet and on the microfilm at the library."

"Like what?"

Hillie took a bite of her sandwich and chewed thoughtfully. She stopped and pulled an obstinate sprout from between her teeth. She held it up for examination. "Why do I eat this healthy shit?"

"Probably to counteract your choice of beverage."

"We can look up the *Tribune* from around the time Logan's wife died. We can look up stuff on his company. If you're looking for a clue as to his secrets, that would be the place I would start."

Amy was uncomfortable about the whole process. "I kind of would like to see the obituary, but they rarely give cause of death. I feel like I'm sneaking around. Logan has been pretty good about telling me things and we've discussed not having secrets. I just want to give him the time to tell me on his own. Because I'm sure he will—eventually."

"You don't think you'd like to know some things before you get any more involved with him?"

"Hillie, aside from having sex with him, I don't think I could be any more involved."

"You're hooked. Do you love him?"

Amy didn't answer. She took another bite of sandwich and chewed longer than she needed to.

"You do."

"I don't know. I just know I have these feelings…"

"Like with Crane?"

"If this is love, I was not in love with Crane, and that scares me, because we had been making definite plans for the future."

"How does Logan feel?"

"I can't put it into words. He hasn't put it into words. He likes me. We enjoy each other's company. He trusts me with his stuff, his house, his workshop, and little by little he trusts me with parts of his life."

"I suppose if you're comfortable with being patient, I can be patient too. I just don't want you to get stung by this guy."

"First of all, 'this guy' is not going to sting me. I trust Logan. I care about him very much. I enjoy his company. I admire him. Hillie, he makes me laugh. I make him laugh. He confides in me and I'm sure I'll know the whole story someday. He's not an axe murderer or a child molester."

"Okay, since you're so interested in his company, let's just start there and leave the family stuff for another time."

"It's just that if he started telling me things, and I slipped and told him that I already knew what he was talking about, he'd think I was checking up on him. Or that I didn't trust him, and since that isn't the case, I'd just rather wait."

Hillie and Amy finished eating and walked to the library next to the coffee shop. There was something very comforting about the smell. All libraries smelled the same. The must and dust of old books, mixing with the paper and ink of new books created an aroma like no other combination. They headed to the desk where they had to sign in to use the computers. There were several that were in soundproof cubicles, which they preferred so they could talk and not disturb anyone.

"Hillie, we could have done this internet work at home."

"I know, but I actually wanted to get into the old newspapers on microfiche."

"We don't have to go back that far. Probably not much more than eighteen months or so."

"I think we can pin down some dates on the internet, and then we'll know which papers to look through."

They pulled up the Carson Creations website and saw some of the same things Logan had showed Amy that first day in his room. Amy was proud of him as she listened to Hillie comment on the quality of products they made. There were quotes from happy customers and some photographs of decks and gazebos that had been built in people's yards.

"Look at this, Ames. This family by the gazebo. Look at their quote. 'We love the quality and we love to show it off to our neighbors. We're just glad the company came back after the fire, because next we're ordering a porch swing.'"

"Logan never mentioned a fire."

"Look at the date. About two years ago. I say we check the newspaper. If there was a fire, there would probably be an article, even if it was a small one."

"Okay, fire only. Nothing personal."

They signed off the computer and went to one of the microfiche machines. Hillary used one frequently in her job, so Amy let her operate it.

"Look for any headline about fire, arson, Carson Creations."

They scanned over two weeks of papers and only found advertisements for Carson Creations, but no other mention of the company in a news-related column.

"Stop!" Amy's voice caused several heads to pop up and look at her. She expected the familiar 'shhh' from the librarian, but it never came. She whispered, "Go back slowly."

Hillie turned the reel back several pages. "What did you see?"

"There, see?" Amy pointed to the screen. "Former employee suspected in arson."

Hillie and Amy read the article together. Amy took a pen out of her purse and tore a deposit slip out of her checkbook. She started taking notes. The date of the fire. Extent of the damage. Possible witness. Bartholomew Winston.

"At least no one was hurt. It didn't seem to stop production for long. I'll try to find a way to get into that conversation with Logan. It shouldn't be too hard. He loves talking about his company."

"It sounds like this was revenge for firing him. I wonder if the police ever caught him."

"Logan told me how strict he is with employees. Not that he's a taskmaster, but he insists on honesty. He even mentioned having to let someone go because of some kind of fraud. I wonder if it was Bartholomew Winston?"

"Should we continue?"

"Well, maybe for a few more days. There might be an article about him getting caught."

They scanned the next two weeks. Hillie stopped and read out loud.

"Carson target of vandal. Blah blah, president of blah blah, reported slashed tires, now accused of endangering the life of a child injured on a piece of equipment purchased, blah blah. Was tampered with prior to shipping. Family bringing suit. Represented by Bolin Carson, brother."

"His brother lives in California. That's who he made the rocker for."

"Amy, if he was being sued, there's probably more in here about the court case."

Amy made a few more notes. "Let's keep on looking."

Pages for a few more days zoomed past on the screen. Hillie stopped.

"Here's more."

Amy read out loud. "Carson settles. Logan Carson, represented by his brother Bolin Carson settled blah blah with the Bronson family out of court. Five-year-old daughter injured blah blah, several incidents of vandalism. Carson paid all medical charges, set up fund for future care, replaced outdoor play set, and built a deck for the family."

"Well, you're right about one thing, he's a real stand-up guy."

"He did the right thing. Several incidents of vandalism. I wonder if they're still suspecting Winston."

"Do you want to keep looking?"

"No. Let's just go, Hillie. I need to think of a way to bring this up in conversation without lying to Logan."

They left the library and Hillie walked back to the train station with Amy. While they waited for her train to arrive Amy filled her in on the Terry-and-Beth situation. Hillie promised to call during the week.

Amy got back to her condo and there was a note taped to her door. It was from Beth. "Don't wake me up. FYI trip to St Louis is on. T. is thrilled. So am I. Love, B." Amy took her note in, turned it over and wrote, "Good for you. Be careful. ASS." She went to her nightstand, found a three-pack of condoms and taped them to the note. She went across the hall and taped them to Beth's door.

CHAPTER 22

A my got up early the next day hoping to see Logan before he left for work. She took two catalogs and her decorating magazines with her. The plan was to show Logan some bedding and hope that he would follow her lead in decorating. She knew he had the money to put some furniture in the rooms and doubted that he planned on making all of it himself. She was sure that he wouldn't be fooling around with fabric. That was something she could do for him, and would enjoy helping him with it. The rooms were looking very nice with the fresh paint, but she wanted it to start looking like a home. Her jobs today were to convince Logan that he wanted the same thing, and to find a way to get into a conversation about the fire.

When she got to the house, Logan had left the coffee pot on for her. He was already gone, but had left a note.

ASS,
Can you stick around?
I won't be late.
Want to show you the desk in its primitive form.
Don't peek without me.
L

This was a good sign. If Logan was excited about the desk maybe it would be finished soon, and she could get the den put together. She was still working on something for the windows and would take him up on his offer to help her on the computer. Today she was doing prep work on the hallway. It was dirty and tiring and she knew her right arm would be sore at the end of the day. First, she was going to sit at the kitchen table with a cup of coffee and mark some pages in her magazines and catalogs.

Logan was still not calling the guest bedroom "feminine." She agreed that "cheerful" would be acceptable and intended to keep the light airy feeling of the room. The light yellow paint they selected would be perfect with the French

Country style she liked so much. The magazine had a huge master bedroom decorated in the light blues and yellows, stripes and florals, and she fell in love with it. She was hoping to do it on a smaller scale—much smaller scale—in the guest room. If Logan saw the pages in the order she planned to reveal them, and then showed him the catalogs from which very similar items could be ordered, her plan might just fall into place. *Why am I worried about his reaction on this? He trusts me. He said so several times,* she thought. Still, she stacked everything in order, anticipating her pitch.

Amy started sanding at the stairway and was working her way to the end of the hall. She finished one side then realized she was standing in front of the door to the room that she would not be painting. Logan made it very clear that this room was none of her concern. He wasn't home. He'd never know. She put her hand on the knob and waited for the feeling to subside—the feeling that she was betraying Logan's trust. It didn't go away. She turned the knob anyway. It was locked. She had a feeling it might be. Oh well. Probably just storage. Maybe some things that belonged to his wife that he just couldn't bear to have around. She understood that. Someday he'd feel better about giving her things away, or maybe even using them again. The one-year anniversary of her death had just passed, and Amy was willing to give him the time he needed.

That morning, Amy finished sanding and wiping down the walls in the hallway and was now putting blue tape on the trim and anything else she didn't want to get paint on. When lunchtime came, Amy ate her yogurt and one of Logan's bananas. She was in the kitchen cleaning up when Logan came in the back door.

"Lucy, I'm home!" He used his best Desi accent.

She knew why she liked him. His life was tough, but he could always make her laugh. "So, did you discover a new reason for killing trees?"

"Hey, hey, hey. Don't make fun. My talent with trees is what pays your salary. You should be hearing 'TIMBERRRRR' whenever you open your checkbook."

"Well, you're probably right on that one."

"So how was your day?" They said it in unison, then laughed.

Logan pointed. "You go first."

"I had a good day. I got the hallway prepped and ready for primer tomorrow, maybe even a little color, depending on how fast the primer dries, how fast I move, when I get here…the usual. How about you?"

"We had a little celebration today. Our three-hundredth gazebo left the shop. I ordered pizza and we had a little lunch. I gave out a few bonus checks. It was a good day."

"Does everyone think you're an awesome boss?"

"We have a really good crew, but it's an assortment of all types, like you find in any workplace. You have the few people who genuinely adore me. Then there are those that kiss my ass to get ahead—they may or may not like me. There are those who are friendly, some who are afraid of me, some who are there for the paycheck—you know, show up on time, do the work and go home. I don't have a problem with that. There are a few who are just using this for a stepping stone. And there are one or two who don't like the job, but are good at it. I think they just don't have the courage to leave and possibly be without a paycheck. I would probably be doing them a favor if I fired them, but I keep them around because they're good at what they do."

"No slackers?"

"Oh, they can slack off for a while. Until I find out. Then they can change their ways or be gone. They're all well paid and most of them earn every cent. That's why when something like this happens, we celebrate. I'd say morale is pretty good."

"It sounds like you have good workers who know when they have a good thing going."

"I've had a few I've had to fire. It isn't easy, even when they deserve it. I had to fire a guy once whose wife was pregnant and bedridden. I hated to do it. He lied on his application and had a serious attitude problem. He practically dared me to fire him, so I did. I felt bad, but not for long. He had some issues and tried taking his troubles out on me."

"Really? How?" *Could this be Winston he's talking about?* she thought.

"He slashed my tires. He set a little fire in the shop and burned a little lumber."

"Logan! Arson! I didn't think you could set just a 'little' fire with lumber. Was anyone hurt?"

"No, it was during the night. Sprinklers came on and the fire department was there pretty fast. They called me and I got down there right away. I was very glad we didn't have a night shift. There wasn't too much damage. Once the wood dried out it was okay. I have a lot of it in the workshop. I cut the charred parts off. It's perfectly good. Some of the equipment was damaged, but insurance helped on that."

"Did he ever come to your home? Was he caught?"

"No and yes. He was caught because he tampered with some of the finished products and they were shipped after they were damaged. That was the worst part. A little girl got hurt on something I made. I still feel terrible about it. She's fine now and we made restitution, but it's something I'll never forget."

"It wasn't your fault."

"Amy, my name is on everything for a reason. The buck has to stop somewhere and it stops right on my desk. The man did what he did because I fired him. I know he was wrong, but I never should have hired him in the first place. Bart was an excellent carpenter so I kept him on when I should have let him go."

"Bart?"

"Bart Winston. In jail. Moved away when he got out. Don't know where he is now. He was in jail when their baby was born. Damn shame."

"Well, that sure cheered me up!"

"You asked, Sugar Plum."

"You're going to show me the desk in its primitive form?"

He nodded. "Then I have something to show you when we get back in."

He saw the catalogs on the table and groaned. "Is this some kind of foo-foo stuff, girly frilly stuff?"

"No. It's just an idea and I'd like your thoughts on it."

"Put your jacket on and let's head out."

Logan took the key for the workshop and a flashlight and headed out across the yard. Amy followed his footsteps. *Nice view*, she thought.

Two of the three parts were almost finished. She was amazed. The roll-top portion would take the longest.

"You've been working hard!"

"I was out here all day Saturday and Sunday, and then last night after work I was out here for about three hours. Once I get going I find it hard to stop. Would you like to help me with the sanding?"

She was stunned. "Oh, Logan, I don't know. You're such a perfectionist and I'd probably..."

"I'd pay you."

"Now that's an insult. If you want my company, all you have to do is ask. You will not pay me. If you insist, I won't do it. If I help it will be because I want to. It sounds like fun."

"Sanding isn't fun."

"That might depend on the company. If I was here with you, it wouldn't matter what we were doing, it would be fun for me."

"Then let me ask again. Amy, I'd really enjoy it if you would like to stay some evening and help me with the sanding."

"My pleasure. Pick the night."

"Tomorrow after supper. I'll bring carry-out."

"Deal."

"And don't bring dessert. My heart couldn't take it! Now let's go in and see what kind of a lacy nightmare you have waiting for me in those catalogs."

Amy glared at him and walked back to the house.

They sat at the kitchen table and Amy spread out her ideas. She showed him the French Country master bedroom. "I think this would be nice on a smaller scale in the guest room. I know it's totally up to you, but I'm just going to blurt out my opinion and you can do what you want with it." She found the pages in the catalogs with the bedspreads, quilts, pillow shams and curtains that were the yellow and blue pastels. "Doesn't this look like a nice little bed and breakfast? That's what this reminds me of. I don't think it's too terribly feminine, do you? I just love it and it's so popular these days that it's very easy to find pillows and things to match."

"Hmm."

She couldn't read his expression. "Logan, any thoughts?"

"It's okay. Do I have to decide now?"

"No. The yellow walls will make it easy to coordinate a lot of things."

"How about I hold on to this catalog and think about it. I mean, since we're not in any hurry?"

"That's fine. I'm on their mailing list and I seem to get a catalog a week. The quality is good and the prices are reasonable. You might even think about a border. No pressure."

"Amy, relax. I'm not feeling pressured. You just don't bring out that reaction in me. I know this place is a mess. Except, of course for the great paint job.

Nothing has been done here in a long time. It was empty quite a while before we moved in. We replaced all the carpeting and did the kitchen, and that's as far as it got. I appreciate any ideas you have because I'm really out of touch."

"I know I'm being paid as a painter, and this decorating thing is just for fun on my part. It isn't often you get a bare space to work with. It's just in my nature to do something with it."

"I'm glad. I'll have fun working on some furniture."

"And in that department, I totally trust you. Now, I have stuff to do this evening, so I'm going to leave you to dinner and sanding."

"Wear your sanding clothes tomorrow. And bring your chopsticks."

"Are there special clothes for sanding?"

"I think Victoria has something you can borrow."

"Funny. See you then."

Amy stood up. Before she could gather up her magazines Logan stood in front of her. He tucked a wisp of hair behind her ear. With both hands on her shoulders, he leaned forward and kissed her forehead. She held her breath and dared to place her hands on his waist.

"Logan…"

"Shhh. Amy," he whispered, "I need to do this to get me through the night."

He tipped her chin up and brushed his lips across hers. She closed her eyes and concentrated on the feeling. Urgency tempered with promise. Passion softened with sweetness. He didn't plunge and plunder her mouth, but teased gently with his tongue, encouraging her to do the same.

"Tomorrow, Sweet."

"See you then, Carson."

Amy turned and waved.

Logan winked and smiled. *Oh my God, woman, you terrify me,* he thought.

Amy got in the van, pulled away and stopped at the end of the driveway. She took several deep breaths and opened the windows. She was chilled, but it didn't matter. *Twenty-four hours. Just twenty-four hours and I can do that again,* she thought.

CHAPTER 23

A my heard the ringing. It seemed too early for the alarm. She knew she didn't get even close to eight hours' sleep. Logan was in her brain and she couldn't get him out. Finally exhaustion pushed him far enough back that she fell asleep. Suddenly, Amy realized it wasn't the alarm, it was the phone. Phone calls in the middle of the night were never good. She hurried to the kitchen and picked up just before the answering machine. She noticed the time. It was 5 a.m. She answered with dread in her voice.

"Amy, it's Logan."

"Good morning. Is this my wake-up call?"

"If I woke you up, I suppose it is. I'm sorry. I just wanted to let you know before you left the house today that you can take the day off."

"You sound awful. Are you okay?"

"Not really. I had a bad night and I feel awful. I'll need the day to recover. I'm not going into work."

"Maybe you need to get to the doctor. Do you have a fever?"

"No, I don't need a doctor and I'm sure I don't have a fever. I just need some time alone. I have some stuff to run through my brain and I need a break."

"A break from me?"

Logan was quiet on the other end. He was searching for words that wouldn't hurt her but he resigned himself to the fact that those words didn't exist.

"Logan, just tell me. What can I do?"

"Amy, I don't want to hurt you, but I need some time. There's nothing you can do to speed this up. I'll be okay tomorrow. Can we reschedule for then?"

"If you think you want to, yes."

"Oh, God, Amy. Yes, I want to. I feel horrible about this. I'm no good for you this way. It will pass. I just have to indulge myself in a little pity party for a while. I didn't want you to make the trip here while I stay locked in my room."

"You know I'd love to come and sit with you. You know I'm a good listener."

"I know and I appreciate it. I'll be fine. Go back to bed. I'll see you tomorrow."

"Bye."

Logan hung up before she did. He sounded dreadful. Her instinct told her to drive to his house right that minute, run up to his room and hold him while he crashed. That may not have been what he needed, but that was what she wanted to do. She forced herself to go back to bed. She reset her alarm for 9 a.m. and tried to fall asleep.

*

Logan sat on the edge of his bed with his head in his hands. He felt terrible about putting Amy off. Part of him wanted to beg her to drop everything and drive over to soothe him. Another part, the part that won out, knew he had to work through this alone, as always.

These episodes had been happening less and less frequently. The last time he had felt this way was well over a month before–actually, before he put the ad in the newspaper for help remodeling. He never knew until it hit him what the trigger would be. The last time it had been a late hospital bill for Sam that had arrived in the mail.

The night before, he'd had a dream. It was a wonderful dream. He was making love to Amy. Then Sam walked into the bedroom wearing a hospital gown. She screamed, fell to her knees, and turned into a pool of blood. It was so real. Logan smelled the sickness and disinfectant of the hospital. He woke up in a cold sweat, ran into the bathroom, and vomited. He washed his face with cold water and looked into the mirror, not recognizing the face that looked back at him.

He had no idea how long he'd been sitting on the edge of his bed. When his alarm clock rang, he knew he had to call Amy and ask her not to come over to paint that day. He would wallow in his misery, talk to himself, and relive that awful day in the hospital. Logan took two aspirins and went back to bed.

*

Amy drifted in and out of sleep until her alarm rang. She was worried about Logan. Her feelings weren't hurt. He was so kind to be concerned about that. She wanted to go to him, but knew he needed private time. She felt sure he'd talk about it when he could. She promised herself she would not rush him.

So, she had a whole day free—a gift in itself. After making coffee and showering, she'd call Hillie at work to let her know their research project at the library paid off. Logan had offered all the information without any prodding on her part.

*

Logan woke up about noon and knew he'd feel better if he showered. He stood as the hot water pounded on his head and back and chest, soothing his nerves. He knew what he wanted to do with the rest of his day. He would plan on telling Amy a little more of his story. She hadn't been scared off yet, but the worst was yet to come. He knew there would be no future with Amy if he kept secrets. They already discussed that and both of them agreed. Tomorrow while they were working on the desk after dinner, he'd tell her more. At least that was what he intended. The general feeling of the evening would determine just how much he would say.

CHAPTER 24

Gibby was on her way home from work when she heard music coming from Amy's condo. She knew her schedule with Logan's project was fairly flexible and wasn't surprised her friend was home. So, she stopped in to say hello.

Gibby knocked, then walked in. Amy was sitting on the couch with her sewing basket, surrounded by various articles of clothing. "Good day for mending?"

"Hey Gibbs. I'm missing so many buttons that with a little sewing today, I will have a whole new wardrobe. Some of these things I haven't worn in a long time just because I'm too dang lazy to sew on a button. How was your shift?"

"No new babies, but three moms in labor when I left. Why are you home?"

"Logan called me when he woke up this morning to ask me not to come over. Seems he had a bad night and needs to crash for the day. I know it has something to do with his wife, but I didn't pry. I'm still debating whether or not I should just go over there to make sure he's okay."

"Feel like doing a little comforting? Thinking maybe a hug would make it all better?"

"Something like that, yes. But I think he wants to talk. He sounded too awful this morning or I would have asked for details. We're having Chinese food tomorrow after work and I'm helping him work on his desk. Probably sanding. We were supposed to do it tonight, but he cancelled. We had such a great time the other night, I wonder if that was what brought this whole thing on."

"Think he might be feeling guilty? I'm sure that happens a lot when someone loses a spouse. Does he feel like he's cheating on his wife with you?"

"I don't know, Gibbs. Maybe. He hasn't really said much about her, except that she died at the hospital."

"At least he's talking to you and that's good. Some people shut down."

"Yes, he's been very honest about that. He knows he needs to talk. I'd like to find out a little more about his family. I just know his dad is a retired plumber and his brother is an attorney in California. Maybe I should ask to see pictures."

"Aren't there any in the house? Nothing on the mantle, nothing in his room?"

"No, the house is pretty empty, and while I was in his room, I was looking at the computer."

"Amy, are you telling me you didn't even go snooping?"

"No. There's been no need to. I'm not kidding when I say the house is empty. He has a couch and coffee table in the living room and some furniture in his bedroom. Other than that, not a clue of any other human being ever living in the house. His workshop tells me more about him than the house does. And, of course, the kitchen. I did ask if his wife was into cooking. He said they both were: that's why the kitchen got remodeled first."

"It sounds like they moved in, then she died."

"That's pretty much it. The one room I wanted to see was locked. It's probably just storage or another closet. Or maybe he has all his wife's stuff locked up until he feels he can cope with it."

"I bet you'll find out. Well, Ames, I'm going to leave you with your buttons. I need to sleep very badly. Let me know what happens with Logan. Remember, you need to invite him here for dinner some night. You know, so we can interrogate him, and humiliate you in front of him."

"If I do invite him, it will probably be a secret. For my sanity. Sweet dreams."

Gibby left. Amy put her head back on the couch and closed her eyes. Her thoughts were reeling. *What if I just drove over there?* she thought. *What's the worst that could happen? He'd throw me out? No, he wouldn't. He'd be very polite and ask me to leave. Would I need an excuse? Did I leave something there that I need? No. There is no work-related reason to go to his house. I care about him. He knows that. He feels awful. If he were physically ill, would I go to check on him? Yes. He needs soup. Could I make soup that would be good enough to make him feel better? No. The deli could. I could just drop off some soup, check on him, and leave. Unless he wanted me to stay. Hmmm. Maybe he'll want me to stay. Gotta take the chance.*

Amy left her mending and her sewing box on the couch and went to her room to change clothes. Something "comforting." Her old soft corduroy pants and a cotton knit sweater would do. Soft was crucial. Huggable.

A quart of chicken dumpling soup from her friendly neighborhood deli was the key that was going to open the door to Logan's house. The soup was very hot and pretty well sealed, but she still secured it under the back seat of the van. She pulled up in his driveway and took a deep breath. She rehearsed her speech. *Just wanted to drop off a little dinner for you. I can't stay, but you sounded so awful this morning, I had to check on you and make sure you're OK. No,* she thought. *Don't rehearse. Whatever happens, happens.*

CHAPTER 25

S he picked up the soup and walked to the back door. It was locked. She used her key. She set the soup on the kitchen counter and headed for the stairs. "Logan?" She called out not too loudly in case he was sleeping. She walked up the stairs trying not to feel like she was being sneaky. "Logan?" No answer. The door to his room was open and he wasn't in it. Maybe he was in the workshop. She turned to go back downstairs when she heard voices. Not Logan's voice. She listened for a moment. It *was* Logan's voice. It was coming from the end of the hall. Suddenly she felt as if she had stepped into a very private, personal moment and was blatantly intruding into his life where she didn't belong. She was just going back to the kitchen and would leave a note with the soup. This felt wrong. Very wrong.

She couldn't help herself. She stood in the hall a moment longer and listened. Just one voice, Logan's. Who was he talking to? He was in…*the room!* The room that was always locked. The room that was "none of her concern." The door was cracked open and she knew Logan was there. *I have to know,* she thought. She headed down the hall.

Logan was sobbing. No, he was screaming in a whisper. He was angry. He was crying, apologizing. She heard the name Sam. *Who's Sam?* she thought. Amy stood just outside the door, afraid to go in, yet wanting to hold him and tell him it would be all right. She gathered up all her courage, stepped into the doorway and knocked gently.

Logan looked up at her. He was sitting in a rocking chair. His face was wet with tears, his eyes red and puffy. He looked rumpled and miserable. He didn't speak. Part of her wanted to run. Part of her wanted to run to him. *Just go to him,* she thought.

"Logan, are you…"

He held his arms open. She rushed into them and fell on her knees in front of him. She held him as tightly as he held her. He sobbed as he buried his face in her hair. It broke her heart to feel him in so much pain. He held onto her as if he would die if she moved. She didn't feel the need to speak and she wouldn't dare let go of him. She knew at that moment she was a lifeline for him. In her whole life she had never heard such a gut-wrenching sound. It came from the depths of him and he couldn't have stopped it if he tried.

"Oh, God! Oh, God!" He groaned into her hair. She held his head to her own and whispered in his ear.

"Logan. I'm so sorry. What can I do?"

"Oh, God, Sam. I'm so sorry." He held her to him with all his strength.

"Logan, who is Sam?"

"It's all my fault. She died. It's my fault."

Amy put a hand on each side of his face and looked into his eyes. "Who is Sam?"

"Samantha. My Sam."

"Your wife?"

He nodded. "I'm sorry, Amy."

"Don't be sorry, Logan. Do you want me to leave?"

He closed his eyes, pushing out more tears and shook his head. She softly kissed each eyelid, pulled his head back down to her shoulder and just held him while he cried. As she held him she looked around the room—the room that was none of her concern. She gasped.

"Logan, this is a nursery!"

He wept harder and groaned into her shoulder. "Oh, God! I killed her!"

Amy resisted the urge to say "no you didn't," because she knew right then he wouldn't believe her. She also knew that when he felt relief from this purging, he would be rational again. They'd already had that conversation at the arboretum.

She pulled him down onto the carpeting. They sat facing each other, legs folded, knees touching. Amy reached onto the dresser and handed him several tissues. He blew his nose and wiped his eyes. They held hands and were quiet for a minute.

"What made you come?"

"Logan, your voice made my heart hurt this morning. I just felt like I needed to be here, and I knew you wouldn't ask me to come."

"I wanted to. But I knew this would be so messy. I can usually handle it. I'm sorry you had to see it."

"How often does this happen?"

"Less and less. More right after Sam died. I went to bed last night after you left. I had a dream. A dream about you." He kissed the back of each hand. "Amy…oh, God." He held her hand to his face. "You were in my bed. It was wonderful. You felt so good next to me. You said you…well, you were…um. Then Sam came in. She was in her hospital gown. She saw us and screamed. There was blood everywhere. It actually made me sick."

"I'm sorry if I prompted that, Logan."

"No, it wasn't you. It was me, I guess, feeling guilty about caring so much about you. Part of me still feels Sam's presence. I know she's gone, but I've been alone for a long time, and you just seemed to slide into a place in my heart that was open. Waiting. It's coming too easy for me."

"Logan, nothing you have gone through has been easy." She looked around the room. "I see you had some plans." She remembered the conversation with Gibby. Touching leads to intimacy. Leads to babies. Hemorrhaging after a miscarriage. Things were falling into place.

He held her hands to his eyes and nodded.

"I can't talk about it yet. It's too hard."

"This is a beautiful room. Obviously built with love. I see evidence of your handiwork."

Logan smiled weakly and nodded.

The cradle was beautiful. The rocker he had been sitting in was very much like the one he sent to Bo and his wife.

"You, Amy are an angel. Thanks for rescuing me."

"My pleasure. Anytime. Just ask. Please, just ask."

Logan laid back on the carpet and pulled Amy down beside him. "Do you have a few minutes to stay here with me? Can we just lay close, holding each other and being quiet?"

She snuggled up against him. He had his answer.

When they woke up it was dark outside. Logan sat up and flipped on a teddy bear lamp. He looked at his watch. Supper time. He was hungry.

He leaned over Amy and kissed her forehead. "Stay for supper?"

"I brought supper. The cure-all—chicken soup. I doubt that it's still warm."

"You brought me chicken soup? You're quite the little nursemaid." He watched her stretch like a cat after a nap. She rolled over onto her back, laid one arm across her eyes, and the other across her stomach. "What are you grinning about?" he asked.

"I can go home and tell my friends I slept with Logan."

"I know women. They'll want details. What are you going to tell them?"

"I'll tell them that you're kind and gentle. You're sweet and sensitive. You're sexy as hell. You have a great ass in and out of jeans. Remember, I saw you in a towel. And, that size doesn't matter."

Logan bent over, picked her up by her arms and tossed her over his shoulder like a fireman. He carried her down the stairs while she laughed and screamed all the way to the kitchen. "If size doesn't matter, why are you so concerned with your butt?"

"Leave my butt out of this conversation, Logan."

"No, really. Why do women always think their butts are too big and their breasts are too small?"

"Probably because most women would rather have smaller butts and bigger breasts. Does that make sense? It makes perfect sense to me. Why do men suck in their bellies when women walk past? We know what you're doing, because suddenly you've stopped breathing. And then there's the comb-over…"

"Now that I would never…"

"Never say never. Some day you may wake up and have more hair on your pillow than on your head, and you'll be moving that part over."

"I promise I won't. And I'll never suck my gut in again."

"You don't have a gut to suck in, Logan. That's where fairness enters into this whole conversation. I can suck my belly in and nothing moves. It feels like my belly button is touching my spine, I look down and there it is— right where I left it. The butt is beyond hope, so forget it. Boobs…well, they're fine, I guess. But gravity will take its toll, and I'm not looking forward to rolling them up and stuffing them in my bra. And that day is coming, Logan, mark my words."

During her ranting, Logan had heated the soup in the microwave and filled two bowls. He got the oyster crackers out of the pantry, sliced some cheese, cut up a Granny Smith apple, and set the table. He sat down and pulled her onto his lap.

"Now you listen to me, Amy Sweet. I may be a perfectionist, but that is only in regards to me. Physical perfection in a woman is a relative thing. You're very close to perfection in my eyes."

She had an arm around his neck and let him talk. She figured he'd stick his foot in his mouth any time now. He stroked her hair. "You're beautiful. I love your hair. You have sexy eyes." Amy batted her lashes. "Your mouth makes me sweat. You have great legs and beautiful hands." He kissed the back of the hand he held. "And these," he said, nuzzling her breasts and nipping at one through her sweater, "are just fine by me." She leaned forward and gave him a sweet little kiss. "If it wasn't for your big old butt…"

"Logan, you're as mean as a snake! If I wasn't so hungry I'd walk out of here right now!" She sat in her chair and tossed a handful of crackers in her soup. She knew his lighthearted teasing was healthy and his dark mood had lifted. She let him have his laugh at her expense. "Watch yourself, Logan. Paybacks are sweet."

They finished their dinner in silence. It wasn't an uncomfortable silence. They were both thinking about the day. Logan was surprised at the way it had ended. He figured he would have gone to bed and not awakened until morning. She came into his misery and rode out the storm with him. She was a rock when he'd needed one badly. He prayed that she wouldn't abandon him when he screwed up his courage and told her the rest of the story. He wanted to tell her. He needed to tell her and she needed to know. It was unfair to make her put her life on hold just because he couldn't bear to see the hurt in her face when he told her. Maybe if he set a deadline for himself, he'd get the script ready in his head. He wanted to give her an out, but he prayed she wouldn't take it.

Amy was thinking about the difference in Logan from when she first arrived and then. He was like two different people. She assumed the dark cloud would have dissipated eventually, but it had probably cleared a little sooner because she arrived. Was he ready to talk about the day? He'd probably rather put the whole thing to rest, but knowing the female mind, she knew she wanted to tear it apart, examine it and put it back together. Was this a good time to ask? He seemed so peaceful and at ease. Why spoil his dinner? She'd give him a little time. Thirty minutes or so. She looked at him and smiled. He winked and finished his soup in silence.

When he leaned back in his chair and wiped his mouth off with a napkin Amy stood up and cleared the table.

"Thank you."

"I didn't make it. I just picked it up from the deli."

He held her arm as she walked past. "No, I mean thank you…you know, for rescuing me."

"Logan, I tried to stay home, but just felt such a strong sense of you pulling me here." She stood next to him while he sat. He wrapped his arms around her waist. She held him and kissed the top of his head. "I was so afraid when I saw that your room was empty, and I heard the gut-wrenching sounds of someone in pain coming from the end of the hall. Then I saw that the door to the room… the nursery…was open. God, Logan, you broke my heart. I was prepared for you to scream at me to get out. So it was such a relief when you opened your arms and welcomed me."

"I was so relieved to see you. I almost called a couple of times but figured this was just something I had to work through alone."

"Logan, you don't have to work through anything like that alone again. I'm a very strong person. You can't scare me off. I know you have issues, and now I've seen you working through them. I know you have more to tell me and I want to know. I need to know. I also know that I can't push you. I've told you I won't push, but you also have to understand that I care about you and want to be a part of your life." She patted his cheek and kissed his head again. *Whew! That was a risk,* she thought. "You can trust me. I won't betray you. Anytime, Logan." She rested her cheek on his hair and he tightened his grip around her.

"I thank God for you, Amy Sweet. It's a miracle that you walked into my life. We need to talk, and we need to do it some day when we aren't both exhausted from work." He pulled her down onto his lap and held her face near his own. "Next Saturday. How does that sound?"

"Come to my place for dinner."

"You're going to cook? Or make a run to the deli?"

"I'll cook, but thankfully the deli is close enough for a Plan B."

"Do we need an agenda?"

"No, Logan, I think we can go with the flow. Dress up—that means a suit and tie. Supper will be basic but good. You can bring wine. We'll eat, chill out, talk a little, at which time you will tell me your deep, dark secrets and I will tell you mine."

"You have deep, dark secrets?"

"Well, they're not all that deep, not very dark, and probably not even secrets anymore, but it's only fair that I share, too."

"Why dress up?"

"Because I think it's incredibly sexy to undress a man in a suit and because I have a cute little black dress that I'm dying to wear. It's slit up to here," she ran her hand up her thigh. "And it's cut down to here," she slid her finger down between her breasts.

"And how am I supposed to concentrate?"

"You'll be concentrating on me. I have a 'to do' list, and that may just be the night I 'to do' you."

"Far be it from me to be the wet blanket on this heat, but you may want to hear what I have to say before you change sheets."

Amy slipped an arm around his neck and kissed him. She caught him off-guard, but it didn't take him long to catch on. He deepened the kiss and probed gently with his tongue. She relaxed and let him have his way with her mouth. She concentrated on his ample bottom lip, imagined it moving lower. Logan slipped his hand under the edge of her sweater and moved it up her back. Her skin was warm and satiny. His hand slid around to her breast and he savored the feel of her filling his hand.

"Logan." It was more breath than speech.

Logan assumed it was a protest but when he tried to remove his hand, she held it in place, pressing, encouraging him to explore. He ran his fingertips over the lace and imagined her creamy white skin showing through. Her nipple brushed across his palm, and he felt branded by the heat it caused. Amy was tempted to grab the hem of her sweater and pull it off over her head. Then Logan reached under the band of her bra and lifted it, freeing her breasts. He pressed and stroked. He lowered his head and lightly pinched a nipple with his lips through her sweater. She gasped and held his head to her chest. Amy was aware of his passion stirring beneath her legs and was afraid to move, concerned about hurting him or encouraging him beyond what she had planned.

"Amy, what are we doing?"

"Logan. You know I want you." She kissed him and ran her tongue across his bottom lip.

"Tonight? Are we doing this tonight? Oh God, please don't move. You're killing me, Amy."

She smiled and squirmed.

"Tonight?" Amy asked the question into his mouth.

"I can't believe I'm saying this. But I really need to tell you some things first. You may not…"

"I'll still want you. You decide."

"If I were a real man, I'd throw you to the floor, bury myself so deep in you, treasure every stroke, and wait for you to cry my name out to the heavens. But I need to be sensitive…"

"Fuck sensitivity."

"Oooh, talking dirty to me, huh? You may push me beyond my limits. Amy, you'll understand on Saturday, really."

She was breathing hard, knowing it was the end, not wanting it to be. "So, you're sending me home like this?"

Logan smiled. He touched her lips with his finger and held it up to her. "I can offer you this."

She held his wrist and took his finger into her mouth, stroking it with her tongue.

"Sorry, not big enough."

Logan smiled and gave her a hug. "I hope you won't be disappointed."

"Not a chance." She shifted on his lap, preparing to stand. Logan winced.

"Yikes! Careful." Amy made it a point to look at the bulge of which Logan was being protective.

She licked her lips seductively. "I can offer you this." She ran her hand up his thigh.

He stood up and took her in his arms. "My sweet Amy Sweet. Be patient with me. I'm a mess and you've just seen the beginning of it."

"You're in luck. Messes are my specialty. Now I have to come here tomorrow, pretend this didn't happen and not think ahead to Saturday."

"Since I took today off, I'll be going in early and staying late, so I doubt that

I'll see you tomorrow. How about I call tomorrow evening just to see how your day went?"

"How about you leave me a note for the next day? I enjoy our correspondence."

"Okay, a note it will be. And Amy...really, I am so grateful you followed your instinct and came over. We can talk about the nursery, Sam, whatever questions you may have. I may not be able to tell you all the details, but I won't dodge anything."

Amy leaned forward, put her hands under her sweater, pulled her bra down and shook her breasts back into place. Logan smiled.

"Can I help?"

"You've done enough, thanks."

She walked to the front door and he followed. "Logan, Saturday? Be prepared." She ran her hand down the front of his jeans. He inhaled sharply.

"I'll be ready."

"I didn't say be ready. I said be *prepared*. Do I have to go condom shopping?"

"Oh, yeah, well, you don't...uh...uh, I mean, I don't think..."

"You're babbling. Snap out of it. We've known each other for a relatively short period of time. It's just the thing to do for now. So humor me. No ribbing, colors or scents. And you'll need more than one."

"At a time?"

"You're adorable."

"Back at ya. Thanks again."

She drove home from Logan's, showered and fell asleep, exhausted from the events of the day.

*

Logan turned on the television, sat on the couch and stared at an old Elvis movie without really seeing it. *I have nothing you need protection from, my dear Amy. And I'm sorry about that,* he thought.

CHAPTER 26

When Amy walked in the next morning and looked for his note, she wasn't disappointed.

Amy,
Since I'm working late tonight, Chinese food and sanding are postponed until tomorrow.
Hope that's okay.
Have a great day.
L

She had totally forgotten about their sanding session. She was spending the day touching up and working on some details, painting switch plates and outlet covers. She wanted to get home early to sift through some cookbooks and do some shopping. She wasn't nervous about Logan coming over. Not yet, anyway. If she got an early start and did her kitchen prep work, she'd be fine. Funny, she was more nervous about her cooking than about the possibility of having sex.

At the end of the day, she left Logan a note.

Logan,
Don't forget the crab Rangoon and hot mustard.
Wash the blue silk boxers. You'll need them Saturday.
ASS

*

Thursday morning Logan was still home when Amy arrived. He was in the middle of writing his note when she walked into the kitchen.

"Don't look, and don't read it until I'm gone."

"Good morning to you, too!" She walked up behind him, patted his back and kissed his cheek. She put her strawberry low-fat yogurt in the refrigerator and dropped a small plastic container of granola on the counter.

"Sorry. Good morning, beautiful. I'm running late. Supper about six? Sanding shortly after, okay?"

"Perfect. Have a good day."

He was gone, Jeep screaming down the driveway.

She read his note.

ASS,
I wasn't going to wear underwear.
What kind of wine do you want?
This is kind of like a date, huh?
Cool.
L

Her plan for the day was to prepare another bedroom for primer. It would take about half a day. If she worked fast she could make it home for a late lunch, clean up, and come back to join Logan for dinner. She also needed another stop at the paint store. She was assuming Logan was okay with the French country idea. She was buying blue and yellow paint.

She responded on the back of his note.

LOGAN!
You are wearing a suit!
Underwear is a must.
Yes, this is a date.
A serious date.
The ultimate date.
Hopefully!
See ya at 6:oo.
ASS

*

Amy got home after an exhausting wait at the paint store. She was dealing with a trainee on the color-mixing machine. Three gallons of turquoise paint would not fly with Logan. Gibby was at the mailboxes, as Amy walked up.

"Taking some time off, I see."

"Yeah, I'm going back to Logan's for supper and sanding. I had some errands to run and some paint to buy. You're home early...or late. I'm never sure with your schedule."

"I covered half a shift for a nurse with three kids. She had school stuff she needed to take care of and it had to be this morning. She's really good about repaying favors, so I don't mind helping out. I can't imagine working and worrying about three kids. And I'm telling you this up front. You may as well lock your door. Marty is coming over and we won't have time to be disturbed."

"The thirty-minute rule in effect?"

"Of course. How's Logan?"

"I know you don't have time for the whole story right now, but he actually had one of the rooms decorated as a nursery, so we have to be right about the miscarriage theory. He's coming for supper Saturday. We're going to share deep, dark secrets, have a little wine and beef stroganoff, and wash it all down with a healthy romp in the sheets...hopefully. For some reason he thinks I'll want to dump him after he tells me about the details of his life. Including Sam. That's her name, by the way. Samantha Carson. We'll have to have a session after I get the entire scoop, so let the others know."

"I'm glad he told you. It sounds like he's going to be honest and up-front with you about his wife's death, and that's good, especially since he seems to have some issues."

"I dealt with one of his issues yesterday. He had a little breakdown of sorts. He was out-of-control sobbing, sitting in the nursery. It broke my heart. It was triggered by a dream he had about me. He was feeling some guilt and...oh... well...it's a long story and I don't have the strength or time right now. Have a good tumble with Marty. Tell him I said 'Hey.'"

"Do we get to meet Logan on Saturday?"

"Maybe on Sunday morning. Bye, Gibbs."

Amy headed to the closet to search for appropriate clothes for sanding. She was fairly certain jeans would work. *Sleeves? Hmm. A sweatshirt might be good, since it was always a little cool in the workshop,* she thought. *Was sanding so vigorous that you could work up a sweat? Layering might be the answer. A t-shirt under the sweatshirt. Did Logan struggle with his sanding wardrobe?* She was sure he didn't.

*

Logan arrived home with a large brown bag containing several cartons of Chinese carryout. He wasn't sure what Amy liked, but she hadn't complained about anything yet, so he felt pretty safe in his selections. He was surprised Amy wasn't there when he arrived, but figured she'd gone home to clean up.

He was setting the table when Amy tapped on the front door and walked in.

"Logan?"

"I'm in the kitchen. Where've you been?"

"Paint store, grocery store, gas station, butcher shop, and shower."

"Is this in anticipation of Saturday?"

"Grocery store and butcher shop yes. Paint store is for here, and I will probably shower again before Saturday."

"Good. I'm looking forward to it."

"What smells so good?"

"Crab Rangoon, at your request, and an assortment of rice and meat chunks and vegetables in some kind of sauce."

"Sounds like Chinese food to me."

"Have a seat. I slaved over these little cartons all day and I'm starved."

"So, Logan, how was your day?"

"My day was good. I worked out in the shop for most of it."

"It's nice you can still do that. I had a surprise when I got home. My neighbor left a note on my table with a phone number of someone she works with that needs to have some painting done. So, it looks like I could have my second job."

"If you need time off feel free to take it. If it's a small project, or if they need it done right away, you can put my place on hold. I'd hate to have you lose a job because of me, especially since you're just starting out. Make sure you charge enough!"

"I only have about two weeks left here, and that's not working weekends, or even eight-hour days."

"Well, I'll be sad to see you go. I'm getting used to being greeted when I come in from work, and it's nice to have someone to talk to when I get home. But then, maybe we can have a few dates and phone calls, you know, more like a normal relationship."

"I think we see more of each other than people who actually live together."

That seemed to be a conversation-stopper. They ate in silence for a few minutes.

Amy spoke first. "So what are we sanding tonight?"

"The desk. I think we'll work on drawers."

"You sand, then stain?"

"Usually, yes. Unless you're not happy with the stain. Then you can sand it down a little. I've been doing this long enough that I'm pretty good at guessing what something is going to look like after it's stained. I have favorite brands that are pretty consistent. I don't have to redo much."

When they finished, Logan put away leftovers and Amy loaded the dishwasher. She washed her hands in the kitchen sink. When she turned around for a towel, Logan was standing very close. He tipped her chin up and kissed her firmly on the lips. "Now the good part begins. Let's go."

Logan took the key for the workshop and led the way. He unlocked the door, turned on the lights and turned the heat up a little. He pointed Amy to a bench.

"Straddle this. It's pretty comfortable and you can put your work in front of you and have a place to rest it. I'll get you some sandpaper. You start with the coarsest and end with the finest."

Amy mumbled under her breath, "Sanding 101."

"What?"

"Oh, nothing. Am I doing the whole drawer or just the front?"

"You can do it all, or just the fronts. You need to use the sanding block otherwise you could end up with an uneven surface. You may think your cute little fingers won't leave marks, but they will. Even if you can't see it, the surface would have uneven spots."

"You're the boss."

Logan sat on the opposite end of the long bench facing Amy. He took a drawer just like the one he had given her and began sanding.

After following Logan's lead for a few minutes, Amy broke the silence. "I can see why you like this so much. It's very relaxing."

"That's funny, because I don't do it to relax. It's invigorating to me. I get excited when I see the progress. Sometimes when I finish a project I actually feel a letdown. I hate for it to end. That's why I like to have a couple things in the works at once. When one is finished, I'm already in the middle of something else, and thinking of what I can start next."

"I think there's a twelve-step program for you somewhere. I can just see it. Meeting once a week. Sneaking in a little sawdust in your pockets, sniffing varnish…"

"At least it's a healthy addiction…I think. It doesn't keep me from my work and it hasn't ruined any relationships. Yet."

"Well, Logan, it isn't going to ruin this one."

He smiled at her. "Good. I thought about putting music out here, but sometimes the silence is good."

"Are you telling me I'm talking too much?"

"Never. How else can I learn about you?"

"Just ask. I'll tell you anything."

Logan stopped sanding and looked at her. *Are you falling in love with me?* he wondered.

"Tell me about the last boyfriend."

"Crane? Well, let's see. He's tall, handsome, thirty-four years old, light brown hair, brown eyes, college-educated, middle child of five, Chicago born and raised. Pain in the ass, lying, cheating, dog-kicking…whew! Didn't take long to get to the core of that one! Next question?"

"Where did you meet him?"

"On the train."

"Does he still call you?"

"He won't if he knows what's good for him. He'll have his hands full in a few months anyway."

"Any chance you'd ever take him back?"

"No chance."

"Good. Did you love him?"

"I thought I did. But I guess lately I've kind of redefined love. You don't treat people that way if you love them. We planned on getting married some day. You just don't go out spreading your sperm everywhere if you're planning on marrying someone. It's just plain wrong. And rude. And mean."

"I agree. Are your parents still alive?"

"Oh, yes, living in Michigan, happy as clams. Are yours?"

"My parents are divorced, but still living. I told you my dad is a retired plumber. I think he has a girlfriend, but he gets embarrassed if I ask about it. They go on a lot of these senior citizen bus trips together. I think he sneaks into her room at night."

"How cute!"

"Yeah, cute. That's the word for it."

"Logan, life is short. Let him get happiness where he can."

"I suppose. I guess I just wish he'd admit it."

"They're from a different generation. That kind of thing is personal and private. Maybe that's not a bad way to be. I get tired of hearing about everyone's sex life on TV, don't you? There's something to be said for privacy. What about your mom?"

"She remarried and moved to Canada, if you can believe that. She makes moose jerky with her new husband. He makes canoes. They're very nice, actually, and he has a nice little business. But to go from Chicago to the wilderness? It's just bizarre to me."

"So, she found happiness. Your dad's working on it. Different method. Sounds healthy to me. Any sibs?"

"I have a brother in California. That's all. We're close, even though geographically we're far apart. We talk on the phone frequently. We're only a year apart. I'm actually a year younger, but I act more mature."

"He's an attorney?"

"Yeah, I mentioned him once before. He gives good advice—keeps me on track since Sam died. Does it bother you if I talk about her? Because you kind of press your lips together when I say her name."

"It doesn't bother me one bit. That's the only way you're going to work through things. She was a huge part of your life and in a way still is. She was a living, breathing human being who existed, and you can't just pretend that what you had never happened, just to make things easier with us."

"You're a treasure. Thank you for saying that. Really, I don't dwell on her as much as when she first died. I mean, it's been over a year. I still have bad days, as you well know, but those are rare. Sometimes I'll hear a song or smell someone's cologne, and I'll look around for her. Then it hits me. Oh, yeah. She's gone."

"Congratulations! You're normal."

"I don't want you to feel like she's your competition. If I dwell on her, try to change the subject, and I'll try to take the hint."

"She is competition in a way, but not in a way that makes me feel threatened. She has a part of your heart that someday I may want to claim. She's in your head sometimes when I wish it was me. But that's okay. She's part of you, Logan. I understand that."

He set his drawer down on the bench. "Look at me, Amy." She stopped sanding and stared at her drawer. "Look me in the eye. I loved Samantha. A part of me always will. She is my past. I want you to be my future."

Amy tried to smile but burst into tears. She pulled off her sweatshirt and wiped her face. "Logan."

"Future, Amy. Do you understand me?"

She nodded and smiled at him.

Logan read her t-shirt and shook his head. It was a picture of Cleopatra with a snake around her neck and it said, "Kiss my asp."

"Amy Sweet, you're a strange and wonderful woman."

They worked for about two more hours and finished four drawers. Amy had the feeling he'd redo hers after she left but she didn't care. It was just good to sit in the quiet and be near him.

*

Later that night, Logan picked up the drawers Amy had been working on, assuming he would have to redo her work. To his surprise, he found very few places that needed touching up. He was proud of her and would have to remember to tell her so the following day.

*

On Friday, Amy figured Logan would be working from home as he usually did. She got to the house a little later than usual to give him time to shower and dress, although she really wouldn't have minded running into him in a towel again. But he was gone and there was a note on the kitchen counter.

Amy,
Checked your work. Well done!
Going in today, since I missed a day this week. Looking forward to tomorrow.
I washed the boxers just for you. I know your aversion to SMA (sweaty man-ass).
The condom store was closed, so I'll just bring plastic wrap. In case there are leftovers.
Time tomorrow?? Let me know.
Ha ha.
L

OK. Add a drugstore run to today's to-do list, just in case Logan catches a big case of stupid, Amy thought. The note did make her laugh, though.

Amy primed the hallway. She worked fast because she wanted to be gone before Logan got home. There was a feeling of anticipation building for Saturday night, and she wanted to revel in it. She noticed her catalog in Logan's reading room—aka the upstairs bathroom—and turned to the pages with the French country bedroom linens and decor. He had turned the corners of the pages down. This was a good sign.

When she finished, she went to the kitchen to write a note.

Logan,
6:30 or 7ish.
I'll be ready but may be putting the final touches on dinner. I'll let you help.
Plastic wrap?? Please!
Amy Sue Sweet
xo

Saturday morning came mercifully fast. Amy took the risk of making another list. This one would not have Logan's name on it. Dinner was not complicated, but she didn't want to feel scatterbrained when he arrived. She wrote down just what she needed to do and the time it took to do each task. She hoped the courses would flow, that one thing wasn't raw while something else was charred.

She had already done prep work, cutting, chopping, washing, draining, marinating and measuring. Romaine, Granny Smith apple, toasted pecans, dried cranberries, and Parmesan were waiting to be tossed with a sweet white wine vinegar dressing. Steamed carrots would be tossed with butter and brown sugar and then baked. Fresh noodles needed to be boiled. The beef stroganoff just needed to be heated, with sour cream tossed in at the last minute. The apple dumplings were prepared, and waiting to be baked. Cream was whipped, with a little cinnamon and vanilla. She added a pinch of cinnamon to the ground coffee. In her mind, everything was in place.

Unfortunately, reality often differed from perception. The phone rang and shook her from her daydreaming. She picked up on the first ring. "Hello!"

"How much coffee have you had this morning?"

"Logan! Hi! Sorry. You just woke me from a trance. I was mentally fixing dinner. You know, kind of a dress rehearsal? Making sure everything turns out okay."

"Was it good? Did I like it?"

"Yes, I think you had seconds and asked for the recipe for the salad." *Smart ass,* she thought.

"Funny, I'm still hungry. Are you nervous?"

"No, I planned ahead, started preparing two days ago."

"For doing me?"

"For dinner. Are you trying to unnerve me? I'm in a fragile state right now and cannot, absolutely cannot, have my cage rattled. Do you understand?"

"What are you wearing?"

"Oh for Pete's sake."

"Right now. What are you wearing?"

She was smiling and was thoroughly entertained by this man. She wanted to say deodorant and nail polish, but was afraid it would push him over the edge. "Flannel pajama pants and a t-shirt."

"What's on the shirt?"

"What do you mean?"

"All your t-shirts have something cute on them. Come on. Is it a bunny?"

"It's a cat, all tangled up in yarn. And it says, 'I didn't do it.'"

"Cute! I knew it. What else? Are you wearing panties?"

"Logan, this is turning into an obscene phone call, and I really should disconnect."

"But you won't. Because you're enjoying it as much as I am."

"I am not." *Yes, I am,* she thought.

"Not what? Enjoying it or wearing panties?"

"What are you wearing?" She tried to deflect the question.

"Amy, panties or not?"

"Not."

"I knew it!"

"Logan, answer me. What are *you* wearing?"

"Belly button lint and a smile."

"One of those two things better be gone when you get here."

"The smile is going to be pretty hard to wipe off my face."

"You *are* showering?"

"Eventually. You?"

"Pretty soon." She heard him moan. "Pervert."

"I had a toe cramp."

"Sure you did."

"Are you wearing a bra?"

"Logan, what would be better for you, if I said I was or if I said I wasn't?"

"That's a tough call. Because a good bra could really make the fantasy. On the other hand…or should I say *in* the other hand, naked is always acceptable."

Oh, he is good, she thought. "No bra, Logan."

"Oh yeah, baby!"

"You need a cold shower?"

"I'm working on it. Take your right hand and put it on your left breast."

"Absolutely not."

"Close your eyes and pretend it's me."

She did. "Absolutely not."

"You're doing it, aren't you?"

Yes, she thought. "No way."

"Your nipple is hard, isn't it?"

Of course, she thought. "I wouldn't know, Logan."

"Just look down, Sweetie. Squeeze it for me."

"We'll have to finish this tonight!" She slammed the phone down, disconnecting.

Within a few seconds it rang again and she let the answering machine pick up.

"Amy, I knew you wouldn't have the courage to pick up. I just need to know, was it good for you too?" She heard him hang up.

"Blast you Logan! I'm trying so darn hard not to be nervous." She walked into the living room talking out loud. "Maybe I do need a shower. Thanks to you, a cold one. Nitwit. Moron." Pacing seemed to help. "If you weren't so damn funny, I'd kick your ass." She headed for the shower.

*

Logan got into the shower with a smile on his face. He loved to tease her. She was always ready with a good comeback, and she challenged his wit. Maybe it wasn't fair to call her, but he figured she was as nervous as he was, and maybe a little distraction would help.

He picked up his dark gray suit from the cleaners, and bought a light pink shirt. He picked out a tie, swirly black, silver and pink, and put it between the mattress and box spring. After sleeping on it, it was good enough to wear without ironing.

He did the normal first-date hygiene routine, which mainly involved taming the wild hairs that seemed to sprout from weird places. He shined shoes, pulled on jeans and a sweatshirt, and headed out to the florist. When he returned home, he put music on the stereo, laid on the couch, and thought about the conversation he'd be having with Amy that evening.

Chapter 28

A my got out of the shower and went into her super-primp mode. After she was polished from head to toe she went across the hall and knocked on the door. Beth and Gibby were having a late breakfast.

"Wish me luck."

"Tonight's the big date, right?" Gibby remembered.

"I'm fixing dinner. You know, I really should cook more often just to stay in practice. Then maybe I wouldn't be so nervous."

"Is it the food you're nervous about or your plans for the evening after supper?"

"Beth, did Gibby tell you? Logan and I have some serious plans for dessert. We'll have a little soul-searching conversation, and then if we still like each other, we may entertain other options."

"Do we get to meet him tonight?" Beth had been asking this since they met.

"Can we not pounce on him tonight? Not that you'd scare him off, but I really want this to go well, and introducing him will add to my stress level."

Gibby went to the fridge. "Want a beer? You need to chill out."

Amy collapsed on a kitchen chair and put her head on the table.

"I was fine until he called and started talking dirty to me."

Beth stood up, hands on her hips and in her sweet southern drawl, said, "Amy, if you can't take it on the phone, what are you going to do when you have the actual naked man in your bedroom?"

"I'm hoping I don't throw up."

"You won't throw up. You got condoms? Rubber sheets? Antiseptic wipes?"

"This isn't surgery. It's just sex."

Beth reminded her, "Just sex? You mean the union of a man and woman that's supposed to happen after marriage?"

"Right. That's the sex I was thinking of. Rubber sheets? What kind of perverted sex do you guys have? Oh, my God! I have to put clean sheets on the bed. Gotta run." And with that reminder she was gone.

Chapter 29

Logan found a small shopping bag with a handle in the pantry. In it he placed his roll of plastic wrap, box of twelve condoms—he was feeling optimistic—and a bottle of California red wine. He took the rose from the refrigerator and headed off to Amy's. He would probably get there somewhere between the times she gave him. He wasn't concerned about appearing too eager. He was, and she knew it. He knew she was excited, too. But he didn't want to wait too long, because she sounded stressed. The last thing he wanted was to have Amy wondering if he was standing her up.

While he was parking in front of her condo, he thought he saw one of the blinds move. He smiled at the thought of her watching for him to arrive.

CHAPTER 30

Amy watched Logan pull up in his old Mercedes. He was carrying a bag. Probably the wine. She scurried to the kitchen, took off her apron, and took a swig of the wine she had just opened. For "medicinal" purposes, of course. Just to take the edge off.

She slipped her heels on, took one last look in the mirror by the front door, and waited for the bell to ring. She heard the elevator open. Mentally, she counted the number of steps she knew it took her to reach her door, and held her breath. She waited. *His feet are larger and his legs are longer. No. It would take fewer steps. Less time,* she thought. And waited. She looked out the peephole. Punkin. Damn cat. Logan had stopped to pet the cat. This was an evil plot by her neighbors, she was sure. Her doorbell finally rang. She opened it, unaware that she was still glaring. Logan stepped back. "Cute cat."

"Pig with fur."

He stopped and stepped back into the hall. "Amy, we're going to try this again. This time, look happy to see me." He pulled the door shut and counted to ten. He rang the bell again.

Amy opened the door, smiling. "Come on in, Logan. How nice to see you."

Logan stepped into the living room, closed the door behind him and stood back to look at her. "You take my breath away. You look awesome."

"Thanks." She leaned into him and gave him a soft quick kiss on the lips. "What's in your bag?"

He handed it to her. "Hand cuffs, Polaroid camera, plastic wrap."

Her eyes opened wide and her mouth fell open. "Logan!" She looked in the bag and saw the wine, the condoms and the plastic wrap. "You're a pervert."

"Time will tell." He smiled, as deviously as he could.

With an "oh-brother," eye roll in return, Amy put the wine on the table, the plastic wrap on the counter, and went around the corner to her room and threw the condoms on the bed. When she came back Logan held out the rose. It was huge, deep velvety red, and very fragrant.

"Logan, it's beautiful!"

"Doesn't hold a candle to you." He took it back and stroked her bottom lip. She closed her eyes and inhaled the scent of it. He pulled her close and kissed her firmly and thoroughly. Logan whispered, "I'm hungry. I want…" Amy held her breath. "…dinner."

"Be nice, or that may be all you get."

Amy took the rose back and headed to the kitchen to look for a bud vase. Logan followed her past the dining room table and noticed that she'd gone to a lot of trouble just for him. "Table looks great. Food smells great. You're looking very appetizing. You smell very sexy. That's a great dress…and don't I just love talking to myself?"

She turned around to face him. "Sorry. I had a little wine for courage, and I may have overdone it."

"Ya think??"

"Logan, come on in and make yourself at home. You look very handsome. Thank you for the rose. It's the biggest one I've ever seen."

"I had it shipped from Texas."

"Really?"

"No. But I did pick it out myself."

"I appreciate that." Amy was stretching to reach for a vase on the top shelf of the cabinet over the sink. Logan didn't have much height on her, especially considering the heels she was wearing. He intended to ask if she needed help, but the slit in the dress was allowing him a very nice view. "Logan would you mind…" She noticed he was watching her struggle with a silly grin on his face.

"You went for the garter belt. I'm proud of you. I'd be glad to get that for you, but I've been enjoying the scenery."

Amy faced him, bent at the waist and pressed her breasts together. "Perhaps you'd like to watch while I get something from the bottom drawer."

"Oh, yeah."

She turned her back to him and bent again, shaking her behind in his direction. "Or take in the view of me removing dessert from the oven."

"You know what I like."

"Do you think you can remove your mind from the gutter long enough to open the wine?"

"Of course. Did you want to continue your binge with the same glass or were you going to switch to a clean one?"

She picked up her glass and held it to the light. It was smudged with fingerprints. "I'll take a clean one, thanks." She pointed to a cabinet and Logan picked one to match his.

He poured the wine, sniffed it, and took a sip. "Can I help with anything?"

"How about we just take the wine and sit in the living room for about ten minutes? Then you can help, because things will come together fast."

Logan carried both glasses into the living room. He waited for her to sit. She chose the couch. Good. He sat next to her and handed her a glass. Before she could drink he motioned to toast. "Here's to the view—a beautiful table and a beautiful woman."

She added, "A gorgeous rose and a gorgeous, sexy man." Their glasses clinked lightly. They both took a sip. Logan took the glass from her and set it on the coffee table with his. "You think I've had enough?"

"Maybe, but I didn't want it to spill when I do this." He put his arm around her shoulder and pulled her close. He buried his face in her hair and inhaled deeply. He kissed her ear, nibbled on it slightly and whispered, "You're killing me, Sweet."

Amy kissed his neck, his cheek, his chin and teased the corner of his mouth. When he moved to claim her mouth, she turned just enough to keep him trying. She caught his bottom lip, the lip that tempted her beyond her strength and took it between hers. She sucked on it and brushed it lightly with her tongue. He held her face still and kissed her the way he dreamed of for days. His intent was that she would know no one else would ever do this to her. He was claiming her mouth as his, marking his territory with his tongue. Logan put his hand on her knee and felt like he was in high school. He loved the silkiness of her stockings. Amy made no attempt to stop him. He slid his hand slowly up her leg, the slit in the dress giving him easy access. His fingertips reached the top of her stocking, and just as he was about to sink his fingers into the smooth flesh of her thigh, they were rudely interrupted by the timer signaling the noodles were done.

Amy froze, torn between the wonderful feeling of Logan's preliminary lovemaking and knowing that dinner would be spoiled if she didn't stand up and go to the kitchen. "Logan, yes, you can help me in the kitchen now."

"Oh good. Let me try to stand up." He did, and took the wine glasses to the table.

"Drain the noodles please. Here's a pot holder. They go in the clear bowl. Pour a little of the melted butter on them and cover them with a towel."

"Yes, ma'am."

"Then come and have a seat." Amy brushed her hand across his behind as she walked past.

She served salad and Logan held out her chair for her. He leaned over her shoulder and kissed her cheek. "Delicious."

"You haven't even tried it."

"Oh, but I have. You're delicious!"

"Have some salad, Sweetie, and put your hormones on hold. I worked hard on this dinner, and I won't be distracted."

"This is very good. The apple makes it. And the dressing. You're a good cook, Amy Sweet. What else is on the menu? Can I have more salad?"

She passed the salad bowl, and Logan helped himself to a refill.

"Are you even taking the time to chew? Because I don't want you using indigestion as an excuse to get out of anything."

"Would I do that? I'm going to need plenty of nourishment."

"So, Logan, how was your day?"

"Uneventful. Just the way I like it. I see you did a little painting today. Have you heard more about the new job?"

"I'll call him on Monday morning. I just couldn't face one more thing to do today. I'm sorry if I seem stressed. I just don't cook often enough...or I should say, I don't entertain often enough to be comfortable with it. And I wanted this to be special. I felt the need to impress you and I didn't want the smoke alarm to go off."

"From the sound of it I thought you had your friends over all the time."

"I do, but that's usually heating up leftovers or eating carryout off paper plates."

"They'd be good for you to practice on, but I can tell you right now, you did a great job here. I am impressed. Very impressed. Can I get the noodles?"

Amy got up and put their salad bowls in the sink. She went to the stove and carried the copper pan with the beef stroganoff to the trivet on the table. She took

Logan's plate, spooned a serving of noodles and ladled on a scoop of the beef. She put his plate back in front of him, went to the oven and removed the carrots and gave him a spoon to serve himself. He waited for her to sit and serve herself.

Logan impaled a chunk of beef on his fork, put it in his mouth and chewed thoughtfully. "This is very good. Good meat…good gravy. Almost as good as…"

Amy couldn't look him in the face. "I couldn't help myself, Logan. I went through your trash and found a receipt for your hush-hush butcher shop. I had to give the secret password before they'd fill my order."

"What cut did you buy?"

"I'm not sure. I told him what I wanted it for, he wrapped something up in plain white paper, and sent me on my way. I'm surprised the guy didn't put me out onto the street blindfolded. This could be horsemeat for all I know."

"I'm probably blacklisted now. You didn't give them my name, did you?"

"Do you like the carrots?"

"You're changing the subject."

"For your own peace of mind, yes. The carrots…"

"They're delicious."

"Thank you." Amy cleaned her plate and watched Logan eat. She poured the rest of the wine into their glasses, making sure Logan got more, since she really wanted to keep her wits about her. "Please leave room for dessert."

Logan gave her a charmingly lecherous grin and raised his eyebrows. "Yum. You, my dear, will be my dessert." He had seconds of the noodles and beef. Amy enjoyed watching him eat. He was savoring every bite.

"No, my dear. An apple dumpling will be your dessert. The crust is homemade. There's cinnamon whipped cream to put on top." Amy turned the coffee on and in a very short time the kitchen filled with the heady aroma of cinnamon coffee.

"Save some of that whipped cream for later."

Amy took the warm dumplings from the oven. They smelled of home, comfort food and cool autumn evenings. Just the sight of them, all golden brown and glazed reminded her of her grandmother. It was one of her favorite desserts and easy to make. "I've never had an apple dumpling. What's in it? I assume apples come into play here somewhere."

"Well, actually you can use any big fruit like peaches or pears. You hollow out the middle, take out the seeds and fill the hole with brown sugar, nuts and butter. You wrap it in piecrust and bake it. It's kind of like a little pie, but round, and the fruit is in one piece."

"They're almost too pretty to eat. And they smell great. They remind me of my grandmother's house."

"Me too!"

"They smell like her apple pie. She was a great cook. No microwave, no fat-free, no artificial stuff. She baked from scratch. Made her own bread."

"My grandma made hot cocoa from scratch. And she made cinnamon toast. I know that doesn't sound hard, but hers was so much better than what I got at home. And she'd cut it into little triangles."

"That's the secret, Amy, the cutting into the little triangles. Maybe we're related!"

"I have too much invested in this evening to find out you're a cousin. Let's not even go there."

"You said there's cinnamon whipped cream?"

Amy went to the fridge and uncovered the bowl. She approached Logan with the topping and a spoon.

"Would you like to try some?"

"Let me taste it before you put it on my dumpling...ooo, that sounded dirty."

Amy scooped up a spoonful and motioned for Logan to open his mouth to taste it.

He licked the spoon clean. "More, please."

"On your dumpling?"

"No, in my mouth."

Amy handed him the spoon. He put some on his dumpling and ate another spoonful. He filled the spoon and pointed it at her. She opened her mouth to taste it and he fed her. "More?"

Amy nodded, "Yes, please."

Logan teased her with the spoon, wiping whipped cream on her bottom lip, chin and the creamy rise of her breast that had been tempting him all evening. She reached for a napkin.

"Oh, so sorry. Let me get that." He licked her chin more meticulously than necessary. He licked the whipped cream from her lip and kissed her. She leaned forward knowing his plan. His tongue played in the whipped cream on her breast. He spread it out, drew swirls in it and licked it clean. He lingered, nudging further into the plunging neckline of her dress. She ran her fingers through the hair at the nape of his neck.

"Mmm. You taste so good."

"Logan. Please." She set the bowl down and kissed him. "Soon. I promise."

"You do realize that when I finish this I will be stuffed like a pig and unable to move for about an hour."

"That's the plan. I made coffee to make sure you don't fall asleep on me."

"Not a chance, sugar. Can I pour some for you?"

"Sure. We can take it into the living room and sit on the couch and listen to some music for a while."

They finished their dumplings, took the coffee and headed for the couch.

"Do you mind if I take my jacket off?"

"Is it too warm in here? Because I can turn the heat down."

"I'm fine, I'd just be more comfortable without the jacket."

Amy set their mugs on the coffee table and walked toward Logan. "Allow me. I love this part." She stood in front of Logan. He went to reach for the button and she lightly slapped his hand away. She slowly unbuttoned the jacket. She ran her hands down the front, feeling the texture of the fabric. "Nice, very soft."

"Words a man loves to hear."

"Hush." She slipped her hands under the jacket and across his chest. He held his breath. She reached up to his neck, slid her hands across his shoulders and slowly down his arms, taking the jacket with her. "You can breathe now."

"You're killin' me, woman."

Amy nuzzled the jacket, drawing in the scent of his cologne left behind and carefully hung it in the closet.

Logan watched her walk. "Those shoes make your ass look really good."

"Don't start." She walked toward the couch, looked him in the eye, and kicked the shoes off.

"Hey, that was a very sincere compliment."

"And I appreciate it, but can we have at least a sixty-minute moratorium on my behind?"

Logan checked his watch. "Fine." He waited for her to sit. She tucked her legs under her and faced him. He sat close without touching. "I don't suppose I can take the tie off yet?"

"Not yet. You look so handsome, and besides, I want to do it."

"Amy."

"Logan."

"Be honest with me."

"I promise."

"How did it come about? This whole appreciation for undressing men? Where did you learn it? Who did you practice on? Not that I'm complaining. But I'm curious."

"I like men's clothes. Not to wear myself, but the feel of them. The structure. They're so different from women's clothes. They're substantial, not fluffy or frilly, not sheer or lacy. And I like watching a man undress. Not like a stripper, although I must say I can appreciate that too, recreationally. But the unbuttoning, the untucking, the unzipping. It's an art form. And I love the reaction. Like just now. All I did was take your jacket off and you were turned on."

"You did more than take my jacket off. You felt me up."

"Don't sound like such a victim. You loved every minute of it."

"True. And part of that was because I enjoyed watching you enjoy it. But I never thought of it as an art form."

"Compare it to this: a beautiful woman undresses for you, but leaves on her knee-hi stockings."

"I'd have to burn the image out of my brain."

"It's the same with men. It's a total turn-off to see a guy standing there in a t-shirt and black socks with his pants around his ankles."

"I see what you mean. I'm so glad you studied this so I don't commit any stripping faux pas."

"I'm here to help you."

"Amy, what would I do without you? I'd probably be one of those geeks standing around in black socks."

"There's a common sense order to removing clothes. First, and we've already taken care of this, the jacket. Then shoes, then tie, then socks, then shirt, then pants, then underwear."

"If he's wearing any."

"You better be. But do you see the pattern? Top, bottom, top, bottom, top, bottom?"

"Did you go to school for this? No, wait…did you practice on Crane?"

"Ugh." She put her head in her hands and mumbled. "Several times, unfortunately. And unless you have specific questions about my relationship with him in some way that would apply to us, I'd just rather leave him out of this evening."

"What first attracted you to him?"

"He's cute, successful, and was nice to me."

"So am I."

"True. But you knock my socks off."

"That's good to know."

"Can we talk about us for a little while?" She picked up her coffee and took a long swallow.

"Of course. Do you want to ask or tell?"

"Ask. Anything off limits?"

"I'll let you know if it comes up."

"Tell me more about Sam."

"I bought a car from her. I thought she was pretty. I asked her out. She said yes. We had sex on our third date and I was hooked, addicted, and in love. We got married two years later. She was about half an inch taller than me and six months older. She was smarter than me. She found out she was pregnant, and we went house-shopping. That's how I ended up where I am."

Amy's heart was pounding. Sam had been pregnant.

"You bought her car?"

"She worked at a car dealer. Any details I can fill in?"

"You have a history of falling fast and hard."

"Yes." He looked at her and smiled.

"Where did you live before you moved here?"

"We had an apartment in the city, which is no place to raise a kid, so we went shopping."

"I know you told me Sam died at St. Mary's. Did she miscarry? Did it have something to do with her pregnancy?"

"Yes. Complications. She hemorrhaged and…"

"I remember, Logan. I'm sorry this is so painful for you, but I'm trying to understand."

He reached out and patted her knee. "That's okay. It's good for me."

"So you decorated the nursery. It's darling. You made the cradle, didn't you?"

"Yes. The anticipation just drove me."

"How often do you go in there…where I found you the other day?"

"Not too much. I was just drawn to it. I could tell you had been down there, painting. I checked the knob to make sure it was locked because I didn't think I could deal with questions."

"I tried the knob."

"I figured you would. And that's okay, really."

"Maybe someday you'll get to use it."

"My turn to ask."

Amy was taken aback but tried not to let it show. Obviously he wanted to change the subject. *Fine,* she thought. He had already revealed a lot of very personal things, and she was ready to back off.

"Ask away, Logan."

"Where do you see yourself in four or five years?"

She took a deep breath. "I haven't really thought about it. My life has changed so much in the last two months that my answer now would be totally different from what I thought of as a plan for my life."

"Why would your plan for your future have changed?"

"Number one, I met you." He smiled at that. "Number two, I lost a job that I thought I would have for a long time and with it a certain amount of security. Number three, my plans for a family went down the tubes with Crane."

"You don't plan on having a family?"

"I'd love to have a family. I just don't want to be forty when I start."

"How old *are* you?"

"Thirty-something…younger than you."

"So there's no huge rush, biological clock and all that."

"No, I feel no urgency, yet."

"Do your parents bug you about getting married?"

"No, do yours?"

"They know better. They're just letting me make my own way back since Sam."

"How are you feeling?"

"Now? Good. A little over-served. Did you want me to catch up?"

"Yes. Anything else pressing that we have to discuss?"

"Pressing? Anything crucial before I make mad, passionate love to you? Can we continue this another day?"

"What? Logan? Sorry. Mad and passionate distracted me."

"Good. Bathroom?"

"Through the kitchen, on your left."

Logan stood up and left the room. Amy went to the kitchen and filled the dishwasher. She shut off the coffee pot, threw the stroganoff onto the noodles, covered the pot with plastic wrap, thanks to Logan, and put it in the refrigerator. She rinsed the wine bottle and set it aside for recycling. Done.

Logan walked back into the kitchen looking refreshed.

"You left a toothbrush out for me. That was very thoughtful."

She grinned. "You're quick. I'm next. Pick out some music if you want."

Amy headed for the bathroom and Logan looked through her CDs. Disco? He couldn't let that pass. Other than that, their tastes in music were very similar.

Amy came back to the living room and Logan was holding up her disco favorites.

"You have to be kidding me."

"Do not make fun of me, Logan. Those are classics."

"Dance with me?"

"The Hustle? Only in private. Where no one, and I mean no one, can see."

"No, something nice and slow." He pressed the 'play' button and she stepped into his arms.

He didn't pull her too close. He wanted her to do that on her own. She felt warm and soft in his arms. He noticed she had brushed her hair. It looked softer than it had at dinner. She touched up her makeup, brushed her teeth and added another drop of perfume. His senses picked up every nuance. Lips were moister, breath was minty fresh, and she smelled great. He wasn't sure where she dabbed the perfume, but it was in just the right place. He brought her hand up to his lips and kissed it. Hand lotion. She was an assault on his senses. His hand on her back felt the almost invisible zipper on her dress. He knew it wouldn't be long and that zipper would be down and the dress would be around her ankles and he would be the happiest man on earth.

"You're grinning, Logan. It makes me suspicious."

"Just planning my evening. Figuring in my mind the order in which I want to remove your clothes."

"Top, bottom, top, bottom doesn't work on girls."

She laid her cheek on his chest and felt his heart beating. He did an excellent job of picking music. Amy snuggled in. He was an exceptional dancer. She heard the music through her ears and felt it through his arms. She closed her eyes and listened to him humming. It reverberated through his chest and she pressed her face closer.

"Amy," Logan whispered into her hair.

"Shh. This is so nice. It feels so good, Logan." She wove her fingers through his hair and rubbed the nape of his neck.

"Amy." Logan lifted her chin and rested his cheek against hers. He kissed her earlobe and left a trail of little kisses across her cheek to her mouth. He kissed her very gently but there was no way she could mistake his intentions. She opened her lips in response to his tender prodding. His tongue teased hers. He tasted so good. She knew it was something she could get used to…no, get addicted to. He reluctantly pulled away and held her face in his hands. He kissed her forehead. "Look at me, Amy."

Amy looked into his green and gold speckled eyes and saw pure passion. She looked into his soul and saw her own reflection. Seeing herself through his eyes pulled on her heart and she would do anything he asked. She wanted to say something, respond to him, but there were no words to express what she wanted or needed from him.

"It's time." He whispered into her mouth and kissed her again.

"I think I'm afraid. I don't want to be afraid. I can understand being nervous, but not afraid."

Logan rested his hand low on her back and pressed her to himself. She felt his rigid strength against her belly and he held her there. "Amy, we're going to your room now. Don't be afraid. It will be good. Besides, you have to help me get undressed."

"Oh, yeah. I want this, Logan. I have for a long time."

"I know. Me too." He put his arm around her waist and they walked side by side toward Amy's room. He slowed down near the kitchen. "Do we need the plastic wrap?"

"Is there something we need to keep fresh?"

Logan was glad the atmosphere lightened. Amy left his side and walked toward her dresser. "Logan, lights or no lights?"

"A little light would be good. I want to look at you."

Amy pulled the cord on a pole lamp in the far corner. The indirect light would keep them from crashing into furniture and falling over each other. She flipped the switch on a small lamp on her dresser with a rose colored shade. The touch of pink made her skin glow.

"Perfect." Logan reached for the knot in his tie, and Amy came over to help him.

"I'd rather not talk you through this, because I want to enjoy every minute of it. I'm just going to give you some gentle direction."

She reached her arms around his neck and kissed his bottom lip. "Shoes."

Logan slipped his shoes off and kicked them out of the way. She kissed him, then pulled back enough to manipulate the knot of his tie. She felt his uneven breath on her hair. She pulled slowly until the ends hung around his neck. She smoothed the wrinkles from the knot and rubbed her hands against his chest. She nudged him gently to the bed and pressed his shoulders down until he sat. She stood in front of him and ran her hands through his hair. "Socks."

Logan crossed one leg over the other and slipped off a sock. Amy reached down and dragged her fingernails across the sole of his foot. Logan gave a startled shriek and jerked his foot away from her hand.

"Whew, that's the most girly sound I ever made!"

Amy smiled and whispered again, "Sock, please."

Logan reached down and removed the other sock. He reached around her back and buried his face in her cleavage, kissing both sides and breathing in the heady sent of her breasts. "Oh God, Amy." He licked and kissed and she let him.

When she backed away Logan stood up. Amy started with the buttons at his cuffs and then worked from the neck of his shirt down, obviously in no hurry, unlike Logan. When she got to his waist she unbuckled his belt but didn't pull it off. She unfastened his slacks and lowered his zipper about two inches. Logan inhaled sharply as Amy untucked his shirt. As she unbuttoned the last two buttons she pressed against his fly.

"Amy Sweet. You have three minutes. If you are not finished, I am throwing you onto that bed and we will make love in whatever clothes are still clinging to my tormented body. It will be hot, hard and fast. With an emphasis on fast."

"Shirt."

Logan pulled his shirt off and tossed it across a chair. He stood in front of her for more torture. Amy pulled the belt from Logan's slacks and tossed it onto his shirt. She reached for the zipper tab, held it and looked up at him. She smiled as she slid it slowly down. It seemed louder than he had ever remembered, and he was sure he felt the vibration of each and every tooth as she teased him. She pushed the slacks down, easing them over his very firm butt. She ran her hands down his thighs as she bent down and followed the slacks to his ankles. She tapped one foot and then the other as he obediently lifted them. She picked up his slacks and laid them over his shirt and belt.

Amy stood in front of Logan smiling, admiring the blue silk boxers that protected her from his weapon of mass destruction. He reached for her and she turned her back to him. She lifted her hair away from the zipper on the back of her dress and he needed no further invitation. He unzipped—without dawdling, teasing, or tormenting. She turned around, and he ran his finger from her chin to the base of her cleavage. He pulled her dress down past her waist and she wiggled as he worked it past her hips. She propped herself on his shoulder as he picked the dress up and laid it across his slacks. Amy stood before him in a black garter belt and stockings, black satin panties and a bra with the sole purpose of giving her cleavage. Logan closed his eyes and mumbled. Amy thought maybe he was praying.

"This is good," he said as he reached for the front clasp on her bra. He liberated her breasts and let the bra drop to the floor. "I'm touching now." He reached for her.

"Please."

He filled both hands and she closed her eyes. "Open your eyes and watch me love you, Amy."

She watched him study her breasts, touch the nipples and compare the different textures. He was mesmerized by the reaction he caused with just the stroke of a fingertip. Amy reached for the hem of his undershirt. He lifted his arms and pulled it over his head. She laid her cheek on his chest, absorbing his heat. She kissed one of his nipples, caught it between her lips and tugged. Logan pulled her close and she put her arms around his waist. He kissed her forcefully as she ran her hands over the silkiness of his boxers. She lowered them slightly, reached between their bodies and gently freed Logan from his shorts. The touch of her hand on the evidence of his passion was the cause of the tremor that shook him. Control lay beyond his reach.

Amy froze as she realized what had happened.

"Oh, God, Amy! Oh, God." Logan held her tight and cried out into her hair.

"Bang," Amy whispered into his ear.

"What?"

"You shot me in the belly."

"I am so, so sorry."

Amy held him and rubbed his back as he moaned. "It's okay."

"I'm so humiliated. I wanted this to be perfect. I couldn't help it. You're so hot and it's been so damn long. I'm sorry, Amy."

He sat on the edge of the bed and with his elbows on his knees held his head and verbally abused himself. She stood in front of him still wearing garter belt and panties. She rubbed his hair and he looked up at her. "Do you want me to go?" he asked.

"Are you insane?"

"It's just that I uh, well…"

"May need recovery time?"

"Yeah, maybe."

"In the meantime you have work to do."

"Anything. You name it. Dishes, laundry…"

She handed him a tissue and pointed to the deposit he made on her soft belly skin.

"Clean-up crew."

"I'm so embarrassed."

"Logan, have I humiliated you or poked fun?"

"No."

"But I probably will in the morning."

"Okay." He gently wiped her belly and kissed it when he was finished. "What else?"

"First, if you notice, I am still wearing something. Second, while you may have felt a spurt of relief I have not. You have a job to do. Finish what you started. I don't care how you do it, but do it you will."

"Of course. I'm an idiot."

Amy took his hands and pulled him off the bed. "Just to be safe I'm approaching from the rear this time."

"Not funny."

"Yes, it is, and you know it." She stood behind him and pulled his silky boxers down, being careful not to get hung up on any protuberances. He kicked free of them and on her way back up Amy bit his ass. Hard.

"Ouch! That wasn't necessary."

"Yes, it was!" Amy sat on the edge of the bed and rested her foot on Logan's thigh. He unhooked each garter and carefully slid off her stockings. She stood up and removed the garter belt and stood in front of Logan in her panties. "On or off for now?" she asked.

"On, I think. I want to take them off but I need to feel them first."

"Take the lead, Logan. You know what I want. I've waited a long time, too. And by the way, I'm impressed." She smiled at him and he actually blushed.

Logan took her in his arms and started from scratch. He teased her with his kisses, stroked every inch of skin that had been covered with clothing. He ran his hands over her behind and stopped.

"Not one word, Logan"

"Only one word. Nice." He gave her a firm squeeze and held her tight against himself. Amy wrapped a shapely calf around his leg and rubbed herself against his thigh. Once again her breathing came in starts and stops and she knew exactly where she wanted him.

"Logan, can we..."

He kissed her thoroughly, enjoying her soft tongue and smooth white teeth.

He pulled away. "Yes we can." He pulled the bedspread down, sat on the edge of the bed and pulled Amy between his knees. He kissed each breast then went back to lavish his attention on one of her nipples. He brushed his lips across it until it blossomed and almost forced its way into his mouth. Logan licked her rosy pinkness then blew gently across it. He watched the texture change and Amy winced as the tightness begged for relief. Logan filled his mouth and suckled as if she offered him the essence of life itself. She held his head to her breast, encouraging him to take his fill. He lavished the same attention on the other side.

After freeing herself from his attentive mouth, she kneeled on the bed and crawled past him. She put her head on her pillow and stretched out. Logan watched, admiring the fluid movements of her muscles under her pampered skin. He lay next to her and watched as she reached for him. Amy stroked the light dusting of hair on his chest and gave his useless nipples a little pinch. He grimaced and gasped. She drew a line with her finger to his belly button. She looked in, blew in it, and winked at him. "Just checking."

Amy placed her hand on his knee and drew circles around it with her fingers. The circles got bigger and her hand slid leisurely up his thigh. She watched his expression as she got closer to parts she was anxious to touch again. "Well, that didn't take so long, did it?" she said.

"You amaze me, Amy Sweet. You have the *magic touch*."

"Well, I'm afraid to *magic touch* you again!"

"I'll be okay this time, I promise."

Logan pulled her close, moved her hands and laid her on her back again. He shifted her legs gently apart and knelt between them. His hands slid up her thighs and met at the crotch of her panties. Amy was afraid to breathe. He slipped his thumbs under the elastic and stroked her. He knew what he'd find there—soft curls, damp in anticipation, a welcoming place. He wasn't disappointed. He leaned over her, placed a worshipful kiss on her belly and smelled himself there. Amy lifted his head and looked him in the eyes. Her lips said, "Please," but no sound came out.

Logan quickly but gently removed her panties, tossed them over his shoulder and gave her a wicked grin. Amy reached under the pillow and handed him a condom.

He had no time for explanations now so followed her directive. "You have to do it yourself this time. I'm afraid of being in the line of fire."

"No jokes until the morning, you promised."

"Logan. Logan. There's a nice warm place waiting for you…"

"Make room, love." He'd apologize later for lack of preliminary warning strokes. He pressed into her until he was certain he'd impaled her to the mattress. Amy took every inch and matched him stroke for stroke. He looked into her eyes in disbelief. Could this really happen to him twice in his life? He thought this part of him was dead, but Amy gave him the kiss of life. "With me?" He was breathing hard. He kissed her haphazardly on the mouth.

"Yes, Logan, now, my God! Oh, please." Logan came with a force that surprised him, and obviously Amy. He called her name into her pillow, thanked her and God, called on Jesus to save him, and collapsed on top of her, forgetting his manners regarding bearing his own weight on his elbows as a gentleman should do. Amy called out, muffling her cries with his shoulder. She bit gently and Logan let her.

"Do not move, Logan. Don't move, please. Please don't move."

"I won't. I can't. Why?"

Her legs were locked around his thighs and she was holding him tight within her. He could feel her muscles inside drawing him deeper. Amy rocked and clenched, holding him inside. "Oh God, Logan. Don't go until I'm done."

"What can I do?"

"Don't move."

"I won't." He felt her hold her breath; her insides quivered. She came again and again, calling his name. Logan was struggling to stay inside so Amy could have the release she needed. He watched her face while wave after wave of orgasm stormed over her. Finally her breathing calmed and he opened his mouth to speak. She arched her back and gave a final shudder.

"Logan."

"Good grief, woman, how long you been storing that up?"

"I've been waiting for you all my life."

A few moments later, Logan rolled over and tended to the abused condom. He wrapped it in a tissue and tossed it over his shoulder, somewhere in the vicinity of Amy's long forgotten panties, and lay on his side next to her. He stroked her cheek, tucking her hair behind her ear, and kissing her earlobe.

She reached under the pillow and Logan assumed she was reaching for another condom. "Already? Again?"

"Can't keep up, old man?"

"Amy-cakes, give me a break!"

She held something in her hand. He pried her fingers open and removed the folded scrap. He leaned over and kissed her as he unfolded it. He'd seen it before. "Congratulations!"

"My list is done."

He read the only task not crossed off. "Do Logan."

"And I did."

"Yes you did." Logan tore the list up and tossed the pieces onto the floor. "You did me. You over-did me. Stick a fork in me, I'm done. I'm damn done. You sapped my strength. You sucked the life out of me, so to speak."

"You shot me in the belly!"

"Not until morning! You promised. Besides, it was your fault."

Amy snuggled close and threw a leg over his. "You're whining. Can you stay all night?"

"It's a tough job, but somebody has to do it."

"Logan?" Amy, on the verge of falling asleep, was too tired to get out of bed. "What, Sweet?"

"Favor, please."

"Anything. Name it."

"Turn off the stereo, lock the front door, close the living room window, turn off the lights, and get back here to rest up for round two."

Logan groaned, rolled over and got out of bed. Oblivious to his nakedness he walked through into the living room, and followed instructions.

Amy watched, fascinated. "Thank you. Very much." Logan stopped in the doorway, posed and flexed. "Just stand there a minute and let me look at you."

"If you move that sheet and let me look at you."

Amy flipped the sheet down and stretched her arms and legs, arched her back and rolled her head from side to side on the pillow. She heard Logan moan and looked up at him. "I don't know why you were so concerned about recovery time. You seem to be doing just fine."

"I haven't put it to the test in a while. It's not like I sat home practicing."

She reached under her pillow and pulled out another condom. "Turn off the lights, big boy, and come here and make me happy."

Logan complied, and they made love again, slower this time, savoring each other, at least until the last few moments.

CHAPTER 31

A my woke up with the sun coming in the window, beaming down on the pillow next to her. But there was no manly mass of tussled hair there. Logan was gone. She sat up quickly and listened for the shower. No. The bathroom door was open. Some of his clothes were still there...his belt, socks, tie, boxers. Then she heard her front door open. "Logan?"

"Good morning, beautiful."

"Where have you been?" She breathed a sigh of relief. *Thank you, God,* she thought.

He was wearing his slacks, shoes with no socks and his shirt buttoned crooked. "I ran down to the car to get breakfast and some clean clothes. I didn't want to bring them up last night, assuming you were going to invite me to stay. But I was hoping, and I wanted to be prepared. I met one of your neighbors... Margaret something. She looked familiar to me."

From the hospital, no doubt, she thought. "Dressed like that? I'm glad you weren't too obvious, or she'd think we spent the night together."

"So what? We did. And I loved every minute of it. Well, almost every minute, and I'm not embarrassed or ashamed. We're responsible adults, respectful of each other, and why should anyone care if we screwed like minks?"

"What did you bring for breakfast, mink man? I was going to make blueberry pancakes and sausages."

"You still can. This is the first course, the preliminary sugar boost for energy. Frosted Flakes and whole milk," he grinned. "Hope you don't mind. Skim milk makes them get mushy too fast."

"What's in your pocket?"

Logan pulled the little black scrap out of his shirt pocket. "Your panties. I'm taking them as a souvenir." He rubbed the silkiness over his cheek and breathed the sent of them in deeply. "Ahh. Amy Sweet."

"You cannot have my panties! Those were eight dollars! What are you going to do, hang them on your rearview mirror?"

Logan pulled out his wallet and laid a ten-dollar bill on her dresser. "There's two extra for gas money to drive to the mall to buy another pair. I'm not parting with these. And no, I'm not hanging them in the car. I'm keeping them in my pocket so I can sniff them whenever I want." He had an exaggerated look of ecstasy on his face and his eyes rolled back into his head. "Oh, baby!"

"You're a pig!"

"Do you want to keep my boxers?" He picked them up off the floor, held them up and twirled them on his finger.

"No. I want you to put them on. Then wear them home and wash them so you can wear them again for me. My imagination is vivid enough that I can recall last night without having to wear your boxers around my neck."

"I'll pull your panties out now and then at work just to show off, you know, make my employees jealous."

"Toss me your undershirt so I can get up without parading naked to the bathroom."

"Do you want to keep it?"

"Logan! I want to pee. I do not need your clothes. I have plenty of my own. I'll be in the kitchen in a minute if you want to get breakfast ready."

"We're eating in here. I'll get bowls and spoons."

Amy slipped his undershirt on. The big scooped neck and open arms didn't cover much, but she had to admit it was an interesting look. She went into the bathroom and looked at herself in the mirror. She whispered to the face looking back at her. "You look like you were rode hard and put away wet. Did you get that out of your system for a while? Of course not. You're obsessed with him. He's wonderful, isn't he? Are you going to say the 'L' word? Think it, but don't say it yet," she warned herself. She washed her face and another more fragrant area. She pulled her hair back into a ponytail and brushed her teeth. She'd pass on the makeup. Logan was going to see her freshly scrubbed. She could shower later.

She came back into the bedroom and sat on the bed with her pillow in her lap. Logan came back in wearing his boxers and carrying his version of a high-energy breakfast: Frosted Flakes, whole milk, two bowls and two spoons. He looked so pleased with himself that she had to chuckle.

"Good morning, beautiful. You look good enough to eat."

"I'm keeping my options open. You're looking pretty sexy yourself."

Logan sat across from her, knees touching, also using his pillow to rest his bowl on. He poured the cereal, kept a bowl for himself and passed one to Amy. He gave her a spoon and let her add her own milk. He dug in, took a big spoonful and crunched away. "Delicious."

"Thanks, Logan. You're good to me."

"Nah, I'm stealing your underwear!"

"No, you bought my underwear."

"Oh. Right." He smiled and took another spoonful. He finished first and poured another bowl, added more milk and motioned for Amy to eat up. She reached across the pillows and plucked a wayward flake out of his chest hair. She tossed it into his bowl.

She touched his face like she had never seen it before. She smoothed his eyebrows and ran the backs of her fingers across his cheeks, noticing that he needed a shave. She followed the curve of his ear with her fingertip and tugged on his earlobe. He stopped chewing and sat still while she explored. Amy kissed her fingertip and pressed it to his lips. He kissed it several times while she held it there. She pulled her hand away and slid it under the pillow on her lap. She arched her back, took a ragged breath, and whispered his name.

"Geez, Amy. What the hell are you doing to me?"

"Finish eating."

"Are you kidding? I can barely swallow." He set both their bowls and spoons on the nightstand and set the cereal and milk carton on the floor.

Amy slid her hand under the pillow on his lap. "Is this for me?"

"If you want it."

"Oh, I want it, alright. And you want to give it to me?"

Logan nodded. "Soon."

Amy rolled her eyes and smiled. "You, my mink man, had better learn to practice self-control."

"I'll be fine." He opened the box of condoms he brought and started to tear one open.

Amy pulled the pillows from their laps and leaned them against the headboard. She pushed Logan back so he rested on them. "You don't need that just yet." She knelt in front of him and grasped the waistband of his shorts. "Lift."

He did and she pulled them down his legs and tossed them to the floor. Again. Once more Logan tore at the foil packet. Amy took it from him and set it next to him on the bed. She got up on her knees, straddled him, put her hands on his shoulders and leaned in to kiss him. He ran his hands up her arms, across her back and down to her behind where his fingers came to rest in her sheltered cleft. He squeezed and pulled her close. He reached farther down and found her ready for him. He stretched her gently with two fingers. She broke off the kiss, arched her back and settled into his hand. She pulled down on the hem of the undershirt until her breasts popped through the neckline. She held one up to Logan. His mouth was drawn to it like a magnet to steel. Amy reached for his unoccupied hand and brought it up to her other breast. He held it reverently, squeezed gently and brushed his thumb across the nipple while he watched her reaction.

His fingers stroked and stretched inside her and she joined his rhythm. He moistened his thumb and probed gently. When he found her sensitive, swollen nub his mouth settled on her other breast and he feasted. She held his head in both hands and cried out. "Logan. I need...I want...please. I need you... more." He withdrew his hand, wet with her slippery essence and massaged it into her breast. He rubbed it onto his bottom lip and kissed her. She reached for the condom, opened it, and before she put it on him, collected a glistening droplet from the tip of his penis. She rubbed it on her lips and Logan leaned forward and kissed her. Their lips and tongues caressed and melded as they took pleasure in the taste of themselves and each other.

Amy rose up and held Logan's shoulders as she lowered herself slowly onto him. He lowered his head and licked her breast clean. He couldn't get enough of the taste of her. She kissed his face, his neck, and pulled his earlobe into her mouth. She whispered her wishes into his ear and Logan adjusted his hips beneath her. She rose up, then lowered herself again so that Logan filled her completely. As he pressed deeply into her she squeezed tightly until he called her name.

"Amy. Okay? Now. Please. Love me." He nuzzled her neck. "Let go with me."

Amy did as he asked. Their bodies were one, slick with sweat from their heated passion. Logan held her in his arms and tried to catch his breath. Then he heard her soft voice. "Logan?" He knew what was next.

"I won't move." He let her ride out the surge for as long as she needed. He rubbed her back, kissed her breasts and let her hang on until she was finished.

"Thank you for that, Logan."

"One of these days you'll finish before me."

"I doubt it, but it would be fun trying."

"Actually, I love watching you come. The passion in your face, the intensity in your eyes, just knowing I'm buried deep inside you. God, Amy. There are no words to describe how I feel about this, about us. Just sitting here. I smell myself on you. I'm tasting myself. I'm tasting you. I know where my cock is… uh…penis is, and you're so hot inside. You have muscles that, oh, my God!"

She knew he was hard again. She leaned forward and gave him room to thrust up into her. She reached behind her and gently cupped him, squeezing and stroking with his rhythm. She couldn't bear to say the words out loud, so she whispered them softly into his ear. "I know where your cock is Logan. I love you inside me. I want you there every day for the rest of my life. So hot, so hard."

Logan stopped abruptly. He pulled out of her and struggled with the condom. Then suddenly he flung it to the floor, and to her surprise plunged back inside her irresistible heat. Before Amy could react to what he had done, he pressed his head back into the pillows and cried out in his climax, filling her with his inert fluid. She laid her head on his shoulder and held him against her as they both contemplated the consequences of what had just occurred.

Amy pulled the undershirt up over her breasts and walked to the dresser. She took a clean bra and panties, a t-shirt and sweatpants into the bathroom. She turned the shower on, and while the water was getting hot, she sat on the edge of the tub and broke into tears. She wasn't sure why. She knew something had drastically changed in the last five minutes. Did she feel differently about Logan? She loved him. That she knew for certain. She trusted him. At least she thought she did. He had made a drastic decision that had put them both at risk. She felt certain he didn't have a disease. She assumed that he must have drawn the same conclusion about her. No, the real risk here was possible pregnancy. Amy thought she could deal with that. She'd rather not, being a single person with no proposals in the wind, but she could deal with it. Could Logan? The last thing she wanted was to make him feel trapped into marriage. Wait a minute! She didn't pull the condom off…he did!

"Amy?"

She didn't answer.

Logan tapped on the bathroom door. "Amy, are you okay?"

"I'll be out in a few minutes."

He walked away. She stepped into the hot water and let the residue of their lovemaking wash down the drain. And with it, the euphoria she had been feeling.

She scrubbed herself, washed her hair, and rinsed longer than was necessary, while she formulated a conversation starter in her brain. She got dressed, took a deep breath and hoped that Logan hadn't left.

He sat on the foot of the bed with his clean clothes in his hand. She smiled at him and he looked relieved. "Do you mind?"

"Help yourself. I'll get you a towel. There's no guarantee how much hot water is left."

"Probably for the best." He stood up and as she handed him a towel he kissed her softly. "Thank you."

"I'll make coffee."

She looked around her room. The bedding lay strewn about in careless piles. Logan had picked up the tissues and other assorted nasty things that had been flung onto the floor. *Thank goodness,* she thought. She went to the window and opened it just a crack to get the air moving. The smell of musk and Logan was overwhelming. She stripped the bed and filled the washer, but she would wait for Logan to get out of the shower before turning it on.

Amy went to the kitchen and started a pot of coffee. So many thoughts were swirling through her head—she needed a task that required concentration. Blueberry pancakes? Cancelled. She pulled out muffin mix from the cabinet, followed the recipe and threw in the blueberries. She preheated her oven and filled muffin cups with the batter. She mixed a little butter, flour and sugar together and sprinkled it over the top of the batter. She set the timer, poured herself a cup of coffee, and added plenty of cream and a packet of artificial sweetener. She set a cup on the counter for Logan, went into the living room, and sat in her rocking chair.

Amy heard Logan turn the shower off. She heard assorted clunking and bumping as he dried and got dressed.

He noticed as he walked through the bedroom that she had removed all evidence of their lovemaking, even the musky sent they had left behind.

As he walked into the kitchen, he didn't have the courage to look at her. He picked up the mug she set out for him and filled it. He walked into the living room and sat on the couch. He was wearing jeans, a Northwestern University sweatshirt, and bright white socks. His hair was fluffy and clean, and he had shaved. He smelled good and looked very huggable. But now she felt afraid.

"Amy."

She looked up from her cup where she was studying the steam rising.

"Do you hate me?"

"Logan, no. Hate you? Why would you think that?"

"I disappointed you. You think I put you at risk."

"You didn't disappoint me. Yes, I think you put me...put us at risk. Disease is a moot point, Logan. But I'd prefer to be a married woman before getting pregnant."

"Will you come here and sit by me?"

She had made up her mind to have this conversation with a little distance between them, but he looked so pathetic that she joined him on the couch.

"Why, Logan? Why did you do it?"

"I suppose we should have had this conversation last night."

"Just spit it out. Nothing will surprise me anymore."

"I can promise you that isn't true."

"Start at the beginning, Logan, and don't spare my feelings. I'm kind of numb right now."

He drank down half of his coffee and set the mug on the coffee table.

"You know most of the story about Sam." She nodded, determined to make him dig himself out of this mess. "You know I blame myself for her death, because if she hadn't been pregnant, she wouldn't have died." She nodded again and tried to keep eye contact. "I was very determined at the time to never again do that to someone that I loved." She had to look away. "Amy, hang in here with me on this, please. I never in my wildest dreams thought I would find someone that I would care about again. I married for life, Amy. I was so knocked off my feet when she died." Tears filled her eyes. The timer on the oven rang, giving a momentary respite. She got up, went to the kitchen, took the muffins out, and wiped her eyes on a napkin. She went back in and sat with Logan.

"Remember yesterday when I asked what your plans were for the next four or five years?" She nodded. "You mentioned having a family." She nodded. "Amy, I had a vasectomy after I killed...I mean, after Sam died." She put her hand over her mouth and didn't speak. So much for her plans. "I can't do that ever again, Amy. Innocent life snuffed out. I won't be responsible for that again."

"Why didn't you tell me before?"

"For several reasons. First, it isn't just something you go around announcing. Second, I have wanted to make love to you for a while. And believe me, I know this is wrong, and I'm not proud of myself, but I was afraid if I told you, you would see no point in continuing a relationship, because there would be no future for us as a family. It was purely selfish on my part. I guess I used you to avoid rejection. Do you know what I mean?"

"I think so. But Logan, give me some credit here. Yes, I want a family. I want to be a mom some day. I think you'll make an awesome dad, but..."

"No! You don't get it. I cannot be a father."

"Please don't raise your voice to me. I don't deserve that, Logan."

He hung his head. "I'm sorry. I'm sorry."

"I know what 'vasectomy' means. I can understand why you had it done. I also understand that even though there are millions of wonderful women in the world that you were too devastated to believe you would ever meet one. And I know this, Logan Carson. I am so glad you met me. I just insist on honesty from you."

He reached out tentatively for her hand. She opened her palm to him and he held her. "I am being as honest as I can be at the moment. You know I'm dealing with this whole situation the best I can. I have come so far. I was a basket case, Amy. There were days when I couldn't even get out of bed. Weeks when I didn't leave my room."

"Is trust an issue? Is there a reason you don't trust me, Logan? Is there something I can do?"

"My gut instinct is to say of course, trust is definitely not an issue. You know I trust you. But then, to be perfectly honest, I don't know if I trust you not to bolt if I were to tell you the whole story."

She pulled her hand back and held it to her heart. He reached over and took her hand back. She stiffened. "Look at me, Amy. Please." She brought her eyes up to meet his. She blinked and tears pushed out and ran down her cheeks. "Now you listen to me. And you hear every word I'm going to say." He wiped her tears with his thumb and wouldn't let go of her hand. "Amy, I am hopelessly, completely in love with you. I was sure of it the night we had supper at my house. Just sitting on the couch, getting to know each other. I was so comfortable with you. Then last night…this morning…making love…my God, I wanted to shout it to the stars. Amy Sweet, I love you! But in the heat of the moment it's just too easy to say, and I didn't want to take the chance that you wouldn't believe me."

"Logan, I don't know what to say."

"How about, 'I love you, too, Logan.'"

She was speechless. She wanted to say the words that he wanted to hear. They were stuck. All wrapped up in his fatherhood issues.

"I'm sorry, Amy, if I caught you off-guard. You certainly don't have to admit to feelings you don't have." He let her hand go. He went to the kitchen and brought the coffee pot in and refilled their mugs.

When he sat down again she turned on the couch and faced him.

"Now you listen to me, Logan, and you hear every word I'm going to say to you. I admitted to myself a couple weeks ago that I was in love with you. It wasn't easy since just a few weeks before that I was supposedly in love with Crane. Obviously, I am not very good at naming my feelings. What hurts me is that you can't seem to trust me. I know you're a kind and loving person. You have a huge heart with a big capacity for love. I guess I don't understand the semantics here. You cannot be a father. Well, I understand that. I also know that vasectomies can be reversed, so if you wanted to be a father, you could be. I also know adoption is an option. But 'cannot' be a father is different from 'will not' be a father, or 'don't want to' be a father. What is it, Logan? And please, respect me enough not to lie to me."

"You love me?"

"Yes, you idiot!"

"Thank you, God." He took both her hands and pressed them to his face. "You, Amy Sweet, love me, idiot that I am, with all the crap in my life."

"I love Logan Carson. I admit it. Life full of crap and all. Come what may. But mark my words Logan, we will get through this. Be stubborn if you must, but I will wear you down. I look forward to the challenge. Besides, you're too good horizontally to let you get too far."

"That's the third reason…you know, why I took the condom off. I wanted to feel you…inside. Skin on skin. Flesh against flesh."

"Logan, that's the best reason. The one I understand."

Logan stood up, pulled her off the couch and she melted into his arms. They held each other tight. Logan whispered, eyes closed, "Thank you, God. Thank you for this woman. She gives me life and love."

CHAPTER 32

They were oblivious to the sound of the ambulance coming up the street until they noticed the siren stopped in front of Amy's building. Reluctantly, she pulled out of Logan's arms and went to the window. Several EMTs ran into her building, two of them rolling a stretcher. There were several elderly people on the first and second floors, so she assumed that's where the EMTs would be stopping. She heard banging in the hallway. She and Logan went to the door and saw one of her neighbors banging on Gibby's door. There was no answer. Amy recognized the young woman, carrying a baby in her arms. She ran into her frequently in the elevator. She had three children, worked hard, and was holding her life together by sheer will power.

"Carrie! What's wrong? Gibby's at work and Beth is at church."

"Amy, thank God you're home. Jack jumped off the kitchen counter and I think he has a broken leg."

"Hi, I'm Logan. So you called the ambulance?"

"Yes…please help. Amy, will you wait here and show them where my condo is? Logan, will you help me until they get here, please?"

Logan followed Carrie to her place. He went into the kitchen and saw Jack on the floor crying. He was holding a teddy bear.

"I'm sorry, Mommy." Jack sobbed, probably more bothered that he upset his mother than he was about the broken leg.

Logan squatted down. He could tell by the angle of the leg that it was broken. "Hi there, Jack. My name is Logan. How are you feeling?"

"My leg hurts."

"I believe you. There are some nice people on their way up to help you. You'll have to be very brave for a few minutes. But don't be afraid of them. It's their job to help people, especially kids."

Amy stood behind Logan listening to his speech in his very comforting voice. Jack saw her come in.

"Hi Amy! I fell."

"I can see that. I think you're going to get a ride in an ambulance! Their lights are on and everything!"

"The sirens too?"

"Of course. You'll be an important passenger."

"Can Mommy come with me?"

Carrie was holding a baby, trying not to appear afraid for Jack's sake. "I'll be there a little later. But you'll be fine. I need to find someone…"

Amy interrupted her. "Jack, your mom will ride with you in the ambulance. We're going to baby-sit until she comes home." She gave Logan a look that dared him to back out.

"Amy, you have company. I couldn't ask you to do that."

"You were going to ask Gibby…"

"She's a nurse; I thought she could help Jack."

Just then, an EMT hurried through the door carrying a large black bag. She was barely five feet tall, petite, and very young. She immediately knelt down next to Jack. The other adults in the room stepped back and let her have room to maneuver. Three uniformed men followed her, two of them rolling the stretcher.

"Mommy!"

Carrie handed the baby off to Logan before he had a chance to object. She got close enough so Jack could see her over the bodies of the strangers that must have looked so big to him. "I'm right here, Jack."

One of the EMTs spoke. "My name is Randy. I'm going to take good care of you. What's your name?"

"Jack. Do you drive the ambeelance?"

"Sometimes, but I didn't today." Randy was a tall, bald black man with a beautiful smile and kind eyes.

"How old are you?" Jack held up four fingers.

"What's your favorite color, Jack?"

"Purple."

"When we get to the hospital, be sure to ask for a purple cast."

"I get a cast? Cool."

"Can you be very brave for me for just a minute, Jack? This nice lady here has to give your arm just a little pinch, but it will help your leg feel better, okay? Maybe you should squeeze your teddy bear for just a minute."

"Ow! Randy, that hurt."

"I'm sorry, Jack, but that's her job. We make her do it so little kids don't get mad at me."

"Is she a doctor?"

"She's going to school to be a doctor. So this is like practice."

"She's pretty."

"I know, Jack. Believe me, I know." Randy addressed Carrie. "Ma'am, you'll be riding with us?"

Amy answered for her. "Yes, she will." She turned to Carrie. "No arguing. We'll be fine."

They lifted Jack very carefully. He looked at Logan carrying his sister, noticing Logan's Northwestern sweatshirt. "Go, Wildcats!" He sang out. "Bye, Logan. I'm riding in the ambeelance now with Randy and the pretty doctor. Come on, Mommy. Bye, Amy."

Amy and Logan stood in the doorway watching them squeeze into the elevator. Amy looked at Logan holding the baby. *Natural. He doesn't even know it,* she thought. Logan finally noticed her staring and handed the baby off to her as if it were on fire.

"Well, I think I'm gonna take off. I want to work on the desk for…"

"Oh, no you don't! Logan, you are not leaving me alone with this…this person…baby, whatever."

"*You* volunteered to babysit. How hard can it be?"

"Logan. Come back here. Logan. Didn't you just say you loved me?"

He stopped and walked back to her. "This is blackmail and you know it. I love you, yes. However, I didn't volunteer to participate in every harebrained scheme you dream up."

"Number one, I did not dream this up. I had a frantic neighbor at my door. You would have done the same thing. Number two, this is not harebrained. What does that mean, anyway? Number three…"

They heard crying from one of the bedrooms.

"Number three, I need you, Logan. She has a twin sister."

Logan stood in the hallway banging his head on the doorframe. *What next, Amy Sweet?* he thought.

They walked into Carrie and Jack's home. Amy held the baby out to Logan to take. He held his arms out to his sides. "I am not touching babies. Believe me, you don't want me touching babies."

"I do want you touching babies. I want you to either take this one, or go get the other one and find out why she's crying."

"I will help with other things, but I am not touching babies."

"Grow up, Logan. They don't bite." No sooner did she finish her sentence than the baby burped and spit most of her breakfast onto Amy's shirt. Logan laughed.

"You want to help, smart-ass? Go get me a clean shirt."

"Gladly. And don't say ass in front of the babies."

"Shut up, smart-ass."

Logan left and went back to Amy's place. He rummaged through her drawers, looking for the t-shirts that looked more appropriate for baby spew. He found one with a big sunflower on the front and another one with a mountain range across the chest with 'Grand Tetons' written below it. *Perfect,* he thought. He grabbed the blueberry muffins on his way out and headed back to the nightmare.

Logan walked in and the place was quiet. Amy was nowhere in sight.

"Amy?"

She didn't answer. He dropped the muffins on the kitchen counter and went searching. He walked into a nursery with two cribs. *Good grief,* he thought. This was terrifying. Amy saw him come in. She held her finger up to her lips and he knew better than to say a word. This wouldn't be too bad if they managed to sleep for the next six hours. Amy had wiped most of the baby puke off her shirt, but the room had a certain aroma to it. Each crib held one baby. There were now two quiet babies, hopefully asleep. Amy held something in her hand and tossed it to Logan. Instinct made him catch it. A diaper. It was heavy. That explained the aroma. He glared at her and she smiled. "You said you'd help. Would you rather hold a baby?"

"Don't goad me, Ms. Sweet." He held the diaper by a very small corner with thumb and forefinger. "What am I supposed to do with this? Flush it?"

"If you want to flush it, be prepared to come back and unclog Carrie's toilet. I suggest the garbage, but I'm not sure if she'd want it in the kitchen."

"This is disgusting. Who puts shit in their kitchen?"

"Don't say shit in front of the babies." Logan wanted to laugh, but this wasn't funny. Amy looked around the room and saw a wastepaper basket—obviously some kind of disposal apparatus for used diapers. She pointed and Logan made the deposit. "You can change the next one."

"No way." He tossed her a clean shirt. "Here. Put this on your Tetons."

Amy changed shirts and Logan went into the bathroom and scrubbed his hands. They met back in the living room and sat on the couch. Logan turned the TV on and Amy pulled the remote out of his hand. She turned the volume down so far he could barely hear it. "If you wake them up, you take care of them." He turned the TV off and laid his head on the back of the couch.

"I never would have dreamed that a few hours after eating Frosted Flakes and making love with a beautiful woman that I would be sitting in a stranger's house babysitting for twins."

"This is why it's futile to try to manipulate life, Logan. Shit happens. The unforeseen suddenly becomes reality."

"Well, aren't you deep?"

"You can kiss my ass, Logan—I know, don't say ass in front of the babies."

"I assume these babies have names."

"I don't know what they are. It's not like they'll come if you call them at this age. Whatever age this is, it probably doesn't matter what we call them, does it?"

"How about we call them Shit and Puke?"

"Because just when you get used to it, Shit will puke and Puke will shit. Then you'll be confused."

"Think Carrie would notice if we switched them around?"

Amy glared at him. "Have you seen them? How about Sweetie and Honey?"

"There's nothing about the smell of this place that would inspire me to call them either Sweetie or Honey. I say we eat a muffin and enjoy the peace and quiet and pray it continues."

Amy went to the kitchen, picked up two muffins and tossed one to Logan. He caught it just like he did the diaper.

"And by the way, stop throwing things at me. I almost stuck my thumb in that diaper. I'm allergic to toxic waste. You would have been sorry. You'd be responsible for two babies, and me having a reaction, needing mouth to mouth resuscitation."

"Stop whining." Amy walked over, sat on his lap and pulled the paper off her muffin. She broke off a piece and put it in his mouth.

"Mmm. Very good. More." He opened his mouth and she put in another chunk and ate a piece herself. She licked a crumb off his lip, his wonderful bottom lip. She kissed him softly, gently, without probing in search of blueberries. "More." She broke off another piece of muffin. He shook his head. "More kiss, please." She kissed him again. He encircled her with his arms and held her close. "I love being able to say 'I love you' right out loud."

"Me too." She kissed his ear and whispered, "I love you, Logan." She rested her forehead on his and looked at the love reflected in his eyes. Their reverie was suddenly interrupted by a baby crying.

"Oh shit."

"How do you know it isn't Puke?" Amy stood up to go check on the girls. Logan didn't move, but finished Amy's muffin and ate his as well.

It seemed to Amy that one of the problems with two babies sleeping in the same room is that if one cried, it woke up the other one. Twins may even have had a deeper connection, but the bottom line was there were two babies crying, and only one person willing to take care of them. Since Logan had said he would help, she decided that help he would.

"Logan, dear! I need you," she called out.

Logan stood begrudgingly and walked to the nursery. He stood in the doorway, not letting even one toe into the room. "What, darling?"

The cacophony was deafening. "I don't know what they want."

"Did you ask?"

"Yes, I did. This is their answer. I think they need to eat."

"Was Carrie nursing? You could do that. You did it so well last night."

"You may have made your last trip to the Grand Tetons, Buddy. Here are your choices: come over and take one of these babies, or go in the kitchen and look for appropriate food. Preferably baby bottles and something resembling formula or milk. It could be liquid or powdered." Logan left for the kitchen.

Amy picked up one baby and sniffed her. She smelled like a baby. She picked up the other one and sniffed her. She smelled okay too, so diapers probably weren't the issue this time. She carried both, one in each arm and walked into the living room. She sat in Carrie's recliner and rocked gently while saying sweet baby words to the girls. Logan listened from the kitchen.

"I'm sorry you sweet little things, that I don't know your names, and I'm sorry I'm not your mommy, but she had to go to the hospital with your big brother. He did some stupid boy thing like jump off the kitchen counter. Be careful around boys. You're never too young to learn this. They may be cute, but they're always trying to get into your pants. They talk real nice and then do stupid things. They smell bad and scratch their balls when they think you're not looking. Just a minute sweet girls, I have to check on your lunch. Logan!"

"I'll be there in a minute. I'm busy scratching my balls."

Amy heard the microwave timer beeping and was hoping Logan didn't just find leftover pizza to reheat for himself. He came into the living room with two baby bottles. Amy breathed a sigh of relief.

"Oh, thank goodness. Logan, you can take Sweetie Pie and I'll take Honey Bun."

"Amy, I told you, I can't do that." He handed her both bottles.

"Oh, right. Then just wait a minute while I pull out my two spare arms! Come on, Logan. It's a baby, not a Hell hound."

"It may as well be. Okay, but Amy, swear to God you will not let me do anything…fall asleep, pinch, anything, please. I'm serious. If something happens to this…"

"Sweetie Pie."

"If something happens to Sweetie Pie while she is in my custody, it is your fault. Do you understand? *Your* fault."

"Logan, you may get tired of me saying this, but we have to talk later about your irrational fear of the soft and cuddly."

Logan reached for a baby.

"That's Honey Bun. You take Sweetie Pie."

"What the hell's the difference?"

"Logan, no cussing in front of the babies!"

He rolled his eyes. The girls were fussing again. Amy and Logan sat side by side on the couch with Sweetie Pie and Honey Bun peacefully sucking away on the bottles. Logan followed Amy's lead.

"Logan, you're looking at me as if I know what I'm doing. This is a shot in the dark here, not instinct. This is what I've seen on TV. I'm faking it, really."

"You seem to be doing fine, so I'm right with you."

He leaned over and kissed her, his heart breaking inside.

Logan didn't take his eyes off Sweetie Pie. Amy watched Logan, trying to figure him out. That could take a lifetime. Amy stood up with Honey Bun and hurried to the kitchen. Logan panicked.

"What's wrong? Where are you going? Please come back here."

Amy came back with a roll of paper towels from the kitchen. "I have a feeling we're going to need these."

"Don't ever leave me alone again."

"Logan, you're doing fine. It seems to me there is some mandatory burping involved here." Amy held up her bottle and saw that it was about half gone. Logan did the same, although he didn't know what he was looking for.

Amy sat Honey Bun up on her lap. She noticed that formula had run down the baby's cheek, through the creases in her neck and had soaked into Amy's shirt. She took a paper towel and blotted up what she could. She tucked the paper towel into the creases of Honey Bun's neck. Logan copied her moves with Sweetie Pie. Her neck was dry and so was Logan. He wanted to gloat, but figured he'd be better off keeping his mouth shut. He made sure Amy noticed, though. Always believing in the preemptive strike, he took the time to tuck a paper towel around Sweetie Pie's neck, preparing for the second wave. Amy tore off another paper towel and handed it to Logan. She took one for herself and held it at the baby's mouth while she tapped her on the back. Logan did the same and was very quickly rewarded with a burp. Sweetie Pie flapped her arms and cooed and giggled for Logan. He grinned, but didn't say a word to Amy.

"Good girl, Sweetie Pie. More burps for Uncle Logan?"

"Puh-leez!"

"Aunt Amy is jealous." He patted and rubbed her back and she burped again. Logan laid her back down and gave her more formula. "They're kinda cute, aren't they?"

"Adorable." Amy patted a little harder and finally Honey Bun burped. Amy looked pleased until the burp was followed by a mouthful of the formula.

"Good thing you went for the paper towels."

"Shut up, Logan."

Both babies sucked the bottles dry and were ready for the second round of burping. Logan was feeling confident but wasn't taking any chances. He had a paper towel ready for any expulsions. What he wasn't expecting was the expulsion from the back end. Amy laughed.

"She farted on me."

"Not possible. Girls don't fart."

"Bullshit!"

"Logan, not in front of the babies."

"I'm telling you she farted on me."

"Then I suggest you be prepared for what follows."

"Oh, no! We're trading right now."

"No way. I already did diaper detail. The next one is yours."

Honey Bun burped. It was only air this time, and the infant snuggled up in Amy's arms. There was a peaceful feeling in holding this innocent life. She didn't ask to be born, yet here she was. Warm, sweet and trusting. For a moment she envied Carrie. Sweetie Pie burped and looked up at Logan as if she adored him.

"Why is she looking at me?"

"She's practicing flirting. She's using skills she'll need for the future."

"Like farting on my leg?"

"Like smiling for no good reason, making goo goo noises, batting her long lashes. Giggling at any dumbass thing you say."

"You do that now."

"I learned it when I was very young. Maybe if you're lucky, later I'll fart on your leg."

"I thought you said girls don't fart?"

"Dang. Caught me."

Logan looked down and Sweetie Pie had fallen asleep in his arms. "Amy, Amy, what's wrong with her?" Logan shook her arm and she woke up and cried.

"Logan, she fell asleep. She must have been very comfortable in your strong arms."

"Jesus Christ, Amy, I told you to watch her."

"She's just fine, Logan." Amy got down on the floor with Honey Bun. "Come on down and let them play for a while." Logan sat on the floor and he propped Sweetie Pie up between his knees.

"How old are they?"

"Well, I remember seeing them in the elevator with Carrie and Jack for the past few months. I'm not very good at judging the ages of babies. I'm sure they're less than a year. They can't really sit up without help, so, maybe four months? Maybe five?"

The two girls wiggled and cooed. Amy and Logan put them close enough to touch each other. They pulled at each other's fingers and touched each other's faces. Sweetie Pie leaned forward and farted again. Then her face turned red and she made grunting noises. Amy grabbed Honey Bun and moved back like something was about to explode.

"What? What's wrong?"

"Logan, I suggest you pick her up and take her into the nursery. There are supplies in there you're going to need."

"No...! Oh, no! I cannot do this, Amy. I really do have to leave now. This is your fault. These are your neighbors. You volunteered. I have to go."

"Logan! Quit whining and be a man."

He put his head in his hands. "No, I don't want to be a man. I can't do this." Then the aroma hit him. "I'm begging you."

"I'll go with you, but you are changing that diaper and anything else that gets tainted."

Amy stood up and took Honey Bun with her. Logan stood up and carried Sweetie Pie arm's length in front of him as if he had a project for the bomb squad. Amy pointed to the changing table. There were stacks of diapers and wipes.

"Oh, God. Please tell me I don't have to wipe."

"Of course you have to wipe. Were you planning to take her to the yard to hose her off?"

"Isn't there some kind of mask I have to wear, you know, for my protection?"

"Logan, it's poop. Just like yours—without the fiber. And a lot less of it, thank goodness. It washes off."

"You're enjoying this," he accused. "This is definitely some kind of cruel torture women like to impose on men. This is for all our sins of past centuries—for chastity belts and mammogram machines!"

"You're stalling, Logan."

"Of course I'm stalling. I'm hoping you show pity and do this for me."

"Not gonna happen. Unsnap the legs, take out the feet, and look before you stick your hand anywhere."

"You're heartless. You don't love me. You're trying to humiliate me. Do you want me to grovel?"

"No, I want you to get rid of that shitty diaper before it stinks up the place."

"Don't say shitty in front of the babies."

"Logan, my darling. I love you. Nothing is sexier than a man being nurturing, caring for the innocent, tending to the needs of…"

"Shut up, Amy. You're bugging me."

Logan followed her instructions. He unsnapped the legs of the little pink sleeper. He pulled Sweetie Pie's cute little pink feet out of her cute little pink…well, not so cute on the inside. He stopped and stared at Amy. She smiled but didn't speak.

"I don't know where to begin. Advice please."

"You told me to shut up."

Logan glared at her.

"Take the sleeper off and set it aside, poopy part in." Logan pulled her arms out and wiggled the sleeper out from under her, careful not to touch anything toxic. He laid her back down and she looked perfectly happy to have Logan changing her diaper.

"I'd suggest you look at a clean diaper, kind of figure out the mechanics of it because you'll have to work fast." Logan took a diaper from the stack and sniffed it. Amy laughed. It was pretty small, considering the amount of residue that had escaped the original one. "Open the wipes. There's no time to fiddle with latches or lids or anything." He opened the wipes, picked them up and sniffed them. Diapers closed with Velcro? He had no idea. Suddenly he felt old and out of the loop. He stood with his hands posed over the baby like a surgeon.

"What next?"

"Remove the offending item."

Logan whined. "Amy."

"Buck up, Carson, you can do this."

Logan made a face and unfastened both sides of the diaper. He stared.

"This is hideous. This is a package from hell. I have never in my entire life…"

"Remove the offending item."

"What the hell do they feed this child? They threw a burrito in the blender, didn't they? She drank a fucking burrito."

"Logan! We don't say…"

"Save it! Stand back."

"Logan, it's poop. It doesn't have a life force of its own. It will not spring itself out of the diaper and land on you."

"This is from outer space. Make sure those windows are locked."

"A burrito from outer space?"

"What next, please?"

"Well, grab a clean spot if there is one." She was trying so hard not to laugh. "You'll probably have more luck toward the front. And just pull it forward, grabbing as much of the poop as you can."

"There has to be a place in heaven for me."

"You'll die of old age before you get this diaper changed."

He glared again.

"Sorry. I'd just kind of tuck the worst part inside and hope for the best. Then you better start wiping fast. You don't want it to dry on there or you'll have a heck of a time scrubbing it off."

"There's shit in every crack and crevice, every crease and fold. How the hell did she do this? This isn't normal. It's half way up her back and she's enjoying it. She's oblivious to the danger we're in here." Logan grabbed a wipe. Then another, and stacked them on top of each other. "I think I need rubber gloves."

"Wipe…and be gentle. This is not her fault," Amy coached.

"No…that's right. It's yours!" Logan wiped fast and furiously. He grabbed two more wipes, moved legs and wiped more. Two more wipes for her back. "Unbelievable." Logan had a stack of about twelve wipes piled on top of the diaper. Amy held the lid of the toxic waste receptacle and Logan made the deposit. Sweetie Pie was naked, happy and cooing. She was holding her foot and sucking on her toes. Logan quickly slipped the clean diaper under her and fastened it tight. Amy handed him a clean sleeper. He put it on her in the opposite order of the one he removed. Carrie was going to have to deal with that when she got home. Logan held her up and looked at her. "Do you hate me? Never again, Sweetie Pie. Do you understand me? Save that for your mother." She gurgled, flapped her arms and kicked her feet. "Da."

Logan looked at Amy. "This is killing me."

The doorbell rang as they walked toward the living room. Amy looked through the peephole and cautiously opened the door.

"Are you Amy?"

"Yes. And you are…?"

"I'm Carrie's mother, Virginia. She called me to come and relieve you." Virginia sniffed the air. "Poopy diaper?"

"Oh, yeah."

"Well, here's her cell phone number. She wants you to call her in the next ten minutes because she'll be in the waiting room where she can use her cell phone. She didn't want to call here for fear of waking the babies."

Amy called and Carrie answered on the first ring. They chatted for a few minutes and Amy hung up.

"Jack will be fine. He's spending the night and will get his purple cast tomorrow. She said thanks for helping out." Logan grunted. "By the way, Virginia, what are the girls' names?"

"Nora and Dora. I still can't tell them apart, though. Carrie can, so that's all that counts."

"Okay, Virginia, we have to go. Thanks for relieving us. Have Carrie stop by when Jack gets home." Amy grabbed her shirts and the remaining muffins, and they headed out the door.

CHAPTER 33

She and Logan arrived at her condo and as soon as the door closed they started laughing. "Nora and Dora? Those poor kids!"

"I like Sweetie Pie and Honey Bun. And I like you, Logan Carson. You did a good thing today. You survived to tell about it. I'm very proud of you."

Logan walked right past her to the bathroom. "I have to scrub with antibacterial soap. This will take me a while."

"I'll never hear the end of this, will I?"

"No."

Amy sat at the kitchen table and waited for Logan to scrub up. She was getting hungry. Breakfast was burned off long ago and lunch never happened. She reached into her junk drawer and found a chocolate bar. She unwrapped it, broke it into squares, and set it on the table. She put a piece in her mouth and let it melt while she folded her arms on the table and rested her head on her arms. She was tired: lack of sleep, lack of food, tussling with twins...tussling with Logan...A nap would be good.

Logan walked back into the kitchen. He stepped behind Amy's chair and started rubbing her shoulders. She moaned and went limp under his strong fingers.

"You'll be a terrific mother some day."

"Maybe."

"You were great with the girls, Amy."

"You were, too. Logan, you looked so natural holding Sweetie Pie."

"I was supervised. It won't happen again. Want to go out for pizza?"

"No, but we can order in." The door opened a crack and Gibby stuck her head in.

"Ames, you decent?"

Logan looked up. "Hi, there. I'm Logan." He walked toward her with his hand out and shook it. "Margaret, right?"

"We met in the hall. You finally letting Amy come up for air? And call me Gibby, please. The only one who calls me Margaret is my mother."

"Well, Gibby, it's good to meet you. And yes, Amy came up for air long ago. We just got back from a mission of mercy that probably would have been yours if you would have been home at the time of the catastrophe."

"What's he talking about, Amy?"

"Jack."

"Cute little Jack from down the hall?"

"Yeah." Her head was still on the table. "He broke his leg, the ambulance came, and Carrie went with him to the hospital. She was knocking on your door for help for Jack, but there was no answer. So, we babysat for Sweetie Pie and Honey Bun."

"You mean Nora and Dora? Aren't they adorable?"

"Gibby, Amy and I were just going to order pizza, want to join us?"

Amy groaned. *Let the grilling begin. Poor guy,* she thought. "Is Beth home? May as well let her know, too."

"Sounds like fun. I'll go get her. And by the way, Ames, you look exhausted."

Logan grinned. "Where do you order from?"

Amy pointed to a drawer. It was filled with carryout menus. Logan flipped through and pulled out three for pizza. He'd let Gibby and Beth choose and clean up whatever was left.

Gibby came back with Beth following her. "Beth, this is Logan, Amy's boss, client, friend."

"Lover."

Amy groaned. Logan smiled. "Why mince words? Hi, Beth. How are you?"

"I'm just fine, Logan. I understand you had a busy afternoon."

"Yes, we did. Never would I have dreamed this morning over my Frosted Flakes that I'd be changing shitty diapers from twins that I didn't know existed."

"You make it sound like you did so much more than you did. You changed one, Logan. I changed one. And I'm the one who got puked on, not you."

"That's because I burped better."

"I'm not the one with the dreaded fear of poop."

"I wasn't afraid, I was repulsed."

"Logan, have you ever looked in the toilet when you're finished?"

Gibby broke in. "Do we need to be here for this conversation? Because really, if you guys need private time to discuss bowel movements we can step outside."

"Thank you, Gibby, for bringing us back into the present. I want pizza. I don't care what's on it as long as the crust is thin. I don't care where it comes from as long as I don't have to go get it. There's a ten-dollar bill on my dresser. It's coming from my underwear fund. Throw that into the pot and let's get this thing going. I'm starved."

"My treat. Amy, stand up please. I have a favor to ask," Logan said. Amy stood up. Logan turned her around to face him. "Your friends think you don't like me and I know different. Can we show them?"

Amy stepped into his arms, hugged him around the neck and let his kiss rattle her to her toes. "I love you, Logan."

"I love you too, Sweet. Would a shower help? A butt massage?"

Amy laughed. "Logan, you're so good to me. I need food."

Beth was smiling as she browsed the pizza menus. Gibby still had reservations. Amy seemed happy, but did she know the whole story?

Gibby called and ordered pizza. Between both their refrigerators they had enough beer to wash down dinner. They sat around the kitchen table waiting for pizza and got the details of Jack's accident.

"Amy, I'm shopping for him tomorrow, picking up some Wildcat stuff from Northwestern. Can you drop it off for me?"

"Logan, he'll love it! It will match his purple cast."

Gibby asked, "Where did they take him?"

"I'm sure they took him to St. Mary's; it's the closest."

"Then I'll stop in and check on him tomorrow. Hopefully I'll catch him before he leaves. Was Carrie spending the night with him?"

"Yeah, her mom is taking care of the babies."

Amy decided to change the subject. "Beth, is the big date with Terry still on? St. Louis, right?"

"Oh, gosh! I'm so nervous. Yes, the weekend is still on. We're staying at the Mayfair. Separate rooms, of course, since we're not married. Not that I'm being judgmental, Logan, but this is just the way I have to do it, and Terry agrees. Of course who knows…it's not like my virginity is at stake here."

"Beth, I have a friend who's a manager there. He owes me a favor. How about if I give him a call and get you a free upgrade. A suite, maybe? A better view?" Logan said.

"Why Logan, that would be very nice of you! Just surprise us. I won't tell Terry. I don't know why I'm so nervous about it."

Amy answered her. "You're nervous because there's the possibility that he may just come knocking on your door. And you're nervous because you just may let him in."

"I suppose that's true. And the Lord would not strike us down or turn me into a pillar of salt, but I'd like to wait."

"You have to do what feels right. Good luck to you, Beth. I hope you find happiness like I've found with Amy. I thought I used up my one and only chance for love, then this peculiar woman shows up wanting to paint my house," Logan said.

"She's a treasure, Logan. You be good to her or you'll have to deal with us. Right Gibbs?"

"Right. She doesn't ask for much...honesty, faithfulness, respect..."

"Hello! I am still in the room, you know. And thanks for looking out for me, but Logan knows exactly what I want and need." Logan looked at her and winked. Amy stood up, took four glasses from the cabinet, poured beer and walked to the laundry room to turn on the washer.

Beth picked up the conversation. "Logan, I understand you own your own company and are responsible for some of the gazebos I see around town."

"Yes, that's right. My favorite is the big one in the park about three blocks east."

"Logan, I didn't know that was yours. It's beautiful," Amy said.

"Amy, isn't that the one where you and Crane were making out and the police chased you out?"

Logan gave her a puzzled look. "Please, tell me more."

"I think the police were afraid we were going to get mugged. It was very late and not very well lit."

"Aren't you a little old to be making out in public?"

"Well, Logan, I'd say we were just swept away by the moment. It wouldn't have mattered where we were. Of course, that's long before he got his new girlfriend pregnant, pig that she is, I'm sure. Actually he did me a big favor. Logan, do you think I should send him flowers and a thank-you note?"

"I think *I* should. If I ever meet him, I'll have to shake his hand and thank him. And maybe we should send flowers to your old boss. If it wasn't for him I don't know how I ever would have met you."

The doorbell rang and Logan took out his wallet. Amy and Beth cleared the table and Gibby passed out napkins.

"I'm starved, but we're going to pray over this pizza. Logan, hope you don't mind."

"Not at all. Do you want me to pray?"

"Logan, Beth normally does that." Amy was trying to save him.

"I think it would be nice to hear a voice besides mine raised to the Lord. Go ahead, Logan." He folded his hands in his lap then noticed that the other three were holding hands. Amy and Gibby both reached out to him. He took their hands.

"Lord, we give you thanks for this nourishment and bless those who prepared it. Be with Carrie today as she worries about her children. Lay your healing hand on Jack and bestow your blessings on Randy and the others in the ambulance. Bless Beth and Terry as they struggle with their futures. Bless Margaret in her work. And, Gracious God, I give you thanks for Amy, a true blessing to me. We ask this in Jesus's name. Amen."

"Thank you, Logan. That was very nice. Amy, you didn't tell us you fell for a religious man."

"I didn't know I did."

Logan kissed the back of her hand and winked at her.

"Can we eat now?"

They finished the pizza and the beer. Beth and Gibby left shortly thereafter. Logan and Amy sat at opposite ends of the couch and looked at each other.

"Do you think they liked me?"

"The prayer was a bit much."

"I'm crushed! That was from the heart and I was very sincere."

"I know, I'm teasing you. Beth loves you, I'm sure. Gibby is just very cautious…with everyone. She sees so much bad stuff in her job that it just makes her question everything."

"I'm glad she's looking out for you. Did she like Crane?"

"No. She told me she thought we would have broken up within two or three months even if he wouldn't have dumped me when he did."

"Funny how she saw it coming and you didn't."

"That's what's weird. I did see it coming, but no one could have convinced me of it at the time. I just didn't want to admit failure."

"Amy, you didn't fail. He failed you. And I'm so glad he did."

He motioned for her to sit next to him and she did. She leaned against him and he put his arm around her and held her close. He kissed the top of her head and she patted his belly.

"Full?"

"Stuffed. Pizza was good. Did you get enough?"

"I don't have much room when I drink beer. I'm good. At least I woke up. I just crashed when we got back from Carrie's."

"I don't know how she does it. Jack must help. She has to be exhausted by the end of the day."

"But that isn't the end. If they wake up during the night, she's right back at it. I wonder where the dad is in all this. I never see him around. I don't know if he's living or dead."

"Well, I give her a lot of credit. She seems to have her act together—as long as her children don't go jumping off the counter."

"Logan?"

"Hmm?"

"Thank you."

"For what?"

"For the day. The incredible breakfast."

"My pleasure."

"For helping with the babies."

"Never again."

She smiled. "For the beautiful prayer."

"Amen."

"For loving me."

"Always. You're my second chance. My sweet second chance. I love you, Amy Sue Sweet."

"Logan, what's your middle name?"

"Merle."

"Logan Merle Carson. Good grief. What did you do to piss your parents off before you were born?"

"Touché!" He pushed her away, pulled her Grand Teton shirt up and blew raspberries into her belly. She laughed and wrestled him but he was too strong.

Threats were her only option.

"Logan, I'm gonna puke if you don't stop that right this minute."

"I can no longer be threatened with toxic waste. I've been to hell and back and lived to tell the tale."

She ran her knee up to his crotch and gently pushed.

"Okay, you got my attention." He pulled her shirt down and smoothed it out. He let her up and kissed her until she went weak in his arms. "I hate to do this to you, Sugar, but I have to get up early tomorrow, and I have spent the whole day here in your wonderful presence. Not that I haven't enjoyed it, but if I don't leave here now I'll have to spend the night again and make love to you until you can't walk. Then my house won't get painted, and I won't be able to give you a good reference for your next job. Then you'll be on welfare…"

"Stop. Please. I know next you'll be blaming me for your taxes being increased. Go home, Logan. I need sleep."

He pulled her to her feet. "I have to get my stuff together, want to help me?"

"Sure. I think I can face the scene of the crime."

They walked back into her room. Amy threw the sheets into the dryer and helped Logan gather up his clothes that were tossed here and there. She noticed he still had her black panties in his shirt pocket. She left them there.

"The bed looks good."

"Go home, Logan."

She walked him to the door. He took her in his arms and hugged her until she couldn't breathe. "I really do thank God for you, Amy Sweet. You're a treasure."

"Love you, Logan."

She locked the door behind him, went to her room, threw a blanket over the bed, lay down and fell asleep.

CHAPTER 34

A my woke up to the sound of a garbage truck making its Monday-morning rounds. She looked at the clock and groaned. If she skipped breakfast she'd have just enough time to shower and stop in to give an estimate for her second painting job. Wisely, neither Beth nor Gibby disturbed her the previous night or before they left for work. She sat up on the edge of the bed, still wearing her clothes from the day before. She showered and made herself presentable. It's not that she didn't care if she got another job right away or not, she just didn't feel the pressure, since she wanted to finish Logan's place and he had certainly been generous with paying her. She grabbed the page of instructions she got from the man on the phone and headed out.

Rush-hour traffic had pretty much dissipated. She had a forty-five-minute ride from her place. She found the house without trouble. The outside really needed paint, but that was something she would not do on her own. She rang the bell and a tired looking mother answered the door with a baby boy bouncing on her hip. He was drinking some kind of fruit juice and was having a good time spitting it everywhere. Amy stood back. *Two days in a row I have to dodge baby spew?* she thought. It was a simple assignment. Two bedrooms needed painting and a few holes from hanging pictures needed to be filled. Amy thought she could do it in two days. She was ready to overcharge for her services until she realized that the family probably didn't have an overabundance of money. She turned in a sensible bid and left her phone number.

She wasn't going to work at Logan's that day, but she was going to pick up the rest of the paint, drop it off, and leave a note for him. She bought more primer and the blue paint for his room. She wouldn't dream of redoing the nursery. Besides, the room really didn't need it. It was very cute, though a little on the feminine side. She wondered if they had known the sex of the baby.

Amy realized that she could be done with Logan's house by the end of the week if she really applied herself. She had to keep reminding herself that just because she finished the house didn't mean she wouldn't be seeing Logan. They'd just have to plan more, like normal people did. She used her key and went in through the back door as usual. She carried four cans of paint and would be making a second trip to the van for the rest.

There was a note on the counter from Logan.

Amy,
I'll be stopping at Northwestern as I mentioned and will leave a little present here for Jack. Deliver please.
I will be out of town on business for a while, will give more details tomorrow.
I'll be late.
L

Amy carried the paint up to Logan's room. There were two huge suitcases and a garment bag on his bed. It seemed a bit much for a business trip, but he said he'd be leaving details, so she wasn't going to worry about it. She went to her van and carried in the rest of the paint. Before leaving, as usual, she would answer his note.

Logan,
Sorry I missed you.
Put in a bid on another paint job—two days at the most.
No painting today. Dropped off the rest of what I'll need and can probably be done by the end of the week.
I'll be glad to drop off something for Jack. He comes home tomorrow.
Will I see you before you go? Hope so!
ASS

Amy locked up and left.

When she got home she ran into Virginia with the twins in the elevator. They had just come from the park. Their cheeks were rosy and they looked very cute in their pink fluffy jackets and hats. Virginia told her that she would be staying on a day or two with Carrie until they discovered just how much extra work Jack was going to be with his leg in a cast.

Amy had the rest of the day to herself. She read the newspaper, finished laundry, finished dishes from dinner with Logan and pizza with the girls. She cleaned the bathroom and baked cookies for Jack. She realized she was just going through the motions, keeping busy to keep from thinking about Logan. She had some decisions to make.

Maybe it was time for a meeting with the girls. Maybe she'd just think about it herself for a while first, sort things out a bit and decide what she realistically wanted in her future.

She knew several things for sure. Sam's pregnancy had come to a bad end. Logan was determined not to be a father after that. Obviously, or he wouldn't have had the vasectomy. Logan blamed himself for Sam's death because it was his baby that killed her. Therefore, if he made no one pregnant, he wouldn't kill anyone else…anyone innocent. Maybe Sam didn't want to be pregnant…that would make her innocent. His thinking was rather convoluted, but she thought she understood it.

So, her job was to convince Logan that she was very healthy and would probably be perfectly able to carry a baby to full term…at least one…maybe more. She had to convince him he would be an excellent father. She had seen him with the twins. There was a soft spot in his heart that they had touched. She had to convince him that adopting or other options were available and okay with her.

Or she had to let him know she would take him as he was—with or without babies. Because she loved him. But did she love him enough to give up her dreams?

*

She had expected a call from Logan, but it never came. She assumed she'd see him at the house since she was leaving very early.

She let herself in the back door. The coffee was on but Logan was gone. His usual note was on the counter.

Amy,

Let me know if I have to do anything before I leave.

I'll be at the airport tomorrow at 6 a.m. Sorry, won't be able to see you before I go.

I'm taking a lot of work with me and will be late tonight.

I called the hotel for Beth. I think they'll be surprised.

Package for Jack on kitchen table. Thanks for delivering.

Love,

Logan

Well, that was something at least...*love, Logan.* She wanted to see him, but obviously that wasn't happening. She finished several small projects, which left only Logan's room. He would not be in the mood to move furniture after working late, but it had to be done. She grabbed pen and paper and responded to his note.

Logan,

Your room is next. Finally.

Can you move the furniture to the center of the room for me? Thanks.

Thanks also for taking care of Beth. Anxious for details on their weekend!

Will drop off Jack's gift. That was nice of you!

Call if you have time. Would like to chat a minute before you go.

By the way, where are you going?

Love,

Amy

ps: miss you

*

That evening, Amy took Jack's gift—a bag chock full of Northwestern University stuff—down the hall. Logan had only met him for about ten minutes. Clearly the man was a soft touch. He could have vasectomies until the cows came home, and she would never be convinced that he didn't want to be a father. Logan Carson was a mystery she wanted to solve.

Jack did indeed have a purple cast. It was signed by Randy, Jack's doctors, and several nurses, including Gibby. Amy picked up the marker to sign. "Get well soon, Amy and Logan" would have to do.

Jack enjoyed the gift from Logan. He dug through the bag and pulled out a purple and white Wildcat football, a purple sweatshirt like the one Logan had on the day Jack got hurt, and two t-shirts that were much too small for Jack. They were pink NU shirts for the twins! Amy almost cried. God, she loved that man. On the bottom was a book about a boy in a cast and how he got people to sign it. Perfect. Jack told Amy that his mom would help him write a thank-you note to Logan.

*

Amy was asleep when the phone rang. It was Logan. He sounded tired.

"Hey, Sweet. Were you sleeping?"

"Sort of. But it's good to hear your voice. I miss you."

"Something came up rather quickly and I have to go to California."

"Will you get to see your brother while you're there?"

"Probably. It would be a shame to go all that way and not see him."

"Do you have a ride to the airport?"

"I'm taking a limo. I don't want to be bothered with remote parking and it's too early to ask a friend to take me."

"I wouldn't mind. Really. It would be nice to see you before you go."

"No, really. My flight leaves at 6 a.m. I'll be getting about four hours of sleep and won't be fit company for anyone. I moved the bed and stuff so you'll be able to get to the walls."

"Logan, are you okay?"

"I'm fine, just dead-dog tired. I'm headed for bed. Just wanted to say bye. I'll leave you a note for tomorrow morning."

"When are you coming home?"

"Not sure.

"Jack loved your gift, by the way. I signed his cast for you."

"Great. He's a cute kid."

"And Logan, the pink t-shirts for the girls..."

"I gotta go, Amy. Love you."

"I love you, Logan. Bye.

"Bye."

Logan hung up and Amy's heart ached. She wasn't sure why.

CHAPTER 35

L ogan's limo dropped him at the United terminal at O'Hare before dawn, in plenty of time for processing and security issues. He was operating on about three hours of sleep, partly because he felt awful about the way he treated Amy on the phone. His intention was not to call her before he left, just leave her his email address. What he really wanted to do was drive to her place and kiss her into oblivion, beg for forgiveness for being an ass, dump his whole load of a nightmare into her lap and hope for the best. In reality, what he was doing was running away, sort of, but not really. At least he could justify it several ways. He hadn't seen Bo in a while. He needed a break from work. Anything pressing he could handle on the computer and through email in California. He had some priorities to set and some decisions to make. Amy was just too much of a distraction—albeit a good one. One that he enjoyed indulging.

Autumn in California was not like autumn in Chicago. Chicago's wind had pretty much stripped the trees of the last of their colorful leaves. The nip in the wind was sharp enough to make a jacket as useless as shirtsleeves. Winter coats and hats had started appearing, and Chicagoans had picked up the pace of their normal brisk strides along the city sidewalks. Logan stepped outside the terminal and found himself enjoying the perennial green surroundings and perfect eighty-degree weather. Southern California had its charms, to be sure, but before long Logan would be bored with it and longing for home and the seasonal changes. At the moment, however, the distance and the climate was just what he needed.

Logan was sitting on his largest suitcase waiting at the curb for Bo, who was, as usual, right on time. Bo picked up his brother in a black Mercedes, which was just two years newer than Logan's. The brothers had bought them from Sam, who had gotten a very good deal from a collector. Bo, living so far south, drove his year-round. Logan, on the other hand, kept his in the garage during the fierce Chicago winters.

Because of parking restrictions, Bo barely had a chance to slow down long enough for Logan to open the back door and toss in his luggage. Logan climbed into the front seat and stretched out, groaning from lack of sleep and from traveling thousands of miles belted into an airplane seat.

"Bo, you look great."

"You look like shit. How was the flight?"

"I sat next to a Puerto Rican man whose wife doesn't believe in eating airline food, so she packed him a cooler of homemade island delights."

"That could be good or bad."

"It was good for about ten minutes because it was still warm and smelled great. Then it got disgusting. He ate the entire trip."

"Did you want to stop for breakfast?"

"Not really, unless you do. I just need sleep. Then I need an ear and some advice."

"This has Sweet written all over it."

"And then some. Will Ginny be home?"

"She can barely walk. She'll be home. Word of caution…do *not* make fun of her fat ankles. No kidding—they *are* fat, man. She's a little sensitive about it. The doc told her they'd go back to normal after the baby's born, but she doesn't believe her. They look funny and when she's in a really good mood I can get away with poking fun, but if she's crabby…her latest favorite mood…I steer clear of the subject."

"Got it. Skip the fat ankle jokes. Other than that, how's she feeling?"

"She feels great. She's never taken better care of herself. It's just that being huge is wearing her down."

"I remember those days."

"Are you sure this was a good time for you to come out here. I mean with the baby due in a week or so?"

"Bo, I had to do something. Really, the baby has nothing to do with it. I'm between a rock and a hard place here with Amy. She knows pretty much all of the story and hasn't walked out on me yet."

"If she loves you she won't walk."

"She says she does."

"Then she's a keeper."

"I even acted like an asshole last night on purpose, just to give her an out if she wanted one. She's being so understanding. I feel like a first-class turd."

"Well, if you're going to be a turd, first class is the way to go."

"She wants a family, Bo."

"And therein lies the rub."

"You know I can't go through that again. I won't."

"So she knows how Sam died."

"Sort of. She asked me, then sort of answered herself. I never bothered to correct her. She knows Sam died in the hospital, but assumed it was complications from the pregnancy, miscarriage or something like that."

"Or something. Think she could handle the truth?"

"Better than I could handle telling her. No, that's not fair. I had a bad day, ended up in the nursery crying my eyes out and being pissed off at Sam for leaving me…you know, normal reaction to falling in love. Amy was supposed to come over to paint, but I called her and told her not to come over, that I was having a bad day and our plans would be postponed for a day."

"You should know better. Females can't stay away when a male needs nursemaid detail. It's a DNA thing. You waved the red flag in front of her face, and she came running, right?"

"I'll give her credit. She waited a while and brought supper with her. I was never so glad to see anyone in my life. She was like the life raft in my sea of self-pity. Of course, then she saw the nursery, and it opened a whole new batch of questions."

"Did you lie to her?"

"No, I just assured her that when I could talk about it, I would. Bo, she has been great through all of this."

"You need to call her to let her know you got in okay."

"No. I'm not going to call her."

"Is this a test?"

"What do you mean?"

"A test to see how far you can push her away before she stops loving you?"

"Maybe."

Logan laid his head back, closed his eyes and slept the rest of the way to Bo's.

*

Bo pulled into the driveway and Ginny came out in her bathrobe and slippers. Logan tried not to look at her ankles.

"Logan! I'm so glad to see you…you look like crap, honey. Bad flight?"

"Bad flight, bad night, but it's great to see you."

Ginny hugged him the best she could with her belly sticking out so far.

"Logan, thank you so much for the rocker. It's beautiful! And so comfortable. I'll treasure it forever. I hope to have several babies to rock to sleep. I may even let Bo sit in it now and then."

"How many are several? When were you going to let me in on these plans, dear?" Bo teased.

Logan grabbed the biggest suitcase, while Bo carried the other two pieces of luggage into the house. He directed Logan to the guest room, where he'd be staying—for an undetermined amount of time.

"I want you guys to promise to throw me out of here if you get sick of me. I appreciate the room, but I don't know yet how long I'll be here. I can go to a hotel, no problem."

Ginny put her finger over his lips. "Now you listen to me, Logan. You're welcome to stay as long as you need to. We have a huge house and your room is at the farthest end of it, so there may be days we don't even see you!"

"Seriously, Logan, you can work, lie around in the sun, shop, visit the homes of the stars, whatever. I would suggest you call Amy. There's a phone in your room."

"Don't start. I need sleep before I do anything. Thanks. Wake me up around noon if you think of it."

Logan closed the door, unpacked, stripped, and was snoring within minutes.

CHAPTER 36

Amy was in no hurry to get to Logan's because she knew he would not be there. Even on days when she didn't see him, anticipating the possibility of seeing him gave her a good feeling. She let herself in the back door and saw a yellow legal pad on the counter. This was not Logan's usual scrap-of-paper note.

> *Amy,*
>
> *Sorry I didn't get to see you before I left. I had a lot to do and it was late, but I'm glad I called.*
>
> *I'm not sure when I'll be home, so take your time with the house. I'm leaving you a check (under the pad). I'm including a little extra because I want you to paint the nursery white.*
>
> *Keep the key until I get back.*
>
> *I'll check email regularly if you need to write.*
>
> *If there's an emergency at the house, call CC and ask for Matt. He can be there in a few minutes.*
>
> *L*

"What an ass! Did I imagine Saturday night and Sunday morning? Was it a dream? Was he even there?" She vented aloud.

She was mad. She was crushed. She was hurt. But mostly she was mad. If Logan had walked through the door that moment, he would have seen the nasty side of a woman scorned. In her present mood, she'd be dangerous with a roller. She took the check, left Logan's and went to the bank. On her way home she picked up six warm Krispy Kreme donuts, inhaled three of them in the car and snarfed the rest when the coffee was brewed.

Back at home, the mental monologue continued as she folded laundry.

Email him if I need to write? Why would I need to write? she thought. *Was he too tired to dip into his vocabulary for a better word? Something's going on, and it definitely isn't all about work. Bo. Maybe he went to see Bo. Work-related trip to California? Please! He doesn't have the balls to break it off with me, that's all. Well, I am not doing his dirty work for him.*

Amy went to her computer. She wrote to Hillie, Beth and Gibby.

Dear Personal Crisis Line:

I need an intervention. We need to meet soon.

Bring your tenderest hearts and your stiffest spines. We'll need both.

Pick a place.

Let me know ASAP.

Amy

Within twenty minutes she had a message from Hillie.

I'll come down tonite. Feed me. I don't have time to stop for food. Rattle the cage next door for Beth and Gibby. 7 or so?

Love, Hillie

Perfect. Amy ran to the bakery and bought a beautiful baguette. Her next stop was the deli. She bought chicken vegetable soup. Her mother wouldn't approve. Fortunately, her mother wasn't invited. Amy's day was a seesaw of emotions. One minute she missed Logan, the next, she was angry enough to clobber him, then she'd feel guilty about picking on a widower with a broken heart. She was determined not to make the first move, unless that was the decision of the foursome tonight, whether it be email or phone call. *Phone call! I don't even know where to call him!* she thought.

Amy was not surprised that Punkin was the first to arrive.

"Where's your keeper, fur ball?"

Beth answered, "I'm close behind. What's for supper?"

"Bread and soup."

"Perfect supper for a chilly evening. No one else here yet?"

"I thought Gibby was with you."

"I think she went out for a paper. When will Hillie get here?"

Amy checked her watch. "She said about seven, so ten minutes or so. Have a seat. Everything's done, thanks to the deli and the bakery."

"Aren't you glad that there are people who like to cook for a living?"

"No kidding. Have you heard from Terry?"

"Yes. He said he had a surprise about our rooms for the weekend. I think Logan had a hand in that, but Terry wouldn't give me any details."

"Logan just mentioned that he arranged something. I didn't get details either. About anything."

Gibby and Hillie arrived together. "Don't tell me you started the party without us!"

"No, Hillie, just warming up. Come on in and have a seat. Soup will be ready in a couple minutes. So, here's my plan. I'll tell you what my dilemma is, then we eat and think. Discussion follows over Frango Mints."

"So dinner will be quiet?"

"No, Gibbs, dinner doesn't need to be quiet, but I don't want to discuss Logan while I'm eating."

Hillie asked, "Does it matter that I haven't even met him yet?"

"I think you'll have thoughts about the whole thing even without having met him. But feel free to ask and I'll fill in the blanks for you. Ready?"

"First of all, I love Logan. He says he loves me. His wife died due to some kind of complications with a pregnancy, so, the natural reaction of the father would be to blame himself. The natural response to accepting that blame would be to go out and have a vasectomy so you could never again harm another person you care about. I would like a future with Logan, and we discussed that just a little bit. I want children, so you see the dilemma. The next part of this whole thing is two days after we 'screw like minks'—and those are his words, not mine—he goes on a 'business' trip to California for an unknown length of time. He leaves me an email address, but no phone number. He pays me in full for the work I've done in his house, plus a little extra to paint the nursery white."

This last comment raised some eyebrows, but no one spoke.

"I'm mad as hell. I'm hurt. I feel sorry for him. I'm afraid that this is his way of breaking things off. I need a little direction here, that's all. Now, let's eat."

No one said a word as they gathered around the table. They automatically held hands and looked to Beth.

"You know, one of these days somebody else here is gonna have to learn to pray. Lord, thank you for this food. May it be a blessing to our bodies. Be with your child Logan as he struggles with some issues. Guide his decisions to live so that your will is done. And Lord, protect Amy's heart. Amen."

Amy sniffled, wiped her eyes and passed the basket of bread. "Thanks."

Gibby stood up and ladled soup into everyone's bowls. Beth talked about her upcoming weekend with Terry. Hillie talked about developing better balance through her Tai Chi classes. Gibby told about a baby born today that was number seven and the whole family was there to watch the big event. Amy told the story about Jack falling, the ambulance crew, and babysitting for the twins, an event that may have helped push Logan over the edge. Dinner conversation was rather benign and that's just how Amy wanted it. They finished eating and settled in the living room around the coffee table.

Amy started. "So. I guess I want a little direction. If we could just throw out a few ideas…because, guys, I'm really flip-flopping on this."

Hillie guessed, "But I bet you know how you want it to end. Maybe we should start there and work backwards to the present. So, where would you like this Logan thing to take you?"

Amy thought a minute. "Long-term, absolutely most optimistic as possible? I'd marry him if he asked me. I'd like a family."

"Well…Not as easy as I thought it would be."

The next suggestion came from Gibby. "Maybe we need to find out why he's really in California. Is it possible that he really and truly is there for business? Plus, doesn't he have some family there?"

"Yes, his brother, Bo."

"So maybe there's just a little bit of running scared mixed in with this business trip."

"That's possible."

Normally Hillie was the most level-headed sensible person, but tonight it appeared to be Beth. "Ames, this whole thing has happened kind of fast. If you think about it, how many people you know fall in love fast and furious in just five weeks?"

"You mean besides you and Terry?"

"Boy, I walked right into that one, didn't I? Keep in mind Logan went from grieving a wife that he thinks he killed, to falling in love—something he didn't plan on doing again in his life. You may have seen a future with him on the horizon, but it sounds like you hit him like a ton of bricks. Maybe he just has some serious sorting out to do."

"We talked a lot. I thought he had things sorted out. Besides, he should have sorted before he slept with me."

"Who slept with who here, Ames? Or is it whom? Seems to me I remember a list. You wanted it for a while, so I'd say that one's a tie. No points or penalties for either side."

Gibby sighed and reluctantly voiced her thoughts. "Amy, you know because of my job at the hospital, since I was there when Sam died, that I can't talk about some of the confidential stuff. That being said, I think you need to do a little research. You and Hillie were on the right track when you checked out his past. The whole business about the factory fire and stuff helped get conversations going and filled in some blanks."

"Yeah, it did, but I just felt like I was prying."

"And maybe you were, but if he's putting his you-know-what you-know-where, that gives you some rights. One of those rights is to know a little of his history. Granted, he has shared a lot with you considering the amount of time he's known you. And the stuff he has shared has been tough for him. But men in their thirties just don't go out and get vasectomies because their wives miscarried."

"But Gibby, she died."

"I'm aware of that. I'm saying, there could be more."

Beth spoke up. "Maybe there's a genetic reason, something in his DNA that caused it. Maybe he just doesn't want to spread any more of his tainted sperm around."

"Gross."

Hillie asked, "So, you just want us to tell you if you should email him first or wait for him to email you?"

"Well, sort of. I want to real bad, but his note was so curt…almost like 'email me if there is a catastrophe, otherwise, see ya when I finally decide to haul my sorry ass home.'"

"Let's try this. What would you say, if you were to write to him first."

Beth groaned. "Do I have to take notes?"

"No, I think Amy will be able to remember this. So, it starts, 'Dear Logan.'"

Amy buried her head in her hands. "Ugh! This is hard. Especially with you guys listening."

"How about this. We each write three or four sentences. That way you can kind of get a feel for what we're thinking. You write one too, okay?"

Amy stood and went to the junk drawer in the kitchen. She came back with four pens and tore off a sheet of paper for each one. "Just remember that this is a person I love. Can we try to do this in five minutes? I really don't want to spend all night on this. And I read mine last." The three friends wrote, scratched out, wrote again, giggled, sighed and wrote more. Finally when they were all finished, Hillie, as usual, took charge of the situation.

"Who wants to go first?" Just like high school—no volunteers. "Well then, I guess I will."

Logan,
Hope you arrived safely and had a smooth flight.
I'm glad you called before you left, but was really hoping to see you.
I miss you already.
Write or call when you get a few minutes.
Love,
Amy

Amy critiqued first. "Well, that sounds almost as uninterested as his note did."

"That's kind of what I was going for, so he can see how it feels."

"Okay, point taken. Who's next?"

"I guess me." Gibby read her note.

Logan,
I was a little surprised at the tone of your note, especially after the great weekend we had.
I'll be busy this week but will try to check email at least every other day.
Write when you get your life sorted out.
Amy

Amy winced. "That's almost brutal. But kind of how I feel."

"That's why I wrote it. Why not write what you feel?"

"Okay, Beth, what do you have?"

"Mine is a little kinder."

Dear Logan,

I'll be thinking of you there in the sunshine as I put on my coat and gloves.

When you get a break from work, I'd really enjoy hearing from you.

You are in my thoughts and prayers as you make important decisions.

Love,

Amy

"I kind of feel like that, too. I guess that's my problem."

Hillie spoke up. "Then, there's your answer. Wait for him to write first."

"What if he doesn't?"

"I think he will, eventually. But if he doesn't, he has just taken the coward's way out. And I have no respect for him."

Gibby added thoughtfully, "Maybe if he has to wait without hearing from you, he'll think about the tone of his note. I think you need to let him know he hurt you."

"I don't think that he thinks he hurt me. I think he was attempting to sound a little aloof, to take the emotion out of his leaving."

"If he really knew you, he had to know that would hurt you."

"I'll wait until I hear from him."

"Hey, wait a minute," Hillie reminded everyone, "I want to hear what you wrote."

"Okay," Amy agreed.

Dear Logan,

I kind of hoped you'd call when you got in. I'm assuming your flight went fine.

I'll finish up your place this week.

As you can imagine, I have some questions about the nursery, but if I don't hear from you, white it will be.

Don't work too hard.
Enjoy the sunshine.
Call me.
Love,
Amy

"Well, I just might go with that, but I'd wait a week."

"A week! I'm hoping he'll be home in a week."

"If he's only going to be gone a week, he doesn't need to hear from you. Make him wait it out. Amy, he said he loves you. If he made it up, write him off. If he meant it, he'll still mean it in a week."

"Gibbs, you're right. I think he meant it. I know he did. I'll wait a week. It will be hard, but I'll wait."

"I don't think he would have paid you if he planned on being home in a couple of days. How much luggage did he take?"

"Oh, Gosh. He could be gone months! He took two huge suitcases and a garment bag."

The friends were silent. They knew she was right. They were just wondering how she was going to deal with it if Logan checked out of her life for good.

Gibby stood up and got ready to leave. "Hate to break up this party, but I have to be at work at five a.m., so I'm going to bed. It will all work out, Amy, really. Give him some space, some time, and don't bite his head off when he finally calls. He's probably working on bigger issues than you know. Finish the house and take a break from the whole atmosphere. Thanks for supper. Bye, Hillie. As always, great to see you."

Beth joined her. "Me, too. I have a call from Terry coming in about ten minutes. We're finalizing weekend plans for St. Louis. The dinner was delicious. Thanks."

Punkin stretched and followed Beth and Gibby out the door.

"Hillie, want to spend the night, or are you just taking a late train?"

"I'm taking a late train, but I want to chat for a few minutes. What does Gibby know that she's not telling?"

"I don't know. She has the whole confidentiality thing going on with the hospital. I understand and respect that, so I don't push her."

"I doubt that it has anything to do with 'tainted DNA.' I think he got a vasectomy because he doesn't want to be a father. I'd like to know the reason."

"Hillie, we've discussed it. He feels his wife's death is his fault and he's not going to risk getting anyone else pregnant. He was very adamant about not wanting to be a father. He really freaked when I volunteered us to babysit the twins. He didn't want to touch those babies. I made him take one. Then he said the strangest thing. He insisted that I watch him. Him, not the baby. In case he did anything."

"Anything…like what? Toss the baby in the air, shake her, swing her around by her ankles?"

"Logan was afraid he was going to hurt her somehow. She fell asleep in his arms and he panicked. Like she had stopped breathing or something. She was just comfy after her bottle and she fell asleep. It was weird."

"He doesn't have kids from a prior marriage or anything, does he?"

"I think he would have told me if he did. I never asked. He always talked like Sam was his first wife."

"Okay, now I know you're not going to like this, but since he is so very far away, I think you need to discretely look through some of his things."

"Oh, Hillie, I couldn't! He trusts me."

"With most things, that's probably true. But he didn't trust you enough to give you the whole scoop on Sam. There's something missing. Gibby knows more, maybe not all, but definitely more. Are you ready to go back through the old newspapers?"

"I just hate to. I think it says something about the relationship. If there isn't trust, why bother?"

"Think about this. Remember when you were at the arboretum and he told you he killed his wife?" Amy nodded. "You know that was totally for shock value. If you were going to be scared off that would do it. You didn't freak out, so he told you the whole story."

"Actually, I was quite calm. For one thing, I didn't believe him."

"How did he tell you he had a vasectomy?"

"Oh, this is embarrassing. He started out by showing me, in a way."

"Did he make you look at his scar?"

"No. Worse. We were right in the middle of doing it."

"You can say the words, Amy. You were having sex, and…"

"And he pulled out and whipped off the condom, plunged back in and finished. It happened so fast I could hardly believe it."

"No shit!"

"We had a few awkward moments, and then we talked about it. Naturally, I was concerned about getting pregnant. Not that I would mind having Logan's baby, but not without marrying him first. He told me that wouldn't happen. Couldn't happen. He couldn't be a father. And it didn't sound so much like, 'I had a vasectomy so I can't be a father.' It sounded like I cannot be a father. Like, 'I'm not allowed to be a father.' And then, of course, Jack broke his leg and we had to babysit for the twins."

"You were deliberately baiting him."

"In a way, I suppose. I could have taken care of them both, but I'd have had my hands full. It was just easier having a helper. It put him in a situation he obviously dreaded and hoped never to experience."

"Well, friend, I think you have the answer somewhere in all those clues he's given you. I have to hit the road now, unfortunately, but I don't think you should feel bad about checking him out. You have a lot at stake here. Wait a few days to email him. I hope he calls, really, Ames. And thanks for supper."

"Thanks for coming out. I always know you'll be straight with me."

"The only way to be in matters of the heart."

Hillary hugged Amy and left for the train station.

*

She knew she'd sleep better if she didn't leave a mess in the kitchen, so she started clearing the table. The soup was gone, thank goodness, because she wasn't in the mood to pack away leftovers. The bread however, was a different story. It had a perfect crust and an airy, chewy texture. Butter turned it into a loaf of heaven. She was glad there was some left for the next day, even though it would be chewier. She hoped the phone would ring. She wondered at what point it became just plain rude that he didn't call her. If she was dumped, better to know it now. But he loved her, she was sure of it. She went to bed secure in that thought.

The next morning Amy was on her way out the door when the phone rang. She dropped everything and ran for the phone, then tried to collect herself so she didn't sound so anxious. She answered, then her shoulders slumped when she realized it was in regard to her second painting job. Yes, they wanted her. She asked them to empty the rooms of furniture; she'd be there tomorrow and the next day. They bought their own paint. Good. She was tired of paint shopping. *Crap. White,* she thought. She had to buy white to paint the nursery.

Logan's room was next on her agenda, and when Amy arrived that morning, she saw that he had moved all the furniture to the center of the room so she could get to the walls. The bed was in the middle, surrounded by his dresser, two nightstands, a chest, and the table he had been using as a desk. She noticed the dresser drawers were facing the bed—not easily accessible. She'd have to crawl across the bed. But the chest...the chest looked like it could be opened by just lifting the lid. It wasn't locked. It was beautiful and she was sure he had made it. There was a cushion across the top of it so it could be used as a seat. Amy sat on it while she weighed the options: open or not.

She decided to have a cup of coffee, paint, think about it while she was painting, and then see if she had the courage to lift the lid. *What's the worst that could be in there?* she thought. *Newspaper clippings showing him as an escaped ax murderer?*

The blue paint looked good. It was very pale and brightened the room. She liked it and hoped Logan would, too. She would come back in three days. If she still hadn't heard from Logan, she would lift the lid.

*

Amy didn't have a name for her business. She wouldn't need one for advertising purposes if she kept getting jobs by word of mouth. The Jacksons, her second client, recommended her to neighbors. She would be painting the inside of their garage. She was appreciative of the work, not so much for the money, but because it kept her mind off Logan. She had put his house on hold while she finished the other projects. All she had left at Logan's was finishing some details in each of the bedrooms and painting the nursery white. She concluded that white—the absence of color—created a symbolic cleansing of Sam's pregnancy from Logan's mind. He probably kept the room locked to protect *himself*, as much as keeping others from going in. It was a shame to paint over it, but Logan was paying her. It was easier on Amy if she treated this as a job rather than a purging of Logan's sad memories.

Three days later, after completing the other two jobs, Amy finished the nursery. What remained was now just a stark white spare bedroom, fit for storage. She sat on the bottom step of her ladder and remembered the day she found Logan in this room, heartbroken and crushed. Her eyes filled with tears and her throat closed as she choked out a curse. "Blast you, Logan! How dare you do this to me! To us! I thought we had something special. I thought you loved me. You shit. You hurt me and you said you never would. If you were here right now I'd kick your ass! Don't ever call me again! Bastard. Bastard!"

She cried until she was too drained to put more effort into her self-pity. She made up her mind to go home and email him. It would be a "shit or get off the pot" speech. Somebody had to have the balls to put this thing to rest. Amy decided she was the one. She carried all her stuff to the van and went back into the kitchen. She took the pad he had written his note on, dated it, and wrote a brief but precise message.

Done.
ASS

Before she left, Amy felt it was her duty to check the chest. She was relieved but disappointed to see it contained...blankets? Blankets.

CHAPTER 37

Amy sat in front of the computer, fingers poised on the keyboard. Being grateful for the chance to edit, she pounded away, just letting her frustration with the whole situation fly from her fingertips. There were no capital letters or punctuation. Her stream-of-consciousness writing screamed with irritation and pain. After five minutes her fingers ached and she felt better. She deleted it and started fresh.

> Logan,
> Just thought I'd let you know I finished your house. I think it looks pretty good for my first job. I've had two other jobs in the meantime, much smaller.
> I was hoping to have a call from you by now. I'm wondering what I did to make you angry. Then I remembered. You left on business. That being said, I hope your business is going well.
> I guess I need to get to the point of this email. We've been honest with each other from the start, I think, so I don't want to stop now. Logan, I need to know what's going on. If you're dumping me, please don't drag it out. You said you would never hurt me and I should never be afraid of you, but I am. Hurt and afraid.
> Please answer by phone or email. I miss you. I'm afraid to say the L word again, Logan.
> As always,
> ASS

She clicked "send," sat back, and waited for a few minutes. The quiet was more than she could stand. Amy got up and headed for the mall.

*

Logan was sitting alone in his room at his brother's house. He was emailing Matt back at Carson Creations, giving instructions on a large order that was going to London. This was their first sale overseas and he wanted it to go smoothly. He was just ready to sign off when he noticed a new email. He assumed it was Matt, since they had been writing back and forth for most of the morning. His heart pounded when he saw Amy's name. He realized there was no sense in putting it off. He had actually been surprised and a little disappointed that he hadn't heard from her sooner. But then, why should she write? He had hurt her. He knew it. He also knew she wasn't the type to just let it go. He opened her email, scanned it quickly, then went back through absorbing each sentence. The only way to respond was line by line.

Amy, hey.
Glad you finished. I'm sure it's beautiful. You do good work. Word will spread fast.
I'm not angry with you, honest!
Business is good. We just finished an order of four gazebos that are going to London. I spent several days in northern Calif. in a logging area. We're looking for another source of trees with wood that will hold up well when left out in the weather. They're doing some great things here with hybrids.
Amy, I'm not dumping you. I'm sorry I hurt you. Please don't be afraid.
Logan

He whispered to the screen, "I love you, Amy." He didn't send his message, but saved it for editing later. He'd send it after he was certain she'd be asleep. There was a knock on his door, bringing him back to reality. "Come in."

It was Bo. "Moss is going to grow on your north side if you don't get some fresh air now and then."

"I was just shutting down for the day. I got an email from Amy."

"Finally! Is she pissed that you haven't contacted her?"

"Maybe, but worse, I hurt her feelings."

"Don't sound shocked. That was your intention. If she's easily shaken off, you'll let her go. I think you're being a real shit about this, Logan."

"You're not in my shoes, man."

"I may not be in them, but I've sure followed them around for enough years to know that this is all about you, not about her."

"Okay, lecture if you must. I suppose I deserve it."

"You're hurting her before she can hurt you. If you piss her off or hurt her enough she'll take off, then you can be the honored guest at your own pity party, once again."

"That's crap."

"It may be crap. Eventually she'll get sick of your crap and she'll hit the road. I found Ginny. I'm a lucky son of a bitch to have her. She's an awesome woman and she puts up with me. If something happened to her I don't know what I'd do. But I do know this. I would have to look high and low for a very long time to find someone who even slightly measures up."

"But you haven't lost her. It's different when you do."

"I'm sure it is. But Lord help ya, Logan, you have another wonderful woman dropped in your lap and you're trying to shake her off. She's the one taking the chances here. She's the one dealing with a person who's been something less than mentally stable for the last year. She's the one out on the ledge waiting to see if you'll jump off into a fresh start with her. You sleep with her then take off. What the hell do you expect from her?"

"I expect time and a little understanding."

"She's given you time. You've hashed things out for a month. She sat home for a week without so much as a 'kiss my ass' from you. I'd say she's given you some time. She's given you understanding, unless you lied to me. She's been patient while trying to drag your life story out of you. She's been supportive and loving. I swear if I didn't have Ginny I'd take her myself, and I've never even met her!"

"Bo, she wants things I can't give her."

"There's nothing you can't give her, if you want to."

"She wants a family. She wants to be a mom."

"You and that fucking spur-of-the-moment vasectomy. I don't want to hear about that sorry excuse. You could get it reversed. You could adopt. You could use a sperm donor. Don't you read? There's almost nothing that modern science can't fix. You'd be a great dad. You think you're afraid, while she's the one with her knees knocking in fear. Get your fucking act together, Logan. Call her. Bring her out here, or go home."

"I'll leave in the morning. If you didn't want me here, just say so."

"If I thought I could finish the fight I'd slap the shit out of you. I don't want you to leave, moron. I want you to do right by Amy."

His diatribe was interrupted by a knock. Ginny walked in, forcing a smile, but in obvious discomfort. She didn't even need to speak. Both men jumped up and each took an arm. Her suitcase was waiting by the front door. Bo and Logan looked at each other and spoke at the same time. "She'll be fine."

Bo hugged him, realizing this was a bit of déjà vu for Logan. "She'll be great! There will be three of us when we get back here."

Logan carried the suitcase out to the car and gave Ginny a hug before he helped her get in.

Bo looked at him and wondered about a bit of the hair of the dog. "Logan, come with us."

"No way, man. This is a family thing and you two need to be focused on each other and that new baby. Just keep me posted. I'll be here all night. She'll be fine."

Logan repeated it trying to convince himself more than Bo and Ginny.

CHAPTER 38

Amy was between jobs with time on her hands. Gibby was working and Beth was in St. Louis with Terry. Logan was…well, who knew where. Hillie was out of town for four days for work.

Amy washed her bedspread and curtains, folded them up and dropped them off at the thrift store. While she was there she saw a beautiful, old sampler quilt that needed a little repair. She could still use it in the meantime. All she needed was a dust ruffle for her bed, some lacy curtains and a new paint job. She was invigorated at the thought of remodeling for herself. She deserved to spend a little time on herself, and she had the money to spend since Logan had overpaid her…at least that's how she saw it. She walked into her favorite paint store.

"Hi, Amy. Back so soon?"

"Yeah, this time for myself. I think I want a nice mauve." She picked through the paint chips and made a decision.

She finished her room in two days. It looked great.

The phone rang and she jumped out of her skin. She had stopped anticipating a call from Logan. Sort of. It was her mother.

"Mom, what's wrong?"

"Nothing, dear. Dad and I were just wondering if you wanted to come up for Thanksgiving."

"Thanksgiving!" She didn't realize it was so close.

"It's next Thursday. Can you take a little time off work?"

"I don't have any painting jobs lined up, so I suppose I could." *I'd like to have plans here…with Logan, but it looks like that's not going to happen,* she thought.

"Well good! We look forward to seeing you. Anything new there?"

"No, Mom. Can I bring anything?"

"Maybe a nice relish tray—something you won't have to cook."

"I'll come up on Wednesday and we can decide then, okay?"

"Good. And you know the girls are always welcome if they want to come. We have plenty of room."

"I'll ask them. See you then."

"I love you, dear."

"Love you too, Mom. Say hi to Dad for me."

Amy signed on to her computer.

Buds,
Did you realize Thanksgiving is this week???
My Mom called and invited me and anyone I want to bring with me. I'm leaving on Wednesday. Let me know.
By the way, she's an excellent cook.
Amy

This was the first time she had signed on since she had read Logan's response. He didn't strain himself much, just responding to her line by line. She didn't answer and wouldn't until she returned to a better frame of mind. He was putting her to the test, and she would not be defeated. Maybe he'd come home for Thanksgiving. It would serve him right to find her gone. But why would he come home? He'd be having Thanksgiving dinner with Bo and family. Or maybe going to his mom's for moose jerky.

*

Logan sat on the couch watching TV and waiting for the phone to ring. When it finally did his heart jumped up into his throat and he was afraid to answer it.

"Hello?"

"Logan...Bo. Things are going fine. It will be a few hours, so I just wanted to let you know not to wait up."

"Ginny's okay?"

"She's tired. She just wants this baby out, and she wants her normal boobs and ankles back."

"What about you?"

"I was really enjoying the new boobs, but the ankles are hideous."

"You asshole. Are you doing okay?"

"I'm fine. Logan. Hear me. Women give birth everyday. What happened with Sam was the exception…rare, understand me? We'll be fine. But thanks for being concerned."

"And thanks for the lecture. I needed it."

"She loves you, man."

"I know."

"I'll call you later."

"Bye."

Logan hung up. He laid his head on the back of the couch and prayed out loud.

"Lord, don't you dare let that little baby die. I forgave you once…twice… but I may not a third time."

He had fallen asleep on the couch and when the phone rang again the sun was up.

"Hello."

"Is Uncle Logan there?"

"Bo? Is Ginny okay? What about the baby?"

"Mom and baby boy are fine."

"A boy! Awesome! And he's fine."

"He's fine and fat with a head full of hair. He's beautiful, Logan." Bo's voice cracked and Logan totally understood the feelings he was having.

"Well you tell him that his Uncle Logan loves him very much and will spoil him rotten. And give Ginny a kiss for me."

"She's a mess. She wants a shower. She wants to eat. She wants to sleep. She wants to hold the baby. She wants me with her. She wants drugs. She wants to go home. We've unleashed a monster."

"Get back in there with her. Do not let her out of your sight. I'm not kidding, Bo. Watch her every minute."

"Logan, it's okay. I'll stay with her. She comes home tomorrow. All three of us. I'll watch her, I promise."

"Please, Bo. I'm serious about this…"

"I understand. We'll be fine."

"What's his name?"

"Well, funny thing. We're deciding between two names. We never quite got that ironed out before she left for the hospital. We have a few hours to make a decision."

"Is there anything I can do here to get ready?"

"Ginny was pretty organized. But one thing."

"Name it."

"Thanksgiving—you're in charge. Buy it, make it, whatever. Ginny will be preoccupied, and you know I'm a walking catastrophe in the in the kitchen."

"Thanksgiving! Already? Well, I'll get right on it."

"Thanks. Gotta go."

"Congratulations, Dad."

"Yeah, imagine that. Bye."

Logan breathed a sigh of relief. "I'm serious, Lord: keep them safe."

Logan got dressed, consulted one of Ginny's cookbooks, made a list and headed for the grocery store. He opened every cabinet in the kitchen to make sure he had enough pans and utensils. He was grateful for the task. It would keep thoughts of Amy at bay and keep him away from the newborn—whatever his name was going to be.

*

The next afternoon, the doorbell rang and Logan opened it to find a florist's van in front of the house and a young man standing on the front porch with a dozen huge red roses. They were for Ginny from Bo. Logan tipped the delivery man and brought the roses in.

Half an hour later Bo and Ginny and baby arrived home. Ginny was moving slowly but obviously happy to be carrying the baby in her arms instead of in her belly. Logan couldn't resist checking her ankles. They were almost there. Bo was carrying Ginny's suitcase and a bag full of stuff from the hospital. Bo went to the table to drop off the stuff he was carrying. Ginny handed the baby to Logan. Instinct left him no options but to take the child. Ginny took off her coat while Logan stood frozen in place.

Bo walked in and saw Logan panicking as he held the tiny package. Bo stopped in his tracks and watched his brother's reaction. Ginny was at the closet chattering on and on about the nurses and staff at the hospital. Logan finally had the courage to look down at the tiny, trusting face. He pulled the blanket off his head and gave it a soft little kiss. "Welcome home, nephew."

Bo was relieved at the progress Logan had made. "Randall."

"What?" Logan turned to look at Bo.

"That's his name. It was Ginny's maiden name. We'll probably just call him Randy, unless we're mad at him."

"Who could be mad at this little bundle?"

Ginny added, "Give him ten years and ask me that again."

Logan carefully handed the baby back to Ginny. She held him close, snuggled her face next to him and breathed in that wonderful, clean baby scent. She smiled up at Logan. "We're fine, really."

Logan went to his room, signed on to his computer and shot a message off to Amy, the only person with whom he really wanted to share his good news.

Dear Amy,

I'm an uncle. Bo and Ginny had a boy, Randall. He's very soft and cute. He and Ginny are both fine. Not sure about Bo, though.

I got to hold Randall and I didn't freak out too much. He's quite a bit smaller than Sweetie Pie and Honey Bun.

Just to take the load off Ginny I'm in charge of Thanksgiving dinner. I think I'll throw the turkey on the grill.

Have a great holiday.

Uncle Logan

While he was at the computer he sent a message to Matt back at CC. He sent similar notes to his parents, letting them know mom and baby were home and doing well. He promised to get the digital camera out and take some pictures. While he was including details to his parents with the assurance that Bo would be writing more when things calmed down a little, he noticed Amy was online.

She answered back right away.

Dear Uncle Logan,

Congratulations! I'm glad to hear everyone is doing well. I hope Ginny appreciates the wonderful rocker now that she can sit in it and hold her precious baby boy. I'd like to meet them some day. Send pictures.

I'm going to Michigan to my parents' house for Thanksgiving. I won't be cooking. I'll just be eating.

Call. I'd love to hear your voice.

Amy

P.S. I painted my room mauve.

She couldn't resist the last line. He was not in charge of colors at her house.

*

Back in Chicago, Amy and her friends had their own holiday plans to think about. Beth would travel to Iowa to meet Terry's family. Gibby had to work, but was going to dinner with Marty. And Amy was picking Hillie up from the train for the drive to Michigan. The weather was holding and that was a good thing. November frequently held surprises for drivers because of the strange effect Lake Michigan could have on the weather. The leaves were gone from the trees but the sky was crystal clear and brilliant blue.

They made three short stops. The first was Tabor Hill winery, where they stocked up in case prohibition was ever enacted again. The second stop was for lunch, gas, and red licorice. The third stop was at a farm stand, where they picked up apple cider.

Amy's parents, Moe and Finola Sweet, met them at the door and gave both girls a big hug. The Sweets first met Hillary when she and Amy were roommates in college. She had spent several Thanksgivings at their home, so this was like the good old days.

"Moe, get their luggage and let the poor girls in. It's cold outside."

Amy stopped him. "We have a lot of stuff, Dad. We can get it. We already have our coats on. We just wanted to say 'hi' first."

Amy didn't want her dad seeing the wine. She knew if he did, he'd bring it in the house and it would be finished before they headed home. "Hillie, just grab two bottles and the cider. This has to last me all winter."

"Gotcha. They haven't changed much, have they?"

"In little ways, but mostly no. They're pretty healthy and I'm thankful for that."

It only took two trips to the car. They visited for a few minutes and decided to run to the store for a few things for the next day's dinner. Moe stayed home to watch football, and Fin and the girls headed out.

"You girls made good time. When I called your house, there was no answer. So, I assumed you had just left. But the Weather Channel said the roads would be clear, so we weren't too worried."

"What did we do before the Weather Channel?" Amy wondered out loud.

Hillie answered, "I think we just took off and dealt with it."

The grocery store was crowded with other last-minute shoppers. It didn't take long to find the few things they needed with the three of them looking at the same time. They were checked out and back home in an hour.

Moe, always ready to set an agenda or make a schedule, asked first. "When are you gals heading back?"

"Dad, we just got here. Are you trying to get rid of us?"

"No, but your mother and I usually have sex on Saturday night, and I just wanted to warn you in case you heard strange noises."

"Dad, you cannot shock me. Mom no longer gets embarrassed, and Hillie got used to it years ago, so why do you still do it?"

"Fin, why do I?"

"Because as your audience gets smaller, your idiocy gets bigger."

"Perfect explanation. See, Amy? Your mother understands me. What's for supper?"

Hillie didn't want to laugh because he would consider that encouragement and would continue.

"Supper is spaghetti, garlic bread and salad."

"I think we'll open Amy's wine."

Fin spoke up quickly, "I think that's for Thanksgiving, dear."

"Oh, I'm sure she has more in the car."

Hillie and Amy looked at each other and laughed.

Dinner was delicious. Afterwards, Moe went to the living room to watch more football. Fin and the girls sat around the dining room table and chatted, just catching up on the news.

Hillie and Amy both talked about their jobs. Fin listened and nodded politely. Then she asked, "What about men? Are there any skulking around in your lives?"

Hillie answered first. "I'm a little short lately. I don't get out much and may have to depend on friends to fix me up. Unless you know of any nice single gentlemen."

"Most of them are ready for Social Security."

"Well if I'm still in the market in five years, I just may take you up on that."

"What about you, Amy, dear? You've been pretty quiet. Any special man hanging around?"

"Special man, yes. Hanging around, no. At least he's not hanging around me. He's in California at his brother's house. He's been there for several weeks on business, supposedly, but I think he's putting me to the test…avoiding me. He has issues."

"Oh, phooey. We all have issues. What's his problem?"

Hillie and Amy took turns explaining Logan and his situation. Fin admitted this was deeper than just issues. Clearly, Logan had problems and needed some time to work through them.

"So you're taking his side and you don't even know him."

"If you love him, I will too. Have you thought about flying out to surprise him?"

"Mom, really. Would you do that?"

"I would if I loved him. If I thought I had a future with him."

"I don't even know where he is. He's visiting his brother, but I don't know where. California is a big state. He mentioned taking a trip to northern California to look at some wood, so I assume his brother lives more south. Email doesn't give you a location, and he hasn't called me."

"As a lawyer, Logan's brother should be easy enough to find. He must be in the yellow pages if he expects to get any business, wouldn't you think, Hillie?"

"You could probably start there, unless he's some kind of private lawyer who doesn't need to advertise."

Fin was undaunted. "Then we'll go next door. Our neighbor is an attorney and he can check through the bar association somehow, wouldn't you think?"

"Mom, please. I want him to come to me on his own."

"He needs a little nudge. Call the brother on Friday."

Hillie's eyebrows rose. "Can't hurt. Maybe he can do the nudging for you."

Fin stood up. "Good. We have a plan. I'm going to bed. We have to get an early start. I want pies in the oven by nine a.m." She hollered into the living room. "I'm going to bed, Moe." Fin winked at the girls. "I like to let him know, just in case."

"Goodnight, Mom."

"See you in the morning, Fin. We'll be ready."

*

Thanksgiving Day started just as Fin planned. She was up at six a.m. making pies. The girls got up about an hour later and helped her. Moe got up in time to finish breakfast early enough to watch the Thanksgiving Day parade in peace.

Big dinners were Fin's specialty. She recruited the girls for washing and chopping vegetables. She laid out ingredients and gave instructions to the girls for assembly, mixing and stuffing. The turkey was big enough for twenty people. That meant plenty of leftovers that would be traveling south on Saturday. Moe's behind was pretty much glued to his recliner for the day, as he napped between football games. Fin woke him up in time to carve the turkey.

"I'm the only one in the house who can cut up a turkey? What are you going to do when I'm gone?"

Fin answered him very calmly. "I'll rent your recliner out to a person who can carve a turkey. Life goes on."

Amy set the table and Hillie made a very festive centerpiece with candles and Indian corn. Moe opened the wine as Fin brought the food to the table. They all took a seat and Fin breathed a sigh of relief. "That's more like work!" Moe gave a brief but appropriate blessing, and like most American families, the meal was over in a fraction of the time it took to prepare it.

Moe belched, kissed Fin on the top of her head and thanked her for a delicious meal. "When it's time for pie, you'll know where to find me."

Fin and the girls cleaned up the kitchen and decided to take a walk before the turkey enzymes kicked in. Fin and Moe lived in a nice neighborhood with small houses, quiet neighbors and wide sidewalks. They passed other neighbors out walking who agreed that the nice days would soon be few and far between. On their way home Fin flagged down her attorney neighbor. She winked at Amy. "May as well ask the question now so we don't have to go ringing his doorbell tomorrow." Fin introduced Amy and Hillary and let Amy ask the question.

"I really hate to bother you with this, but is there a way to find an attorney in California if I have no idea where he lives?"

"With the internet you could probably find anyone, especially someone who is in the public eye, like an attorney. You don't know what city he's in?"

"No, southern California, probably, but that doesn't narrow it down much. His name is Bolin Carson."

"If it was William Smith we'd probably have a problem, but that name should be pretty easy to find. Fin, you and Moe still don't own a computer, do you?"

"No, and we probably never will."

"Then I'll check through the California Bar Association for you. What do you need, address and everything?"

"I think just a phone number and city for now. I just want to talk to him, not drop in on him. Although it crossed my mind."

"Fin, I'll give you a call when I find him. You girls here for the weekend?"

"We'll be leaving on Saturday to avoid the crunch through Gary into Chicago."

"Smart move. Fin, tell Moe I said Happy Thanksgiving. Send him over tomorrow when you're sick of looking at his ass in that recliner. We'll go to the mall to hit on chicks or something."

CHAPTER 39

Logan woke up early to start on Thanksgiving dinner. The nice thing about California was he didn't need a coat to cook on the grill in November. He expected no help from Ginny and Bo was useless in the kitchen. He had a lot of prep work. As he walked quietly down the hallway toward the kitchen, he passed the nursery and Ginny called to him in a whisper.

"Logan. I'm in here. Come on in for a few minutes."

She was sitting in the rocker he made, nursing Randy, just the way Logan pictured she would. It was a beautiful, peaceful sight.

"Are you sure? I don't want to disturb you."

"Sit with me a minute. Logan, this chair is wonderful. Thanks again. You did a beautiful job."

Logan tried not to stare, but Ginny was very modestly covered while Randy had his breakfast. "Can I get you some coffee or something?"

"No, that's okay. He doesn't need the caffeine. I'll get some breakfast after I lay him down."

Logan was sitting on the floor with his legs crossed. "Would you mind if I got my camera? I'd like to send a picture to the folks and maybe have one made for Bo."

"I'm not going anywhere. Sure, that would be fine."

Logan sprang up and went to his room to find the camera. When he returned Ginny looked so beautiful as she looked adoringly at the little life she was nourishing. Logan took several shots and sat back down.

"How are you feeling?"

"Except for my…uh…when I sit, I'm fine. Just a little sore. I really appreciate you taking care of dinner today. I can't wait. You're doing turkey on the grill?"

"Yeah, I'm taking advantage of the weather."

"Are you going to call Amy?"

"You too? Has Bo been talking to you?"

"Just a little. I know you have a very special woman sitting on the edge of her seat, waiting for you to make a move."

"She is very special. The fact is, we haven't known each other very long and I'm just not ready to jump into something with both feet yet."

"You jumped into her bed with both feet."

"Bo told you more than just a little, didn't he?"

"He cares about you. He thinks you know that you've found a person you want to spend the rest of your life with and you just aren't admitting it."

"She's awesome, Ginny."

"Trust her to love you back, Logan. Give her a call today and tell her she's one of the things you're thankful for."

"She's at her parents' house and I don't know where they live. I'd email her, but she probably wouldn't get it until she got home anyway. I'll just wait until next week. You have to trust me on this, Ginny. I can't call right now."

"Don't blow it, Logan."

"I won't. How does it feel?"

"How does what feel?"

"Nursing. I never got a chance to ask Sam."

"Oh. Well it feels kind of like it does when um…like when there's no milk there."

"You mean it kind of turns you on."

"Well, sort of. It helps the uterus get back into shape after being all stretched out. But it's not really like being turned on. I guess it's just one of those things that are hard to explain to someone with useless nipples."

The initial embarrassment was gone. Ginny sat Randy up for a little burp and then switched sides. Bo walked in and noticed Logan watching in awe.

"Hey, you lookin' at my woman's boobies?"

"Bo, don't be silly, Logan and I were talking."

He addressed Logan. "Stop looking, Logan."

"Bo, she covers up. You can't see anything. Besides, Randy's fluffy hair covers the good stuff."

"Bo, we've been through this. Nursing is a perfectly natural thing."

"So is taking a shit, but you wouldn't do that in front of Logan, would you?"

In stereo, Logan and Ginny scolded, "Don't say shit in front of the baby."

Logan stood up and headed for the kitchen. "Give me half an hour and I'll have some breakfast ready."

"Bo, he'll be a good dad some day, don't you think? I'm asking my doctor for the name of a good urologist so he can get unfixed. Do you think he'd do it?"

"Let's see how he is with Randy. After he fixes dinner."

Later that day, when dinner was finally on the table, they all agreed that turkey breast cooked on the grill was absolutely delicious. Logan also prepared the corn on the cob and the potatoes on the grill. He cheated on cranberry sauce, however, and had also purchased the dinner rolls. No way was he making a pie. Luckily, he discovered a bakery nearby. Logan also made sure the coffee was decaf, so Ginny could enjoy it. She passed on the wine, but Logan and Bo made fast work of it.

It was Bo's turn to give instructions. "Ginny, you have an hour to take a nap. I'm loading the dishwasher and cleaning up in here. Logan, you'll put a football game on the TV. I don't care who's playing who. You'll hold Randy until I get in there. Then he's mine. No argument from anyone."

Logan protested. "Bo, I know what you're trying to do."

"Then shut up and go with the program. Ginny, are you worried about Logan holding the baby?"

"Absolutely not."

"See? Neither am I."

Logan walked into the living room and turned the TV on. It was hard to find a channel that didn't have a football game, pre-game or post-game show. He lay down with his head on the arm of the couch. Ginny arranged a baby blanket on his chest and gave him easy access to a burp cloth. She laid Randy on the blanket and covered him lightly. There's no way he'd get a chill laying on Logan. Randy was asleep and Logan watched his back rise and fall with each breath, almost as if he was willing him to inhale and exhale. He rubbed the baby's back and kissed the top of his head, feeling Randy's pulse through the soft spot. *How can they trust me with this?* he thought. Eventually Logan relaxed, watched football and succumbed to the turkey-induced coma.

Ginny had a nice nap. She woke up and walked into the living room expecting to hear Randy squawking, ready to eat. Her eyes took in the same sight women all over America were looking at on a Thanksgiving Day afternoon. Three men asleep in front of a TV tuned to a football game. She went into Logan's room, brought his camera out and took several pictures. It was a sight that gave her great comfort.

*

The phone rang Friday and Fin answered it.

"Fin! Survived the holiday, I see."

"Yes, we did. And feel free to come get Moe anytime. Do you need to speak to Amy?"

"Yes, I have a phone number for her. Put her on."

Fin handed the phone to Amy.

"Hello?"

"Amy, dear, get a paper and pencil. I have a phone number for you. It's a Los Angeles area code, so mind the time difference."

Amy scrambled in her mother's kitchen. She didn't have a junk drawer! The nerve! Amy motioned to Hillie to hand her her purse. She found her address book and a pen. She took the phone number for Bolin Carson. She'd call him later in the day. She thanked her parents' friend and hung up.

"Ames, you going to call him?"

"Yes, later. He wouldn't even be in the office yet because of the time difference. He probably won't even be in at all today. I'll probably just end up calling back on Monday. Maybe I should just wait."

"Chicken."

"I'm not a chicken. I don't want to intrude on his holiday."

"If he takes your call, you won't be intruding."

"Fine. When it's nine a.m. in California I'll call."

"What city?"

"I don't know. He just said it was a Los Angeles area code. Could be in the city, could be a suburb. I'm not sure."

She slumped in the chair and poured herself another cup of coffee.

At 12:10 p.m. she took the cordless phone and went into the guest room. She dialed the number and waited for an answer.

A woman's voice answered. "Bolin Carson, attorney-at-law, how may I help you?"

Her mouth went dry. It must be his secretary.

"I'd like to speak to Mr. Carson please."

"Mr. Carson isn't in right now. This is his answering service. If this is urgent I'll be glad to give him a message."

"Well, no, not really. Wait. Yes, actually I do think I'd like to speak with him as soon as possible, if it's not too much of an inconvenience."

"That's not a problem. Leave your number. He'll be checking in for messages several times today."

Amy left her name and phone number at her mom's. Now she'd wait. Hopefully he wasn't as rude as his brother.

*

Bo checked with his answering service after lunch of leftover turkey sandwiches with mayonnaise, lettuce, and tomato on wheat bread. Ginny wanted him to ignore work just for the weekend, but he assured her he just wanted to know what's going on. He promised he wouldn't go into the office. He called the service and was quite surprised to hear the name Amy Sweet. She was calling from a Michigan area code. Probably at her parents' house. It was the only call he had, but he went through the motions of writing info down, nodding his head and mumbling into the phone. The answering service had already disconnected, but Bo didn't want to look too obvious. He avoided looking Logan in the eye. "I'm going to return just one call." He looked at Ginny and winked. "I'll be in the bedroom for a few minutes." He was a little nervous about making this call. Why? He had nothing at stake here. But he was concerned about Logan. He dialed her number. She picked up on the second ring and took the phone into the guest room again.

"Hello?"

"This is Bo Carson calling for Ms. Sweet."

"Bo, this is Amy."

"Well. Hello there. How was your Thanksgiving?"

"Very nice, thank you. And congratulations on the new baby. Logan emailed me with the news."

"Well, thanks. We're still pretty much on a high around here."

"And your wife…she's okay?"

"She's doing great. Amy, what can I do for you?"

"Gosh, this is harder than I thought it would be."

"In that case, let me start. Logan and I have talked about you every day since he got here. First of all, let me tell you that he is here mainly on business. But personally, I think that's just a convenient excuse for hiding out for a while."

"Bo, that's exactly what I figured. I think he panicked."

"You scared the shit out of him, Amy."

"I'm sorry. I didn't mean to."

"Don't apologize. This is a good thing. You knocked him off that ridiculous fence he's been sitting on for months, wallowing in self-pity."

"He has every right to wallow. He lost his wife."

"How quickly you come to his defense! You must love him."

"You know I do. If you've been talking to him, he probably told you that we've gotten pretty close…at least I thought we were. Now the way he's avoiding me, I'm not so sure."

"He thinks you want things from him that he can't give you."

"Like what, sperm?"

"Basically. A family, motherhood."

"Bo, that's not fair. He told me about his vasectomy and essentially hit the road. We haven't had time to discuss the options or the impact of that. I love the man. And yes, I'd like to be a mother. I think he'll be a great dad, but there are ways around his alteration."

"Well, we're on the same page with that thought. He told you about Sam, how she died?"

"Yes, there were complications after a miscarriage and she bled to death."

"Amy. I hate to do this, but I'm going to fill in a little detail that Logan hasn't had the courage to share with you. Swear you will not ever tell him we spoke of this."

"Bo, you're scaring me. I promise. What do you want me to do?"

"First, you will go to the cemetery where Sam is buried. You will read her headstone. Are you writing this down?"

"Yes. Where's the cemetery?"

"Check the old newspapers for the obituary. I don't remember the name of it. If you want me to tell you the rest of this you have to promise to do the research. Talk to someone from the hospital."

"No problem. My neighbor works at St. Mary's."

"Good. See if you can get access to Sam's records."

"Bo, that will be impossible. The privacy restrictions are so rigid."

"I know. But I think what I tell you may help. And remember, I feel like an asshole telling you this. But I think you're good for Logan, and hopefully when he gets his head out of his ass, I'll feel better about telling you."

"Good grief. Spit it out, Bo!"

"Sam didn't miscarry. She had a baby girl."

"What?"

"You heard me. Are you writing this down?"

"Yes. Bo. What happened?"

"They named her Rebecca. Logan was in Sam's room. Sam was resting and Logan was sitting with her. He was holding Rebecca. It had been a long night and all three of them were tired. Logan fell asleep holding the baby. While he was holding her…well, he thinks he smothered her. She stopped breathing."

"Oh, my God! That explains so much! He's terrified of babies. He made me watch him while we were babysitting so he wouldn't hurt one of the twins he was holding. He said he was already responsible for taking one innocent life, he wouldn't do it again. I thought he was talking about Sam."

"Oh, he blames himself for that, too. Anyway, he woke up and thought the baby was sleeping. When he handed her to Sam, she noticed that Rebecca wasn't breathing. She started screaming and calling for a nurse. When Logan finally realized what was going on, he thought Sam was blaming him for killing the baby. The nurses and doctors came running in and took the baby and tried to resuscitate her, but it was too late. Sam kept screaming. Logan thought it was because of the baby. He didn't know that she was actually in pain and bleeding out. He was trying to comfort her instead of going for a doctor. There was no way he could have known, but still to this day, there's no convincing him of that."

Amy was in tears and speechless.

"Are you still there, Amy?"

"Yes. Oh God, Bo. My heart breaks for him."

"Personally, I think Sam knew that the baby was dead and didn't have the will to live, so she didn't even try to get Logan to help her. I think her heart hurt worse than the bleeding."

"Logan probably thinks she died blaming him for the baby's death. Was he responsible, Bo?"

"That's where the records come in. I say no, he wasn't responsible; it was like a crib death. They did an autopsy against his wishes, but that was the rule at the hospital for an unexplained death. He was in Sam's room after they took her to the funeral home. He was packing up some of her things to take home and he heard her roommate telling someone on the phone that he killed the baby and everyone knew it. But since his wife died and everyone felt bad they weren't going to pursue it. The curtain was pulled, but I'm sure she knew he was there."

"How cruel! Who was she?"

"Check the records, Amy, and confront her. I think she was just a rumormonger and was out for the attention. Logan was so crushed that he would have believed anything bad about himself at the time. He thought he was the lowest life form on earth and killed two people. He would never pursue it. I've asked him to research it many times."

"I will. He's too kind, Bo. I think I love him even more, if that's possible."

"Do the research. Check the newspaper. Go to the cemetery. Check with the hospital. Find out who the roommate was. Question her. She played a cruel trick, Amy, and my brother is hurting."

"Bo, I swear, he'll think this all came from me. He knows I'd just dig until I got to the bottom of something. You're off the hook."

"Good. Let me know before you let him know. Call my office number when you find something out."

"Bo, why hasn't he called me? I miss him. I need to hear his voice."

"Shit, Amy, I don't know. I cuss him out daily, if that helps."

"Obviously not. His emails are few and far between and very vague. He has such passion and I want to read that. I'm afraid to tell him how I feel now because it's like I'm putting myself out there and getting nothing return. It's a little embarrassing. And it hurts me."

"Amy, I'm nudging him all I can. My goal now is to get him used to holding Randy without freaking out. He's getting better. He actually fell asleep Thanksgiving lying on the couch with Randy sleeping on his chest."

"Oh my. That must have been hard for him. And you. Were you afraid?"

"Actually, no. I fell asleep in the chair right next to him and Ginny was in the bedroom taking a nap."

"Well I'm certainly glad all four of you woke up!"

"Me too, but I never doubted it. For all we know Sam could have been bleeding the whole time she was sleeping or the stress of Rebecca dying could have triggered it. Either way, there was nothing Logan could have done to prevent it."

"I think he finally believes that. We had quite a chat about him killing his wife, as he put it. It was a deliberate effort to scare me off. I was very calm, actually. I hadn't known him long, but I knew he didn't have the heart of a killer. Then when he told me the whole story...or most of the story, I knew he still was blaming himself. Did he tell you he had a little break down in the nursery?"

"Yes, he told me you rescued him."

"Well, that's rather dramatic. Actually I just held him and let him talk it out. Did he tell you he asked me to repaint the nursery white?"

"Like that would erase the memories."

"I think that's what Logan was thinking. Kind of elementary psychiatry on my part. But it makes sense. Well, I'm not going to keep you from your family. Just know this: I love your brother. I think he loves me. Anything you can do to get his sorry ass back into my life would be greatly appreciated, Bo."

"Amy Sweet, it has been a pleasure talking to you. Logan is a fool if he lets you go, but I don't think he will. Ginny has something in the works for him on Monday, but I have spilled enough of the beans. Any more will have to come from Logan himself. I'll nag him a little about emailing, but don't count on a call. Your voice would do him in and I think we both know that."

"Thanks for calling me back, Bo. I look forward to meeting you someday."

"The pleasure will be mine, Amy. Bye now."

Amy hung up the phone and sat in stunned silence. Logan was a father...for a few hours. The pieces fell into place and she needed to see Gibby. She dialed her number and left a message on her answering machine to keep Saturday night open for an important discussion. Confidentiality be damned.

*

Bo walked back into the living room. Logan was alone and Ginny was in the nursery feeding the baby.

"That was a long call. Anything important that can't wait?"

"Important, yes, but it will wait until Monday. Excuse me while I go into the nursery to confront the rascal who has claimed my wife's tits for his own."

Bo headed toward the nursery, peeked in and reveled in the sight of Ginny holding the baby. Ginny waved him in and he closed the door behind him.

"Amy tracked you down, didn't she?"

"Good guess. I like her, Gin."

"So, what's the scoop?"

"She loves my idiot brother."

"Does she know the Sam story?"

"Most of it. I filled in the rest. And don't you ever tell Logan! She's sworn to secrecy. I sent her on a few errands. She'll do the research herself and then she can confront Logan. Maybe he'll believe her."

"I can't wait to meet her."

"She's got her head screwed on straight. Do you know that SOB had her repaint the nursery white?"

"Erasing the past?"

"So it seems. Since you have two spigots, can I try the other one?"

"Absolutely not."

*

Amy and Hillie left for home Saturday morning. The visit with Moe and Fin was a nice break. The food was delicious and they had leftovers for home. Amy filled Hillie in on the phone call with Bo, on what was a mercifully uneventful trip back to Chicago. She was anxious to get home to start the little research project Bo sent her on.

First stop would be Gibby's place. Amy needed to send her on the quest for hospital records. Amy needed to find out who Sam's insensitive roommate was. In the meantime, she planned to go through microfiche at the library to look for the obituary. That should give her the name of the cemetery. She wondered why Bo was so insistent that she go there. If they were dead and buried there would be a headstone. Maybe she had to see it just so she could let Logan know that she was actually there and had followed the trail from the obituary. Bo had his reasons. He trusted her and she would respect his wishes on this.

The train was already at the station when Amy dropped Hillie off.

"Perfect timing! Thanks for inviting me. I had a great time with your folks as always. They crack me up."

"I was glad for the company on the drive. I'll keep you posted on what I find out. And remember, this is never, ever to be mentioned in Logan's company. I'm only telling Gibby enough to convince her that I need her help and there's no other way I can get it."

"Safe with me, friend. Bye."

Amy waited for the train to pull out, then drove home. She carried her luggage and cooler in. She put food in the refrigerator and clothes in the washer. She changed into sweats and a t-shirt that said "Will work for chocolate." She crossed the hall and knocked on the door. Marty opened it.

"You still here?"

"Hello to you too, Amy. I was just leaving. My thirty minutes are up." He turned around, kissed Gibby on the cheek and said, "Bye, Sugar."

"Bye, Marty."

He left and Amy closed the door a little harder than she needed to. Gibby was wearing a t-shirt…only.

"I don't know why that man bugs me. I should be nice to him since you seem to care for him, but I swear Gibby, sometimes he gets on my last nerve."

"Mine too. I totally understand. No need to apologize. How was your Thanksgiving?"

"It was good. I'm glad Hillie could go. The drive gets tedious after a while."

"How are Fin and Moe?"

"Slowing down a little, but they're good."

"You stop at the winery?"

"Of course. And we got some cider."

"Good. Hear from Logan while you were gone?"

Amy sat at the kitchen table. Gibby handed her a Michelob and a glass. "He sent me a very pleasant email…as if he was writing to a sister. He let me know that he is now an uncle. Bo and Ginny had a baby boy named Randy, who, he says, is very soft and cute."

"That sure beats the names he had for the twins. Hell hounds, or something, wasn't it?"

"Randy won't be so cute once he shits on Logan, believe me."

"Did he say when he's coming home?"

"No, but he has been so kind as to inform me of his effort to find some wood that will hold up in nasty weather. Like I give a shit about that stuff. Well, it's not that I don't care about his company, but geez, I need to hear about his life. The life where I am supposedly included as part of the future. Toad."

"Did he give you one of these 'I need space' lectures?"

"No, not really, but that's the feeling I get. I called Bo."

"Really! Ames, you got balls! Good for you!"

"Someone around here needs them, since his have been revised. I just wanted the truth. If we're breaking up I want to know now, so I can sweep up the pieces of my life again and move on. I don't want to wait two months while mink man decides what he's going to do."

"Who?"

"Never mind. I have a huge, really big, very important favor to ask of you."

"Why don't I like the sound of this?"

"First of all, it does not involve confidentiality at the hospital."

"Good. Because you know how I feel about that."

"I am going to tell you what I think I am pretty certain I know. Then you will know why I need your help."

"Spit it out. Sugar coating it won't help, I can tell."

"Logan's wife didn't have a miscarriage."

Gibby didn't looked surprised and she didn't respond.

"You knew that along, didn't you?"

Gibby nodded. "You know I couldn't talk about it."

"I know, and really, I respect you for that."

"I hear a 'but' coming here."

"And it's a big one. But I don't think of it as a confidentiality issue."

"Well, let me know, and maybe I can make that decision."

"I need to know who her roommate was."

"Can't do it."

"Gibbs, listen. She heard something. I know it. Oh, shit. I didn't want to tell you this, because I pretty much promised Bo that Logan would never know that he told me some details about Sam's death."

"Let me save you the effort. I know. I was on duty when it happened."

"Rebecca?"

"Is that what they named her? I always wondered."

"Do you see now, why he's such a mess?"

"Yes, I'm sure it's rough to lose a wife and a daughter in the same day."

"Gibby, it's beyond that. He thinks he killed the baby."

"That's ridiculous. That was a SIDS case."

"Not according to the roommate. That's why I need to find out who it was, so I can get her to retract that. Otherwise, Logan will believe that it was his fault the baby died."

"I can't go into records, but I will mention it to some people, just to see if anyone remembers a name."

"And Sam…"

"Neither the baby dying nor Logan had anything to do with her hemorrhaging."

"I figured as much."

"No more."

"Thanks. I have about an hour to get some work done at the library."

"Want some company?"

"Throw on a coat…and some pants, please, and let's get moving."

*

There weren't many people at the library on a Saturday evening. They didn't have to wait for a microfiche machine. Amy sat down and Gibby borrowed a chair from a neighboring table. Amy wasn't sure of the exact day Samantha Carson died but knew it was in early October, over a year ago. It shouldn't take too long if all you have to look through is the obituaries.

Amy was flipping rather quickly, and a name caught her eye. It was a small headline on an inside page. "Winston arrested."

"Gibbs, look. This is the guy who torched Carson Creations." She read the article. "Bartholomew Winston being charged with arson and vandalism at Carson Creations...allegedly retaliating after being fired from his position there...held at county jail while awaiting trial. Carson has agreed to press charges to the full extent of the law. No injuries, damage to machinery and property."

"He's the one Logan told you about, isn't he?"

"Yes. There was more to it, involving injury to a child, but everything worked out well. Logan told me they caught him."

"Okay, then, back to the obituaries."

Amy scanned, one day at a time. It didn't take long.

"Here, Gibbs...look...Samantha Rae Carson. Passed away at St. Mary's Hospital, survived by husband Logan M. Carson...her parents...interment at Roseneck Cemetery."

"How sad."

"There's no obit for the baby. She died the same day, didn't she?"

"Actually, the baby died first, as you know, but yes, it was on the same day."

"So this is what Bo wanted me to see. I'm going to the cemetery tomorrow. Want to go along?"

"Why not, may as well see this mystery to its end."

Amy decided to buck up and be prepared for being ignored once more. She checked her email and was surprised to see something from Logan, albeit brief.

MAUVE! Revenge is sweet, yes?

Hope your T-day was great. I cooked up a storm on the grill. Of course, the people I was feeding had no choice. So they ate it.

Have a safe trip home.

L

"You're pissing me off, Logan," she answered him aloud.

L,

You're not the boss of me.

I'm home safe, alone.

ASS

Gibby stopped by Amy's for breakfast and they left for Roseneck Cemetery. They stopped at the office for directions to the grave. It was a very old cemetery, but very well tended. The headstone was not hard to find. It was modest but elegant.

BELOVED WIFE AND MOTHER
SAMANTHA RAE CARSON
INFANT REBECCA

They both knelt down to read the stone. Amy brushed some leaves away. They were very quiet there in the presence of evidence that could have such a huge effect on Amy's future. Gibby spoke first.

"Ames, do you notice something strange?"

"Aside from the fact that two very young people died?"

"That's part of it. Two. There's only one grave here."

Amy broke down and sobbed. "Poor Logan. You're telling me they're in the same casket? Mom and baby buried together. God, it's so sad I can barely breathe. I can't even imagine how Logan felt. His future, buried."

They stood up and Gibby put her arm around her friend as they walked to the car.

"Now that you know, maybe you can help him more."

"I can't do it in an email. It has to be in person…I have to see his face."

"Could you do it on the phone?"

"Maybe. I could let him know what I found out. It won't matter. He still thinks he's responsible. Gibbs, I need a name."

CHAPTER 40

Logan unenthusiastically called the phone number of the well-regarded urologist Ginny had given him. He was looking at this appointment as research. Nothing was scheduled, planned, or pre-certified. This was informational only. He wanted to know percentages, long-term effects, risks, pros and cons. He had an appointment in two days.

Bo pushed, as usual. "Did you call?"

"I told you I would."

"Do you have an appointment?"

"Yes."

"Do you want me to go with you?"

"If you want to see my balls, why don't you just ask?"

"I've seen them. Nothing to write home about. This could be a good thing, Logan."

"No promises. I'm going to see this guy under protest."

"Okay, first you need to know…"

"Bo, could I see you here for just a minute…right now?" Ginny interrupted the conversation.

"Sure." Bo walked to the kitchen where Ginny was holding the baby.

"Do not tell him this doctor is a woman. He'll cancel his appointment."

"Oh, please, I want to go along very badly. I have to see his face."

"Shh."

Bo walked back into the living room grinning.

"Now, what were you saying? What do I need to know?"

"Uh, that there are no guarantees. But um, this is a very common procedure now. You'll do fine."

"This is an appointment for information only. Not surgery."

"Right."

*

Amy called Bo at work the next day.

"Hi, Amy. I assume you had a safe trip home."

"Yes. Is Logan still at your place?"

"Actually, today he's at a factory checking into an environmentally safe stain. But I'm sure he'll be home this evening sometime."

"I had an interesting trip to Roseneck Cemetery."

"Oh, yeah, that sounds familiar."

"They were buried together, weren't they?"

"Yes."

"Was it just very awful for Logan?"

"It was awful for all of us, but yes, especially for Logan."

"He never told me. I guess he didn't trust me with that."

"I think he's ashamed."

"He did nothing wrong. It was a sudden infant death syndrome case. I'm sure someone must have told him that."

"Yes, but he didn't hear it. All he knows is that he handed his wife a dead baby."

"Bo, I want to see him."

"He has a little project he's working on. I think you'll be pleased."

"Tell me."

"Can't. This one is definitely Logan's story to tell."

"You're as big a tease as he is."

"It's genetic."

"How are Ginny and Randy doing?"

"Amy, this is such an awesome thing. I hope you get to experience it someday."

"Me, too. Well, just wanted to let you know what I learned. So you're off the hook. I have someone checking on a roommate name. I'll let you know if I find out anything new."

"Thanks. Hang in there."

Amy got off the phone and went to the kitchen to fix lunch. There was a piece of paper slipped under her door. She picked it up and unfolded it. She did not recognize the handwriting. It had a name printed on it. Bobbie Winston.

Amy sat on the floor in front of the door and read the name over and over. Could it be a relative of Bart? Winston was not an uncommon name. She tried to think back to the day Logan told her about the vandalism. He fired Bart. Did he tell her anything about his family? *Think, Amy, think!* she thought. It hit her. *His pregnant wife was bedridden. Bart was in jail when the child was born.*

Amy hit redial and Bo got on the phone again.

"Amy, what's wrong?"

"I think I know what happened. Samantha's roommate was Bobbie Winston. I think she's…"

"She's Bart Winston's wife. I remember from the trial. She had just had a baby…Oh, wow. Good job. I'm sure she's the very same Bobbie who's married to Bart."

"Do you think she deliberately made that comment so Logan would hear it?"

"I'm positive. Retaliating for putting her husband in jail."

"I need to find her. I want her to admit what she did. It was cruel."

"Amy, don't go looking for her yourself. I have people…"

"You're in California. She's probably still here in the area."

"I know when Bart got out they moved. I don't want you near him. Let me look for her. If Bart is out of the picture, I'll let you know where she is. If he's still living with her, no way. If anything happened to you Logan would kill me."

"Bo, this could really help him, couldn't it?"

"Yes. And you get an award for being a great investigator. But leave it alone now. I promise I'll let you know what's happening."

"Thanks, Bo. I feel better already."

*

Amy went back to fixing lunch and Beth knocked on the door and popped her head in. "Hey there, neighbor. How was your Thanksgiving?"

"Come on in. Want some lunch?"

"Depends on what you're having."

"Leftover turkey on white bread with mayo."

"Make two."

"I haven't talked with you for a while. Tell me about the St. Louis trip."

"Well, next time I see Logan I'll have to thank him. We had a suite with a beautiful view and a huge fruit basket waiting for us when we got there. Then we had appointments for massages in the spa. It was wonderful."

"Tell me about the suite set up."

"There were two bedrooms connected by a living room and a bathroom."

"How many sheets did you rumple?"

"Why don't you just ask me if I slept with Terry?"

"Did you?"

"No. But we came pretty close. That's why I have to ask you what you're doing next July 20th."

"Now how would I know that?"

"Well I know what I'm doing that day. I'm getting married."

"What? For real? That's great!"

"Well, will you be a bridesmaid?"

Amy came around the end of the counter and gave her a hug. "I'd be honored. I know you'll be sensible when it comes to picking out dresses...no pink, no puffed sleeves, no tons of lace..."

"Whose wedding is this, anyway? You know my taste. Gibby is maid of honor. I still have to ask Hillary. This will be a fun wedding. And by the way, it will be in Iowa."

"I'm not afraid to leave the state. We can get a hotel room and have a fun weekend. No ring yet?"

"No, he'll give it to me at Christmas. He wants to shop and surprise me. He does have an idea of what I like because we did a little preliminary shopping in St. Louis."

"This is very exciting. Are you going to be able to hold out until July?"

"Who knows? We'll do our best, but what happens, happens. It helps that I have to drive several hours to get there. It's not like I can just take the train for thirty minutes. If we saw each other more often, then we'd be in trouble."

"How did he ask you? Where were you?"

"We were taking a little walk in a park. It was full of mums and autumn flowers and it was so pretty. We were holding hands and all of a sudden he stopped, turned me around to face him and said, "Beth, I can't imagine a future without you in it. Would you do me the great honor of being my wife and the mother of my children?"

"Oh, Beth! How sweet!"

"I said I would be very happy to be his wife and the mother of his children."

"Laying down the ground rules from the start, that's good."

"Amy, I can't believe how this happened so fast. Life can sure throw you a curve now and then, can't it?"

"Well…Sit down while I tell you about *my* curve."

As they ate lunch, Amy explained the whole story of Samantha, Rebecca and Bobbie Winston. She told her about Logan still being in California, the shortage of email, and the lack of phone calls.

"Amy, he loves you. It's so obvious. Better he takes his break now than after you're married. And I do believe that's where you're headed."

"I thought so too, once. Now I'm not so sure."

"He's living with his brother and taking care of business. I think you're making more out of it than you need to. I understand you want to see him and talk to him. And I am slightly annoyed with him for not stepping up and including you in some of his decisions. But I'm going to give him the benefit of the doubt here. He hasn't exactly had a normal life for the last year or so. Just pray for him and let him be for now."

"I have no choice. He isn't here for me to beat up."

"Well, gotta run. I have a haircut appointment."

"I'm going to check my email. Congratulations, again. See ya later."

Beth left and Amy headed for the computer.

She had email from Logan.

Hello, Amy!

I plan on being home in about three weeks.

Could you do me a favor at the house? Just run over, run the water, flush the toilets, and make sure things are as they should be.

Watch your mail. I just sent you and the girls a box of oranges to share.

Can you believe I'm watching Randy while Ginny takes a nap? I suspect I'm his favorite uncle.

L

Three weeks! Good grief. She started pacing while she was thinking of how to respond to his impersonal note. As she walked by the window she noticed the snow. Perfect. Autumn's gone. Winter was bearing down, and she was alone again. Loneliness swept over her.

Logan,

I'll check on the house.

You'll need to shovel, though, unless we have a warm front come through. It's snowing here.

I'll watch for oranges. Thanks.

Beth and Terry are getting married next July. Thanks to you.

Three weeks?

Logan, I miss you.

Amy

*

Logan turned down Bo's street and into his driveway much too fast. He slammed the door of the rental car and stormed into the house. Ginny was on the couch with the baby. That let the wind out of his sails. He wanted to holler and rage. He scowled at Bo, pointed a finger at him and growled. "You. Right now. In the back room."

Bo looked at Ginny and grinned. He was going to get his ass chewed and he knew why. So did Ginny.

Bo peeked around the corner into the spare room that Logan had been calling home for the last month.

"Is it safe? Are you armed?"

"You get in here right now you son-of-a-bitch."

"Don't hit me. What?"

"A woman! That's what!"

"What woman? I don't know what you're talking about."

"Oh, yes, you do, you weasel! Dr. Andersen. The urologist. The *female* urologist."

"Really?" Bo tried to act surprised but Logan wasn't buying it.

"I have been totally humiliated."

"Why? Because a woman had her hands on your balls? Would you rather it was a man? Is there something you're not telling me? Do you have a secret life I should know about?"

"I'd rather not have a stranger's hands on my balls, but the situation is just a little easier to discuss with a man."

"Women have been going to male gynecologists for years. What's the difference?"

"Don't try to change the subject. The difference is…this is me. These are my parts, and I would like to be the one to decide which women I want touching them."

"You kept the appointment, didn't you?"

"Yes."

"Logan, what did she say?"

"I'm not sure I heard everything because part of my brain was plotting on how I was going to kick your ass into next week."

"But the part you did hear…what does she think about a reversal?"

"Technology is very advanced and success rate is very high. I can't be any worse off than I am now. It's a tedious procedure. It's easier to snip things than to put them back together. I have to ask myself, what kind of an idiot has his balls sliced on twice?"

"There's a mirror."

"There is nothing funny about this situation."

"I agree. What does she look like?"

"She's beautiful. That didn't help. She was wearing Amy's cologne."

"Now, I get it! You got your feet in the stirrups, so to speak, she's got the flashlight out, rubber gloves on, pinching, squeezing, pressing, and she smells like Amy and you got hard, didn't you?" Bo kept his distance as Logan started pacing. He was grinning and he couldn't help himself. "Was it worth two hundred and fifty dollars? A hooker would have charged less and at least you'd have gotten off."

Logan was silently grinding his teeth and glaring at Bo. "Yeah, but I couldn't file charges for a hooker with my insurance," he quipped back. "And I did get off. In a little cup, in a little room, with dirty magazines."

"Why, just to make sure no swimmers were making it through?"

"Maybe. I think she just wanted to make sure the surgery was successful."

"So, you gonna do it?"

"I have an appointment day after tomorrow. With Dr. Andersen and her long, slender fingers."

"I may have to keep her in mind when it's time for a prostate exam."

"You're a pervert. I don't know how we could possibly be related."

"Oh, we're related all right. It's just that I say out loud what you're thinking."

"That's why you're the attorney."

"Well, Logan, I'm sure, given the nature of her business, that yours is not the first erection she's ever seen. Maybe the smallest, but not the first."

"Amy said she was impressed, so that's all the validation I need. And also thanks to Amy, I get an erection whenever I walk past the paint store, so my brain is warped for life."

"So, what's the time line on this?"

"A little pre-op testing, surgery, rest—thank God. Then a test run."

"When can you have sex?"

"You mean with a person?"

"Yes, someone besides your hand."

"Not sure. She said everyone is different. It will depend on my level of discomfort."

"That means your balls are going to ache."

"Probably. So you better be nice to me."

"Are you going to tell Amy?"

"Eventually. Not until it's over."

"Well, good. This is a step in the right direction, I think. I hope it all goes well. Really, Logan. I'll be pulling for you."

"That's not funny."

They walked into the living room and Bo gave Ginny the "thumbs-up" sign.

"Logan, how did it go?"

"This is just a continuation of the female plot to dominate the world, isn't it?"

"What do you mean?"

"Dr. Andersen, the female urologist. Really, what kind of a woman gets into that business?"

"Women go to urologists, too, Logan. Men don't have a corner on peeing."

Bo couldn't stay out of the conversation. "But men have an easier time peeing on the corner."

"Stay out of this, troublemaker."

"Oh, come on. This is a branch of medicine with mostly male patients. There's just more plumbing on men. What kind of a woman wants to spend her days looking at…geez, Ginny, what did you do to me?"

"I think after a while, they all look the same. Let's face it, that is one ugly patch of skin. Lumpy, bumpy, hairy, stretchy…it's just nasty. I'll tell you what I'm grateful for. I'm grateful that when God created human beings, he decided to give that to men. What if he decided…ah, yes…the woman. I think she needs this little leftover patch of skin right here. And he slapped that on our forehead. Pretty sight, huh? We'd all have bangs."

"Ah, Ginny, that's where you're wrong. They don't all look the same because Dr. Andersen got to see the expanded version."

"Logan! You didn't!"

"He says she smelled like Amy."

"Now, Logan, you know I've pretty much left you alone when it comes to Amy, but really, you better get home to that girl. When you start embarrassing yourself in public, you need a little personal attention. I think she's waiting to give it to you."

"Can we please leave my sex life, such as it is, out of our conversations?"

"So, you gonna do it?"

"Day after tomorrow. Under the knife. Again. On the most delicate part of my body."

*

Amy was sitting at her kitchen table designing a small advertisement to put in a local newspaper for her painting business. She got up to refill her coffee cup and the phone rang. It was Bo.

"Hi, Amy. Keeping busy?"

"Actually, I was just working on an ad to drum up a little more business. Do you have some news for me about Bobbie Winston?"

"Actually I do, and I'll give it to you if you promise me something."

"That depends. What do you have?"

"I know where she is. I also know Bart is in jail for auto theft."

"Do you have her address?"

"I do, but I'm not going to give it to you."

"Bo, this is important for Logan, not just for me."

"Let me tell you how this is going to work. I have a guy: a private investigator. I trust him completely. I want you to call Bobbie and ask her to meet you in a public place. My man will be there with you, where he can watch you to make sure you're safe. If she doesn't want to meet you, that has to be the end of it. You can't harass her or stalk her."

"Okay. So she must not be far."

"Probably less than an hour if you live near Logan."

"Not presently, but yes, I know what you mean. Is it okay if I give her my phone number in case she changes her mind and wants to get in touch with me?"

"My instinct is to say no. But kind of feel out the situation. If you feel threatened, don't do it. If she seems mellow or remorseful then go ahead. But do not give your address."

"So, who is this guy?"

"His name is Barney. I'm going to also give you his phone number. After you set a meeting time and place, call him. And I am dead serious about this. You must call him, Amy. I don't trust anyone who is in any way related to Bart Winston. Keep in mind she has already done something very mean. Maybe being a mother has calmed her down, but we can't count on that. Promise me you'll call Barney."

"Yes, I promise."

Amy took both numbers from Bo and planned to call Bobbie Winston as soon as they hung up.

The phone rang six times and Amy was ready to hang up when Bobbie Winston answered.

"Is this Bobbie Winston?"

"Yes it is. Who's calling?"

"Bobbie, my name is Amy Sweet."

Suddenly her brain went blank. She hadn't even planned what she was going to say to Bobbie. How was she going to describe herself? Maybe the direct route was best.

"I'm a friend of Logan Carson and I'd like to meet you somewhere to discuss your hospital stay when your baby was born."

"He's a heartless bastard! Put my husband in jail. He didn't even get to see his own son be born!"

"I can understand your anger about that. Can we meet somewhere? I'd like to buy you lunch. You name the place and time."

"I don't know. I have a baby to take care of—by myself, thanks to Carson."

"Bobbie, please, I just want to talk. I can be in your area in about an hour."

"Denny's. I'm in the mood for a strawberry waffle. One hour. How will I know you?"

"I'll wear a red sweater. I have brown hair."

"I have blonde hair and will wear a brown leather jacket."

"Great. Thank you, Bobbie."

Amy's next call was to Barney. She described Bobbie, but then realized he probably already knew what she looked like since he was the one who found her. He would be at Denny's where he could keep an eye on them both. She decided that she would be glad to have Barney close by. He would arrive before they did.

The drive went faster than Amy thought it would. Of course, it wasn't rush hour, so traffic wasn't too bad. Denny's lot had plenty of parking. She scanned the other cars in the lot and took a space close to the front door. A waitress seated her. She took a table facing the door and waited with a cup of coffee. She glanced at the menu, looking up every few seconds. Then she remembered Barney was supposed to be there. She looked at the men eating lunch. Most were in groups of three or four or with families. Then she spotted him. He was in a booth reading a newspaper. She caught his eye and he winked. He stopped a waitress and she changed his seat. He was sitting closer now with an unobstructed view of her and within earshot.

Amy spotted Bobbie first. Blonde hair, brown leather jacket. She was pretty, but her life had hardened her features a bit. Bobbie scanned the lunch crowd and Amy stood up. The waitress followed her to Amy's table and left a menu with her.

Amy extended her hand. "Bobbie, I'm Amy Sweet."

Bobbie took it, but only briefly, to be polite. "Bobbie Winston. Of course you already know that. Your treat, right?"

"Yes, of course."

The waitress came to their table. Bobbie ordered the strawberry waffle as she had mentioned on the phone. Amy ordered blueberry and they both had coffee.

Bobbie started. "Well, plead your case, or whatever."

"First of all, how is your little boy? I thought you might bring him."

"He's fine. My mother is watching him." Amy smiled and thought how this person could be a friend if it weren't for her husband.

"I want to talk about the day when Mrs. Carson and the baby died."

"Pretty horrible. I was in the bed right next to her. Of course, they didn't know who I was. And why would they, really. You know, in the hospital with all the excitement of a new baby and everything. It's not like women are in the hospital for a week anymore. You pop it out and go home the next day. Not exactly the atmosphere for making lasting relationships."

"When did you recognize the name and realize who your neighbor was?"

"The nurse called him Mr. Carson and the Mrs. called him Logan. How many Logan Carsons can there be on earth?"

"Only one that I know of."

"Well they were just there enjoying their baby. She was tired, as you would expect. I was just mixed up. So happy with the baby, so pissed that Bart wasn't there."

"Pissed at whom, Bobbie?"

"I don't know. Pissed at Carson for firing Bart. Pissed at Bart for getting fired. It was really a good job. Pissed at Bart for taking revenge and getting his ass thrown in jail. Again."

In true Denny's style, the waffles arrived on platters and were edged in whipped cream. After the waitress left the conversation continued.

"Bobbie, let me tell you my place in all of this."

"I wondered when you were going to get to that."

"I'm in love with Logan."

"Don't piss him off."

"I try not to. It's taken him a while, as you can imagine, working through the death of his wife and daughter. We'd like to have a life together. I'd like to have a family."

"So, what's stopping you? What do I have to do with it?"

"Logan was packing up his wife's things when he overheard you on the telephone with a friend or family member."

"Really? I don't recall."

"You may not. It was over a year ago. But he heard you tell someone that it was his fault the baby died. You knew he was listening, didn't you?"

"Oh, that. Well, I was really in the mood for revenge, but unlike Bart, would never go set fire to something. I wanted to hurt him like he hurt me."

"Bobbie, he took your comments to heart. He thought you really overheard nurses talking about him being responsible for Rebecca's death."

"Rebecca? That's what they named her? That was the name I had picked out if I had a girl. Shit. I wanted to hurt him."

"You did. Still to this day he thinks he killed that little girl. He's afraid if he has another child he'll kill it."

"Well, now, why after all this time would he still believe that?"

"You caught him at a very vulnerable time. He felt guilty anyway—that his wife died while he was at her side. It was just easy for him to believe you. He still to this day doesn't know who you were. He doesn't know you said it out of spite."

They ate their waffles in silence and had refills on coffee. Amy looked up and saw Barney. She had forgotten about him. Bobbie spoke next.

"I suppose after a year of suffering I could let him off the hook. But I want you to know how hurt I was. I had a horrible pregnancy. Bart got fired in the middle of it, and believe me, that did not make things better. Then he got caught in the whole arson thing, and the vandalism, and some check bouncing thing. I was so busy being mad at Carson that I didn't think I should be angry with Bart."

"Bobbie, Bart had choices. He made the wrong ones. Logan is in a business where people can get hurt if his products are inferior. One little girl did. Bart lied on his application. Really, I don't think Logan had a choice."

"I know that...now. And I'll tell you this...promise not to spread it around..."

Amy nodded. Who would she tell? They didn't exactly move in the same circles.

"I'm filing for divorce. This whole auto theft thing is the last straw. What kind of an example can he be? Who will hire him when he gets out? I need to make a fresh start. Bart will be mad and may even beat the crap out of me when he gets out, but it will be worth it to be out of his life."

"Bobbie, go far, far away. A fresh start is a good idea. You have a baby to think of now. Bart's not a good person, Bobbie. You are."

"Suppose there's a way I can apologize to your boyfriend?"

"Well, how about if I just tell him. If he doesn't believe me, can I call you back?"

"Sure…for another waffle!"

"You're doing the right thing, Bobbie."

"I feel like I am. I feel better about it."

"When does Bart get out?"

"Five and a half months. That's time to take action, I think."

The waitress dropped off the check. Amy took it and pulled out a credit card.

"Thanks for lunch, Amy. I'm glad you called. Logan has himself a good woman, whether he knows it or not."

"I'm glad I got to meet you."

Bobbie left and Amy went to the register to pay. Barney was behind her in line. She turned around and looked at him, making sure Bobbie was pulling out of the parking lot.

"Barney, I presume?"

"Miss Sweet?"

"I'm calling Bo when I get home. I think everything went well. Better than I would have imagined."

"Good. Glad to be able to help."

"You were very discreet. Almost invisible."

"That's my job."

He paid for his coffee and left.

Logan deserved a phone call to share this news, but she did not want to be the one that made the first call. She would take a little advice from Bo, since he seemed to have a good grasp of the situation.

Amy dialed the California number that was becoming so familiar. "Bo, I'm sure Barney already checked in."

"Just hung up, actually. So it went well."

"She admitted it, you know, that she made up the whole thing. She knew who Logan was and she wanted to hurt him."

"Well, it worked."

"I asked her if it was okay if I tell him that she apologizes. She said yes. Also if he doesn't believe me, she said it would be okay if we called her again. Hopefully Logan will be home before Bart gets out of jail in five and a half months."

"Do I sense a little sarcasm, Ms. Sweet?"

"From me? Nooo."

"Do you think he'll believe you?"

"Do you think he'll believe me, Bo? You know him better than I do."

"I used to think that, but I think you know him best. I knew the old Logan. You know the new Logan, the invigorated Logan, the hopeful Logan."

"The absent Logan."

"Do you trust me, Amy?"

"I don't have much choice. You're holding my boyfriend hostage."

"I think he'll be home in about three weeks. I almost guarantee he'll be home before Christmas.

"Bo, what's happening? Why won't he call me?"

"He's afraid of you."

"Okay, that's a box of crap."

"You're the only one right now with the power to crush his healing heart."

"I would never do that. He knows that. He trusts me, he told me so."

"Trust is a big thing."

"No kidding. I'm trusting that he's going to come back home, but believe me, the longer he stays away, the harder it is to believe it."

"Amy, I have an appointment that I really can't be late for. But let me promise you this, I'll put the pressure on for him to call you."

"As long as it's a promise."

"You bet. And Amy? What we did today? It was a good thing."

Amy hung up and went to her computer.

Logan,
Please call me. I have news that I don't really want to put in writing.
Not to keep you in suspense, but I spoke with Bobbie Winston today.
I'm going Christmas shopping. Is there anything special you want?
I miss you.
Love,
ASS

CHAPTER 41

While she was contemplating what to do for supper, she walked across the hall to visit with Beth and Gibby for a few minutes. She was greeted at the door by Punkin who wove in and out of her ankles, depositing orange fur on her socks.

"Well, you'll never guess who I had lunch with today."

"Don't tell me Logan's home."

"Beth, think. If Logan were home, would I be here?"

"Probably not. Then don't make us guess. Just spit it out."

"Bobbie Winston."

Gibby asked first. "Who is Bobbie Winston?"

"Come on, Gibbs. You know who she is. And by the way, thanks for the note under the door."

"What note? I don't know what you're talking about."

"Really. In that case, Bobbie Winston is the wife—soon to be ex-wife—of Bart Winston."

Beth remembered the name. "Is that the guy who burned Carson Creations?"

"Yes, the very same. The guy Logan fired for lying on his application, among other things."

"What made you want to have lunch with his wife?"

Amy told an abbreviated version of the story. "It seems she was the roommate of Samantha Carson on the day Sam and the baby died. She deliberately spoke to someone on the phone while Logan was within earshot, mentioning how he killed his baby and everyone knew it. It just reinforced the guilt he was feeling. The thing is, I don't think he knows who Sam's roommate was. Bobbie, however, did know who Logan was. She knew he was the reason her husband was in jail during the birth of their first baby. She was hurt and angry and struck out the only way she knew how—a blow to Logan's heart."

"Amy, you're telling us that Logan doesn't know who she was?"

"No. I don't know why he'd believe someone he overheard behind a curtain."

"Are you going to tell him what you know?" Gibby asked.

"I just emailed him and asked him to call me. I told him I had lunch with Bobbie Winston. Maybe that will inspire him to call. I also asked him what he wants for Christmas."

"In other words, he better start shopping for you, right?"

"Beth, you're quick. No lame excuses. By the way, have the oranges arrived yet?"

"What oranges?" Beth asked.

"Logan is sending a case of oranges for us to share."

"Isn't he sweet?"

Amy growled. "He is going to have to kiss my ass for a long time to make up for this bullshit he's putting me through. Bo said he thought Logan would be home in about three weeks. By Christmas, for sure."

"If he comes back a better person, more secure, more sure of his feelings for you, then that's a good thing. Two short months out of your very long life doesn't seem like so much to me."

"Well, Miss Gibson, could that be because someone is regularly coming over to rumple your sheets? Believe me, it seems like a long time to me. What are you guys doing for supper?"

"Tuna noodle casserole. Can't you smell it? That's why Punkin is pacing."

"What color of wine goes with that?" Amy asked.

"Any color that I don't have to go out and buy. Want to stay?"

"Can I have a carryout? Just in case Logan calls?"

"Go home. I'll bring you a plate."

"Thanks, Gibbs." Amy left, picked up her mail and waited at the kitchen table for her dinner. And a phone call.

When she woke up the weatherman was gesturing at a map of the Midwest describing the hint of winter weather predicted to descend on them for the next five days. She watched the end of the news, and on her way to bed, she noticed that she had email waiting. She sat in front of the computer and spoke to the screen. "Well, it's not a phone call, but it's better than nothing."

Amy,

Stay away from the Winstons. They're dangerous. Please, do not go to see her again. Bart hurts people. I couldn't bear it if you were one of his victims.

What I want for Christmas...hmmm.

I want to go to church with you Christmas Eve. I want to hold you in my arms in front of the Christmas tree. I want to see the candlelight sparkle in your eyes.

See you soon!

L

She answered right away.

Logan,

Bart is in jail for at least 5 more months. Bobbie is divorcing him. She's a nice person and wants me to apologize to you for something.

I won't do it in an email. Call me, or I'm calling Bo.

You do realize, to get what you want for Christmas, you have to actually BE HERE.

I have a very nice cashmere sweater. It's white and very, very soft and clings in just the right places. I'll be wearing it with a short, dark red skirt that does amazing things to my ass. Imagine black strappy pumps.

Dance with me, Logan. Hold me close again.

Hurry home to me.

Amy

CHAPTER 42

The next morning Bo drove Logan to the hospital outpatient surgery department. Logan checked in and was hooked up to an IV while he sat in a wheelchair. Confidence and independence dissipated when he had to leave all his clothing with Bo. The open-backed gown made a real fashion statement, and Bo let him know that.

"Did you call Amy last night?"

"No, I sent her an email. She actually met Winston's wife. I told her to stay away. I don't trust him. He's an angry, violent man. If he hurt her, it would be my fault."

"If he hurt her, it would be his fault. Quit taking on the guilt of the world—that job has already been taken. But I must say, you're probably a better carpenter."

"Speaking of Jesus, do me a favor and pray that this works. I really don't want to have to get into creative fertility measures with Amy...surrogates and all that petri dish stuff. I just want this to work, Bo."

"Do you want me to call her?"

"No. Give me a couple of days. I'll call her."

A nurse approached wearing a smiley face smock. Logan cringed. Bo introduced himself and shook her hand.

"This is my brother, Logan. He's putting some very delicate parts in your hands, literally."

"Actually, I'm just taking his vitals. Dr. Andersen will be taking his very delicate parts in her hands. She's very good." She addressed Logan, "Try to relax. You'll be getting a little something to help you in a few minutes."

"Chivas?"

"No such luck, Mr. Carson, or I'd join you. It's been a long shift." She gave Logan a heated blanket and tucked it in around his legs. "Don't want you catching a chill."

She pushed him in the wheelchair. As they passed the waiting room she motioned to Bo. "You can sit in here and wait. If you need to use your cell phone, though, you'll have to go down to the lobby or outside. There's coffee, an assortment of newspapers, and now and then someone even brings cookies, so you may get lucky. The doctor will come out and speak to you when Logan is finished."

Logan put out his hand and Bo shook it. "Good luck, man. I think my first stop will be the chapel. This is the first time I ever prayed for sperm."

Logan discreetly gave Bo the finger, and Bo chuckled as he headed for the elevator.

"I saw that. Shame on you." The nurse mussed his hair. "Brothers!"

Bo was reading *Sports Illustrated* when Dr. Andersen came into the surgical waiting room. "Mr. Carson?"

"That would be me." Bo stood and shook her hand.

"I'm Dr. Andersen." She spoke in a low voice and stood very close to him. Logan was right—she smelled good. "Logan's surgery went very well. He'll be swollen for a while, so we won't know for a few days just how much of his normal function is returning. You can come and sit with him in recovery for a while if you like."

"Yes, please." Bo left the magazine on a table and followed her down the hall. "He's staying with me. Are there any rules?"

"Pages of them, most of which he will ignore. I'll give them to you to read over so you can keep him in line. He had very delicate surgery and we don't want to jeopardize that. He'll be sore and he won't want to walk, but make sure he does. No jogging, just gentle walking for a few minutes at a time. If he just sits around, recovery time will be longer than it needs to be."

"He can walk with my wife. She has the same instructions. We just had a baby."

"Congratulations. Some of these instructions I'll discuss with Logan when he wakes up. Otherwise, I don't think he'll believe you."

"Oh, this is sounding interesting."

"You'll have to check his stitches. If they get infected or bleed, call me right away." She handed him three prescriptions. "Get these filled on the way home. Make sure he doesn't miss a dose. The pain meds you can back off on, if he feels he doesn't need them."

"He's a baby."

"Most men are when their testicles are involved."

Bo winced. "You're probably right about that."

"He's young and very healthy. I think his recovery will be quick."

When they arrived at Logan's room he was sleeping and still had the IV hooked up. Bo walked up to his bed and looked at the doctor. "Can I wake him up?"

"Sure."

"Logan. Time to wake up, man. Surgery is done. Doc Andersen wants to look at your balls."

Logan groaned and covered his eyes with his arm. He was in for a hell of a week and he knew Bo would not make it any better.

Once the hospital staff were satisfied that Logan was ready to leave, Bo dropped him off at home, and headed for the pharmacy. Ginny walked Logan down the hall to his room. He sat down very slowly on the edge of the bed.

"Can I get you anything, Logan?"

"Water bottle. Spill-proof. I want to lie down."

"Can you undress yourself?"

"Probably not, but I'm going to try."

"Call if you get stuck. I promise not to look."

"Comedians. I'm surrounded by comedians."

CHAPTER 43

Amy answered the phone and the woman on the other end sounded in a panic.

"Yes, this is Amy, can I help you?"

"Oh, thank God! Amy, Margaret Gibson gave me your name. I have a painting emergency. Please, please, I know you're busy this time of year." Amy wondered who she had been talking to. "But I'm having a holiday party and my living room is ruined."

"Well, depending on the damage, I can probably give you a couple of days."

"Oh, dear. The party is in two days."

"What kind of damage are we talking about, fire or what?"

"Nothing quite that serious. I have white walls. My son had a party and someone threw a jar of spaghetti sauce and it went all over the wall. I just can't wash that orange tomato stain off. And I mean I have scrubbed and scrubbed. There's no way to hide it and I don't have artwork big enough to cover it. Can you come and look at it and tell me what you think? I'll pay you double your usual rate. Triple. Please."

Amy slipped on shoes and a coat and headed out in the van. When she got to the house the guilty party answered the door and apologized for inconveniencing her during the holiday season. Amy tried not to laugh. She appreciated the distraction. Actually two walls were involved. It was quite a sight. Definitely not a Christmas color. She explained that the prep work would take one day and she could paint the next day and hopefully the smell would dissipate before the party. Scented candles would be a good idea after she finished. The woman handed Amy a sizeable check as she glared at her son. Amy left, stopped at the paint store and went home to change into work clothes.

She checked email. Nothing from Logan—the dog.

She drove back to the sauced house to get started on the mess. Maybe it was time she designed a business card for herself. She preferred not to be known as the person who deals with painting emergencies, but if they all paid triple her going rate, it was something to consider. This freed up a little extra money for Christmas gifts. She wanted to get something for Bo and Ginny, especially since Bo had been so supportive during the whole Logan situation. And something for the baby. She tried it out in her mind. *Uncle Logan and Aunt Amy.* It was definitely better than being an aunt to a mutant cat. As always, here she was again, presuming—presuming that Logan was still serious about her being part of his future.

*

Logan was trying to sleep when Bo knocked on his door. "Logan, wake up. I have drugs for you."

Logan groaned. "This torture...it's deliberate, isn't it?"

"Just following Dr. Andersen's instructions. And I have to check your stitches to make sure they aren't infected."

"I haven't had them long enough for them to get infected. You just want to see my balls, don't you?"

"Yeah, because that's such a thrill."

"Well then, make yourself useful and help me get up. I have to use the bathroom."

Logan twisted, turned, moved one leg at a time while he whined, cussed, and groaned. To help him out, Bo reached behind him and grabbed a pillow for him to hold. Bo stopped and stared.

"Black satin panties...are those your size?"

"Shut up, Bo."

"They're Amy's, aren't they?"

"Not today, okay?"

"You know, Logan, you can have the whole woman, you didn't have to steal her panties."

"I'm gonna piss on your carpet if you don't help me up. And find a mirror for me. I'll be checking my own stitches."

"Ginny has one with a handle. I'll go get it once you're in the can."

Bo tried to wipe the smirk off his face as he caught up to Logan heading back to his room. Bo had a mirror in his hand from Ginny's dresser. Logan got situated in bed and threw the pillow back over the panties. "Shut up."

Bo tried the innocent act. "I didn't say anything."

"You didn't have to. I know you. Give me the mirror and turn your back."

Bo handed him the mirror and leaned against the door frame. He heard Logan grunting and whimpering while he was trying to situate himself for a good vantage point.

"Oh, my God! They're huge. I know she said there would be some swelling, but really, this is awful."

Bo couldn't resist turning around. "You're using the magnifying side, asshole."

Logan flipped the mirror over and breathed a sigh of relief. Bo left the room laughing. Logan wanted to laugh too, but it just hurt too much.

Bo hollered back down the hall. "You have time for a one-hour nap, then we're taking a little walk."

*

As Amy was picking up the last of her painting supplies, her client, with a very relieved look on her face, handed her an envelope. "You already paid me…"

"I know, dear, but I'm so grateful that you could take care of this so fast, it's an invitation to the party tonight. If you want to come back after you clean up, that would be nice. Bring your boyfriend, if you like."

"I appreciate the thought, but I have plans. Thanks for asking, though. I hope you're happy with the results."

"I am, and if any of my friends need painting done, I'll give them your name."

"I'd appreciate that, too. You have a nice holiday."

Amy tossed the invitation on the seat next to her and went home. She wasn't in a party mood. She carried her things in, tossed the invitation and her purse on the kitchen table and checked the answering machine. No messages. Tomorrow she would call Bo. She headed for the computer to check for email. It just glared at her. She wrote again.

Logan,

It's just plain rude not to answer a person.

I'm calling Bo tomorrow.

Whatever you do, don't call tonight. I had a painting emergency and I'm tired.

ASS

*

Logan had been avoiding the computer, sure that there was a message—at least one—from Amy. He wanted to have news for her when he finally did write. He thought he'd pick a time for a phone call, just to make sure she was going to be there when he called. He had just come in from another walk with Ginny and was going to sit and rest for a few minutes. He signed on to his computer and was rewarded with two messages from Amy. He read the oldest first.

You're killing me, woman! he thought.

"Email from Amy?" Bo stuck his head in Logan's room.

"You want to know why I'm screwed up, come here and read this."

Bo leaned over his shoulder and let out a low whistle. "Cashmere sweater, huh?"

"I don't think I should be reading this until I heal a little more."

"You thinking about what tits feel like through cashmere?"

"Well, I am now!"

"She sounds hot."

"Fahrenheit or centigrade, man. I have to go home."

"Amen."

"Let me read this other email." It was short. Logan felt chastised. "She's pissed because I didn't answer her. She says she's calling you. I didn't give her your number."

"She seems to be clever enough to find it."

"If she calls, don't talk to her, please."

Too late for that, Bo thought. "If she calls me, I'll talk to her. You just have to trust me. Or better yet, call her first. That will head off the call to me. Besides, maybe she's bluffing."

"She'll call. She doesn't bluff. Don't tell her things that should be coming from me."

"Then call her, man."

Amy,

You sure know how to stimulate my hormones.

I'll call you tomorrow night about 10 your time. Cut me some slack if I'm a few minutes late.

Looking forward to it.

Love,

L

Amy read his email and was filled with a warm feeling—something she had missed since Logan left for California. She actually had something to look forward to. That was one of the benefits of being in love. It put a grin on her face that she couldn't wipe off. She knew she'd sleep well that night.

First thing the next morning, Amy dialed Bo's number.

"This is Bo."

"Hi, Bo, Amy here."

"He's calling you tonight."

"I know. I just wondered if there was anything I needed to be prepared for before I pick up the phone."

"Are you missing a pair of black panties?"

"Yes."

"He stole them. He sleeps with them under his pillow."

"He didn't steal them, he bought them."

"Why?"

"I caught him stealing them and made him pay me for them. So they are now his black satin panties."

"He's goofy over you, you know."

"He's goofy, alright."

"Amy, I think he's ready to come home. It would be good if you were ready to have him back."

"Bo, I never wanted him to leave."

"I know. He asked me not to talk to you if you called. What do you want me to tell him?"

"Tell him I found your work number and called you. I don't lie to Logan."

"And you don't bluff."

"That's right. Thanks, Bo…for everything."

"Good luck tonight."

*

Since Punkin was standing in the hallway waiting for her, Amy stopped in to let Beth and Gibby know that Logan was calling that evening. She ate dinner, did laundry and took a shower. She was going to calmly enjoy a quiet evening at home. She turned the TV on and flipped through all the channels twice. Nothing caught her eye. Nothing tempted her to linger. She picked up her checkbook and a calculator and was doing a little math. The phone rang. It wasn't even 9:30. It couldn't be Logan yet. She answered the phone on the third ring.

"Hello?"

"I thought you were going to make me talk to your answering machine for punishment."

She smiled at the sound of his voice and took the phone into her room. She propped pillows against her headboard and sat down.

"I should have. Hi, Logan. How are you?"

"Much better, thanks. And yourself?"

"I'm better now, now that I've heard your voice. I've missed you terribly."

"Thank you for that. I've missed you, too. Sounds like you've been busy painting."

"Not really what I'd call busy, but I have had a couple extra jobs. I'm thinking about business cards."

"We can do that on the computer when I get back."

"When is that going to be, Logan?"

"Pretty soon. I'll let you know when I know for sure."

"How is the new baby?"

"He's pretty tiny, just sleeps the day away, except for the time he's attached to Ginny's breast. Bo is jealous. It's pretty funny."

"Have you changed any diapers yet?"

"Just one, under Ginny's guidance. It was nothing compared to the twins."

"Jack said to say 'Hi.' His cast is coming off in a few days."

"And Beth is getting married?"

"Yes, next July, in Iowa. She's very happy."

"Amy."

She waited for him to continue, but she just heard him breathing.

"Logan, what?"

"I love you."

"I love you, Logan." She wiped the tears on her pillowcase.

"I have things to tell you, but not over the phone."

"Good things, I hope?"

"Very good things."

"I have things to tell you, too."

He repeated her question. "Good things, I hope?"

"Actually, I think I'll tell you right now. Just because you've waited for this for so long."

"Okay, now you have my curiosity aroused."

"I told you I went to see Bobbie Winston. And don't start scolding me. Bart is in jail and Bobbie is divorcing him, so he was no threat to me. I found out she was Sam's roommate in the hospital."

"What?"

"She knew who you were and she was very angry with you, blaming you that Bart couldn't be with her when their baby was born."

"How did you find this out?"

"Bobbie admitted to me that she did something very hateful to you and it was totally deliberate, as revenge for firing Bart and starting him on his downhill slide."

"He started himself on that slide."

"Yes, and she realizes that now. She wanted to apologize for the conversation you overheard when you were taking Sam's things out of the room after she died. She knew you were in the room and could hear her…"

"Oh, my God, Amy. How do you know about this?"

"You left me no choice. I had to do some research. I know about Rebecca,

Logan. It just filled in all the blanks for me. I'm so sorry. I wish you could have trusted me enough to tell me the whole story."

"It's not that I didn't trust you to deal with it. I just had trouble admitting that it even happened."

"Bobbie knew you could hear her, so she told whoever she was talking to that everyone knew you killed your baby. Logan, she did it deliberately to hurt you."

"It did." His voice was soft and choked.

"She's sorry, Logan. She realizes now that she struck out at you because she couldn't strike out at Bart. I asked her if you didn't accept it from me, if you could call her, and she said yes."

"I don't know what to say. Her words have been haunting me for over a year. I thought she really overheard nurses talking."

"No. Rebecca's death, like Sam's, could not have been prevented by you."

"Rebecca, my little Rebecca. Amy, she was so tiny and perfect. She was beautiful."

"You didn't hurt her, Logan. You don't have to be afraid of babies anymore."

"How did you find out about Rebecca?"

"Old newspapers at the library. I read Sam's obituary and went to the cemetery."

"Amy, I should have gone with you."

"You weren't here, Logan, and I had to find out what was tormenting you."

"I'm glad you know. I just wish I would have been the one to tell you."

"Logan, do you want to hang up and just be alone with your thoughts for a while?"

"No, I've been alone with my thoughts enough. I want to share them with you. I just don't know where to go with this information from Bobbie Winston."

"I'm going to make it easy on you, Logan. Take some time and go talk to Bo. Call me again tomorrow or the next day."

"Okay, maybe I will."

"I'm going to bed now. I've had a long day."

"Think about me, ASS."

"No doubt about that, mink man. Come home to me."

"I will. I love you."

"Love you, Logan"

*

Amy and Logan spoke on the phone once a day for the next two weeks. He was still very vague about returning home. Amy, now more secure in his feelings for her, decided she would just charge ahead with her holiday plans. She knew Logan was aware that she was Christmas shopping for him. She remained vague as to any material items that he wanted, however.

Herself in his arms was easy enough to provide, but she wanted to get him something she could wrap up and tie a ribbon around. Just how fast was Logan going to move now that he supposedly had his family issues resolved? If not resolved, at least everything was out in the open, finally...she hoped. The thought of an engagement ring flashed through her mind and she had a brief moment of panic. Would he ask? Would she say yes if he asked? No doubt. If he didn't, would she be crushed? No, it would happen eventually, she was sure of that. What if she asked him? Fresh out of courage.

Ring or not, she would shop for him. She almost wished she were overbooked with painting jobs, since she did her best shopping under pressure.

That's when she decided. She would buy a tree, take it to his house—she still had the key—and decorate it with her ornaments. Now the pressure was on. Now she had a plan and felt ready to shop. She picked up her mail, separated it, and tossed the bills on the counter. She opened a couple of Christmas cards. One from Bo, Ginny and Randy. How sweet of them to think of her—although, Logan probably didn't give them a chance to forget her. She remembered the party invitation she had never gotten around to opening. She slit open the seal, slid out the card, opened it, and watched, surprised, as five one-hundred dollar bills floated to the table. She read the Currier and Ives Christmas card with its winter scene and handwritten invitation.

Amy,
I would be honored to have you return this evening for our party. 8 p.m.
Thanks again for the emergency paint job.
Merry Christmas,
The Burns Family

Well, that sure made shopping easier! she thought.

Amy found gift-wrapping one of the best traditions of the Christmas celebration. Watching people open her carefully wrapped packages was another. She made several stops while shopping for Logan, as this year she had included the California Carsons, Jack, Carrie, and the twins on her list, in addition to Hillie, Gibby, and Beth. Her parents were easy to buy for: she would purchase gift certificates for several restaurants. As she was nearing the end of her list, she realized there was one more person she'd forgotten—Bobbie Winston. She made a quick detour to Denny's for a gift certificate. And now, the final stop for Logan: Victoria's Secret.

*

Amy knew how much Beth missed Terry, so she thought it would be a good idea to bring her along on her secret mission at Logan's house—"Operation Tannenbaum." Beth welcomed the distraction.

The girls picked out a fresh eight-foot Balsam Fir. The fragrance of the tree brought back warm childhood memories for both of them. Fortunately, with Logan's house finished, Amy was able to remove painting gear to make space for the tree and two boxes of decorations and lights she had selected. They watched as the Boy Scout who sold them the tree, carefully wedged it in place.

Before long, the two partners-in-crime were rolling down Logan's driveway and Amy was jiggling her key into the lock at his back door. There was a strange feeling of invasion of privacy, since officially she no longer worked for Logan, but she gave Beth a quick tour anyway.

Beth admired Amy's work. "And you did this by yourself? Amy, really, I think you have found your niche!" Beth's hand was drawn to the railing, as Amy's had been. "I assume this was made by your darling Logan. It's so elegant."

"He's a perfectionist. Well, I guess we'd better get to work. How are your elf skills?" Amy asked.

"I love decorating! Let's do it!"

Amy and Beth juggled and grunted as the tree settled into the sturdy stand. By the time they were finished, their hands were sticky with sap, but they both agreed that the smell alone was worth it. Stringing lights was a task Amy always dreaded, but she found it was much easier with two people. She added red lights randomly in a string of white lights. The effect was quite nice. She opened a box of new ornaments and mixed them with some of her favorites she'd brought from home. She thought about looking for Logan's Christmas decorations, but decided against it when some of her own brought forth so many memories. That was definitely a job she would leave for him. If he wanted to include her, it would have to be his decision.

With two of them chatting and working diligently, the tree was finished in no time. Amy and Beth stood back and admired their work. The tree— strategically located in front of the picture window—looked great, from both inside the house and outside.

"Perfect," Beth whispered.

"Well, I guess we should clean up a little. I'll find the vacuum and take care of this carpet, if you'll fill the tree stand with water, Beth."

When these tasks were completed, Amy unplugged the lights, took the boxes, and locked up. She was anxious for Logan to discover her surprise.

"Ho, ho, ho!" Beth called out as they drove down the driveway and onto the road.

"Now, that's what I call Christmas Spirit," Amy agreed, grinning from ear to ear, tingling with anticipation.

*

When Amy got home, she found a message on her answering machine.

"Hey, Sweet. Check your email," Logan's mellow voice urged.

Darn, she thought. She'd missed his call. Before signing on to her computer, however, she needed to get the remaining tree sap off her hands. She rubbed baby oil on them until the goo finally broke down, then washed her hands.

Amy, Love,

I'm flying in on Friday. Matt is picking me up at O'Hare, and I'm going directly to CC to drop off some work and pass out the staff's Christmas gifts.

I'll be late. So, can we do breakfast Saturday morning? I'll pick you up at 8 a.m.

I'm leaving Bo's tomorrow—heading to Sacramento on business for a few days.

See you soon.

Love,

L

Perfect. That feeling of being under pressure kicked in. She needed a haircut. She had baking to finish and gifts to wrap. Thank goodness the shopping was done. Since her ornaments were at Logan's, she wouldn't put up a tree, but she had plenty of other decorations to scatter around. Amy remembered that the candle store had been calling her name. Their candles were handmade and very fragrant. This would be a gift to herself and would add the final festive touch to her home.

With all these odds and ends racing through her mind, she typed her reply, hoping Logan would check his email before leaving Bo's.

Logan,

How dare you be so close and not see me!

I suppose I can stand it until breakfast. 8:00 is fine. I have some last minute holiday stuff to deal with anyway. I'm trying to stay on Santa's "nice" list.

Have a good flight.

I miss you.

Love,

ASS

*

On Wednesday, Beth and Gibby stopped by after work. The smell of snickerdoodles was only part of the reason for their visit.

"Hey, Ames. You blowing that wonderful smell out into the hallway on purpose?"

"Not really. There's just something about cinnamon that gets in the air and draws people in. I can't give you a lot of time, but I can give you hot chocolate and a few cookies. I'll try to work and talk at the same time. If you can stand it, you're welcome to stay."

"For cookies and hot chocolate we can stand just about anything, can't we Beth?"

"Oh, it will be tough, but we'll manage. You just keep on working and I'll put some hot water on."

Gibby came back to the main reason for their visit. "Amy, have you realized that this is going to be the first Christmas in a while that we won't be together on Christmas Eve?"

"Why? I guess I hadn't thought about it. Hopefully Logan and I will have plans later in the day, but I thought we could do something in the afternoon."

"Sorry, y'all, but I'm going to Iowa to spend the holiday with Terry's family… you know, big engagement deal and all. Hillie is meeting a cousin in Paris of all places. Didn't she tell you?" Beth asked.

"She said it was a possibility, but didn't sound very sure of anything. Actually, she didn't even sound very excited. I just assumed the trip was off."

Beth was curious. "I think Paris would be very romantic at Christmas, but who is this cousin?"

"She's about five years older and lives in New York City. I met her once. We went to New York on spring break one year and stayed with her."

"That's why Beth and I were wondering if you'd like to get together for a few hours on Friday. You don't have a paint job, do you?"

"No, I haven't really been pushing. I've got enough going on and then the whole mental thing of Logan coming home has me exhausted by the end of the day without doing a darn thing. Friday would be okay with me. How about supper?"

"I checked with Hillie and Friday is okay. Beth, Friday still okay with you?"

"I took the day off to pack. I'm headed to Iowa the next day. I can't make a late night of it, but sure do have time for a little supper and gift exchange."

"I have Friday off, too. I traded Christmas Day with a friend at the hospital. She has kids and is into the whole Santa thing and all."

"Gibby, you're so thoughtful."

"It's easy when you have no life."

Amy set out three Christmas mugs and spooned in the instant hot chocolate mix. "If my grandma were here, this would be homemade from scratch. There'd be a big fat marshmallow floating in the middle of it." Her expression changed from sad to thoughtful. "My mom is a great mother, but I just don't think she'll be the kind of grandmother that I had. Then again, maybe she'll surprise me."

"Ames, does this mean something is happening with you and Logan?" Beth asked.

"Beth, the man hasn't been around for about two months. What could be happening?" Gibby asked.

"You've been talking on the phone and emailing. I just thought that maybe you made some decisions."

"I think we both decided we want to be together, but no details beyond that. I think his definition of 'future' and mine may not be the same. To me it means forever and ever, amen. I haven't pinned him down yet. When he looked in my eyes and said he wanted me in his future, I envisioned marriage, babies, the whole works. I know that sounds like sappy teenage girl stuff. I just don't know if that's how he sees it," Amy said.

"Look at it this way," Gibby said, trying to be optimistic. "He had two months to get his shit together. Let's hope he did. I would think with the big revelation from Bobbie Winston, things would kind of sort themselves out for him."

"I agree, Amy. I think Logan will come back with a whole new outlook on life."

"I hope you guys are right."

The warm, buttery cookies took their minds off more serious matters for a few minutes.

Amy got back to the issue at hand. "So, tell me about supper. Are we going out, carrying in, cooking or what?"

"We're taking the train to Hillie's. The city will be beautiful. We just have to bring a few things. Besides, she's the only one with a tree."

"I thought you guys had a tree."

"Punkin pretty much tore it up last year. You know cats—they have to attack anything dangling."

Amy winked at Gibby. "So, I assume Marty takes protective measures. And what is the life expectancy on these beasts?"

"Amy Sweet, that was just plain mean. Punkin probably has about four of her nine lives left."

"Her? So now this is a female?"

"Depends on my mood. When I'm feeling kind, she's a girl. When she's being a beast, she's a boy."

"Gibby, why don't you write that down for future reference?"

They finished their hot chocolate and Amy gave them each some cookies for the next day.

"Ames, if you think these cookies are going to see tomorrow, you don't know us very well."

"Bye, Beth. Gibby. Show some self-control, huh?"

*

On Thursday, Amy stopped at the post office to drop off her last batch of Christmas cards, including a thank you note to the Burns family for the Christmas surprise. She stopped at Logan's to fill the tree stand with more water. The living room smelled wonderful. Fortunately, the paint smell had been replaced with the balsam.

Friday morning found Amy full of energy. It was too cold to go for a walk, she had nothing to paint, and the cookies were finished. The only other activity that could burn up that much energy, besides sex, was cleaning. She stripped her bed and cleaned the bathroom. She put Christmas music on the stereo and washed windows. Before she knew it, it was time to get ready for the ride downtown to Hillary's apartment.

Finally, the three holiday revelers set out for the Metra station. They purposely planned to ride the train between rush hours, to maximize spread-out room for comfort and packages. The girls took seats facing each other, removed their hats and gloves, and opened their coats.

Amy shook her head and wondered, "Doesn't this seem strange, that three people drag stuff downtown and then drag it back home again in different bags, when it would be so much simpler for one person to do it? Exactly why are we doing this?"

"Because, if you'll remember, Hillie is the only one with a tree."

"I don't know that I see the necessity of the tree. Jesus didn't have an evergreen tree in the stable, did he? That didn't stop the Magi from bringing him gifts."

Gibby developed Amy's thought further. "If Jesus had been born in

Chicago, he'd have had a tree. It would have been plastic, but it would have been shaped like an evergreen tree. And he would have gifts: Goldschlager, franks and beans, and mirth."

Beth couldn't stand it. "Now don't you two go perverting the gospel!"

"Are you kidding?" Amy couldn't let it alone. "If Jesus were here right now, he would love mirth. Who doesn't? And franks and beans? Come on! Boys love that stuff. Goldschlager, I'll admit, would be overkill. But I bet Mary could have used a shot of it."

Beth pretended not to listen, but she was pinching back a smile.

Gibby picked up where Amy left off. "It's a good thing he was born so long ago. Imagine the Christmas story…they wrapped him in Huggies and a silky and laid him in a bouncy seat. DCFS would visit to make sure he was being taken care of properly, since the parents weren't married. They'd fill out forms that would get lost, and no one would ever check on him again."

"This is not funny."

"Come on, Beth. Look around you." A little boy across the aisle pulled something out of his nose and wiped it on the seat. "Don't tell me God doesn't have a sense of humor."

Beth glared at the little boy. He grinned at her and said, "Mewwy Cwismas. I'm going to my gwamma's house."

"That's nice. And Merry Christmas to you."

"Wheh you fwom? You talk funny."

Gibby and Amy were laughing so hard they were crying. Amy choked, "Go ahead, Beth, tell him where you're from."

"Young man, I have lived here for more years than you have been born. And I don't talk funny."

The boy's mother gave her an apologetic look and pulled her son closer. He leaned toward Beth and whispered, "Yes, you do."

To end the conversation, Beth leaned her head back on the seat and closed her eyes. "Let me know when we get there."

The train pulled into Union Station, and they had no trouble finding a taxi. The ride to Hillary's was short, but the women were bogged down with packages and the fare was well worth it. Hillie buzzed them up, relieved them of their packages, and gave them hugs and holiday greetings.

"Hillie, this is great! Everything looks so festive. Who did the food? I know it wasn't you."

"Thanks, Ames, you do know me pretty well. Actually I have a new friend, male, gay of course, and he has a catering business that he's trying to get off the ground. Just knowing you guys, I figured we could make a meal of canapés, finger sandwiches and appetizers. He wants our honest opinions, and I assured him we'd give them."

"Well, on appearances alone, I give him an A plus," Amy said while chewing something made out of a cucumber.

Gibby wondered, "How much is he charging you for this?"

"Half price. Mainly because he has a couple of experimental things that he's trying out on us. But don't ask which ones, because he wouldn't tell me."

Beth didn't bother with a plate. She just looked each item over, sniffed and popped it in her mouth. "Nothing here I don't like. Just stay out of my way."

Hillie watched, amused, as her friends grazed. "I'm sure glad the plan was to eat first." They all stopped chewing and looked at her, but only for a few seconds, then continued sampling. "I'll open some wine while you pigs enjoy the trough."

"Oink."

The four friends gathered in the living room with their wine glasses, surrounded by brightly wrapped gifts. Since none of them had family nearby, this had become their tradition. Hillie lit several candles and they turned down the lights. The Christmas tree was beautiful, adorned with red and green ornaments, cranberries on a string, and white lights.

Hillie laid out ground rules, and for a good reason. It could easily become a free-for-all. "One at a time, so we can ooh and ahh over everything. And we start with the person next to the tree and we go clockwise. Do not deviate from this direction or you will lose your turn at opening and your gift will be forfeited to the hostess. Me."

Amy raised her hand. Hillary acknowledged her. "What now?"

"I think we need to deviate. I think you need to start, because I know what's in that gold box and I want a piece."

Cheered on by Gibby and Beth, she acquiesced. The Godiva chocolates were passed around and everyone thanked Hillie, who in turn, thanked Amy.

One by one, they opened their gifts, holding up sweaters, sniffing cologne, flipping through books, and opening more chocolate. When the last paper had been torn and ribbon set free, they thanked each other for the thoughtful gifts, but truly feeling much more grateful to be part of one another's lives.

"I really appreciate you guys moving the celebration here this year. Our annual Christmas dinner means a lot to me. It makes me sad to think that this little group could fall apart soon, with Beth getting married and Amy attached to Logan."

"Change isn't always bad, Hillie." Beth reached out and patted her leg. "Besides, as Amy keeps reminding me, Iowa isn't Egypt. Terry's is only four hours away."

Gibby added, "I bet next year Amy and Logan will have other plans."

"I hope so, but I hope they are in addition to my plans with you guys, not in place of them."

"Of course, I'm just sitting around waiting for one of my gay friends to introduce me to one of his straight friends."

"Hillie, you have friends. Period. That's a blessing."

"I know it is. Believe me."

Gibby stood up. "I swear, if you cry I will come over there and kick your ass. Where are the tissues?"

They sat a few minutes treasuring the warm feeling, remembering fondly Christmases past and apprehensive of the unknown future.

Beth was the first to make the move to leave. "As much as I hate to leave even a crumb of this food, I have to get up very early tomorrow. And Gibby has to work. And Amy will probably need all this time to primp for the return of Logan."

Hillie gasped. "Tomorrow! Are you nervous? Are you ready? What are you going to say? Are you going to ask him what the hell he's been doing? Are you going to threaten him with bodily harm if he ever does it again?"

"Whoa, Nellie! I'm going to screw his brains out. And then we're going to talk."

"I thought you were going for breakfast."

"Whatever."

"Keep us posted. You know we're living vicariously through you."

"Merry Christmas, Hillie, and thanks again for inviting us."

The friends hugged, thanked each other one more time for the gifts, and wished Hillie Merry Christmas. She waited with them for a taxi, then went back in. The train ride home was quiet. They contemplated their lives and how quickly things changed sometimes. Amy was counting down the hours until breakfast with Logan. Beth was imagining her engagement to Terry, and Gibby was hoping Christmas would be a joyful time for the parents at the hospital nursery.

CHAPTER 44

When Amy got home she spread the gifts from her friends on the coffee table. She locked the door and put on the free t-shirt she received for buying a pair of running shoes. Across the chest it read "Just do it." She washed her face, brushed her teeth, and climbed between the clean linens that still smelled like the dryer sheet. She hugged her pillow, inhaled the clean scent, and fell asleep.

She had been asleep for about an hour when the phone rang. She went to the kitchen, picked up the cordless and took it back to bed with her.

"Hello." Her voice was thick with sleep.

"Is this Amy Sweet, the most wonderful woman in the world?"

"Logan, are you drunk?"

"No, Sugar, just missing you. You asleep?"

"Not now. Where are you?"

"I'm on my way home. Dreaming about me?"

"I don't think I was asleep long enough to dream. How are you?"

"I'm just fine. Horny, I think. Or maybe it's gas."

"Figure it out before you get here, okay?"

"Thank you for the tree. It's beautiful."

"You were home already?"

"I had to drop off some stuff and pick up some stuff. I saw it through the window and hoped you were hiding behind it, waiting to surprise me."

"It crossed my mind. I even bought a big red bow for my butt."

"My kind of gift."

"Are you done being a shit, Logan?"

"I think so. I'm going to have to kiss your ass for a long time to make up for this, aren't I?"

"Pucker up, baby."

"That's one of the reasons I love you. You never let me off the hook."

"Never will. Logan?"

"What, Sweet?"

"What are you wearing?"

"That's my line."

"Not tonight. It's my line."

"I'm wearing jeans. Old ones. Tiny hole in the knee. Color worn off the seat and thighs. I'm wearing an old sweater, soft and red. White running shoes and socks, white t-shirt, and blue silk boxers."

"Geez, Logan. I bet you look good enough to eat."

"Yes, I do. Want a snack?"

"Run your hand up under your sweater."

"Amy, it doesn't work this way."

"It's working for me. Are you touching yourself, Logan?"

"No. What are you wearing?"

"Ratty t-shirt. This is my game." There was a knock at the door. "Shit."

"What's wrong?"

"Someone with incredibly bad timing is at my door, probably Gibby or Beth needing to borrow something." She took the phone with her and went to the door. She opened it. Logan stood looking at her with his cell phone to his ear, a huge smile on his handsome face. She stood back, let him in and said, "Gotta go. There's a horny stranger at my door, and I think he wants to molest me."

Smiling, Logan took the phone from her hand, hung it up and laid it on the table with his. He slipped off his jacket and hung it on a hook by the door. When he turned around, Amy had stepped back and was holding her hands over her mouth. She was crying and suddenly Logan looked concerned.

"What's wrong?"

Rushing toward him, she pounded her fists into his chest. He didn't try to stop her. She pounded and admonished him.

"Damn you Logan, don't you ever leave me again!"

When she calmed down, Logan wrapped his arms around her and held her close. He whispered into her hair. "Shhh. Amy, I'm sorry. But I'm glad I left. I figured stuff out. I know that I don't want to live my life without you being part of it, and I couldn't be awful enough to scare you off. Please forgive me. I missed you so much." He kissed her hair, her ear, her neck. He held her wet cheeks in his hands and wiped them gently. Slowly her arms went around his back and she looked up into his bottomless green eyes. He kissed her eyelids, her forehead and the tip of her nose. She tipped her head back and parted her lips as he kissed her tentatively. She held him tighter and he whispered into her mouth, "Love me, Amy."

"Logan, I do."

He claimed her mouth with his and she gladly relinquished ownership. Logan ran his hands down her back and pulled her tight against himself, as if reassuring her that he was home to stay.

"Can you spend the night?"

He put his hands on her shoulders and grinned. "I look at it as arriving early for breakfast. Can we talk for a few minutes?"

"Do we need to?"

Logan put his arm around her shoulder and walked her back to her bedroom. "Yeah. Just updating you on the latest developments."

Logan took in the newly remodeled bedroom and nodded. "Mauve isn't as bad as I thought it would be. You did a nice job. I like the quilt."

"Thanks. I had a lot of energy to expend and redirect."

Logan stretched out his arms and looked at Amy. "Well?"

"Well what?"

"Are you going to undress me or is that for special occasions?"

"The full blown version is for special occasions. But tonight we can start with the sweater." She ran her hands underneath the sweater, caressing Logan's chest. He reached down and pulled it up and off, tossing it on a chair. He knew what was next and sat on the chair to remove his shoes and socks. She stepped between his knees, held his face and kissed his mouth, enjoying the bottom lip she had missed for almost two months. His arms went around her waist and he nuzzled into the softness of her chest. Amy noticed that he hadn't had a haircut in a while and she liked it. Running her fingers through his hair, she held him to her and kissed the top of his head.

"I missed you, Logan. I missed everything about you. I got used to seeing you almost every day, so it was terrible being without our conversations, our meals together, the silliness."

"Yes, it was. Do you want me to stay dressed while we talk or can you control yourself?"

"Don't talk to me about self-control, mister. We can do this. We're grown-ups, aren't we?" She pulled the t-shirt off and tossed it across the room, standing in front of him in her everyday white cotton panties.

"Well, well. That's some industrial strength underwear you got going there, Ms. Sweet."

"Don't make fun of my panties."

"Nothing that big is panties. Them's drawers, plain and simple."

"Be nice, or my drawers will stay on all night."

Amy pulled Logan up by the hands and he pulled his t-shirt off. Slipping her fingertips beneath the button on his jeans, she pulled him closer to the bed. He sucked his belly in as she started to unbutton the jeans. She stopped and looked up at him.

"Are you trying to impress me? Keep in mind I've already seen you trotting naked through…"

"Okay, number one, I don't trot. Number two, I know you're impressed. Number three, I was just giving you a little slack to make it easier to go for the gold."

"Had it gold-plated while you were gone, did you?"

"You'd like that, wouldn't you?"

"Add a few jewels for texture and I just might!" She unbuttoned the jeans and lingered on the zipper while resting her forehead on his chest. She looked up into his eyes, smiled and yanked it down quickly, causing Logan to suck in his breath. He reached down and held her hand still.

"Jewels, indeed. That's just what we need to talk about." Logan sat on the edge of the bed, pulled off his jeans and Amy's favorite silk boxers. "Lose the drawers and we'll talk."

Amy dropped her panties to the floor, caught them on her big toe and flung them into the laundry basket.

"Now, I'm impressed."

She bowed and sat with her legs folded on the bed facing him. He reached across and touched her breast with one finger. She reacted and whispered, "Cheating. No fair."

"Sorry. I've wanted to do that for a while.

"You'll get your chance in a minute. Talk to me, Logan."

"I'm going to ask you to do something, and just go with it, don't think it's weird."

"Okay, I trust you, you know that."

"First, give me your hand." She did. He held it to his face and kissed her palm. "Now be gentle, and I'm not kidding." He guided her hand between his legs and pressed her fingers to the scar, still slightly raised. She held him gently and with her other hand covered her mouth.

"Logan! Oh, my God! Did you? Did you do it?"

He nodded and smiled at her.

"Did it work? For real?"

He nodded again. "How do you know?"

Logan's brow wrinkled and he rolled his eyes. "Well, I had to visit a hooker... and she..." Amy gave a little squeeze. "Hey, hey. Gentle, please. This is delicate tissue we're dealing with. The lab checks for swimmers, that's how I know."

"Logan, you have swimmers?"

He smiled and nodded. "Yes, Amy, we have swimmers."

"So your daddy issues..."

"Pretty much dealt with—between the twins and Randy, and my brother beating common sense into me."

"And knowing Bobbie Winston lied."

"Well, there is that. And thanks, Amy. Thanks for digging that out. You're quite the detective."

"Logan, can I let go now?"

"Never."

It was Amy's turn to roll her eyes. "So this means we're back to condoms."

"Unless you want babies tonight, Amy, yes."

"I want babies, but not tonight. Logan, you know you could have had this surgery here. I could have been with you for support."

"I know that. I was fairly certain that I was going to try for the reversal when I left for California. And really, it isn't that I didn't want your support. Mainly I had to deal with what I was going to do if it wasn't successful."

"Logan, I love you, that wouldn't have changed."

"I know, but I had to figure out how I felt about the options. I had to come to a decision about that even before I knew if the surgery worked. Once I was sure that I could tell you that the reversal didn't work, and we'd need to adopt, or do something in a petri dish, then I knew that I'd try it, even if it failed. It wasn't that I didn't trust your reaction. I had to come to terms with it myself."

"I'm trying not to have my feelings hurt…"

"Oh, Amy, please, don't. It would have been dangerous to have you around, for one thing. It was bad enough that my doctor wore the same perfume that you wear."

"You had a woman doctor for this?"

"Yeah, don't be jealous…but she had her hands all over me…she couldn't help herself. I think she enjoyed it."

"And then she sent you a bill, right?"

"It's not like paying for sex. I didn't enjoy it. Even if she did have long blonde hair, great hands, big…"

"She better have a big ass, that's all I can say. Just remember, I won't send you a bill."

"Well, then, the decision is made…I'm dumping her. I needed a little break from stimulation, if you know what I mean. I was swollen and sore and crabby. Believe me, it was better that you were here."

"Well, since you came home with such good news, I'll forgive you."

Logan placed his warm hands on her knees. Amy looked down at them as he started moving them very slowly.

"Look at me, Amy." She was mesmerized by the warmth of his hands and the heat from his eyes. She didn't look away and neither did he. He left a trail of heat where his hands had been. Her breath came in starts and stops as she anticipated his final destination. Logan was excited just watching passion and anticipation rise in the expression on her face. She licked her lips and whispered his name as she reached across and pressed her fingers to his lips.

"Logan. Logan, make love to me. Please, Logan."

He kissed her fingertips and pulled her legs out straight. She lay back on her pillow and watched him stretch over her as he reached for the nightstand. The condom box was right where he left it. "You sure you don't want babies tonight?"

"I'm sure of very little at this moment, except that I want you to touch me all over, kiss me until I can't breathe, and come deep inside me where I've been keeping a place warm for you."

He handed her the condom, leaned back and let her put it on him. She was being very careful, and for that he was grateful.

"I'm afraid time is of the essence here once again."

"Logan. We have to do this more often. That will help."

"I agree. But right now…" He ran his fingers through her soft, inviting curls, gently probing her warmth until her back arched. "I need to be inside where you hold me so tight." As he pressed and probed, he kissed her breast and pulled the nipple deep inside his mouth. His tongue teased and Amy held his head to her, not wanting him to stop.

"Come home, Logan." She moved her leg, wrapping it around his thigh. She drew him closer and guided him into her with her hand. Logan's lips found her other breast. He tugged on her nipple before licking and sucking the puckering skin. "Logan, don't make me talk dirty to you."

"Do it…whisper in my ear."

She put her lips on his ear, traced it with her tongue and made demands in a whisper. Fervently he kissed her until she gasped for breath. "Logan. Please. I missed you so much."

As Logan thrust deeper into her welcoming warmth, she matched his rhythm and urged him to finish with her. Logan's face was buried in her silky hair spread across her pillow. He groaned, "Okay? Amy. Come on, baby." He thrust one final time, filling her and groaning his release into her pillow.

Amy held him tight to her, enjoying his weight pressing her down. "Logan?"

"I won't move. I promise. Love me, Amy. Just love me."

"Mmm. I do. Oh, Logan. God!" She clenched him between her thighs and let go. "Thank you. I needed that, really. Logan. I love you. I love you." She kissed his shoulder as she tried to catch her breath. He collapsed on her and that's just where she wanted him to be.

The bright winter sun hitting Logan in the eye woke him up. He watched Amy for a few minutes. They were wrapped in a tangle of sheets, and he wasn't quite sure where she started and he stopped. She was making a little humming noise and a lock of her hair was stuck to her lip. Very gently, he moved the top sheet and looked at her breasts. When he leaned forward he blew across the tip and watched it harden. Amy shifted, freed her hand and rubbed her breast as if to warm it. Logan groaned and reached to pull the hair off her mouth. He touched her cheek with the back of his fingers and licked her bottom lip. She opened her mouth and reached for him, but he had backed up to watch her reaction. When she opened her eyes she saw Logan studying her.

"Good morning, my darling."

"Logan, how long have you been watching me?"

"Long enough to get this." He guided her hand beneath the sheet and wrapped her fingers around his erection. She squeezed and stroked.

"Logan. Condom right now. If I get up to go to the bathroom I'm not coming back."

As agile as a gymnast, Logan turned, trying to reach the nightstand while not dislodging Amy's hand. Condom in place, Amy continued instructions.

"And don't breathe on me. What on earth did you eat last night? Never mind. Don't answer."

Logan rolled her to her side and snuggled from behind. He pulled her close and she lifted her top leg over his. With her hand she guided him exactly where she wanted him to be. He pressed deeply and held her breast with his hand, the hard nipple branding his palm. She moved his hand lower and he stroked her sensitive, swollen flesh. As wave after wave of her climax rolled over her, she called his name.

"Logan, thank you. God, I missed this." He was still full inside of her and she gave him a final squeeze, which nudged him over the edge.

"Amy, my Amy." He moaned his release into the back of her neck. "Finally, I got to finish last. I love you." He pulled her close and kissed her shoulder. When he collapsed onto the pillow they were now sharing, Amy heard a rumble then a noxious cloud rose over the bed and threatened to smother her.

"Logan, you didn't!"

"What?"

"Don't pull that shit with me! I just remodeled in here! Now the paint will be peeling off the walls. You stink, you beast! Get your stinking ass out of my bed! What the hell did you have for supper?"

"A burrito as big as my ass."

"New ground rules: never again, unless there are at least three days between the burrito and seeing me. Sorry, Logan, you have just stepped into the PIG zone. You have twenty minutes. I'm getting a shower. The smell better be totally gone when I get out of the bathroom. Clear it out! And no lighting candles. I'm afraid of an explosion. Open the windows, whatever. If I smell it when I get out, we're finished. No breakfast, no life together, nothing. There is a special place for that lethal discharge, and it is not, I repeat, not in my sheets."

"Sorry," he mumbled. He pulled the sheet over his head to hide from her wrath and quickly pulled it back down. "Yikes. Sorry." He ducked as she threw a can of deodorizer on the bed. He picked it up and read the label. "Lavender doesn't stand a chance against this."

"Shut up and spray, Logan." She slammed the bathroom door.

Logan, leaning against the pillows laughed and shouted to the bathroom door, "I love you, Amy Sweet."

He knew she replied, but didn't quite understand what she said. Probably just as well. He opened the bedroom windows, sprayed the entire room, threw the sheets in the washer and tossed her quilt over the balcony railing. He went to the kitchen to start coffee and sprinkled the grounds with cinnamon. Any additional fragrance would be welcome. He sat on the couch in his boxers hoping he wasn't infringing on any new rules. He was next to use the shower and hoped she'd save him some hot water. He'd be lucky if he got a towel.

The bathroom door cracked open and Amy took a preliminary sniff of her room. The linens were stripped from her bed. She smelled a hint of lavender and coffee and noticed that Logan was gone. She slipped on fresh underwear, old jeans and a warm sweater, then followed the scent of the coffee into the kitchen.

Logan was sitting at the kitchen table with a cup of coffee, trying to look innocent.

"Morning, Sweet."

"The shower is yours now. Take a clean towel."

"Thanks. Kiss good morning first?"

Amy leaned over his shoulder and kissed his cheek. "Blueberry pancakes okay?"

"I'll hurry."

She smiled as she watched Logan's strong back and blue silk boxers leave the room.

After making pancakes and pouring orange juice, Amy poured herself a cup of coffee and sat to wait for Logan.

He kept his word and hurried back. When Logan joined her at the table she stood up, wrapped her arms around his neck, and ran her fingers up into his clean, fluffy hair. He kissed her, thoroughly claiming her as part of his life. He rubbed her back, buried his face in her hair, and whispered into her ear. "I love you, Amy. I'm so glad to be back."

"Logan, don't ever leave me again."

"I won't, my darling. Can I have some pancakes?"

They sat down to eat breakfast. Logan chugged his orange juice and waited while Amy placed several pancakes on his plate. "Tell me all about your California trip."

"I found new places to order lumber and stain. I hired a carpenter."

"Logan, I mean the personal stuff."

"Gosh, there was so much. Ask specific, I'll tell you specific."

"Boy, that's the male brain at work. I want to hear about your thoughts and feelings, not what you wore while you were there."

"Khaki shorts, polo shirt, Birkenstock sandals."

"Typical. Tell me how you felt when Ginny went to the hospital."

"Oh, God." He set his fork down and took a deep breath. "Bo was actually great. He just kicked into high gear and dealt with it all, cool and collected."

"I asked about you, Logan."

"Well, part of me was watching how Bo reacted. I had a flashback to Sam. I remember driving her to the hospital, so hopeful, you know, nervous, but excited. Ginny saying, 'It's time,' just threw me back. Bo brought me back to the present. They invited me to go along, but there was no way I could relive that. Finally Bo called after Randy was born. I made him swear to keep an eye on them both."

"But are you better with that, now that I've told you about Bobbie Winston?"

"Oh yeah. I mean, it's still horrible, something I'll never forget. And when I drive you to the hospital nine months pregnant and ready to deliver our baby, I'm sure it will cross my mind again."

"Logan."

"What?"

"Our baby? You actually said the words without flinching or sweating."

"Because I know it will happen. I want it to happen. I need it to happen. Amy, I love you. I want you in my life forever. I want to hold you close and feel our baby moving in your belly between us. Please, Amy, want that with me."

"I do. I'm glad you finally feel that it can happen for us."

"Amy, will you move in with me?"

Not quite the proposition she was expecting, she said, "No."

"Okay. But after we're married, will you move in with me?"

"I'll let you know when you propose."

Logan got out of his chair, knelt next to her, took the fork from her hand and kissed each finger. "My darling, beautiful, sweet Amy Sweet, will you do me a great honor and be my most wonderful wife for ever and ever, amen?"

"Can I check my schedule?"

"I'll turn you over my knee right now."

"Logan, nothing would make me happier than having you for my husband. I love you. You fill my heart. You make me a better person. You make me laugh."

"I give you multiple orgasms."

"Well, there is that. Yes, Logan. I would love to be your wife."

"Thank God. And after we're married, can I assume you'll move in with me?"

"In your house? The one I just painted?"

"If you're not comfortable with that, we can sell it and buy another one."

"Logan, I love the house. Can you deal with the Sam-Rebecca-nursery issues? I know I can. I feel no threat from any part of your life. You love me and I know it and I know we'll have a fresh start."

"I have a feeling by the time you finish the house, it will totally be ours, not Sam's and mine. And of course I'd love to keep the workshop."

"I'd hate to have you give it up."

"Great." Logan sat back in his chair. "I have a few surprises for you. I was assuming you'd say yes. I was hoping. I want to go to the house. I have a couple things to show you."

"Today?"

"As soon as we clean up our breakfast dishes. You'll find I have little patience with keeping secrets or surprises."

"Okay, I'm intrigued. I was just at the house to water the tree."

"I've actually been home for a while."

"You dog! Here I sit moping, missing you, and you've been home?"

"It wasn't easy for me, believe me, but it was necessary. You'll see." He helped her clear the table and load the dishwasher. She turned off the coffeepot, then they grabbed their jackets and headed for Logan's.

Brisk was the best word to describe that wintry Saturday morning. The sky was crystal clear blue. The sun warmed their faces and snow crunched under their feet as they walked to the back door.

Logan used his key to let them in. He pointed to her last note on the counter. It was only one word, but emotion shouted from the four letters: *Done.*

"Snotty little note you left me."

"I was pissed at you and hurt." She crumpled it and tossed it in the trash. "I think I'm over it but don't push me."

He held her close, rubbed her back and kissed her mouth with the familiarity she had missed. He reveled in the taste of her. She responded by leaning into him and relaxing with the warm feeling of coming home. Amy surrendered her lips as she concentrated on his taste and textures, committing them to memory.

Slightly pulling back, she whispered, "Is this the surprise? We're going to do it on the kitchen floor?"

"Do you want to? I was thinking more like on the counter."

"Stop kissing me or that's where we're headed."

"No, you stop kissing me."

"I can't. I've missed you."

"Amy, trust me, within the hour, you will once again be begging me not to move."

"Oh, good. The surprise?"

Logan helped her with her coat and they kicked off their shoes. He turned the heat up and Amy filled a pitcher with warm water and carried it to the Christmas tree. She filled the reservoir as Logan turned the lights on. Its simple beauty filled the room.

"Thank you so much for doing this for me," Logan said.

"I didn't look for your decorations, so these are mine."

"Mine are gone. One of my more stupid moves after Sam died."

"Right up there with vasectomy?"

"Oh, yeah. Live and learn, baby."

"Surprises, please."

"Upstairs."

Logan wound his arm around her waist and side by side they ascended the stairs.

Amy assumed they'd be going to his room, but at the top of the stairs he turned her in the opposite direction. As she turned she noticed the door to his room was closed. She walked side by side with Logan to the end of the hall. The door to the former nursery was closed, as usual. Even after painting it white she had closed the door.

Logan opened the door, stepped into the room and held his hand out to Amy. She grasped it and he pulled her in.

"I'm sure you were thinking bad things about me when I asked you to repaint the nursery white."

"Not bad things, exactly, but I was sad because it was so cute. It seemed you were trying to erase memories by painting over everything."

"Symbolically, I can see where you would think that, and maybe that was partly true. I'm sure it was true. But my real reason was so that you'd have a blank canvas to decorate for our babies."

"Logan." She threw her arms around his neck and burst into tears. "That's so sweet, so thoughtful."

"These are happy tears, I assume?"

"These are very happy tears. I love you, Logan. Thank you very much."

"You're very welcome." He returned her hug. "Amy, promise me, anything else here that you think may be too much 'Sam' or too much my life 'BS' before Sweet, please tell me. We'll remodel, knock walls down, whatever it takes for you to feel totally welcome here. Even the kitchen."

"Thanks. The kitchen can stay."

"Good. It was a lot of work. You can hire someone to decorate or you can do it yourself. You have a good eye and I trust you."

"Maybe hire a decorator for ideas and I'll do the work myself."

"I'd like to help."

"We'll see."

"Next stop." He led her out into the hall, leaving the nursery door open.

She stopped at the study. He had carried part of his desk up and had his new chair in place in front of his computer. He added a brown leather recliner and had measured for book cases, which she assumed he would make.

"You did a great job with the paint, Amy."

"Thanks. We still need to work on windows."

"The rest of the desk is almost done. I'm happy with it." He nudged her down the hall to the next door, the more feminine guest room. The yellow walls were so cheerful. Then Amy realized the room was finished.

The bed and dresser were from Logan's room. He had added lace curtains and an antique quilt covered the bed.

"Logan, it's darling!"

"That's what I was shooting for. I'd like to add a little dressing table and maybe a rocker. What do you think?"

"That's just what it needs."

"Look under the pillow."

Amy pulled back the quilt and reached under the pillow to find a box of condoms.

"We're breaking it in properly right now."

Before she could respond, his sweater was off, he had pulled his socks off and unbuttoned and unzipped his jeans. He pulled her sweater off over her head. She was wishing she had worn a bra; he was glad she didn't.

"Isn't it kind of bright in here?"

"Exactly. I want to look at you. You're not shy, are you?"

"Logan, please, every crease and roll…"

"Relax. I love you. All of you." He unsnapped and unzipped her jeans and smiled. "Yellow panties; you match the room."

"Not for long." She pulled off her socks and jeans. "You're not wearing underwear? Logan, please."

"I'm going commando just for you, baby."

"Ugh, gross! Panties on or off?"

"Off." Logan pushed his jeans down and hopped around on one foot while pulling at the other leg. Off-balance, he landed on the bed.

"Underwear, please. This is not a good look for you. Hopping and bouncing parts…really, Logan."

He held out his leg. "Pull." She did, and tossed his jeans on the floor with the rest of their clothes. "Just remember, I'm still healing."

The sun warmed her face and lit her breasts. She stepped between his knees and he held each breast very gently while alternating kisses on each one. She held his head to her chest, not wanting him to stop. She inhaled, rubbing her face in his hair. His tongue circled a nipple, and when she gasped and clenched her hands in his hair he drew her deep into his mouth.

"Logan. Logan. God, I missed you. More please. More. Oh, God."

"Amy, you're so beautiful." He slid his hands down and encircled her waist. As he kissed her belly, he reached behind and sank his fingers into her bottom.

She warned, "Not one word, Logan."

"I love your ass." He turned her around, placed several kisses on each cheek and reminded her, "Remember, I have to kiss your ass for a long time to make up for the California trip."

Amy sat on his lap and pushed him down on the bed. "I won't let you forget it. You're not afraid of getting girl cooties from this room?"

"No. If I haven't gotten them from you, I'm not going to get them from lace curtains."

"Kiss me until I faint."

"I think I'll stop just short of that." They explored with lips and tongues, making little noises and murmuring love words. Amy ran her knee between Logan's thighs, stopping just short of making him wince.

"It's time, Logan. I need you inside me."

Logan reached for the condoms and Amy stopped him with a hand on his wrist.

"Amy?"

"Logan, we're getting married?"

"Yes, my love."

"Soon?"

"Whenever you want."

Amy took the box and tossed it to the floor. "I want you inside me, Logan. I want to feel you."

"If you're sure, because I don't mind."

"I want the heat and texture, the wet and messy, the hard and slippery. And

I want it now, Logan. Love me. Please love me."

He knelt between her knees and ran his hands up her arms, over her breasts and down to her belly. She brought her knees up and held him. "Logan, I need you." She reached down and being careful of his healing incision, gently drew her nails over the snug, textured skin.

"Amy, what are you doing to me?" She stroked his hardness and guided him to her warmth.

"It's where you belong, Logan." She clenched her muscles and he groaned as he pressed deep inside her.

"Don't let me go, hold me tight. Come with me, Amy."

"One of these times, we're going to slow this down a little."

"This isn't the time. Oh, God, Amy. Come with me."

She pressed her heels into his bottom and held him inside. With her arms around his back, she held him close, nuzzled his neck and rose to the pinnacle of passion with him. He collapsed on her, whispering her name in love and thanks.

After Logan caught his breath, he rolled off Amy, raised himself on an elbow and brushed her hair back from her face.

"You're so beautiful when you have that exhausted, satisfied look on your face."

"You wear me out, Logan. Thanks for the surprise."

"There's more."

"I don't think I have the strength."

"First, you're going to have a refreshing, invigorating shower."

"I could use one."

Logan stood and pulled her across the bed. She stood up and walked with him into the bathroom. Logan turned the shower on and handed her the bar of lavender soap that she used once before. He stepped into the tub and offered his hand to her. Holding her close, they stood under the spray together. He handed her the shampoo and bent so she could easily reach his head. She scrubbed and caressed, enjoying the feel of his thick hair. He rinsed and washed her hair, combing with his fingers so there were no tangles. Amy lathered the washcloth with the lavender soap and scrubbed Logan's back. He returned the favor.

He lathered his hands and slid them over her breasts, gently squeezing. Amy's breath caught as he stroked her nipples. She held onto his shoulders. "Logan, again?"

"I want to wash you."

"Really, I can do that myself."

"I want to." He reached between her legs and very tenderly lathered her. He caressed and rinsed her and she was surprised at the gentleness of his touch.

"Well, I guess modesty is out the window."

"I've kissed you there, Amy. Don't tell me you're embarrassed?"

"No, but it's different in the dark, under sheets."

"Wash me."

She lathered her hands and standing behind him, reached around to his front. Logan leaned forward with his hands on the wall. She rubbed his belly and went lower, not missing any crease or fold. He was slippery with soap and she stroked his penis until he became hard in her hand. "Do you want me to finish this?"

"No. I think it's clean enough, don't you? Besides there's another surprise."

"Logan, you're wearing me out."

They rinsed and Logan wrapped her in a thick, fluffy, yellow towel. She took another towel, fluffed his hair, dried his back and handed it to him. He wrapped it around his waist and picked her up.

"Logan! Where are you taking me?"

"To the next surprise." He carried her down the hall and opened the door to his bedroom. "Close your eyes." He walked to the center of the room and set her down. "Open."

With her eyes wide open, Amy covered her mouth with her hands, unable to speak. Logan wasn't sure how to interpret her reaction.

"Well…?"

"Logan, it's beautiful! When did you have time to do this?"

"It's been done for about a week. I'm surprised you didn't run into someone when you came to water the tree. I had Matt arrange everything."

"The bed is beautiful. Did you make this?"

"I ordered it from Freddie." The bookcase headboard matched the other furniture in the room and looked perfect with the French Country comforter and accessories that Amy had originally pointed out to Logan from the catalog she left with him.

"It must have cost you a fortune!"

"You know how I feel about quality handmade furniture. It's worth every penny. You saw the kind of stuff Freddie makes. He's a perfectionist…probably more so than I am."

She gave him a doubtful look and smiled. "You took my suggestion with the decorating."

"I was feeling very positive and optimistic. I was hoping you'd say yes when I asked you to marry me. I was hoping you'd want to keep the house."

"This is for me?"

"Merry Christmas."

She stepped close and reached her arms around his neck. "You are an amazing, wonderful man and I love you from head to toe. Thank you, Logan." She nuzzled his neck and kissed his chin.

"Want to break it in?"

"No. I want to save it. I want it to be a special place for Mr. and Mrs. Carson."

"Okay. I'll stay in the guest room until after we're married. There's one more thing." Logan, still wearing his towel, walked to the closet and brought out a big box wrapped in red foil topped with a gold bow. "This is for you."

"Isn't it a little early for Christmas gifts?"

"This one can't wait. I have other things for you under the tree, but this you have to open now."

Amy lifted the lid and looked in. Logan reached into the box for her and pulled out a beautiful wooden box. She slid her hands over the finish and knew that Logan had made it himself. She sat on the floor with her legs crossed, holding the box.

"Logan, it's beautiful! You made this. I can tell."

"Open it."

There were several drawers. Amy slowly opened one. It was lined with red velvet. She ran her fingers over the cloth, appreciating the softness.

"Open the top."

She slowly opened the lid and looked in. Her eyes filled with tears as she spotted the engagement ring.

Logan picked up the ring and held her hand. He looked into her eyes. "Are you sure?"

She nodded and whispered, "Yes."

"I can exchange it if you'd rather have something else." The large marquise cut diamond set in platinum sparkled, even in the subdued lighting of the bedroom.

"Not a chance. I love it and I love you."

Logan slipped the ring on her finger and kissed the back of her hand. "Perfect."

"You have excellent taste."

"I closed my eyes, pictured your face, and this just popped out at me."

"I need a manicure! Did you get this in California?"

"Yes. Bo has some convoluted friend of a relative of a client's cousin or some such nonsense that knows the great-aunt's neighbor of someone at some fancy-ass jewelry store. So I got a deal. There was only one hitch."

"You had to meet the guy in the parking lot of a deserted warehouse at midnight?"

"It isn't stolen!"

"I'm teasing you, goofy! What was the hitch?"

"I had to buy the matching wedding band and matching earrings...but forget I told you that, because it's part of your Christmas gift."

"Logan, it's all too much. Can I pick out your wedding band or do you have to come with me?"

"I trust you. You can pick it out. Surprise me. Just a few requests, if you don't mind, no jewels, yellow gold, very shiny."

"Whatever you want."

Logan reached over and wrapped a damp strand of her hair around his finger. "Kiss me please, soon-to-be Mrs. Carson."

Amy pulled her towel off and sat on Logan's lap. "My pleasure, future husband." She ran her hands through his damp hair and kissed him softly on the mouth. "Can I sit on your surgery?"

"If you don't get too rambunctious."

"Me? Please." She reached down, opened his towel and pushed his shoulders back until he lay on the floor. "I'm going to make love to you from head to toe." And she did.

The Following October

After surviving a harrowing ride on the expressway, watching Logan lose his cool, nearly falling when she slipped on wet leaves, it was a relief to be in the maternity ward while professionals dressed in cheery smocks fussed over her from head to toe.

"Logan, are you sure you don't mind coming back to St. Mary's? Really, we could take an ambulance somewhere else."

"Are you kidding me? You are not leaving this place until that baby is born. Nurses, doctors, aides, and I will not let you out of our sight for a minute. I promise."

"I made you a promise, too. Remember? I said I would give you better autumn memories. This is just the beginning. Okay, this is starting to hurt."

Logan made his way past two nurses and held her hand.

"When is her doctor getting here?" Logan asked a nurse who looked much too young to be in charge of anything, let alone someone as important as his wife.

"Mr. Carson, she'll probably be in labor for a while. You called the doctor before you came in, didn't you?"

"Yes, we did. She said she'd be here soon."

"She will. You have quite a night ahead of you. Can I have someone bring you something to drink?"

"Like beer?"

"If we had it, I'd bring you one. Next time remember, there are some things you need to smuggle in with your wife's overnight bag."

Amy butted in. "Next time? What makes you think I'd do this again? I have stretch marks that glow in the dark, I can't see my feet, I'm dead-dog tired, and I think I have hemorrhoids!"

"Mrs. Carson, when you look at that sweet little baby's face and kiss the top of its pointed little head, you'll fall in love with your husband all over again and you'll be pushing the limit of the six-week break from sex that you're supposed to observe."

Amy clenched Logan's hand and winced. "Will not."

"If nurses were allowed to gamble, I'd give a week's wages."

"She can barely resist me now. I don't know if I could take much more."

"Shut up, Logan. Aren't you supposed to be helping me breathe?"

"You could breathe better if you stopped chatting."

"Shut up, Logan."

And so the evening began. Logan was torn between flashbacks with Sam and Amy begging him to make the pain stop. She needed more comforting than Sam did. Or maybe he just didn't remember Sam needing his presence as much as Amy did. He felt like a player in every movie he ever saw with babies being born. The sweating, miserable mother-to-be in pain while the inept, bumbling father-to-be did his best to make her comfortable and assure her that he loved her. When Logan told Amy he loved her, she rolled her eyes. He had her fingernail marks in his hand, just short of drawing blood. He needed to use the men's room very badly, but he was afraid to leave her. Gibby's shift started in twenty minutes. He would feel safe leaving, if Gibby would stay at her side.

Gibby and Dr. Butler walked into Amy's room together. Logan hugged Gibby with the enthusiasm of a long-lost friend. Dr. Butler shook Logan's hand as he reached around Gibby's back.

"So, how's the mommy?"

"Hi, Doc! I'm just fine in between contractions. But I'm thirsty and hungry, sore and tired."

"Pretty normal, then! Good. I'll be popping in and out every twenty minutes or so. I understand Gibby here is a friend of yours?"

"Best. And neighbor."

"You have two other friends in the waiting room."

"Gibby, did Beth and Hillie come too?"

"You're the first one of us to do this, and I think they wanted to be a part of it. If you scream too much, you'll scare them off. Don't forget, Beth is due in two months."

Logan interrupted. "Gibby, please, if you don't mind, will you hold her hand while I run to the men's room?" He pried Amy's fingers from his hand and shook it until the circulation returned.

"Sure. I have a little work to do while I'm here, vitals to check. Stop in the waiting room and say hi to the girls."

"Good idea." He kissed Amy on the forehead. "I love you, darling. I'll be right back."

He left the room, leaned against the wall in the hallway and sunk down to the floor. Dr. Butler almost tripped over him when she left Amy's room.

"Mr. Carson! Are you alright?"

Logan wiped his face on his sleeve. "I'm fine. I just don't know if I can do this again."

"Do what again? I didn't know you had other children."

"She died. So did her mother. There were complications and a lot of bleeding."

"Amy is very healthy. She has had a very uneventful pregnancy and although I can't make promises, I expect no problems."

"I'm trying to be very strong for her, but I'm so scared."

"You're doing great. She's counting on you."

"I know. I'll be fine. I love her so much. She's an awesome woman."

"I like her. She'll be a great mother. She has a big heart."

"Thanks, Doc, for stopping. I have friends to visit."

Logan headed for the waiting room after a much needed stop in the men's room. Unlike waiting rooms of past years, there were no pacing, cigarette-smoking fathers. The fathers were right at their wives' sides, and smokers were banished to the farthest corner of the parking lot. Hillie and Beth were sharing a *People* magazine, discussing Brad, Angelina, Madonna and Denzel. They both stood when Logan walked in. He approached them with open arms and hugged them together.

"You look like crap, Hon." It was Hillie's greeting, but Beth agreed.

"Logan, she's the one in labor, and you look like the one who's working hard."

He held out his abused hand and Hillie took it in hers, turned it over and exclaimed, "Good grief! You'll need therapy to get this back in shape! Amy did this to you?"

"She has quite a grip. The nails dig in as she cusses me out and blames me and my parts for her misery."

"Normal."

"That's what I hear. I'm trying to let it just blow by me."

"Water off a duck's back, Sweetie."

Beth made room for him on the couch. "Sit a minute, Logan."

He sat between them and Beth rubbed his back. "Thinking about Sam?"

"Well, off and on. I just can't help it. This is where we were two years ago. I know in my rational brain that babies are born every day that live into old age. I know that moms normally survive to raise them. I doubt that what happened to me once could happen again. But still…"

Hillie patted his knee. "She'll be fine. And you'll be a great dad."

"Thanks. She's lucky to have good friends. So, how about it? I know she'd love to see you. I think Gibby should be done with her poking and prodding by now. Just a word of warning, she's a sweaty mess, her makeup is gone, and I keep telling her she's beautiful, so don't spoil it."

"I'll be in this spot myself in two months, so I'm going to take lessons so I don't scare Terry to death."

Logan walked them to Amy's room and walked in first just in case something was happening that they shouldn't see.

"Where have you been?"

"Hello, beautiful. I brought someone to see you."

"This is all your fault."

"I know, believe me, I know. I love you."

As the contraction ended, Amy got her normal, sweet voice back and greeted her friends. "Hi! I'm so glad you guys came! Don't let Logan scare you, Beth. You actually get a few seconds to breathe now and then."

Logan stayed back while Hillie and Beth went to both sides of her bed and each held a hand.

"Amy, is it bad? Can you have drugs?" Beth was curious.

"I'm not having drugs…yet. And no, it isn't bad…well, yes. It's bad. It hurts like hell, but supposedly I'll just be thrilled when it's over and won't remember a thing."

"I'm glad you're first, Ames. I just may be satisfied with my boring life and my gay men friends."

"Hillie, your time will come. Scout the halls for a doctor."

Amy felt another contraction beginning. "Logan!"

He hurried to her bedside and Beth gladly gave him Amy's hand. "I'm here. Hang in there."

"Logan! Oh, God! It hurts!"

"I know, darling. I'm sorry."

Gibby walked Beth and Hillie to the door. "We're going to give you guys some privacy. My guess—you'll be parents before midnight."

"Two hours! I can't do this for two more hours! Logan!"

"Will you hit me if I tell you to breathe?"

"Yes! I'm breathing! Can't you tell?"

Gibby winked at Logan. "I'll be back in a few."

The three friends walked to the waiting room. They all looked exhausted and concerned. Gibby reassured them.

"She's doing fine. The baby is doing fine. She's right on target. Everything will be fine."

"I was more concerned about Logan." Beth spoke out loud what they had all been thinking. "He's a mess. I know he had nine months to prepare for this, but it has to be a horrible déjà vu thing for him. Last time, he left here empty-handed."

"I think he'll tough it out for Amy. He'll watch her and the baby like a hawk."

"I'm off at eleven, but I'll stick around until she delivers. I have another mom in labor down the hall, so I have to go now, but please come and get me if...well, if you need to. She has a great doctor."

Gibby went back to work. Beth and Hillie pumped coins into the beverage machine and sat back down on the couch. Beth laid her head back, closed her eyes and Hillie was certain she was praying. It came so naturally to her. Hillie prayed in her own way—like she was having a mental discussion with God in her head. In either case, Amy was blessed to have good friends and a wonderful husband. Beth sat back up and found a parenting magazine in the rack. Hillie found a tattered trashy novel and started reading. Time passed quickly for them, and before they knew it, Dr. Butler came into the waiting room with the news they had been waiting for.

Hillie jumped up. "So?"

"Eight-pound, five-ounce, healthy baby girl."

Hillie and Beth hugged and cried.

"How's Amy?"

"She's tired, but fine."

Hillie remembered their earlier conversation. "How's Logan?"

"He won't let either of them out of his sight. I got the story about his first wife, so I can understand his reaction. But really, they'll both be fine."

"Thanks, Doctor. Can we go see her…them?"

"Sure. She'll be in her room in about twenty minutes. I'll tell Gibby and she can meet you there after her shift."

Dr. Butler left the waiting room. Beth and Hillie looked at each other, held hands, jumped up and down, and did a silent scream.

"Thank you, God! Hillie, this is one of the happiest moments of my life."

"Mine too. No more jumping for you. One delivery a night is all I can take. Did they ever decide on a name?"

"I tried to pin Amy down, but she was always pretty vague. I think she was planning on having a boy, hoping for a boy, actually, to make it a little easier on Logan."

"How about Hillary Beth Carson? It has a nice ring to it."

"Let's get Gibby. We'll run it buy her and then make the suggestion."

*

Amy's bed was wheeled into her room. She was holding the baby. Logan was two steps behind her, looking very exhausted, but not planning on resting until he had his family home.

Dr. Butler checked on Amy, then left her in the capable hands of St. Mary's nursing staff. An aide scurried around Amy, making sure she was comfortable and had everything she needed.

"Dad, would you hold the baby for a minute while we get this bedding straightened out?"

Logan looked panic-stricken. He took a deep breath, smiled at Amy and said, "Sure. She'll have to get used to looking at me sooner or later. I'll be dropping her off at kindergarten before you know it."

He walked to the side of the bed and Amy passed him the little bundle. He remained standing, pacing and talking to the peaceful little face.

"Amy, we have to get serious about a name."

"Are you disappointed we didn't have a boy?"

"I thought it might be easier, having a boy, but now that I hold her, it wouldn't have made one bit of difference. She's beautiful and I'm thrilled."

"Leah Rebecca Carson."

"What?"

"Leah, for my grandmother. Rebecca, for her sister. Would it be too hard for you?"

"It's perfect. Sisters. I never thought about that. She lives on then, doesn't she?"

"Logan, you'll be a wonderful father."

"I hope you're right. Keep me in line. I'm sure I'll be a much better father if you can step up to diaper detail."

"You're not weaseling out of this. Besides, we won't feed her burritos. You'll be safe."

There was a soft knock on the door. Gibby stuck her head in.

"Feel up to a couple of visitors?"

Logan, looking very proud, stepped up.

"Come on in, ladies. I want you to meet Leah Rebecca Carson."

Beth held out her arms and Logan carefully handed her the baby. He went to Amy's bedside and held her hand.

"I just can't wait to have my own. She's beautiful!"

"Don't be offended if I doze off. I'm exhausted."

Logan looked at Gibby. "She can sleep, can't she?"

"Logan, yes, she can sleep. She probably needs to sleep. We'll be leaving as soon as I get a chance to hold that baby!"

Beth reluctantly gave her up, and Gibby kissed Leah's forehead and whispered sweet little baby words to her. She passed the bundle to Hillie, who looked apprehensive about accepting it.

"Okay, I have absolutely no experience with this. Am I holding her right? Is her head okay? Am I holding her too tight?"

"Relax, Hillie. You're doing fine. They're a lot more durable than they look."

Logan surprised himself with his instructions. It seems someone in the delivery room just said the very same words to him. Amy's eyes were closed, but she smiled, knowing that Logan would eventually be very comfortable with the baby.

"Welcome to this strange and wonderful world, little Leah. We'll see you later at home." Logan took the baby and walked her around the room, refusing to sit down. "Congratulations, you guys. We'll be by the house for a visit once you get settled."

"And don't forget, we're doing the baby shower!"

Logan whispered, "Thanks for hanging around, you guys. It meant a lot to Amy, and to me, too. When Amy wakes up to nurse, I'm running to make a phone call. My folks and brother don't even know we left for the hospital."

"Hillie called Amy's folks. Anyone else you can think of that needs a call?"

"No, thanks, Beth. I think we've got it covered. Good night."

After the trio left the room, Logan watched Amy sleeping peacefully and began to pray. He thanked God for his healthy family and begged that it would stay that way.

*

Logan made sure Amy was comfortable in the Mercedes and securely belted. Leah's car seat looked ridiculously big for the tiny bundle he was strapping in. For good measure, Logan covered her with two blankets.

"Things will never be the same, will they?" he pondered.

"No. Logan, they'll be different, just wonderfully different. We'll adjust. Think of it as an adventure. Every day a surprise."

She put her head back and closed her eyes.

"Tired, Mama?"

"I'm exhausted. You're in charge... Daddy."

They had an uneventful ride home. Amy carried Leah, and Logan carried everything else. Babies sure had a lot of equipment. The hospital loaded them down with formula, diapers, wipes, booklets, and other assorted samples, coupons and instructions. Amy headed up the stairs and Logan held his breath. He'd get used to it all.

Amy stopped outside the nursery. The closed door reminded her of things she didn't want to think about. She needed to remain in the present. Logan dropped his bags and opened the door for her.

Amy couldn't believe her eyes. "Oh, Logan! It's beautiful! When did you have time?"

Amy went to the rocking chair, custom-made for her, and sat down carefully.

"I made it at work. I wanted it to be a surprise."

"The other one?"

"We'll give it to Beth."

Amy kissed Leah's forehead. "Thank you, Logan, for everything."

"Thank you, Amy... for a second chance."

J ACKIE FANCHER was born in Evanston, Illinois. Aside from six years spent in Germany and Michigan, she has never lived more than a ninety-minute commute from Chicago. The invigorating pace, the lakefront and skyline, and the endless list of things to do keep her close by. Though she now lives and works south of the city, in Wilmington, Illinois, Chicago is a frequent destination for renewal and entertainment.

While active in her church, local ACS Relay for Life, and diakonia™ training, Jackie spends her spare time reading and writing.

Jackie has two sisters and three brothers who support and inspire her. Her son, Andrew, a constant source of pride, is the reminder that single mothers can work and raise thriving, successful children.